P9-EFJ-585

Signed First Edition

Eleventh Grave
in Moonlight

DARYNDA JONES

St. Martin's Press

Eleventh Grave in Moonlight

Also by Darynda Jones

The Curse of Tenth Grave

The Dirt on Ninth Grave

Eighth Grave After Dark

Seventh Grave and No Body

Sixth Grave on the Edge

Death and the Girl He Loves

Fifth Grave Past the Light

Death, Doom, and Detention

Fourth Grave Beneath My Feet

Death and the Girl Next Door

Third Grave Dead Ahead

Second Grave on the Left

First Grave on the Right

Eleventh Grave in Moonlight

Darynda Jones

ST. MARTIN'S PRESS ❧ NEW YORK

ELEVENTH GRAVE IN MOONLIGHT. Copyright © 2017 by Darynda Jones. All rights reserved. Printed in the United States of America. For information address St. Martin's Press, 175 Fifth Avenue, New York, N.Y. 10010.

Library of Congress Cataloging-in-Publication Data

Names: Jones, Darynda, author.
Title: Eleventh grave in moonlight / Darynda Jones.
Description: First Edition. | New York : St. Martin's Press, 2017.
Identifiers: LCCN 2016043107| ISBN 9781250078216 (hardback) | ISBN 9781466890527 (e-book)
Subjects: LCSH: Davidson, Charley (Fictitious character)—Fiction. | Women private
    investigators—Fiction. | Women mediums—Fiction. | Gods—Fiction. | BISAC: FICTION /
    Mystery & Detective / Women Sleuths. | FICTION / Fantasy / Paranormal. | GSAFD:
    Occult fiction.
Classification: LCC PS3610.O6236 E44 2017 | DDC 813/.6—dc23
LC record available at https://lccn.loc.gov/2016043107

Our books may be purchased in bulk for promotional, educational, or business use. Please contact your local bookseller or the Macmillan Corporate and Premium Sales Department at 800-221-7945, extension 5442, or by e-mail at MacmillanSpecialMarkets@macmillan.com.

First Edition: January 2017

10 9 8 7 6 5 4 3 2 1

For Trayce
Because, day-um!

Acknowledgments

Some times getting the words out of the head and onto the page proves more difficult than others, but the people who push and plead and beg for another Charley book make it all worthwhile. I am insanely grateful, dear readers. You are my everything. You are my Grimlets.

Thank you to my fantabulous agent, Alexandra Machinist, and my spectacular editor, Jennifer Enderlin, as well as everyone at ICM, St. Martin's Press, and Macmillan.

Thank you to the woman who brings Charley to life so vividly, Lorelei King.

Thank you to my team members: Dana, Netters, Jowanna, and Trayce. You guys are the best of the best. You're the bestest!

Thank you to the Collas family, for letting me share your story here. Your angel stole my heart and is in my thoughts always.

Thank you to my amazing family, for being so patient and supportive and pretty. Because that's what's most important.

Thank you from the very deepest and most cavernous depths of my heart to the incredible Trayce Layne. I have no words. You have gone so far above and beyond, I'm pretty sure you've landed among the stars. The only way to express how much I appreciate everything you've done is through interpretive dance. So, you have that to look forward to.

And thank YOU, for picking up this book. May it bring you bouts of laughter, a few surprised gasps, and a squirmy kind of pleasure.

Eleventh Grave in Moonlight

1

Lord, help me be the sort of person
my psychiatrist medicates me to be.
—T-SHIRT

I lay on a psychiatrist's couch, a couch I'd named Alexander Skarsgård the moment my gaze landed on its buttery curves and wide back, and wondered if I should tell Dr. Mayfield about the dead kid scurrying across her ceiling. Probably not.

She crossed her legs—the psychiatrist, not the kid, who was male—and gave me her most practiced smile. "And that's why you're here?"

I bolted upright, appalled. "Heavens, no. I'm totally over the whole evil stepmother thing. I just thought, you know, full disclosure and all. FYI, I had an evil stepmother."

"Had?"

"She died."

"I'm sorry."

"No worries. She had an ugly demon inside of her at the time."

"I see."

"Wait, no, that was her outfit. The demon wasn't that ugly."

"Ah."

"No, seriously, her outfit was hideous."

"Perhaps we should get back to the fact that you're the grim reaper?" She pushed plastic-framed glasses up a slender nose. Thankfully, it was hers.

"Oh, right." I relaxed again, falling back into Alexander's arms. "I pretty much have the reaper thing down. It's the godly part of me I'm struggling with."

"The godly part." She bent her head to write something in her notebook. She was quite lovely. Dark hair. Huge brown eyes. Wide mouth. And young. Too young to be analyzing me. How much life experience could she possibly have?

"Yes. Ever since I found out I was a god, I've felt a little off balance. I think I'm having one of those identity crisises."

"So, you're a god?"

"Wait. What's the plural of *crisis*?" When she didn't answer, I glanced back at her.

She'd stopped writing and was looking at me again, her expression mildly expectant. And ever so slightly taxed. She was trying to decide if I was playing her. I wasn't, but I could hardly blame her for thinking that. Dealing with delusions of grandeur was probably an everyday aspect of her life. Trying to sort out the legit from the cons.

When she continued to stare, I said, "I'm sorry, what was the question?"

"You're a god?"

"Oh, that. Yes, but to quote a very popular movie, I'm *a* god, not *the* God." I snorted. Bill Murray was so awesome. "Did I forget to mention that?"

"Then you're *not* the grim reaper?"

"Oh, no, I'm that, too. I volunteered. Kind of. Long story. Anyway, I thought you could hypnotize me. You know, give me a full-access pass to my pre-birth memories so I won't be blindsided again."

"Blindsided?"

"Yes. That's why I'm here. Because my sister refuses to do regressive therapy with me, and—"

"Your sister?"

"Dr. Gemma Davidson?" The shrink-wrap community couldn't have been very big. Surely she knew my sister.

"Dr. Davidson is your sister?"

"Is that a problem?"

"Not for me."

"Fantabulous." I rubbed my hands together. "Okay, so, you know how you're going through life, remembering everything that ever happened to you since the moment you were born—"

"You remember the moment you were born?"

"—and suddenly someone says, 'Hey, remember that time we singed our eyebrows lighting that bowling alley on fire?' only at first you don't remember singeing your eyebrows while lighting a bowling alley on fire, but then you think about it and it suddenly comes to you? You totally remember singeing your eyebrows while lighting a bowling alley on fire?"

She blinked several times, then wrenched out a "Sure."

"It's like that. I remember being a god, but not totally. Like parts of my celestial life have been erased from my memory."

"Your celestial life."

"Right. Before I became human? I think I have a glitch."

"It's . . . possible, I suppose."

"I mean, who knows? I might already have a way to defeat a malevolent god that's loose on this plane and not even realize it."

"A malevolent god?"

"The malevolentest."

"And he's loose on this plane?"

"Yes. And trust me when I say you do *not* want him here. He takes his death and destruction very seriously. And he has zero respect for human life."

"Mmm." She nodded and went back to taking notes.

"Zero," I added for emphasis, making an O with my fingers. Then I waited. She had a lot to write down. When she kept at it long enough to outline a novel, I filled the silence with, "It's funny. My husband thought it would be pointless to come here."

She laid her pen across her notepad and gave me her full attention. "Tell me about him."

"My husband?"

"Yes." Her voice was very soothing. Like elevator music. Or summer rain. Or Darvocet. "How's your relationship?"

"How much time do we have?" I snorted, cracking myself up.

My husband, a.k.a. Reyes Alexander Farrow, didn't find my joke as funny as I did. It happened. I felt him before I saw him. His heat brushed across my skin. Sank into me. Saturated my clothes and hair and even warmed the cool gold band on my ring finger.

As he passed over me, all darkness and billowing smoke, he paused to whisper sweet nothings in my ear. I barely heard him over the rushing of my own blood. Whatever he said made my nether regions clench in anticipation. Then he continued on his journey, materializing on the other side of the room where he stood in a corner to watch from afar. Ish.

"Just kidding," I said as his eyes glistened in the low light. "He's kind of awesome. He's from down under."

"Australia?"

"Hell."

His eyes narrowed, but any threats he may have been trying to hurl my way were nulled and voided by the smirk playing about his sensual mouth. He crossed his arms at his wide chest and leaned back into a corner to observe my goings-on.

He'd been doing that a lot lately. Popping in to check up on me. It could have had something to do with the fact that I had waged war with not one god but two. The malevolent one and the Good One. The Big Guy upstairs.

I decided to ignore my husband to the best of my abilities. I was here on a job. If I couldn't stay focused despite being bombarded with the most delicious distraction this side of the Flame Nebula, I was no better than a gumshoe-for-hire PI.

Oh, wait. I *was* a gumshoe-for-hire PI. Which would explain the job I was currently on. It paid the bills. Sometimes.

"Okay, let's get back to your husband. You mean he's from hell metaphorically?"

I refocused on the good doctor. "Oh, no. Quite literally. Technically, he's a god, too, but he was tricked by two other gods—one of which I've already trapped in a hell dimension and the other of which I'm currently trying to trap and/or horribly maim—and handed over to Lucifer, who created his only son out of the god's energy."

She frowned and squinted her eyes like she was trying to imagine it all.

"Okay, so, basically, you take the energy of a surly god"—I held up an index finger to demonstrate—"toss in some fire and brimstone"—I wiggled my other fingers around said index—"top that with a little sin"—I pretended to sprinkle sin over the mixture—"whisk for five minutes, and voilà." I flared my fingers as though I'd just done a magic trick. "Rey'aziel incarnate."

When Reyes scowled at me, I fought the urge to giggle. Nothing like having your entire existence boiled down to its basest elements.

"Rey'aziel?" Dr. Mayfield asked.

I bounced back to her. "Sorry. Reyes Farrow. My husband. You know, I used to think explaining the particulars of my less-than-ordinary life to a total stranger would be difficult, but this hasn't been bad. I was born the grim reaper: check. I was still learning about my abilities when I found out that I had once been a god with my own dimension: check. I'm married to the son of Satan, a.k.a. Reyes Alexander Farrow, who we recently found out is also a god, through no fault of his own: check. My stepmother was a hell-bitch extraordinaire: check. Somehow that seems important in this situation. And there is yet another god, a malevolent one, on this plane who is in cahoots with Reyes's dad and wants to kill our daughter, whom we had to send away to keep safe." I beamed at her, purposely ignoring the pang in my chest at the reminder that my daughter had to be sent away from me just to be safe. Just to have the barest glimmer of hope to live. "This has not been bad at all."

When it looked like Dr. Mayfield was going to try to refute something I'd said, I raised a hand to stop her. "I know what you're going to say. And, yes, technically being the son of Satan, among other things, makes my husband an iffy prospect." I shot him a grin. "But he was a god first. The God Jehovah's little brother, in fact, and I like to think that *that* part of him, the good part, is stronger than the evil part that emerged when he was forged in the fires of sin and raised by demons in a hell dimension. Though," I said, scooting closer, "the minute you get a load of him, your first thoughts will definitely be the carnal kind, if you know what I mean." I gave her a conspiratorial wink. When she only stared, I added, "Boy's hot."

Reyes dipped his head, trying to hide a grin, as the doctor picked up her pen and started outlining again.

"Nice T-shirt," Reyes said to me. Apparently, no one else in the room could hear him.

I was wearing my I LIKE IT WHEN MY PSYCHIATRIST PLAYS WITH MY MARBLES T-shirt. It was either that or my EXCUSE ME WHILE I FREUDIAN SLIP INTO SOMETHING MORE COMFORTABLE pajama top, but I didn't feel that wearing pajamas to a shrink session would send the right message. I was a professional, after all. Also, I'd gotten mustard on it and had to change.

The kid on the ceiling had stopped moving. He was gawking at the ol' ball and chain commanding the room from the corner pocket. That happened a lot when Reyes was around.

I nailed him with a fake scowl. I was on an assignment, after all.

"We need to talk," he said.

Uh-oh. Nothing good ever came out of a conversation that started with "We need to talk." I mouthed, "Later," and shooed him away while the doctor took a few more notes.

He laughed softly, and for a split moment, the doctor lost her focus and let her gaze dart, just for a second, over her shoulder.

He winked, the saucy flirt, and dematerialized, leaving me alone with my psychiatrist again. I was pretty sure he'd been breaking a few HIPAA laws by being there, anyway.

"Did you hear something?" she asked.

"You mean besides the thunderous and devastating ramifications if I can't figure out how to take this god down and he completes his mission?"

"Yes. Besides that."

"If I could just get all my memories back . . . I know there's something hidden, something important that will tell me how to deal with him. Like it's on the tip of my tongue, only with more of a brain analogy."

"Okay. So, why does your sister refuse to do regressive therapy with you? Besides the obvious?"

"Oh, that whole ethical dilemma thing on account of her being my sister and all? Yeah, well, she's afraid it will bring out some strange new power in me and I'll accidently blow Albuquerque off the face of the planet. Which is ridonculous." I snorted and rolled my eyes. "I can totally control my powers now."

She took more notes.

"Most of the time."

She continued to write.

"I don't think the 'Lumpy's Taco Hut incident' should count. That place was an eyesore. People should be thanking me."

She offered me her attention once again. "Lumpy's Taco Hut? That was you?"

Shit. I forgot that whole thing was still under investigation. "Pfft, no." Thank Reyes's Brother, Lumpy's had been closed due to code violations at the time and no one was hurt.

"Ah." She shut her notebook. "Is there anything else you want to share? Anything you think I should be aware of?"

"No." I shook my head in thought. "Not especially. Unless you count the fact that I'm going to take over the world."

"The whole thing?"

"Well, I'm going to *try* to take over the world."

"And you feel you're prepared for world domination?"

I lifted a noncommittal shoulder. "I'm taking a business class."

"Good for you." She opened up her notebook again and jotted down a few more ideas.

"I told Jehovah, through his archangel Michael, of course, that I was going to do it, too."

"Take over the world?"

It sounded silly when she said it out loud, but I could hardly turn back now. "Yes."

"And how did He take that?"

"Not well, but you don't know what He did. He created an entire hell dimension just to lock my husband inside and throw away the key. Though we weren't married at the time. This was a few thousand years ago."

Ever since informing Michael of my plans, God had sent a legion of His minions to follow my every move. They were like the heavenly version of the Secret Service. I'd threatened, and, for some reason only they knew of, they'd taken it seriously. But why? I was angry when I said it—and I certainly meant it—but that doesn't explain why they would take me seriously. Unless I was a real threat.

Hell.

Yes.

"So, God talks to you?"

I snapped back to reality. "Oh, no. Not directly."

"Right. He talks to you through His archangel, Michael." She wrote down every word as she said it.

"Yeah. Kind of old-school, if you ask me, what with today's technology. You know, I thought psychiatrists just sort of listened while the patient talked. You're gonna run out of ink there, missy." I laughed nervously.

She gave me a patient smile. "I have more pens in my desk."

"Gotcha."

"So, God is upset because you threatened to take over His world?"

"That's the word on the street."

"Are you worried?"

"Not especially."

"Fair enough. Let's get back to these powers. What do you plan to do with them?"

"Excuse me?"

"Your powers. I mean, surely you're going to use them for good?"

I got the sneaking suspicion she was humoring me. I was good with that. I threw an arm over my face. "There's so much, you know? So much I could do. I could cure cancer. I could end famine. I could stop all wars and bring absolute peace to the world."

"And why don't you?"

I lowered my arm slowly. "I'm still kind of figuring the whole thing out. I'm saying I *could* do all those things. Not that I know how."

"That would be difficult."

"That and I think that's why the angels are here. Not, like, in this room, but all around me. Following me. Watching me. I don't think He wants me to do any of those things."

"And why wouldn't He?"

"Autonomy." When she raised her brows in question, I explained. "That was the deal. After that whole Adam and Eve fiasco—Eve got screwed, by the way—that was the deal. He gave humans complete autonomy. Earth is ours, and it's up to us to help our fellow man or harm him. To heal ourselves. To do good things. No matter your religion, no matter your beliefs, the lesson is the same: be kind."

I fought the urge to add another word to the end of that statement.

I lost. "Rewind."

Damn it. I sucked at fighting. Urges or otherwise.

"It's a good message," she said when she came back to me, a microsecond before she started writing again.

"It is. And I have to tell you something else."

"I'm all ears."

I released a lengthy sigh and fessed up. "The whole regressive therapy thing? That's actually secondary to the real reason I'm here."

"Which is?"

I dropped my feet over Mr. Skarsgård and sat up to look her in the eye. Or the part in her hair. Either way, I wanted to study her reaction since I couldn't feel her emotions. "Dr. Mayfield?"

"Hmm?" she said without looking up.

I cleared my throat and steeled myself. It had to be done. She needed to know the truth. To accept the things she could not change, so the prayer went, and there was definitely no changing this. Without further ado, I said softly, "I'm sorry to have to tell you this, but you died two years ago."

She kept writing. "Mm-hmm. And you can see me because . . . ?"

"I'm the—"

"—grim reaper. Right. Oh, and a god, no less."

Wow. I sat back. She took that really well. Either that or she didn't believe me.

Nah.

I bit my lip while she continued to take notes, but my attention span was only so long. "So, yeah, I've been hired, in a manner of speaking, by the new leaser of this office. He's been experiencing strange events. Just the usual stuff. Cold spots. Magazines moving from one corner on a table to another. Pictures falling off the walls."

"I see. And he hired you because he thinks the place is haunted."

"Actually, no. He thinks the landlord wants him to break the lease to use the office for his new juicing business, which is dumb because this would be a horrible location for a juice bar. But he thinks the landlord is trying to scare him off. To frighten him away. To send him fleeing in terror. In a word, he thinks he's being punked."

"But you disagree?"

"I do."

"You think it's really haunted?"

"Yes, I do. And I have to admit, at first, I thought it was you."

"Naturally."

" 'Cause you're dead and all."

"But you've changed your mind?" She had yet to look up at me.

"Yes. I'm pretty sure it's that kid crawling around your ceiling."

She stopped writing, but she didn't want to bite. I could see it in her expression. She looked at me at last. Eyed me a long moment. Probably wondered if she should give in. If she should feed my delusions by looking up. After a lengthy struggle in which I lost focus and contemplated the origins of marshmallows—seriously, what mad genius came up with that delicacy?—she slowly raised her lashes and looked toward the ceiling.

Thankfully, only I could hear her earsplitting screams. She dropped her pen and pad, fell to the ground, and crab-crawled backwards. In heels and a pencil skirt, no less. I was impressed.

In her defense, the kid crawling on her ceiling looked a little like that monochrome girl who crawled out of a television set in a horror movie I once watched about an hour before a DOA popped into my bedroom, wanting me to tell his wife where the insurance papers were, only the kid was a he. A he who looked about ten years old, with long black hair and a shiny black cape. An odd fashion choice for a boy of any age. And from any era.

The good doctor cowered in a corner, the look of horror on her face both sad and strangely amusing.

"Dr. Mayfield," I said, easing toward her with my palms patting the air. "It's okay. He's perfectly harmless."

Of course, the second I said it, the little shit landed on my shoulders and sank his teeth into my neck.

Insanity takes its toll. Please have exact change.
—MEME

I screamed. I had a small vampire on my back, and I screamed. I tried to fling him off, but he'd latched onto me like a leech. Only with teeth. I twisted and turned, knocking over chairs and a side table, as he sank his teeth farther into my neck.

Just as I got a handful of the little shit's hair, I heard laughter from somewhere in the distance. Somewhere far, far away. Like three feet. So not that far.

I stopped, turned, and gaped at a thirteen-year-old gangbanger who'd died in the '90s. Angel. He was one of my investigators. Not to mention the bane of my existence. And he was on the floor, laughing so hard he had to hold his stomach.

"What the fuck, Angel?" I asked, turning toward him.

I was now wearing the kid like a backpack, but at least he'd stopped biting me. The glass half-full and all.

The kid jumped down and doubled over laughing, too.

While I graced them with my best look of horror and disgust and betrayal, Angel stood, and the two urchins, who were clearly in cahoots, fist-bumped.

I rubbed my neck where the kid had bitten me. "That was wrong on so many levels."

Angel snorted, and they doubled over again. I finally got a good look at the kid. He was closer to Angel's age than I'd originally thought, though a lot shorter. But he really was made up to look like a vampire. His long black hair was real, and his face had been painted white with thick black liner and fake blood dripping from his mouth and down his temple.

When I folded my arms under the girls, a.k.a. Danger and Will Robinson—names I'd given my double Ds because of their propensity for inviting trouble—the kid explained. Or he tried to. His words came out muffled. Partly because of the laughter but mostly because of the fake teeth.

"Ha-oh-ween." He held up a finger, then spit out the teeth, the kind that glowed in the dark, and wiped at his mouth with the back of his hand. "I can't talk with those things in. Halloween. Hit and run."

A soft Native American accent accompanied his speech. Syllables that flowed without effort from most Americans were stopped short in the smooth, rhythmic staccato distinct to native people, only he was from a newer generation. His accent had been diluted by all the Anglo-Saxons running about, mucking shit up. Still, there was just enough of one that, if I had to guess, I'd say he was from the Zuni reservation northeast of Albuquerque.

And his costume was pretty awesome. Or it was before it dawned on me that the blood dripping down his temple and off his chin wasn't part of the gig.

"The blood's real," I said, astonished and sad.

"Oh yeah." He waved a dismissive hand. "No big."

My chest tightened, and I fought my natural instinct to pull him into my arms. It fought back, but I held strong this time. Mostly because being accused of groping a child was a real thing.

"This is Logan," Angel said, sobering.

Logan held out his hand. I struggled to find a smile as we shook.

"Angel told me all about you. Why you're so bright and all." He nodded in approval. "Pretty badass, if you ask me."

"Then I'm askin'," I said with a grin.

He ducked his head, hiding a bashful smile, just as I gasped and turned. I'd almost forgotten about Dr. Mayfield. She was still holding down the carpet by an oak filing cabinet, a look of sheer terror lining her face.

And we'd made a mess. A costly one. No telling what that pile of glass that used to be a vase would cost me.

I could chalk this case up to another entry in the red column after I paid for the damages. I totally wasn't pulling my weight. While my husband was earning enough in interest alone to buy a small country—daily—I was still struggling to earn enough to buy toothpaste and pay my assistant at the same time. One simply had to go. And I could hardly be expected to live without toothpaste.

But I was bound and determined to make my own way in the world. Right after I bought that yacht I'd been eyeing. And those thirty-seven pairs of boots I had in my wish list on Boot Bliss. After that, it would be all me, baby.

"Dr. Mayfield," I said, easing closer to her, "are you okay?"

She was shaking visibly, her eyes wide and wild and more than a little panicked.

"It's a lot to take in," I said.

"How . . . ? I don't . . . when . . . ?"

"Breathe." I knelt down and scooted closer. "Just breathe, Doctor."

She took in a deep breath before she realized the fruitlessness of her endeavor. "It doesn't do anything."

"I know. I'm sorry. It's just, the act tends to calm some people down. I've actually seen a departed hyperventilate. No idea how, but it happened. But once he got his breathing under control . . . well, you get the idea."

She continued to pant, to force air in and out of her nonexistent lungs. The boys calmed down the minute they realized Dr. Mayfield was having difficulties. They knelt beside us, and Logan took her hand.

"Dr. Mayfield?"

She let her gaze travel slowly toward him.

"It's just makeup," I assured her. Just in case. "He's not really a vampire."

"Oh. Okay." She nodded, then recognition dawned on her pretty face. "Wait." Her gaze traveled the length of the boy. "You're . . . you're Cynthia's son."

I had no idea who Cynthia was, but the doctor had apparently nailed it.

The kid nodded and flashed a nuclear smile that shot straight to my heart. "You helped her so much after the accident . . . after I died, I wanted to help you, too."

Both hands flew over her mouth as she studied him. "You really are . . . you really were . . . you're here. She said she felt you."

"Yep. And instead of telling her she was crazy like everyone else, instead of making her feel stupid, you went with it. Even though you didn't believe her, you helped her work through her grief."

"It was what she needed at the time." She took his hand again. "I'm so sorry I doubted her."

"But she didn't know that. That's all that matters."

"Oh, my God," she said, pulling him into her arms. Her shoulders shook with her newfound knowledge. Her new circumstance.

Angel and I stood to give them a moment. It didn't take him long, however. It never took him long.

"So, we gonna make out now? All the cool kids are doing it." He gestured toward the pair on the floor.

"You've been hanging out with me way too long." I took a good, long look at him. He still wore the clothes he'd died in, as did almost all departed. And those that didn't flummoxed me. He wore a dirty A-line T-shirt, the blood from a gunshot wound still on his chest. His jeans rode too low on his hips and the bandanna he wore rode too low on his brow, but he was an absolutely gorgeous kid. "Hey, aren't you supposed to be somewhere?"

He was supposed to be tailing my curmudgeonly uncle. What good did it do me to have minions if they didn't . . . min?

"Swopes is on it. I couldn't miss this."

"Of course not. How are you?"

His lashes narrowed in suspicion. "Good. I'd be better if we made out."

"How's your mom?"

He lifted a shoulder. "She's good. She's dating a really nice guy. It's weird."

I laughed. "She deserves a nice guy."

"She always did."

I raised a hand to his jawline. Stroked my fingers over the dark peach fuzz there. He had barely begun life when he passed. His death was so senseless. So utterly needless.

He took my tenderness as a cue. Stepped closer. Buried his face in the crook of my neck. Pressed in to me, then let one hand drift around my waist. After a minute, it drifted some more. Lower and lower until it rested on my left ass cheek.

I rolled my eyes and tried not to laugh. The kid would try anything, but he was thirteen. It was in his adolescent DNA. And hugging him pretty much made my day. I felt like an older sister even though, if one counted the fact that he'd died at thirteen in '95, he was older than I was.

Before he could protest—or molest me further—I wrapped my arms around him and hugged. Hard.

This was the point where I usually threatened him. Pushed him back. Slapped his hands away. My response surprised him, which was the reason I did it all stealthlike. He didn't have time to react. I could get in a good hug before kicking him to the curb.

I placed a brisk kiss on his cheek, then stepped out of his reach.

"I win." I smirked, but he only stared at me.

After a few seconds, he asked, "Not that I didn't enjoy that, but are you okay?"

"I'm grand, beautiful boy."

He grimaced. He hated it when I called him that. Sucked to be him.

"And you didn't win," he said. "I got to cop a feel. Doesn't get any better than that."

"Damned sure does, Skippy." I reached up and fondled his peach fuzz again. "You sure you hit puberty?"

He caught hold of my hand and rubbed the backs of my fingers over his mouth, the move entirely too sensual considering the age difference.

"I could prove it to you," he said, a confident challenge in his eyes. The little shit.

With the help of Logan the Vampire, Dr. Mayfield got to her feet.

I rushed forward to help steady her. "How are you, Doctor?"

She wobbled as we helped her to a chair.

"You know, you can cross through me if you'd like. I'm sure you have family—"

"No," she said quickly, then swallowed and started over. "Sorry, no, thank you. I'd like to check on my sister. Can I do that?"

"You sure can. I bet Logan would help you."

He nodded, his enthusiasm evident.

"You don't have to," I said to him. "You can cross as well."

"I'm okay here for now, but thanks. I can show her the ropes. My dad . . . he still goes into my room every night and cries. Maybe you could get a message to him?"

"Absolutely." I put an arm on his shoulder. "But I think he'll still cry."

"I know. But he'll feel better knowing that I'm there with him."

"Yes, he will. And if you change your mind, you know where to find me."

"You're hard to miss," he said with a soft chuckle.

And so I was. As I turned to leave, the current occupant, a.k.a. my client, stood at the door, coffee in one hand, briefcase in the other. He took in the state of his office. His well-manicured jaw hung loose on its hinges, his mouth open in what I could only assume was shock. Or he'd been infected by the Thing. Pretty much all versions of that movie were creepy.

Logan spoke first. "Um, we should probably go. Now."

"Later, gorgeous," Angel said. The deserter.

The coffee in my client's hand fell and spilled onto the cream-colored carpet. I took another look at our surroundings. It wasn't that bad, for heaven's sake.

I pointed. "That's not on me. I'm not paying to have that cleaned."

"What the hell?" he said.

So, *not* infected by the Thing.

"Oh, this? Yeah, your landlord isn't trying to get you to break your lease." I bent to grab my jacket and bag. "The place really was haunted, so to speak." I waltzed past him before he became indignant. "It no longer is." I poked my head back in and added, "And you'll get my bill."

I hit the head before starting back to my place of employment. Could I call it a place of employment if I owned it? I was so bad with business etiquette. Good thing I was taking a class.

My phone rang as I sat on the loo.

A female voice filtered through the airways and into my ear. It was like magic. Or science. Mostly science. "Charley, what have you done now?"

God only knew. It was a friend of mine who took the concept of habit to a whole new—or really old—level. As in, she wore one. And they were not the least bit flattering.

Sister Mary Elizabeth was also clairvoyant, though she hated using that word. But what else was I supposed to call someone who could eavesdrop on the conversations of angels?

"Hey, sis. How's it hanging?"

"Heaven is in an uproar, that's how."

"Isn't it usually?"

"No, Charley, it's not. I check out for a few days, and when I check back in, all hell has broken loose. And guess what the topic of conversation is?"

I tried to tidy up while holding the phone to my ear. The toilet paper was not cooperating. "Angels are such gossips. Don't they have anything better to do?"

"Did you actually threaten our Lord and Savior?"

I snorted. "No. I threatened our Lord and Savior's Father. You know, the Big Guy."

"You . . . you . . ."

"Use your words," I said, finally managing to make myself presentable. I stepped out of the stall and around a departed homeless woman who was busy trying to get a paper towel out of the dispenser. Her hand kept slipping through. That had to be frustrating.

"Charley, you can't just threaten the Heavenly Father."

"Can, too." Yes. I was seven.

"Charley," she said, appalled.

When she didn't follow up, I said, "I know. I get it. But I was just really mad at the time."

"At the Almighty?"

"At the almighty jerk who stole my memories and tried to put my husband in a hell dimension for all eternity."

I was pretty sure she didn't hear a thing I'd said. The moment the word *jerk* left my mouth, she gasped. Loud and long. For, like, sixty seconds. Girl had a set of lungs.

"I'm sorry." I looked up and said it again. "I'm sorry. I get it. Threatening the Big Kahuna is a bad idea, but He started it."

"This isn't the third grade, Charley. And even if it were, you don't pick a fight with the principal."

"No, but I did pick a fight with my first-grade teacher, Mrs. Hickman. That woman was bat shit."

We hung up a couple of minutes later, once I convinced her that even if I did threaten Him, what could I do? For reals?

After drying my own hands, I took a paper towel and handed it to the homeless woman. It slipped through her fingers to the floor, but it seemed to satisfy her nonetheless.

Homeless departed, by and large, rarely wanted to cross. And when they did, it was disorienting, their mental illness often putting the whammy on me for days. So I didn't offer, though she could have crossed at any time. I had little say in the matter.

She noticed me at last. Flashed a gap-filled grimace. Leaned closer. "The Jell-O didn't set. It'll never work now."

I looked up to where heaven supposedly resided. "Don't I know it."

———

I called Cookie, my "best friend slash receptionist slash research assistant slash shoulder on which to cry," on the way to the parking lot, ignoring the angel perched atop a minivan, watching me with hawklike eyes.

Angels had a way of setting me on edge. They were all business. And terribly perceptive when it came to said business. They had a mission, and they would not be swayed. I'd tried. A couple of days ago, I'd offered one a C-note to scram. He didn't bite. Didn't flinch. Didn't even look at the hundred I'd waved at him. Steel resolve if I ever saw one.

And angels were unreadable when they wanted to be. They had the best poker faces this side of Vegas, and their emotions were impenetrable unless I was really close. And close was not a place I wanted to be. Their power felt like an electrical current rushing over my skin. It was unsettling and breathtaking at once.

As far as looks, they hardly resembled the pictures in the Bible. No curly hair or golden crowns or togas. Nope. This was one area where Hollywood nailed it. Angels wore long dark jackets that flared out at the shoulders, like the riding coats of yore, or perhaps dusters. Their wings arched behind them and folded in at their backs and down their legs, reaching to the bends at the knees. The vision was one of such majesty, such splendor, it was hard to see them as my adversaries. But adversaries they were. At least for the time being.

The angel staring me down from above had short black hair, eyes just as dark, and mocha-colored skin. And he was stunning. Like all angels, I'd come to realize. They were nothing if not heartbreakingly beautiful.

Cookie finally picked up on the twelve-hundredth ring, panting and out of breath.

"Are you getting a quickie at the office again?" I asked, climbing into Misery, my cherry-red Jeep Wrangler.

"No, Charley, I have never gotten a quickie at the office. I was trying to put paper in the copier."

I did not even want to know why that would have her so out of breath.

"It's acting up again."

I turned Misery's engine over, put her in reverse, and sped out of there, all the while keeping an eye on the celestial being keeping an eye on me. It was all very cyclical.

"Did you check the carburetor?"

"I don't think copiers have carburetors."

"Did you check to see if it had one? Maybe you need to be on top of these things instead of judging others."

"You're absolutely right. I apologize."

She didn't mean it. I could tell.

Once out of his sight, the tension in my lungs eased, though just barely. "So, I have bad news."

"Uh-oh."

"I'm going to have to let you go."

"Did we lose money on a case again?"

"This one was not my fault. I was attacked. And I hate cheap toothpaste, so it's either let you go or buy cheap toothpaste. Sorry, hon."

"That's okay."

"Of course, at the rate I'm going, I might need to find a new job as well. Or go back to my old one. My former pimp said he'd hold my corner for me should I ever go back to him."

"Aw, that's so sweet."

"Actually, I think his exact words were, 'If you ever come crawling back to me like the ungrateful bitch you are.'"

"Well, still, it's the thought that counts."

"Right?"

"So?" she asked.

"So?" I asked back.

"How'd it go?"

"Not horridly, if that's what you're implying. But I didn't get to say good-bye to Alexander Skarsgård."

"Don't tell me. A chair?"

"No."

"An end table?"

"No."

"A floor lamp with really nice curves?"

"A couch."

"Ah."

"Seriously, Cook, if stealing weren't illegal, I would've taken him home with me. And slept on him. And possibly licked him." Parting was such sweet sorrow.

"Well, you've licked worse."

"Why? What have you heard?"

3

I parked in front of our office building, partly because I worked there and partly because there was an actual space open. On Central. In the middle of the day. That rarely happened. Of course, I usually parked at the apartments behind our building. Partly because I had my own parking space with a sign that warned any would-be trespassers of car booting and disembowelment should they even think about parking there, and partly because I lived there. Mostly because I lived there.

But, hey! Free space!

Just kidding. There was a meter.

I fed it a few quarters, ignored yet another angel watching me from the building top next to ours, and took the outside stairs to our second-floor offices. Mr. Farrow, my slightly sexier half, would be at work in the café below, and I wasn't sure what all he'd wanted to talk about. Thus, I decided to avoid him at all costs.

Cookie was at her desk, looking rather perky in a hot-pink, frilly thing. I could totally use that in my streetwalking gig. It would be a tad big, but that's what bondage straps were for.

"Hey, Cook," I said, hanging up my jacket.

"Hey back."

Uh-oh. Doldrums. I could feel them coming off her in waves and hoped it wasn't contagious. I was already depressed. I'd recently found out that, as a god, I couldn't die except at the hands of another god. What if I became suicidal? What would I do? The fact that I couldn't die would make me even more depressed, and there wouldn't be a damned thing I could do about it.

Oh, well. Best cross that bridge when I got to it.

"What did you do last night?" she asked, her gaze glued to her computer screen, her voice listless, which was completely at odds with the searing pink she was wearing and the spiky black hair that framed her round face and cerulean eyes.

I sat in the chair across from her, the one I'd secretly named the Winter Soldier. It had a mysterious vibe with a murky, possibly sordid past. "I went onto the dark web. I thought it might be a chat room for demons. Figured I could get some inside info."

"And how'd that turn out?"

"Bad. Very bad. Hey, is it inside-out day again? I used to love that in, like, the third grade."

She looked down at her blouse, then pulled it out at the neck, and either searched her seams for a clue or checked out her girls. "Damn it. It is inside out." She let out a lengthy sigh, stood, and headed for the rest-room.

"Hey, you okay?" I asked, noticing the matching earrings and pink bracelet.

"Sure."

"Cookie?" I said, drawing out the vowels in my best I-know-you're-a-lying-skank voice. Only without the skank. Cookie was as much of a skank as I was a saint. "What's going on? You've never been into color coordination before."

She pursed her lips and sat back down. "I don't know. I feel like something is wrong."

"It's the chafing. Once you turn it the right way—"

"No, not with the blouse."

"Of course."

"I was trying to be sexy. He didn't even notice."

"Our Lord and Savior?"

"Robert."

"Oh, yeah, that makes more sense."

Every time I spoke with Sister Mary Elizabeth, my thoughts tended to lean toward Catholicism for a few days. She and my uncle Bob had gotten hitched a while back—Cookie, not Sister Mary Elizabeth—so it made sense that she would try to be sexy for him.

I leaned closer and put on my best sympathy face. "Cook, what's up?"

"I think I'm losing him."

"Oh, please. You couldn't lose him if you were seventeen, on a date with Thor, and he was your virginity. The man is so into you, Cook."

She filled her lungs. "Maybe at one time. I think he's having an affair."

If I'd been drinking coffee, I would've spit it out in a fit of coughs. Thank God for small miracles. "Oh, hon, you know that's impossible, right? He has ED."

She gaped at me. "He most certainly—" When she realized I was teasing, she stopped gaping and glared instead.

She was right. ED was no joking matter. "Okay, he doesn't have erectile dysfunction, but it's fun to say out loud, and the thought of Ubie having an affair is hilarious either way."

"Why? Because he loves me so much?"

"No. Well, yes. But seriously. There's just no way. That man is head over heels, and he would never do anything to hurt you like that."

"I don't know." She punched a few keys on her keyboard. "He hasn't touched me in three days."

It was my turn to gape. For a solid minute.

"What?"

"Three days?"

"Yes."

"You're ready to call it quits after three days in desert conditions? The key is hydration. And possibly a vibrator."

"What? No, I'm not ready to call it quits. I'm just worried is all."

"Oh, good, 'cause I ain't taking him back. He's yours now. You signed all the appropriate documents. In triplicate. I witnessed, remember?"

"I know. He's just been so preoccupied."

"Well, he is a detective for the Albuquerque Police Department. That comes with a certain amount of stress, hon."

She shook her head. "No, there's something else. Something's bothering him. I just can't put my finger on it. It's like, I don't know, like he's in another world all the time. And he's had—" She caught herself. Cleared her throat. Shook her head. "Never mind. You're right. I'm just being silly."

"Oh, no, you don't. He's had what?" No way could she leave me hanging now.

"I don't want to worry you."

"Cook."

"He's had a bit of a temper."

This time, I was stunned. Uncle Bob? He'd always had a bit of a temper, but never with Cookie. "What happened?"

"It's nothing. Really."

"Cookie Kowalski Davidson." If he did anything to hurt my best friend or her daughter, blood be damned.

"He burned a roast last night."

"Oh, well, I guess that could be considered abusive. For the roast, anyway."

"When he pulled the pan out of the oven, he cursed and threw it across the kitchen and into the sink."

"He threw it?"

"Hard. It actually scared Amber. Then he stalked off to our bedroom and refused to come out even after I'd heated up some leftovers for dinner."

My blood came to a slow simmer. It didn't reach a full boil. I understood frustration as well as the next girl. But that whole macho temper tantrum bullshit didn't fly with me. "I get your point, but that's not affair behavior. That's something else. Something is eating at him."

Did he know?

One of the cool—or not-so-cool, depending on one's perspective—things about my husband being born in hell was that he could see when a person was slated for his homeland and what he or she did to get the short end of the stick.

I'd found out only days ago that my uncle Bob was slated for that very destination because of something he did for me. Something he did to save me from a Colombian drug baron who believed that cannibalizing people with any kind of supernatural ability would transfer that ability on to him.

He was wrong, of course, but he believed it, and there was no telling how many people died as a result of his obsession.

When some of his henchmen found out about me and my connection to the supernatural realm, they'd planned on gifting me to him to slither into his good graces. But Ubie had found out, somehow, and from what

Reyes told me, he'd killed them all in a shoot-out before they could inform the baron about me.

That was a few years ago. The reason it came up at all was because, unbeknownst to me, Uncle Bob was scheduled to die at the hands of a low-level thug named Grant Guerin. In fact, he was destined to die two days ago, but we'd thwarted the attempt.

Thanks to my husband's keen powers of perception and the fact that killing my uncle was how Guerin had been slated for hell himself, we'd known exactly where and when Ubie was to die at his hands.

We'd staked out the place, but he must've spotted our guy there and taken off. Thus, when Ubie showed up, Guerin wasn't there. Ubie was saved. Kudos for us.

But until Reyes actually saw Guerin again, we wouldn't know if we'd only postponed the inevitable. If Guerin killing Ubie was still in the works.

Because of this, we kept up the round-the-clock surveillance on Ubie. And why I'd scolded Angel in the psychiatrist's office. He'd been on Ubie detail for the last few days.

We thought we'd found Guerin a couple of times, but he continued to slip through our fingers. I needed to know if the threat on my uncle's life had been neutralized or only postponed. And we wouldn't know that until we found the little snake.

Cookie lowered her head. "I was worried that might be the case. And all I can think of is that he's lost interest in me. How pathetic am I?"

"On a scale of one to Kanye? You don't even register. You're not pathetic. Trust me, I'd know."

She sniffed. "Yeah?"

"Absolutely. Or you won't be once you turn your blouse right side out."

The front door to the office opened, and a tall—very tall—blond guy walked in.

I stood to welcome him to Davidson Investigations when recognition flooded my cells and rushed down my spine like a jolt of electricity.

There are moments in life that leave you stunned. Moments that take your breath away and make you forget your native tongue.

Reyes's brother walking into the office was one such moment. Not *that* brother. Not the godly one. The other one. The one that could have been his brother by kidnapping had the people who kidnapped him as a child not handed him over to a monster. That was my suspicion, anyway.

I'd been investigating the Fosters before my world got turned upside down, before I'd ended up, first, living in an abandoned convent for eight months while the bun I'd popped in the oven baked to simple perfection, and after, living in upstate New York for a month under the throes of amnesia because of having to give up said perfect bun.

As far as I could tell, the Fosters panicked when their families got suspicious. That was my best guess, anyway. Why else kidnap a child and then get rid of him weeks later? So, instead of handing Reyes back to his birth family, they sold him to Earl Walker. Or just handed him over. Either way, they gave Reyes to a monster. And not in the supernatural way, either. Earl was a man so evil, so vile, it wafted off him like a toxin.

Cookie and I had yet to figure out if Shawn Foster, the man standing in my office waiting for me to speak to him, was a legitimate adoption or if he, too, had been kidnapped.

"Are you Ms. Davidson?" he asked, his voice low and smooth.

When Cookie had first described Shawn Foster to me, she'd commented on how opposite he was in looks to Reyes. But that applied only to his coloring. Where Reyes was dark, Shawn was light. Literally and celestially. His aura was stunning. Brighter than most. More pure. He had blond hair cropped short and pale skin. But his features were bizarrely similar. Beautiful. Angelic. Very much like Rey'aziel's. Which would explain why my suspicions shifted into overdrive.

"Yes." I stepped forward and took his outstretched hand. "Sorry, you just look really familiar."

"I should," he said with a grin. "You've been investigating me for a while now."

We stood in an awkward silence, mostly because it took me a moment to recover from his statement. He knew I'd been investigating him. His parents. Did he know about Reyes? He was younger than Reyes. My age, actually. And from what we found out earlier about him, he was living with his parents again while he went to graduate school at UNM. He was in engineering. And he was still gazing at me, waiting for his statement to sink in.

"Oh, right. Well"—I shot a *save me* expression to Cookie, who was still busy trying to reset her jaw—"not so much you as . . . your parents." I realized too late that investigating his parents could seem worse than investigating him.

"Good," he said, dropping my hand and acknowledging Cookie with a nod. "Then you'll have a jump start on my case, should you choose to accept it."

"Your case?" I asked, gesturing toward my office, which was just past Cookie's, a.k.a. our reception area.

"Yes. I'd like you to find my real parents."

I almost tripped, then closed the door, giving Cookie one last *holy crap* look before it closed completely.

"Please, have a seat." I offered him the chair across from my desk, then went straight for the Bunn. "Coffee?"

"No, thanks." He was still standing, checking out the digs. "This is nice."

"Thanks. My husband recently had it redecorated."

"Right." He sat down at last and put a folder he'd been carrying on my desk. "He owns the bar and grill downstairs."

Was that all he knew? I could only hope at this point. "Yes, he does."

I'd been having strange encounters with both the living and the dead, with both demons and angels, with poltergeists and the mentally unstable, my entire life, but I could honestly say this rated really close to the top.

I sat across from him and took a sip of liquid courage. "How did you know about the investigation?"

"I didn't. Not at first. But when I saw you drive by my parents' house the other day, I remembered seeing you parked down the street about a year ago."

"You have a great memory."

"You were there for quite a while."

Try days. "And that's unusual because . . . ?"

"You parked. You never got out. You didn't live in the neighborhood, but you sat down the street for some time."

"Of course." Wasn't he the perceptive one.

"So, the next time you did a drive-by, I took down your license plate and had a friend run it."

"Isn't that illegal?"

"Very."

"And resourceful," I added.

He lifted a shoulder in modesty.

"What have your parents told you?"

"That my mother was in labor for thirty-six hours. That she eventually had to have a C-section. That she nursed me until I was two."

"I see." When we'd looked into the case before, we were almost certain Shawn Foster had been abducted by the Fosters as well, and that they'd gone through a shady adoption agency, one that had only been open a few months and had facilitated only three adoptions, Shawn Foster being one of them. "But you don't believe them?" I asked. Why would he be here if he did?

"I don't. For several reasons. And I don't think you do, either."

I still had to wonder if he knew anything about Reyes. I gestured toward the file. "May I?"

"Of course."

He leaned back while I thumbed through the folder he'd brought. It was mainly pictures, notes on inconsistencies in his parents' stories, statements from relatives who didn't remember Mrs. Foster ever mentioning the pregnancy to them, and one final slip of paper in the back that pretty much sealed the deal. A DNA test. The Fosters were most definitely not his parents. Not even close.

"Do your parents know you did the DNA test?"

"No."

"So, you believe you were adopted?"

"Do you?" he challenged.

"What do you mean?"

He rubbed a hand over his mouth in thought, his blue eyes studying me. "You've been looking into this for quite some time. I'd like to know why. And what your thoughts are."

"Mr. Foster—"

"Shawn, please."

"Shawn, all I have are thoughts without a single shred of evidence to support any of them. I couldn't possibly divulge my ramblings without proof. It would be very irresponsible."

"Well, that answers that."

"What?" I asked as he stood, grabbed the file, and turned to leave. "Wait. That answers what?"

"You're just like them."

"Wait, please."

He swung around and marched toward me until I had little choice but to take a step back. When we were nose to nose, he answered, his voice low, his face flushed. "Lies. Runarounds. It's all I've gotten my whole life, and I'm done. I'll find out the truth myself, one way or another."

The anger in his expression, the pain emanating out of him, the glittering wetness between his lashes, cut sharply into my chest. I wanted to help him, but I didn't know what to do. I'd promised Reyes to stay out of what he considered his business and his business alone. But Shawn had come to me. Surely Reyes would understand.

And, quite frankly, Reyes could bite me. He *was* my business.

Shawn turned again, but I took hold of his arm. He stopped but didn't look at me, and I could tell he was embarrassed by his behavior.

"There is a reason I was looking into your case. I have no evidence whatsoever, but I believe you were abducted by the Fosters."

He must've believed the same thing. He registered no surprise at all. "Why do you think that?"

"Because—" I stopped. Took a deep breath. Wondered if I was taking my life into my own hands. I could only be killed by another god. And Reyes was another god.

Oh yeah. He was going to kill me.

"Because," I continued, opening the bag to let the cat out of it, "because my husband was abducted by them as well."

After two hours and seven cups of coffee split between the three of us— since Cookie had helped me with the initial investigation, I'd invited her into the meeting—we came to the conclusion that Shawn was definitely one of the three adoptions that the shady agency had overseen.

I couldn't imagine how the agency got away with it. There were rules and regulations up the wazoo for a business like that. State inspections and licenses that had to be approved. The paperwork must have just slipped through somehow. Or perhaps someone was paid to look the other way.

We went over everything Shawn knew and everything we'd found out with a fine-tooth rake. Shawn wanted to know more about Reyes. I had already said too much. And besides, I got the feeling he knew a lot more about Reyes than he was letting on.

Thankfully, he understood when I told him I needed to confer with my partner in crime before filling him in. Of course, one search and he could know way too much about Reyes, if he didn't already—namely, that he'd spent a decade behind bars for a murder he didn't commit. But what little I did say about Reyes hadn't surprised him in the least. Almost as though he already knew him.

The longer we talked, the stronger the feeling that there was more to Shawn Foster than met the eye. I would catch him studying me. Not in the usual way a man might study a woman, but in a curious way. Like he was trying to figure me out. But that was cool. I was trying to figure him out, too.

"Okay, we'll get started on this. Are you sure you want to go home, Shawn?"

He'd stood and taken his cup to the counter where the Bunn sat. "What do you mean?"

I walked over to him as Cookie gathered papers. "I mean, are you going to be able to keep up the charade a little longer? I don't think you should tell your parents—"

"You mean the crackpots who abducted me?"

I bowed my head. The resentment was already getting a foothold.

"Yes. I don't think you should tell them just yet. Let us look into this a little more. See what we can dig up."

He nodded. "I won't say anything."

"I'm worried what will happen if you do."

"Charley, I've been living with this for a long time. The doubt. The suspicion. A few more days isn't going to make any difference."

"I live in the Causeway, the apartments behind us. Third floor. First door on your left. You are welcome anytime, day or night."

"Thanks," he said. It was a brush-off. He didn't believe me.

"No, I mean it. In fact, I think you should come stay with us either way. Just until we get this sorted out."

He let a grin overtake his features. "And what would my brother say?"

I laughed softly. His brother. Reyes.

"Maybe you should tell him about all this first."

"He's kind of awesome, actually. He'd be totally cool with it."

"Okay, well, I'll think about it." He said good-bye to Cookie, and just as he was about to walk out the door, he turned and said, "There is one more thing I've been meaning to ask you."

"Shoot."

He narrowed his eyes, looked me up and down, then said, "Why the hell are you so bright?"

4

Why yes, I have discovered the joy of cooking.
It's when my husband does it.
—MEME

"What does this mean?" Cookie asked.

I'd put Shawn off for a while. No way was I going to tell him about my whole grim reaper gig. Or better yet, the god thing.

"He must be like Pari," I said.

One of my besties, a tattoo artist with more ink pigmentation than skin cells, could see just beyond the veil that separated this plane from the next. The one that lies between the tangible world and the intangible. But instead of seeing the departed, instead of seeing an actual being, she saw mist. But she also saw my light. In fact, she had to wear sunglasses around me.

Shawn seemed fine without the shades, but he definitely saw my inner glowworm. I decided to leave it at that. If I pried further into what he could see, he would've had cause to pry further into what I was, so I didn't ask if he could see the departed. If he could see ghosts. I just told him I had a connection to the supernatural realm that was . . . complicated.

That seemed to satisfy him. For now.

"Okay," I said, snapping out of my musings, "how about you look into that agency some more? And maybe do a more thorough background check on the Fosters. I want to know everything about them. Where they were born. Where they went to school. How they met. Surely there is something in their past that will help explain their present."

"Already on it. You know, there's something we haven't discussed yet."

"Yeah?"

"If this does come out, especially your husband's part in it, the Loehrs could be summoned for a deposition or even to testify in court."

"Crap. I hadn't thought of that."

"Since they're in hiding with your daughter, I thought that might be a bad idea."

"No, you're right. We'll just have to keep Reyes's abduction out of it altogether. If that's possible."

"Shawn will go along with that. I'm certain."

"I think so, too. He seems like a great guy."

"He does," she said. "Wait. What about the other two?"

"The other two?"

"The other two adoptions that shady agency facilitated. Where did those kids come from?"

I sat behind my desk again. "Yeah, I wondered about that, too. Maybe you should look into those. You know, in your spare time." I was such a slave driver.

"Do you think your friend Agent Carson could help?"

"With the case, probably. With the fact that your blouse is still inside out?" I eyed her doubtfully.

"Oh, for heaven's sake. Why didn't you remind me?" She took off for the restroom, appalled. "I'm meeting Robert for lunch."

"Get a quickie while you can!" I said with a giggle.

———

I sat at a table in Calamity's, Reyes's bar and grill, and watched my husband leave his office and head toward me. I'd offered to make him lunch. He was the master chef in the family, but I'd watched just enough Food Network to be dangerous. I figured it was high time I cook for him. There was just one problem with my master plan. I'd gotten so busy this morning that I didn't have time to cook, so I'd had to improvise.

He moved with the grace of an animal, his dark hair and intense gaze captivating the room. Most eyes turned toward him. Most breaths caught. Most conversation came to a standstill.

When he sat down, I pushed one of two plates toward him. Each had three rows of crackers with tuna salad on top and a fat, orange carrot on the side as garnish. The carrots still had their peels and stalks on them, stalks that took up half the table. But I'd run out of time.

He eyed his plate, his expression filled with traces of humor and doubt.

"Don't knock it until you try it," I said. "We're having *whores-de-vours*." I gazed up at him. "Who doesn't adore *whores-de-vours*?" When he didn't answer, I took the opportunity to add, "And carrots."

"I had no idea you were so fond of hors d'oeuvres."

"Love. Them." I snapped off the tip of my carrot and ate, crunching it as loudly as I could.

"More than my huevos rancheros?"

Damn, he had me there. His huevos, rancheros or otherwise, were pretty fantastic.

He lifted a cracker as though it had a viral infection and took the whole thing in one bite. Then his face—no, his doubts!—transformed. He nodded in appreciation and ate another.

I took a bite, too, and marveled as I savored the best tuna salad I'd ever had. It was tuna salad, for his Brother's sake.

"This is really good," he said, a little surprised.

"It's phenomenal." I was even more than a little surprised.

He finished off his first line of whores, then asked, "What's your secret?"

"No idea," I said with my mouth half-full. "I didn't make it. I got busy."

He cast me a look of horror but recovered quickly. "Who made it?"

"No idea again. I scraped it off the sandwich Sammy brought for lunch."

He choked, coughing lightly before asking, "And how did Sammy take that?"

"I don't think he knows yet."

"And the carrots?"

"They were there. Just seemed kind of fitting."

He leaned back in his chair. "An entire kitchen at your disposal and you had to resort to thievery to feed me. What kind of billion-heiress are you?"

For that, I stole one of his crackers. "Billion-heiress implies an inheritance. I married into money, thank you very much. I'm officially a trophy wife." When he continued to watch me with an uncomfortable mixture of appreciation and humor, I put down the cracker and said, "So, what did you want to talk about?"

"I think you know." His deep voice washed over me like warm water. Or honey. Or rum. Add some lemon and I could pass for a hot toddy.

"What did you do to ruffle Jehovah's feathers?"

How did he know I did anything to ruffle his Brother's feathers? "How do you know I did anything to ruffle your Brother's feathers?" When he only stared, silently judging me for, like, ever, I caved. "What gave it away?"

"That would be the army of angels tailing you."

Damn. I knew he'd notice. Then again, they were a little hard to miss. They were just so . . . there. Angels. Everywhere. With their wings and their swords and their dark eyes following my every move. Make one tiny threat to take over the world and *bam*! Heaven's version of the Secret Service rains down on you, throws you to the ground, and puts you in a headlock. Metaphorically.

"Fine. Michael and I had a bit of a tiff."

"The archangel?"

"That's the one."

"You had a tiff with an archangel?"

"Just a little one. Nothing to worry about."

"And it's like angel stew on Earth because?"

"I kind of told him I was taking over the world, but he got all up in my face."

"Ah. When did this big showdown happen?"

"A few days ago. Right after—" I bowed my head, thinking of that horrible day. Of how many people we could have lost. Of what Reyes *had* lost. "Right after the incident. Speaking of which, how are you doing?"

He folded his arms. "We're not talking about me."

"But don't you think we should? You lost your sister, Reyes. It's okay to grieve, you know. We all do it. All of us humans, that is."

A laugh that was full of sorrow escaped him, but he brushed it off. As usual. "What are we going to do about this?"

"About what?"

"About the angels on your ass."

"Oh, that. Don't worry about them. They're just watching. Waiting. Making sure I don't actually follow through on any of my threats."

"There was more than one?"

"Well, there was the one biggie and then a few that were more or less implied. They apparently take that crap really seriously."

"I can't imagine why."

"Right?" I took another bite, then asked, "Do you miss her?"

He filled his lungs and eyed me with frustration before giving in. "I miss her. Of course I miss her. How could I not? But just knowing that she's out there watching over Elwyn helps."

"I agree." I said. Having someone like Kim watching our daughter eased the discomfort about one one-hundredth of a percent. But every little bit . . . "It's like a salve. Like a Band-Aid on an open, gushing wound."

He looked away, unwilling to give me any more. I didn't push.

"I've come to a decision," he said, looking back at me.

"Oh yeah?"

"Yeah." He gave me a long, slow once-over. "I think you need a bodyguard."

I laughed out loud that time. "A bodyguard?" I thought about it while poking my carrot with a fork. "Well, I already have a guardian, and she's pretty awesome." That guardian was a departed Rottweiler named Artemis.

"I know, but she can't protect you against an angel. They're powerful, Dutch. Very powerful. And just because they can't kill you doesn't mean they aren't going to give it their all. I don't think you'd be willing to do what was necessary to stop one if it came after you."

"But they're the good guys."

"In most situations, yes. But in this situation, I'm not so sure."

"I did threaten Him."

"You had a legitimate complaint. Jehovah—that's not His real name, by the way—knows that better than anyone, but I don't think He's going to give up His toy box just because you're angry with the way He governs His action figures."

"Yeah, I didn't expect He would. Wait. That's not His real name? What's His real name?"

"I'm not going to tell you something you already know. When were you going to tell me about your conversation with Michael?"

"That is an excellent question. Are you going to tell me His name or not?"

When he looked at me that time, his irises shimmering with something deep, something dark, he asked, "Why? So you can trap Him in the god glass, too?"

I gasped, completely offended. Not that I'd had any doubt that our conversations would one day lead to the pendant I carried in my pocket 24-7. The 600-year-old pendant that contained a substance called god glass, an opalescent stone that shimmered like a thousand galaxies. Inside it was the aforementioned hell dimension, the one Jehovah created for His rebellious little brother, a.k.a. my husband. And it all sat in an intricate glass-covered pendant, barely bigger than a quarter, with delicate scrolls and ornate markings.

Because I hadn't known how Reyes would take the news when he found out he, too, was a god, because I hadn't known if he would change into the malevolent being I'd been led to believe he was, I kept it hidden. Until I had to use it, that is. I'd trapped one of the two truly malevolent gods who'd joined Team Satan in it. And now that god, along with a nasty demon named Kuur, was locked in a dimension with dozens of innocent souls.

Getting them out without releasing the evil entities inside had been on my to-do list for a while. But Reyes had figured out I'd kept the god glass a secret from him. And why. So, I decided to do what I did best. I changed the subject.

"About this bodyguard position, you offering?"

He sat watching my mouth for the longest time, causing my insides to tingle. Then he bit his bottom lip and wet it. The movement was so innocent, so everyday, yet it sent a jolt of pleasure straight to my core.

"I don't know," he said at last. "What does it pay?"

I cleared my throat. And my dirty mind. "I can't afford much. I'm already having to switch to cheaper toothpaste just to keep Cookie on."

He tsked, the sound both humorous and sensual. "The sacrifices we make." He had yet to lift his gaze from my mouth, and I could've cut the pheromones hanging thickly in the air with a switchblade.

The way I saw it, I had two choices. I could take him to the broom closet and tear off his clothes, or I could wish that I'd taken him to the broom closet and torn off his clothes for the rest of the day.

Broom closet it was.

Just as I'd decided to jump on the idea—and him—I remembered my latest gig. The one that he was not going to be happy about. The one that I really should have discussed with him before accepting, not that my PI business was any of his, but it had been a sensitive subject in the past. Like third-degree-burn sensitive.

Best to get it out in the open. Rip off the Band-Aid, so to speak. Cut open a vein and hope he still cared enough about me afterwards to apply pressure.

I cleared my throat and straightened my shoulders. "So, yeah, I got a new case today."

"You don't say."

"I just want you to know that I already accepted it."

He finally met my gaze, his curiosity getting the better of him. "What do you mean?"

"I mean . . . I mean Shawn Foster. The Fosters' son came in today."

He stilled but gave no other clue as to his thoughts.

"He knows, Reyes. He knows he's not the Fosters' biological son. And the adoption agency that supposedly did the paperwork should the Fosters ever have to prove they'd gotten him through legitimate means? He knows that was bogus as well. He believes, as do I, that he was abducted as a child. Just like you were."

I could feel rather than see the darkness slide over him like a cloak. His poker face was top notch, but he was not a happy camper shell. "He asked you to look into it?"

"He just waltzed into the office and hired me."

"How did he know to come to you?"

"See, now here's where it gets interesting." I was so good at lightening the mood. Not so great with lightening my hair, though. Peroxide and I did not get along. "I've done a few drive-bys past the Fosters' house since we've been back. You know, just to check on things. Totally, 100 percent innocent. But he noticed. I know, right? My bad."

"I thought we'd agreed you weren't going to look into the Fosters."

"We did," I assured him, jumping to explain. "And I wasn't looking into them. I was looking around them. Like, peripherally. Shawn just happened to notice." When Reyes didn't say anything, I continued. "But it's all good. Shawn and I are on the same page. He had a lot of great information. I had a lot of great information. Combine that with what you told me, and I think we could put them away, Reyes. I think we could get a conviction."

"And you think that's what I want?"

"Don't you? I mean, how can you not? They abducted you, Reyes. Then they allowed you to be abducted again by a monster, if that's what really happened, and you just want them to get away with it?"

"I want you to drop it."

"Reyes, I've already accepted the case. I was hoping you'd understand. Shawn wants to know. He wants to find out where he comes from. Find out who his real parents are. What his real life would have been like. He has questions just like you did."

"Drop the case."

It was an order, plain and simple. And the fact that he actually thought I'd follow it was comical. Or it would've been if he weren't seething underneath that calm exterior.

"No. I'm sorry, but I can't. This isn't just about you anymore."

He leaned forward, so close I could feel his breath on my mouth when he spoke. "Drop the case or I'll drop it for you."

Oh, no, he didn't. I narrowed my lids and set my jaw. "Try."

Heat exploded out of him. It was an inevitable part of who he was, of what he was, but this time the heat hit me like wall of fire.

He struggled to tamp it down. I could feel at least that much in the strangling density of his emotions. He fought to regain control.

And I struggled to stand my ground. This was important. The Fosters were criminals. They needed to be brought to justice. And the moment he believed he could threaten me into doing anything against my will was the moment he and I were going to have to seriously reevaluate our relationship.

My phone rang just as he stood to leave. "Wait," I said to him.

He stopped but didn't look back at me.

I checked my phone. It was Cookie. "This'll just take—"

"We'll talk about this later," he said, and then he strode away. Just like that. His anger leaving heat streaks on the air.

I answered. "Hey, Cook. What's up?"

"He's having an affair."

I'd started to get up, too. Several sets of eyes watched me, mostly women's, curious about Reyes and me. I sat back down. "Did he tell you that?"

Her breath hitched. "He didn't have to. I practically threw myself at him, and he barely noticed."

The sigh of relief I let loose made me light-headed. "Cookie, he is not having an affair. I'd bet my bottom dollar on it. Or even just my bottom. But I'll look into it for you if you'd like."

"I'd like. But that's not why I called."

"I'm downstairs. Heading up now."

"I'm still at home. I've been looking into the Fosters' backgrounds."

"At home?"

"I go into research mode when I'm upset."

"Ah, okay," I said as Valerie, Reyes's manager in training, cleared my table. "Hit me. What'd you find?"

"Well, they don't make sense."

"Child abductors rarely do."

"No, it's like they were never born."

"So, they were hatched?" I teased. I smiled at Valerie. She almost smiled back. It was so much better than the sneer I usually got from her. I got the feeling she didn't like me much.

"That makes about as much sense as what I'm finding. Neither one of them have birth certificates on file in the states they say they were born in."

"Oh, now that's interesting."

"Isn't it? Right now I'm looking at their employment records. Mrs. Foster has a copy of a birth certificate on file at the pediatrician's office she manages. It was issued in West Virginia, but according to the state records there, there was no female child born on that day in that town. Eve Bathsheba Foster was never born."

"Her birth certificate is fake?"

"I believe it is."

"Wait. Her middle name is Bathsheba? For reals?"

"The thing about the birth certificate is, who's going to double-check something like that? When someone hires you, unless it's a job where you need a certain level of clearance from the government, your employer will just get a copy of your birth certificate and call it good. They only need it to cover their asses should any problems arise later on."

"True."

"And how hard can it be to get fake documents in today's day and age?"

"Have you looked up Mr. Foster's?"

"I'm looking for the actual record now. His was a little harder to track down, but he filed for a conceal carry permit a few years ago under the name Abraham Boaz Foster."

"What the hell is up with their names?"

"No idea. I don't have a copy of the actual certificate, but get this— according to what was written on the application, both Mr. and Mrs. Foster were born on the same day, in the same town, at the same hospital."

"Okay, that's weird, right?"

"Oh, it gets better. Mrs. Foster's birth certificate lists her maiden name as . . . are you ready for this?"

"Cookie, you're killing me."

"Foster."

I sat back down. "Are you sure?"

"As sure as Shirley."

I didn't know who Shirley was or why she was so sure of herself, but Cookie seemed pretty confident in her findings. "Okay, let's say they did fake their birth certificates for some reason, who would go to all that trouble to fake one only to put the wrong surname on it?"

"Maybe the forger messed up?"

"I'd say."

I needed to get up close and personal with Mrs. F. To get a feel for her. She was clearly capable of kidnapping. What else was she capable of?

We'd been hired to find Shawn's real parents, but this case provided the perfect opportunity to delve further into Team Foster. If we were going to prove that Shawn had indeed been abducted, we'd need all the ammo we could get when we went to the DA.

"I think I should pay Mrs. Foster a visit today."

"Okay, she's at lunch right now, but she'll be back at two, and she's working until six. I checked."

Man, she was good. "Perfect. Now I just need a reason to visit a pediatrician's office and not actually see the pediatrician."

5

She has moments when she seems stable,
but then so does nitroglycerin.
—MEME

Since I had a few minutes, I decided to hit up an old adversary for info on said adversary's CI, his confidential informant. The confidential informant I had yet to find. The one who'd been slated to kill my uncle Bob, according to Reyes, who could see exactly when people were penciled in for a visit down under and what they did to get there.

Reyes had met Guerin in prison. He didn't think much about it at the time. Many of the inmates had locked themselves into a visit to the fiery pits long before they ended up behind bars. But Reyes had recognized Uncle Bob as the detective who'd put him away. No animosity. Just fact.

Guerin had been in prison for stacking up too many petty crimes, but he had yet to do the deed that would get him sent under. That wouldn't happen for a few years. Still, Reyes saw it the moment he met the kid, and though the time had come and gone, the threat was still there.

Since we'd been unable to locate the petty criminal, there was no way of Reyes seeing into him. Of him being able to tell if the kid's inevitable trip to the netherworld had been postponed. Or rescinded altogether.

And that was where Parker came in. I'd had a run-in with ADA Nick Parker a few days ago. ADA, surprisingly, did not stand for Abnormally Dimwitted Asshole. Who knew?

He'd basically blackmailed me into solving a case for him. I solved the case, mostly because it needed solving, but I never liked being black-mailed. It brought out the worst in me. Especially when the leverage was a threat against my daughter. My claws came out. In a fit of anger—and right around the same time I threatened to take over the world—I let ADA Parker know that. I did something I didn't even know I could do. I touched my mouth to his and showed him the supernatural world that raged around us in all its glorious detail. I showed him what I was, but more importantly, what I was capable of.

If nothing else, he'd never blackmail me again. I just hoped he was okay. Mentally. I'd left him in a state of shock. But hopefully he learned Rule #1 in the *Charley Davidson Handbook*: don't fuck with the reaper.

Just kidding. I didn't have a handbook, but I did have a handbag. A Prada knockoff.

Wait.

I stopped halfway in and halfway out of Misery when the realization of a lifetime dawned. I was a gazillionaire now.

Well, Reyes was. Dude was a genius.

Still, I could totally afford a real Prada handbag now. Holy cow. I scooted my ass across Idris Elba, my driver's seat. The one that hugged me in tight curves and kept me safe under the most hazardous conditions. The one that heated up with the push of a button. That warmed my nether regions to exquisite perfection.

Damn, I'd lost my train of thought. Oh, right. Prada. This would take some thought. I couldn't rush into such a big decision. Should I go with the fall line or wait for the new spring line to be out? My brain was going to explode with all the possibilities. Maybe I should just go to Target. Get my usual.

I turned Misery on, literally, and started to back out. But first, I flipped off the angel—this one with long black hair and pale skin—that was crouched on my hood, gazing at me through the windshield.

I floored it. The angel, completely unimpressed, simply spread his massive wings, rose up a few inches, and landed with his feet in front of my grill. His moves were more graceful than a ballet dancer's. Smoother than a mocha latte. And cooler than Christopher Walken, though not by much.

Then, with two fingers, he saluted me. It was a very human gesture. I stared for a moment in surprise before realizing my foot was still on the gas pedal. I slammed on the brakes. Then I sat for a moment, stunned. I'd almost backed into oncoming traffic. I surveyed my surroundings, made sure I hadn't run over any pedestrians, then offered the angelic being my best glare. He tipped an invisible hat. Not knowing how to take the gesture, considering the source, I shoved Misery into drive and headed to Parker's office.

Fifteen minutes later, Parker's assistant told me he was in court, so I meandered that way. I didn't know what case Parker was prosecuting but found the courtroom easily enough. A few spectators in the gallery were just going back in after a break, so I fell in line and went with the flow, following a tall white-haired man who reminded me of Colonel Sanders.

We sat behind the prosecutor's table. Hopefully, Parker would see me and I could pass him a note to meet for coffee. I needed to know if he'd heard from Guerin.

But Parker was too busy to look up when he walked back into the courtroom, shuffling papers and speaking quietly to his colleague. All very important. Very Zen. I didn't want to screw up his Zen, so I sat patiently, searching for my own Zen.

We stood as the judge came into the room, much like one would when a king entered, or the president, or a male stripper when the women in front of you are really tall.

Parker called his next witness, a woman who'd been held up at knife-point by the defendant. This seemed a pretty open-and-shut case. The guy was guilty. I felt it on him the moment he walked in. The woman was nervous. She stuttered and mumbled and had to be asked to speak up more than once, and every time she had to repeat herself, the defendant smirked and shook his head.

The poor woman was scared. Terrified. And he was enjoying it. She was a mouse, and the defendant, a large, hairy man with sideburns straight out of the seventies, was a cobra. And his behavior caused her to stutter even more.

Normally, this was the point in ADA Nick Parker's life where he turned a hilarious shade of red. He had the patience of a pit viper and zero empathy to boot. But not this time. He was frustrated. I could feel it. But no red or purple or even a soft shade of pink. What the hell? Where was the entertainment value in that?

"Let the record reflect that the witness has pointed to"—Parker had turned toward the peanut gallery and met my gaze at last—"has pointed to the defendant, James Wi . . ."

Parker's voice trailed off, and he just sort of stood there, staring at me.

"Mr. Parker?" the judge said, trying to get his attention.

I smiled and wiggled my fingers as inconspicuously as I could. Then I flashed him a piece of paper. I'd planned on gesturing toward his associate, letting him know I was going to give my message to her, but Parker did something I never expected. Something pretty much no one expected, so I wasn't the only one having to scrape my jaw up off the floor thirty seconds later.

He stilled.

I stilled.

He blinked.

I blinked.

He took in a sharp breath.

I blinked.

He dropped to his knees in the middle of the room, clasped his hands over his head, and bent forward, laying his forehead on the carpet and rocking.

Was he . . . ? No. He couldn't be. I mean, why would he worship me? Was *worship* the right word? Maybe he was seizing.

I blinked.

The judge blinked.

The bailiff blinked.

We all sat speechless for several long minutes.

"Mr. Parker," the judge said at last. "What are you doing?"

Parker's shoulders started to shake, and I realized at that moment that there was a chance, an ever-so-slight chance, that showing him the supernatural world around us may have affected him a tad greater than I'd imagined.

The judge called the bailiff over and pounded the gavel, calling for a recess.

I rushed past the bar to Parker's side. "Dude," I whispered, patting his head, "you can't worship me. I'm not that kind of god."

But he was gone. Praying and chanting and kind of whimpering. The bailiff helped him up, and I followed them into the judge's chambers despite the bailiff's stern, questioning brows. He had great brows.

"He just needs water," I said. "He does this all the time. It's a nervous condition."

Parker wouldn't look at me. On the bright side, his face was finally that hilarious shade of red I knew and loved. He kept his hands clasped and his head bowed.

"Do we need to call an ambulance?" the judge asked.

The court reporter had followed us in as well. "I'll do it."

The judge nodded. The bailiff went for water. And I kicked ADA Parker in the shin.

His head snapped up, and he looked at me at last.

"Cut it out," I said from between gritted teeth. "What the hell?"

"You. It's you."

I leaned closer as the bailiff brought him a tiny white cup of water. "Yes. It's me. Now cut this shit out."

"But you . . . you're—"

"I don't get it. You've known me for years. You've never worshiped me before."

"You're . . . a god."

I pushed the cup to his mouth and chuckled at the bailiff, dismissing Parker's statement with a wave of my hand. "I think it's his blood sugar. I solve one case for him, and suddenly I'm *a god*." I added air quotes for effect.

The bailiff shot me another warning. With his brows. They were very expressive.

Parker slowly slid off the chair onto one knee, his head bowed again.

I lifted him back up. "Stop it," I said, my voice more of a hiss than an actual whisper. "I mean it. Stop worshiping me. Jehovah is already pissed."

"Okay," the court reporter said. "An ambulance is on the way."

I was beginning to think he really needed one. He was sweating and panting, and his red face was turning more of a fuchsia. I figured he was somewhere between a panic attack and a heart attack. Either way, the guy had to calm down.

I took his jaw into both of my hands and lifted his face to mine.

"Nick," I said softly, soothingly, "be still."

He calmed instantly. A cool warmth left my fingers and soaked into him, like a supernatural version of Icy Hot.

Whatever it was, it worked. His breaths slowed, and his face paled to leave red splotches along his cheeks.

"I think he's okay," I said to the others.

He just stared at me, unable to speak. When the ambulance arrived, they gave him oxygen and started an IV before wheeling him out. I followed until they loaded him in the van.

"I'm sorry, Nick," I said as he watched me. "I just wanted info on your CI. We never found him."

He took off the oxygen mask. "My wife is pregnant."

That was fast.

I showed my palms. "I swear it's not mine."

"What do I call you?" He was serious.

"Charley. Charles. Chuck. Goddess Divine."

He didn't crack. I was losing my touch.

"I'm kidding about that last one. Parker, I'm just Charley."

"You were never just Charley."

Damn. What the hell did I show him?

"I—I had no idea." He was shaking, and the ambulance guys really wanted to head out.

"Grant Guerin?"

"I don't know." He wasn't lying. "But I can try to find him."

I squeezed his hand before turning to jump out. "Thank you."

"Nobody knows, do they?"

I turned back. "Knows?"

"What's coming. Nobody knows."

I scooted closer again as the EMT took Parker's blood pressure. "What are you talking about? What's coming?"

He'd been a million miles away. He blinked and focused on me again. "You."

"Miss, we need to go."

"Me? Parker, what do you mean?"

"Miss." The guy was getting more impatient.

So was I. Left with little choice—aside from knocking the guy out with a defibrillator, which was probably bolted down—I slowed time. First, to buy more of it. And second, to shut the guy up.

His movements came to a complete stop in suspended animation. A roll of tape he'd dropped hung in midair, his hand just below it ready for the catch.

Parker didn't notice. Nor did he notice the shadow pass by. I looked over my shoulder. An angel stood at the doors to the ambulance. It was the one that had been crouching on Misery. His massive wings blocked the sun as he looked in the van.

I ignored him. At least, I pretended to. As I spoke to Parker, I reached toward the ground, my palm facing the floor of the van.

"What do you mean?" I asked, just as I felt Artemis, my guardian Rottweiler, rise into my palm.

She paced around to my back, her teeth bared, her growls low as she watched the angel. Her sharp eyes would miss nothing, and I would have some sort of warning should the celestial being try anything. Though what he would try, I had no idea.

Parker's eyes filled with moisture as he thought back. "You should warn them not to make you angry," he said, his voice full of sadness. "They should never make you angry."

"Who? Those guys?" I gestured toward the EMT.

"No. Everyone. All of them. Any of them." He gave me a chastising frown. "You were a hungry, hungry hippo."

Ugh. This was like talking to Rocket, a savant friend of mine who'd died in the fifties. He'd had electroshock therapy before he died. Had I done the same thing to Parker? Had I scrambled his brain?

"Parker, what did you see?"

"You." He lifted a hand to my face. Parker wasn't the tender, loving type, so it startled me. Time slipped, but only a little before I caught it again. "I saw you."

"I don't understand."

"You ate too much, and now your power is too great even for you, god eater."

Had he somehow gained access to memories I'd lost? Or had he seen the future? No. That was impossible.

"I saw seven become one. The thirteenth. The most powerful. I saw you devour them all and become . . . become what you are. All for him."

Artemis growled by my side, but when I turned back, the angel was still standing stock-still. His head bowed, he gazed at me from beneath thick lashes. His stunning face void of any expression. But time was screaming toward us. I could only hold it for so long.

"Parker, enough with the cryptic shit. What did you see?"

"Ice." He smiled, then a soft laugh overtook him. "Ice. First hell, in your infinite anger, then everything else."

"Hell? You saw hell freeze over? Like literally?"

But it was too late. Time had bounced back with a thunderous roar. Parker said something else, but the rebound of time drowned it out.

"In or out," the EMT said, oblivious. "Now."

"Fine." I rose and stepped down from the van.

The angel was gone. Artemis followed me out, and I called to Parker just before they closed the door, "Grant Guerin!"

He nodded, then disappeared.

I could only wrap my head around three words: *What, the,* and *fuck.*

I called Cookie on the way to the pediatrician's place where Mrs. Foster worked as an office manager.

"So, you know how you go into a situation expecting one thing and something else comes along and blindsides you? Something you never saw coming?"

Which is the definition of blindside. "I do, actually. What happened?"

I relayed what happened in tremendous detail, telling her how Parker began worshiping me in the middle of a cross-examination, how he knew I was a god, how he believed I'd somehow managed to get his wife preggers which, oddly enough, I had. It was a whole transfer of mystical healing elements when I'd kissed him, but I wasn't about to go around claiming I could help couples get pregnant. I'd have to change the name of my business to Davidson Investigations and Fertilization Clinic. Then I gave Cookie time to absorb it all.

After a few minutes, she asked, "Charley, what the hell did you do to that poor man?"

"Fuck if I know." I was just as lost as the next person. "He called me a god eater. He said he saw seven become one."

Artemis had hitched a ride. She was sticking her head out the window. The closed window. *My* closed window. She may have been incorporeal to the rest of the world, but to me she weighed about a thousand pounds. And driving with her in my lap was like trying to steer in a full-body cast. This could not be safe.

"Well, let's think about it. He saw seven become one. That makes perfect sense. You are the descendent of the seven original gods from your dimension, right? Once all the other gods merged down to one, you were all that was left. You were the thirteenth."

"Oh, right. I hadn't thought of that. But I had nothing to do with their joining. Two gods merge to become one. To become stronger. And they just kept doing it until I was the only one left."

"He called you a god eater?"

"Yes. What the hell is a god eater?"

"I don't know. Sounds ominous."

"I was going to say pretentious, but okay. Hey, I know. We should call Garrett. He's our research and development guy. Maybe he's come across something like this in his reading."

When one looked at Garrett Swopes, *research and development* was so not the first thing that came to mind. He was more a combination of GI Joe and a Chippendales dancer. But he'd really gotten into the whole research gig. He could know something.

"I'll get right on it."

"You okay?"

"I will be just as soon as you figure out what's going on with my husband."

I loved it when Cookie called Ubie her husband. I was such a romantic. "You didn't happen to come up with a reason for me to be visiting the office manager of a pediatrician's practice, did you?"

"How much do you know about copiers?"

"Copiers?"

The young girl behind the desk took the tried-and-true attitude of sheer boredom and transformed it into an art form. She barely looked out of high school. Nobody mastered the epitome of boredom like a teenager. Sadly, as we aged, we lost the delicate intricacies of the skill set. It was rather like losing an ancient language or a potato soup recipe.

"Did you say *copiers*?" she asked again above the earsplitting screams of a surly toddler. I'd fought demons and malevolent gods and even Lucifer himself, and nothing terrified me more than an angry two-year-old.

"Yes. If I could just talk to your office manager—"

"We already have a copier." She popped her gum and continued to stare.

I forced a smile. A plastic one I'd found on sale at a consignment store a few weeks back. "Yes, but you've never tried the Eureka Mighty Mite."

"That's a vacuum cleaner."

"Or the CLS550."

"That's a Mercedes."

Holy shit, she was good.

"Look, is the office manager in or not?"

After drawing in a long, deep breath that sucked most of the oxygen out of the room, she called out, "Eve!"

I froze in anticipation as Mrs. Foster, a.k.a. Reyes's abductor, walked around a corner. Reyes had been right when we talked about them a few weeks ago. While Shawn Foster had light coloring to the extreme, Mrs. Foster had dark hair and eyes. She looked in her early fifties, her short hair curled and styled to perfection. Her crisp business suit and thick-heeled pumps perfectly matched. She looked about as much like a child abductor as I looked like, well, the grim reaper. But the moment her gaze landed on me, her emotions rocketed into overdrive.

She stopped short and stared a long moment before catching herself. "Can I help you?" she asked, walking forward.

Did she know who I was as well? Shawn Foster, her would-be son, had busted me casing their house. Had she done the same?

"Hi," I said, offering her the same plastic smile I'd flashed her colleague. Thank goodness it was BPA-free. "I was wondering how happy you are with your copier."

I tried to register the emotions bombarding her nervous system, but they were all over the place. Surprise. Dread. Suspicion. Distrust. But mostly extreme interest sprinkled with a healthy dose of fear. So, mostly negative.

"Salespeople aren't supposed to come to the front desk during business hours. What was your name again?"

I held out my hand. "Buffy. Buffy Summers-s-s-sault." I seriously had to quit watching Joss Whedon reruns.

"And you work for?"

"Malcolm Reynolds? Maybe you've heard of him? He owns Serenity Office Supply?"

Holy crap on a crack pipe, I was usually better at this. It was her reaction to me. She either knew who I was or . . . or what? Knew *what* I was? But how could she? Shawn could see my light. Could she as well? Was it a family thing? But he wasn't even her biological son. I didn't get it.

Or maybe she knew Shawn had hired me, which would make a lot more sense. I'd have to warn him.

"Okay, well, I think we're pretty happy with our copier. Do you have a card, though? Just in case?"

"Yes." I nodded to emphasize the fact that, indeed, I most definitely had a card. Just not on me. "Yes, I do. In my car."

"How about a brochure?"

"Yep." I nodded again. "In my car as well. I seemed to have forgotten everything." I knocked on my head to make sure it was still attached. "Still there," I said with a nervous laugh.

The entire time we spoke, the receptionist's jaw dropped in increments until her mouth hung open at an odd angle. Add a little drool dripping down one side of her chin, and I was right there with her. Idiot. Of the blithering sort.

"You know what? I'll go get our extra-special promo pack with all my information and be right back."

Mrs. Foster inclined her head as though agreeing that might be best, but she reminded me of a duck. Or that saying about a duck where it's just chilling on the surface, all calm and collected, but underneath the water it's paddling its little webbed feet like crazy. She looked cool on the outside, but her insides were churning like a gathering storm.

I took off before I could do any more damage. So much for stealth. I only hoped she wouldn't connect any of the dots. Shawn had come to me, after all. Unless he told her of his pursuit, she couldn't know. I crossed my fingers just in case the act really did have some magical ability to bring one luck.

The look on my husband's face when I stepped off the elevator, however, would suggest otherwise.

6

A lot of people are only alive because
I shed too much hair to ever get away with murder.
—MEME

I stepped off the elevator into the parking garage and stopped short as I spotted my husband leaning against a concrete column about fifty feet from me. But he graced me with only a quick glance. I could feel his anger from where I stood. I'd been having problems lately deciphering his emotions, he was so tightly wound, but there was no mistaking the quiet rage pulsing around him.

He was angry about my investigation. Well, he'd just have to get over it. I raised my chin and started toward Misery. That's when I noticed what he was glaring at, and my apprehension eased. A bit. He stood between me and an angel.

I considered walking over to him, but he shook his head and said softly, "Go."

He didn't need to tell me twice.

I hoofed it to my bright red Jeep, but when I got in, I propped my head against the steering wheel and just sat there. What the hell just happened in that doctor's office? I was normally so cool under pressure. Buffy

Summersault? If I'd just risked the safety of one of my clients, I'd never forgive myself. Shawn had come to me in the strictest of confidences. It didn't get much more delicate than investigating your own parents for child abduction. What would they do if they found out he knew?

When I looked back at Reyes, he'd shifted his attention from the angel and onto Mrs. Foster. She rushed out of a side door and hurried to a gold Prius, her movements harried, her expression lined with worry.

"And just where might you be going?" I asked no one in particular.

I turned the key, but the moment I threw Misery into drive to follow the nice kidnapper, a knock sounded on my window. My heart jumped into my throat. I turned to see the receptionist motioning me to roll the window down.

"Hey." I couldn't help but notice the stiff line of her mouth.

"You upset Eve," she said.

"Yeah." I watched as the taillights of the Prius disappeared around a corner. "Sorry about that."

"You don't really sell copiers, do you?"

"Sure I do. I have a card right—"

I looked around Misery, ignoring the smirk my thirteen-year-old investigator sent me from the passenger's side. Artemis bounced up in the backseat when Angel popped in, whining in excitement, her stubby tail wagging at the speed of light.

I understood. That was often my reaction when Reyes appeared.

Angel reached back and rubbed her ears, before nodding toward the actual angel loitering in the dark garage, and asking, "What's with all the angels?"

"Oh," the receptionist said. "Okay. Sorry." She started to turn. I was clearly about to lose a lead. Her demeanor was one of concern and apprehension, not triumph for having busted me for fraud.

"Okay," I said, stopping her. "I don't sell copiers." I let it go there. If she had something to say, she would. If not . . .

She faced me again.

"She's hot," Angel said.

"Then what were you doing here?"

"I was just getting a feel for the place. You know, should I ever need a pediatrician." I bowed my head and tried to ignore the fact that I would've been in need of one had I been able to keep my daughter. But she was safe. That was my mantra. Beep was safe. Safer than she would be around me.

"You'll get her back," Angel said.

I had one hand on the gearshift. He covered it with his. I turned mine up and laced our fingers together.

"You know, we could make out and she would never know."

I rolled my eyes, then held up an index finger to the receptionist. "Excuse me." I took my hand back and picked up my phone so I could pretend to talk on it, but first I had to set up my pretend conversation. "Hello? Yeah. Uh-huh. Uh-huh. Uh-huh."

"Are you going to do this all day?" Angel asked.

I cast him my evilest grin. And continued. "Seriously? No way. Uh-huh. Uh-huh."

Angel laughed, then slowly leaned forward like he was going to kiss me. The little shit.

"You do realize my husband is not fifty feet away."

And he was now watching us from beneath hooded lids.

Angel snorted and moved in even closer. "I'm not afraid of your husband." When Reyes's arm snaked around his neck and he pulled Angel back against his chest as he materialized, locking him in an inescapable chokehold, Angel added through a strained larynx, "Much. I'm not afraid of him much."

Artemis pawed at them, wanting to play, too. Angel chuckled, ducked under Reyes's arm, and lunged into the backseat to wrestle with her. Thank goodness the laws of physics didn't apply. There was no way all three of them would have fit in my backseat had they been corporeal.

"Aren't you supposed to be watching Uncle Bob?" I asked him.

"I have been. He's perfectly safe. Swopes is on watch now."

"Oh, okay." I'd trust Garrett Swopes with my own life, so I felt Ubie was safe in his hands.

Angel let out a squeak that I assumed was a plea for help, but I ignored it.

"Sorry about that," I said to the receptionist, pretending to end my pretend call.

"That's okay."

Reyes materialized in my passenger seat but stayed firmly planted in the supernatural realm. Otherwise she would have been in for quite the shock.

She kicked at the ground. "Well, I'll let you go. I got off early and—"

"I guess Mrs. Foster did, too?" I asked, nodding toward the exit.

She lifted a shoulder. "I guess."

"Do you know where she went?"

The girl narrowed her lids. "Why do you want to know?"

"No reason." Either a paw or a foot landed on the back of my head. I coughed to cover up my sudden lurch forward, then refocused on her as Reyes shot a warning glare over his shoulder. "But if I did have a reason, is there anything you'd like to tell me?"

"Drop the case," Reyes said.

But the receptionist's reaction caught my attention. A sadness came over her. She looked down and took a long drag off an e-cigarette. "Not really. I just thought maybe you were, I don't know, investigating or something. Like undercover maybe."

Unless she knew what I did for a living, that was an odd thing to think. "Why would I be undercover?"

She shrugged again. "Because there was an investigation, but then nothing happened."

"Really?" I was having a hard time hearing her over Angel's screams. Apparently Artemis was going for the jugular.

"I'm not kidding, Dutch," Reyes said. He leaned close until his mouth was at my ear. "Drop the fucking case."

I tried to make my next move appear completely innocent, as though I were just looking around when I turned to face off against my husband.

His gaze sparkled with a mixture of interest and frustration. His expression hard. His full mouth set. Until I dropped my gaze to it and whispered the one question I knew he wouldn't answer: "Why?"

He eased back, the muscles in his jaw working as he turned away from me, propped an elbow on the window frame, and rested a hand at his mouth in thought.

We had agreed a few days ago no more secrets between us. Ever. Funny how long that accord *didn't* last.

"Besides, if you were undercover," the girl continued, "you'd know more about copiers than you do. You would have brushed up on them so you didn't look like you were undercover."

"Ah"—I raised an index finger and turned back to her—"but maybe that was all part of my master plan. Maybe I went in without knowing that much about copiers to throw you off my scent, so to speak. If I'd known too much . . ." Okay, that sounded dumb, even to me. "Never mind. What's your name, hon?"

"Tiana."

"Tiana. That's gorgeous."

She shrugged and nodded a shy thank you.

"Can we go somewhere to talk?"

As she mulled over my proposition, I ignored Angel's pleas for help and my husband's sudden shift into a draconian style of domesticity. Thankfully, Angel's cries were more laughter than agony. But Reyes's mistaken impression that I'd actually comply with his ridiculous demands lay somewhere in that gray area between adorable and assault with intent to kill.

Tiana nodded and said, "Okay. As long as it's far away from here."

To say that the receptionist was paranoid would have been an understatement had she not had good reason. We sat in an out-of-the-way restaurant in Rio Rancho called the Turtle Mountain Brewing Company, which was about twenty minutes from where she worked.

Reyes had dematerialized the moment I started Misery, his heat scalding my skin and leaving it warm the entire trip. I'd lost both my other two passengers when Artemis plowed into Angel as I was going seventy on Paseo Del Norte. I watched as they fell onto the pavement. Cringed as car after car rolled over them. Or, well, through them. They were so into re-creating the Battle of Gettysburg that they didn't notice, thank goodness.

The devastation of losing my passengers didn't affect my appetite in the least. I was enjoying a killer green chile pizza called the Chimayo. I wanted to marry the pizza and have its babies, but the server said it was already spoken for. Damn it.

My jesting, however, had eased the tension roiling in Tiana's stomach. She chowed down on a sub called the Sun Mountain. It looked amazing, and I had to resist the urge to ask for a bite. At least until we got to know each other better. I gave it ten minutes.

"You don't understand. It's not any one thing," she explained. We were, of course, discussing her coworker. "I can't really put my finger on it. I mean, Eve and her husband are, like, super religious."

"Religious?"

"Yeah, but not your everyday kind of religious. They're like the nut kind of religious. They believe they are here for a reason."

"Here?"

"On Earth. They think God put them here to . . ." She laughed softly as though the very thought made her uncomfortable. "I can't even say this out loud without cringing, but they think God put them here to fight evil."

"Okay," I said, a little taken aback. "Well, it's good to know we have someone on our side, yes?"

She let out a breath that was part amusement and part relief. It must have felt good to talk with someone about her concerns.

"You don't think they're the good guys?" I asked.

"I think they *think* they are, but they go about it the wrong way. I'm surprised Dr. Schwab hasn't fired Eve. Especially after her latest catastrophe."

That perked me right up. I encouraged her to elaborate by inching closer.

She met me halfway. "She told one of our mothers that her son was evil. Told her to be careful and watch for signs of the beast."

I sat stunned, torn between laughter and alarm. "The beast? Who would tell a mother something like that?"

"That's what I mean. She's crazy. Said the kid had a darkness about him."

A darkness? Could she really see into the supernatural realm? "And she told her that at the doctor's office?"

"No." Tiana shook her head and took a drink of water. "That's the only reason she still has a job. She doesn't work directly with the patients unless she has to contact them for billing or insurance information. According to Eve, she just happened to run into the mother at a grocery store in the South Valley. A store that's all the way across town from work and the Fosters' house. Why was she shopping for milk all the way across town?"

"Good question. What did the doctor say?"

"Well, it was the woman's word against hers. She denied saying it, of course, but why would that mother make up something so bizarre?"

"I agree. I don't suppose I could get the woman's name?"

Tiana was more professional than I gave her credit for. She shook her head, albeit regretfully. "Sorry. They have pretty strict laws about stuff like that."

I was beginning to like her more and more. The girl had ethics. I had ethics.

No, wait, that was epics. I had epics. Epic ass. Epic boots. Epic looks, but only when I was drunk. Tons of epics.

"I understand." Besides, if I really needed the info, I could get Uncle Bob to get it for me. But I didn't want to cause the woman any more grief than was necessary. And I certainly didn't want to get Tiana in trouble or cast any suspicion her way in the workplace. "So, I get that this is a little disturbing, but I'm sensing something more."

She put down her fork and shifted in her seat. "There was another incident. The cops came, but they could never connect the two."

"The two?"

"That's why I thought you might be undercover or something. You know, like they were still investigating, but I guess not."

"I can't tell you everything," I said to her. "But I can promise you, if I find anything to implicate Mrs. Foster of any wrongdoing, I have a ton of connections with the APD." A ton meaning one in the form of Uncle Bob. Some might say he weighed a ton.

Okay, he wasn't that big. In fact, he seemed to be losing weight lately. And not in a healthy way.

"Well, after that incident, Eve kind of eased up on the whole religion thing. At least while at work. Personally, I think Dr. Schwab ordered her not to bring it up again. But this one mother came in with her two kids and . . . it was so weird. When Eve saw the kids, she had the strangest reaction. Like all the blood drained from her face. She turned white. And the look she gave the mother. If looks could kill."

Okay, even if the kids did have some kind of dark aura or something, why look at the mother that way?

"Did she say anything about it to you?"

"No. Saint Eve doesn't exactly confide in me."

"Saint Eve?" I asked with a grin.

"That's what we call her at the office. All that holier-than-thou crap. Her husband is just like her."

Interesting.

"So, no, she didn't say anything to me. I just kind of overheard her on the phone talking to her husband."

"Nice. And?"

"She told him that a little girl had come in with her mother and baby brother. She said the girl was marked."

I stilled. Swallowed hard. Then asked as nonchalantly as I could, "Marked?"

Tiana shrugged. "No idea what she meant. And I wouldn't have thought much about it except for the fact that . . ." She shook her head and took another drink. "Never mind. It's crazy."

"No, Tiana, please tell me. What happened?"

"It's going to sound crazy. One thing can't possibly have anything to do with the other."

"You might be surprised."

"It's just, later that night, the little girl disappeared."

I covered my shock by wiping my hands on a napkin and sitting back in thought.

"It was all over the news. About two months ago?"

About two months ago I'd been sequestered away in a convent. I missed a lot. "Did they ever find her?"

She shook her head. "No. She's still missing. I can't tell you who it is, but it's public knowledge." She took out her phone, pulled up a webpage, then laid her phone on the table and looked away. Girl was good. Nobody could prove she'd told me a thing.

I leaned over and glanced at the page entitled Find Dawn Now. It had been set up by friends of the family and offered a reward for any information on the whereabouts of three-year-old Dawn Brooks. Brown hair. Blue eyes. And beautiful.

I could look into it more later and ask Uncle Bob what he knew about the case.

Tiana's phone darkened, and she pulled it back to her. "The mother came in a couple of weeks ago with her baby boy, Dawn's little brother, for a checkup. She was a basket case. So different from when I first saw her." Tears shimmered in the young girl's eyes. "She broke down in Dr. Schwab's office. I don't think she's doing very well."

The walls of my chest tightened. "I can't imagine that she is." At least I knew where my daughter was. I knew she was safe. Well cared for and loved. This poor woman had no clue, and statistically, children missing that long, those that weren't taken by an estranged parent, were rarely found alive. "Do you think Mrs. Foster had something to do with her disappearance?"

"I know how it sounds." She sat back, dejected. "I get it. I just found it odd. The whole thing. They had just come in for a one-month well child visit for the little brother. It was just weird, you know? Eve gets all pale and freaks out. Goes to the bathroom to call her husband. Makes some excuse to leave work early, then that very night the girl is abducted from her home, and Eve is out sick the rest of the week."

"She called in sick?"

"She missed four days of work." She bowed her head as though ashamed. "I know how thin it sounds, but something just wasn't right. So, I . . . I'm the one who called the police. Or, well, I had my cousin Elias call the police and talk to the detective in charge of the case. I was afraid someone would get the recording and know it was me. I could get into a lot of trouble."

"Not if there was a threat of danger or wrongdoing, Tiana. Don't feel guilty."

"Maybe. But it didn't do any good. They looked into it. Eve and her husband said they were home that night, watching a movie. Their son corroborated."

A current of electricity rushed over my skin. It carried dread and suspicion. "Their son?"

"Yeah, I guess he lives with them? He's getting his graduate degree or something. He's really nice looking. I met him when he came to pick up his mom for lunch one day."

"Tall? Blond?"

"That's him. Shawn Foster."

"I'll look into it, Tiana. I promise." If Mrs. Foster was still up to her old abduction tricks, I wanted to be the first to know. But what startled me most was the whole supernatural slant to all of this. Could she really see auras? Had she seen my light? Had she seen Reyes's darkness when he was a baby?

Considering everything I knew thus far, it was a strong possibility Reyes's darkness was why she took him in the first place. That would also explain, to a degree, why he wanted me to drop the case. He was so sensitive about the whole son-of-Satan thing.

"Also"—I pointed to her sub—"are you going to finish that?"

———

I thought about skipping my business class, but I'd need those skills once I took over the world. Still, I was running a little early, and since Osh's digs were close, I decided to pay him a visit.

Osh was a Daeva, a slave demon, who had escaped hell much the same way Reyes had. Only Reyes had used a map. The tattoos on his shoulders and back were literally a map of the void between hell and this plane. Osh navigated the void using only instinct and skill. Few demons were that clever.

I hadn't seen him since I forced him to swallow my soul so I could sneak up on one of the malevolent gods without my bright-ass light giving me away.

But swallowing a god's aura, even for a Daeva, was lethal.

I trapped the malevolent god and got back to him before he exploded with all the energy he'd ingested, but the ordeal had taken its toll.

All the lights were out at Osh's. Before I'd tried to disintegrate his innards with my energy, he'd been on Ubie patrol, taking a shift, tailing my rascally uncle to keep Grant Guerin from killing him. But since the incident, he'd been lying low.

I knocked lightly, waited a whole three seconds, then let myself in. He never kept his house locked, in the hope of a thief stopping by. I'd agreed, when we first met, to let him feed off the souls of those who did not deserve them, but I mostly meant murderers and rapists and pedophiles. Still, if someone had the gall to break into another person's domain, that someone had better be willing to accept whatever may come.

His house, a really nice two-bedroom in the traditional Santa Fe style with muted colors and warm hues, was completely dark. I took out my phone and turned on the flashlight.

A voice originating from a dark corner startled me. "You're not a thief."

I turned to see Osh—or Osh's shadow—sitting in a recliner. "Am too. I stole a Jolly Rancher from Circle K when I was seven."

"So, I can sup on your soul?"

He sat with his knees apart and his hands on the arms of the chair. When I shined my flashlight on him, he squinted and frowned at me.

I walked closer and turned on a lamp beside his chair. That time he scowled.

"I think we tried that already." I took a seat on his sofa. "You almost exploded. Which, thank goodness, you didn't. You'd never have come out of Garrett's carpet."

He tried to charm me with a lopsided grin. "I said *sup*. Not swallow in one, nuclear gulp."

It worked. Osh, or Osh'ekiel, as he was known in the supernatural realm, looked about nineteen in human years, but he was hundreds of years old. Since time was different down under, it was impossible to tell how old, exactly, but his pale skin, shoulder-length blue-black hair, and shimmering bronze eyes made him quite popular with humans of all ages.

Still, I'd known for months he'd play an important role in things to come. I knew he'd be by my daughter's side. I knew she'd love him. But I also knew he was created and raised in a hell dimension. Still, I trusted him. He would love Beep. He would give his life for her. But the prophecies that foretold of Beep's coming trials also said that there was one who would either lead her to victory or be her downfall.

I believed that prophesied entity to be Osh, though I had no way to know for certain. I saw through the veil, but most of what I saw was vague, and none of it was set in stone. If Lucifer won, if he found Beep and killed her before she could fulfill her prophecy, he would be unstoppable.

For some reason, Reyes and I had not been in the visions I'd seen. We were either dead by the time she came of age or unable to assist her, which led back to the being dead part, because nothing but nothing would keep me from helping my daughter short of that.

But she would love him. Osh. Beep would love him with all her heart. And he would love her back. Mythology in every culture in the world had stories of infants being promised to royalty or celestial beings or hideous beasts, but for it to be real, for it to actually exist, was both surreal and disturbing.

"You keep looking at me like that."

"Like what?" I asked.

"Like you're trying to figure me out."

"Sorry. I just wanted to make sure you were okay."

"I swallowed a god and lived to tell the tale. I'm good."

He had yet to move, but his glistening gaze missed nothing. The cracks in his skin where my energy had seeped out of him had almost completely healed. Only faint purplish lines remained on his face and neck. He wore a black long-sleeved T-shirt and jeans, so I couldn't see much beyond that.

"And you're sitting here in the dark because . . . ?"

"I was waiting, but you've scared them off."

I sat up straight, alarmed. "Them? Who were you waiting for?"

"Two men have been casing my house. I did a rather elaborate ruse to get them to think I was out for the night. They were just about to break in when you pulled up."

"Don't tell me you're hungry already," I said, teasing him. "I wasn't enough for you?"

"I told you, I could live off you for all eternity. But a guy likes a snack here and there."

"Are you okay, really?"

He didn't answer for a long time, and when he did talk, it had nothing to do with my question. "Why are you here?"

"I told you. I'm checking on you."

"You don't look good in guilt."

I dropped my gaze. "I'm so sorry, Osh. I almost killed you."

He leaned forward. Took my chin into his hand. "You did what you had to do. And what I never in a million years thought you could do. One of these days, I'm going to stop underestimating you."

"Yeah, well, one nasty god down and one to go. Any suggestions?"

"Only that I don't think I can take you in again and live to defend my strip poker title."

"I would never do that to you." When he cast me a dubious stare, I added, "Not a second time."

"Then you'll lose." He said it so matter-of-factly that I glanced up at him in question. "If you aren't willing to do anything, to sacrifice anyone, then you will lose and your daughter will be dead before she's old enough to know what a wuss her mother was. Which is probably for the best."

"Because I'm not willing to sacrifice you—"

"Anyone."

"—we will automatically lose?"

He stood and raked a hand through his hair. "This god, this Eidolon, doesn't play by the same rules you do. The odds of you trapping another god in that glass . . . let's just say they aren't in your favor." When I didn't respond, he changed the subject. "How's your uncle?"

"Still slated for hell."

"Why?" He sat down again and leveled a curious stare on me.

"What do you mean, why? Reyes saw it. He killed people. It doesn't matter that they were horrible and were planning on abducting me so their boss could eat me. Uncle Bob made the decision to hunt these men down and take human life, so he's automatically penciled in for an eternity of agony."

None of it made sense. Nor was it fair. Why would a noble pursuit sentence Uncle Bob to hell? Reyes explained it once. Said that Ubie had taken lives on purpose when there were other options. It was not self-defense, but premeditated. Still . . .

When Jehovah and I finally meet face-to-face, we are going to have a serious discussion.

"No, I know all that," he said. "I was just wondering why. Want a beer?" He stood and turned on several lights before heading to the kitchen. I followed him.

"What do you mean, why? I just said why."

"Okay." He took out a beer and popped the top off.

"No, not okay. What do you mean, why?"

He grinned at last, and I felt like the joke was definitely on me. I just still had no idea what the joke was.

"I just figured since you were the reaper, you'd do something about it."

"About what?"

"About your uncle being slated for my birthplace." He walked back into his living room and picked up the TV remote.

I took it from him. "Osh, what do you mean? Spill or I'll . . . I'll melt your remote with my . . . my fire."

His brows inched higher, unimpressed. "You aren't the quickest rabbit in the race, are you?"

"That's it." I focused all my energy on his remote and—

"Okay," he said, jumping up and grabbing it from me. "Chill. All I'm saying is, you're the freaking reaper. Just, you know, do what you do. Unmark him."

He sat back down and turned on the TV while I stood there in a sea of confusion.

When I didn't move out of his way, he leaned to the side, unfazed.

"I can do that?" I asked at last.

"Of course. Isn't that your job, anyway? Part of it, at least."

I sank back onto his sofa. "But I didn't even know he was marked."

"You just didn't look. It's there, plain as Dayton, Ohio. Want to watch *Buffy*?"

"Oh, hell, yes," I said, snuggling into his cushions. Then I remembered I had places to be. "Crap. I can't. I'm going to be late for class."

"Class?"

"I'm taking a business class so I can run the world once I take it over. You know, from a fiscal standpoint." I hadn't really grasped the whole fiscal concept as it applied to world domination, but I loved saying it out loud. It made me sound smart.

"Ah. Well, get your ass out then. Maybe I can still salvage my evening. Snack on a couple of thieves."

"Osh." I took his hand in mine.

He eyed me warily.

"Are you mad at me for almost killing you?"

The once-over he gave me, the one filled with appreciation and interest and humor—mostly humor—warmed me to my toes. "No, sugar. I'm honored you think so highly of me to entrust me with your light."

"Also, you were the only one who could have handled it."

"There's that," he said with a grin.

I considered everything else I was willing to entrust him with— namely, my daughter, the future of the world, my daughter. Mostly my daughter.

"I thought about selling it on eBay," he added, "but I had no idea how to ship a box full of all-powerful, omnipotent light."

I laughed, leaned in, and kissed his cheek before heading for the door. Just as I was about to go through it, he said, "Oh, I meant to ask you, what's with all the angels?"

7

I just ordered a Life Alert bracelet, so if I get a life,
I'll be notified immediately.
—BUMPER STICKER

I called Uncle Bob on my way to class. I'd considered telling him about his impending doom, but I didn't know how. Or what to say. Or where to start. He'd want to know exactly how we knew. Did I then tell him about his inevitable trip to Lucifer Land? How could I?

He picked up on the first ring. "Hey, pumpkin."

"Hey back. So, I was wondering if I could find out who was in charge of the abduction of Dawn Brooks. And if you could get me everything you have on it."

"I can look into it. What are you doing?"

"Right now?"

"Yes."

"Heading to class."

"Class?"

Why was everyone so surprised I was taking a class? "I've decided to become an exotic dancer."

"Sounds good. Do you think you could do me a favor?"

"Anything."

"Could you, maybe, stay home for a few days?"

I waited for a solid minute for him to clarify and/or explain. When he didn't, I asked, "Can you tell me why?"

"Oh, you know. Just a lot of crazy in town lately."

That was so amazingly lame. "That's the best you got?"

"At the moment, yes."

"Then, no."

"I could make you stay home."

I'd pulled up to a stoplight, and thank goodness I had. His statement stunned me. "What do you mean?"

"I mean I'd like you to stay home for a few days."

"I'm heading to class."

"Skip."

"No."

"I insist."

"Then I desist."

"I don't think that means what you think it means."

"Uncle Bob—"

"I could order you to."

"Well, you'd best be ordering your coffin at the same time."

"I mean it, Charley."

"I suggest a nice mahogany." The car behind me honked before I realized the light had turned green. I pulled into South Lot and shifted Misery into park. "Uncle Bob, until you can give me a legitimate reason—"

"I'll have you arrested. How's that for legitimate?"

Boy howdy, did Cookie nail his mood. What the frackin' hell? "I'm going to pretend you didn't just threaten me."

"I'll have campus police pick you up in ten."

He hung up before I could gasp in his face. Via an electronic signal transmitted through radio waves. But still.

I made it to my classroom on the main UNM campus with few incidents and fewer arrests to speak of. Two men in my life, two of my favorite, were suddenly ordering me around. Like they had the right. Just no. Besides, Ubie had no grounds for an arrest. Not without signing his own warrant as well. He was an accessory to many of my out-of-the-box crime-fighting procedures. If I went down, he went down.

Men.

Our business teacher, a Mr. Hipple, was a fine instructor as instructors went, but he seemed to lack my enthusiasm. My vision. My complexity.

I raised my hand.

He kept talking.

It reminded me of grade school when my PE teacher wanted us to climb a rope and I asked her if she could apply that skill to a real-life situation. You know, so I could understand why I had to climb the rope. I hated the rope. It chafed. And made my arms shaky.

I kept asking Mr. Hipple, a very tan man in the prime of his midlife crisis if the shiny new Corvette he drove were any indication, to apply a broader scope to his principles. Like, say, in a world domination kind of way.

I raised my hand again. Mr. Hipple let loose a loud sigh and said, "Charlotte?"

"Oh, just Charley. Okay, so let's say the world was headed for another economic crisis and the housing market were to totally crash again—how would, say, a god fix it?"

Mr. Hipple scrubbed his face with his fingers, then pinched the bridge of his nose before replying. I took that as a good sign. Like he was really mulling over how best to answer my question.

"Charley, would you like to ask a question that actually pertains to this class?"

A couple of students snickered, and I folded my arms over Danger and Will and sank down in my seat. What was the point of my taking the class if I couldn't use the information in the future?

Reyes must have felt the same way. He was still following me. Still incorporeal. Still dark and brooding and hotter than a sidewalk in August. As Reyes's heat blasted across my skin, his anger at Mr. Hipple's answer apparent, Mr. Hipple went on with his pointless lecture.

I supposed I couldn't blame the guy. It was an odd question, but I was beginning to think that taking over the world might not be such a great idea. I knew nothing about management beyond my own PI firm, and Cookie handled most of that. I knew nada about performing miracles or parting seas or calming storms when asked.

I was in way over my head. Mr. Hipple was right. Not that he said that, but I felt it was implied.

Reyes had taken the seat behind mine. They were the kind where the desk folded away to the side if you didn't need it. As quietly as I could, I folded my desk away in anticipation of our break. Since the class only met once a week, it was almost three hours long, and I'd had a lot of coffee before coming in. My bladder was screaming at me.

No, wait, that was the departed girl who ran up and down the halls screaming for someone to lend her a pencil. I'd had that nightmare a few times myself. She was in a hospital gown, though, so I wasn't sure why she was haunting the UNM campus instead of, say, a hospital.

She'd rush into the room, scream for someone to lend her a pencil before it was too late, then run back out again, disappearing through the wall in which she came. Poor kid.

I felt the warmth of Reyes's gaze on my back before he returned his focus to the angel leaning against the wall in the front of the classroom. This one was probably the most surprising I'd seen yet. He was a ginger, and while he wore the requisite long black coat, he wore something I could only describe as a kilt underneath. It wasn't a true Scottish kilt, but it resembled one in that it was a man-skirt. A black leather man-skirt that came to his knees. The belt at his waist was wide and held a variety of weapons, and his sword was strapped to his back.

He was a scrapper, through and through. And Reyes kept a close eye on him. Close enough to be mistaken for aggression. I swore if those two threw down in the middle of my business class, someone was getting an ass kicking. Most likely me if I tried to step in, but I needed to pay attention. We had our first test next week. I didn't have time for rumbles.

"Miss Davidson," Mr. Hipple said, drawing me out of my musings. "May I speak to you?"

I glanced around as students rose and filed out of the classroom. He'd called break, and I missed it. I had no idea how long we had.

I nodded and wound my way to the front of the room, coming way too close for comfort to William Wallace, the highland angel. But he was too busy staring down my main squeeze, who'd followed me, putting them within fist-throwing distance. Damn it.

"Miss . . . Charley," he corrected. "Can you tell me what you hope to get out of this class?"

"I put that on the questionnaire you sent around the first night."

"Yes, you did." He pulled out my answer sheet. "You are taking this class to learn more about business administration and management should you succeed in taking over the world."

"Was that redundant? Putting down both administration and management?"

"Not at all. My point is, I assumed you meant that metaphorically."

"Which part?"

"The part about you taking over the world."

"Oh, right." I was leaning against the desk, and Reyes leaned against me. Leaned into me. His warmth soaking through to the marrow of my bones. "No, I meant it quite literally, though I probably should have phrased it differently."

He braced an arm against the desk, putting a barrier between the angel and me. It was protective and kind. Despite his anger at my taking the Foster case, he still protected me. It would've even been romantic had the kid not come in again and screamed in my face.

My shoulders wilted. I had to help her.

"I did mean it metaphorically, Mr. Hipple. I'm sorry. I'll stop asking questions."

"I hope not," he said, surprising me. "I'd just like them to be something I can answer. If you really are taking over the world, I think you need to take a class that's more advanced than Intro to Business 101."

I laughed softly. "Thanks. I'll look into it."

Just as I was headed out the door, he called out to me. "I think they cover world domination in Business 350."

I laughed again and left, knowing I wouldn't be back. I couldn't learn how to run the world, possibly the entire universe, from a classroom. I needed real-world experience.

Issues girl got all up in my face. She did it to everyone. What she didn't expect was for me to see her.

"I need a pencil!" When she screamed, her mouth opened really wide, and her tongue was a little blue. Of course, that could have been a side effect of her being dead.

I did a mom thing and grabbed her ear.

"Ouch," she said as I dragged her into the restroom. "What the hell?" She rubbed her ear when I let go. "How did you do that?"

"Haven't you noticed that I'm a little brighter than the other kids on the playground?"

"So, I still need a pencil."

"You don't need a pencil. And your screaming is the most grating thing that's happened to me all day. That's saying a lot. Trust me."

"Wait. You can hear me?"

I finished checking the stalls and then went to a sink for a hair check. Still longish and brown. Okeydokey, then.

"Yes, I can hear you. What the hell is up with the pencil?"

Now that I had her attention, she seemed perfectly sane. "I just . . . I needed a pencil for a test." She turned around in circles like a dog chasing its tail. Maybe not that sane. "Is this a hospital gown? Does it open in the back? Can you see my butt?"

"Do you remember what happened to you?"

She stopped twirling. Thank goodness, because I could indeed see her butt.

"I was . . . I fell. I remember I leaned over to ask another student for a pencil and the room started spinning. I . . ." She looked at her hands. Then the gown. Then her bare feet. "Am I . . . am I dead?"

"I'm sorry."

"I was two semesters away from graduating."

I hitched a hip onto the sink and waited for her to absorb it all. She walked into a stall and sat on a toilet.

She buried her face in her hands. "How is this even possible?"

"I don't know, hon, but since you didn't cross when you died, you can cross through me. I'm sure you have family waiting."

"Cross?"

I nodded.

"Like, to the other side?"

Reyes materialized then, but he kept his distance this time. Not that it

was a very big restroom. He crossed his arms at the farthest end and
leaned against the back wall.

"I believe you missed the sign on the door outside," I said, teasing him
even though he was a grumpy bear.

He took me in from head to toe, then back up again, pausing at my
mouth. Both times. Sizing me up?

The girl rose and peeked around the stall door.

I refocused on her. "Yes, hon, to the other side."

"But I can stay if I want to?" She had yet to look back at me. Her gaze
was laser locked onto my husband.

"Or you can go. Just walk right through me," I said, encouraging her.
"Your family will be excited to see you."

"That's okay." She wiggled her fingers at him. "I think I'll stay."

That time, I crossed my arms and glared at the man. Two. Two in one day
who had refused to cross. Or was it three? Either way, I was losing my touch.

In a move that was part supernatural necessity and part theatrics,
Reyes slowly dematerialized, cell by cell, disintegrating into a cloud of
billowing smoke. Then he was gone.

The forlorn look on the girl's face said it all. No way was she leaving
now. Damn it. I thought about telling her about the butt thing but decided
against it. She'd leave when she was ready. At least she'd stopped screaming.

I ended up going back to class after all, after talking to some of my
classmates, then I hit an all-night diner with a couple of them. We'd
bonded instantly the first day of class. Mostly because they worshiped
coffee almost as much as I did. Almost.

Reyes joined us incorporeally, as did our Scottish friend. They spent
the whole time eyeing each other as though waiting for the other one to
make a move. Which neither ever did.

Our group eventually got kicked out of the all-night diner. Apparently my definition of *all-night* and theirs were two totally different things. We said our good-byes, which would have gone better if I could've remembered their names. I was so bad with names. And the one girl I thought I knew the name of kept looking at me awkwardly every time I used it, so I finally gave up the struggle. Which was real. The struggle.

Oddly enough, they all knew my name. Probably because Mr. Hipple had used it so much in class. For better or worse, I did tend to make an impression.

By the time I got home, however, Reyes was already asleep. Or he was faking it. Either way, boy was hot. His lean body shimmered in the low light, one arm thrown over his eyes, the other wedged behind his pillow. His wide chest took up half the bed. He had one leg out from under the covers. One hip open to the moonlight streaming in from the massive windows. He was like a Greek god. Sleek. Surreal. Temperamental.

Did the Fosters see the darkness in Reyes? Is that what compelled them to take him when he was a baby?

I shifted. Not all the way. Just a little. Just enough to see what they might have seen. Darkness, yes, but so much more.

The world around me changed from the blackness of night to bright, bursting colors. Oranges and reds and yellows, swirling in a perpetual storm where lightning and tornadoes converged. And Reyes, seemingly so serene, burned brightest of all. Engulfed in flames, a true child of hell. But at the center, at his core, was the darkness. The same darkness he tried to hide. He tried to overcome.

I shifted back to the tangible plane, changed into a nightie that fell just past my hips, and slid in bed beside him to spoon, my favorite utensil. I was only there for about five seconds, nestling against him, burying my face in his hair, when he spoke, his voice deep with sleep.

"Did you do it?" he asked, the tenor of his voice as smooth as he.

"Did I do what?"

He took the hand I'd draped over him and lifted my fingers to his mouth, scalding the tips one by one as he tasted me, then said, "Drop the case."

I decided it was high time I broke in our new sofa: Captain Kirk.

Captain Kirk wasn't as comfortable as I thought he would be. Not after snuggling with a hell-god. I was able to get in about three hours before Mr. Coffee began serenading me. Whoever invented a coffeemaker with a timer deserved a Nobel Prize. He'd probably saved more lives than Prozac.

I slipped on a pair of bottoms and tiptoed past the angel lounging against my living room wall, the arch of his wings brushing our twelve-foot ceiling, to get to the kitchen. The same kitchen I was fairly certain used to be my neighbor's apartment. Reyes had remodeled the entire apartment building.

Thankfully, he bought it first.

But he took out all the apartments on the entire top floor and reconstructed it to create only two: ours and Cookie's. Now I lived in an apartment that resembled a Park Avenue penthouse. And it had the kitchen to back that up. Gorgeous industrial appliances. Deep Tuscan hues. And my favorite part: a butler's pantry.

I cracked up every time I thought about it. Still, if we ever did get a butler, he'd have his own little corner of the world. With running water and a wine rack. The lush.

Part of me wanted to offer the celestial stalker a cup of joe, but I didn't want him to stick around. If Reyes found one of them in our apartment, he could come unglued. And gluing that man back together was not an easy task.

It was still dark out when I padded back to the captain and sipped on my cup o' panacea. But even with a cure-all flooding my cells, my brain felt like one of those inflatable bounce houses. I had so many question marks jumping and colliding and twisting arms and breaking ankles, pretty much like a real bounce house at a seven-year-old's birthday party.

What had ADA Parker meant when he called me a god eater? I mean, Reyes was a god and I liked to nibble on him, but what an odd thing to call someone. Unless I was drunk when I hit an all-night drive-through and ordered chicken McGodlets—with fries, of course—I'd never eaten a god in my life. Still, I bet they'd be good with ketchup.

And hell was going to freeze over? I just thought that was a saying.

Then there was Uncle Bob. No idea what got his panties in a twist, but he'd best iron them out pronto. And Reyes. I could only take men ordering me around for so long. It was like we were in the Middle Ages. If they'd had programmable coffeemakers. And cell phones. And water bras.

But possibly the most important question mark bouncing around my brain was that of Dawn Brooks, the little girl who was very likely abducted by the Fosters. If that were the case, however, where was she now and why would Shawn corroborate their alibi?

I needed to bring in my FBI BFF ASAP, but I doubted Agent Carson got to the office before eight o'clock. I checked my Bugs Bunny watch. Two hours to go.

Which meant I had two hours to get to know the newest member of our clan. When Reyes remodeled, he opened up the storage units on top of the building, leaving the metal beams exposed and turning the whole thing into a massive skylight.

But there was something else really special Reyes had left exposed. A little blond boy. As in tiny. As in way too young to be hanging out—literally, his feet dangling over the side of whatever beam he happened to be on—in the scaffolding of a twenty-four-foot ceiling. He'd been there since we moved back in, and I had yet to coax him down. Although, admittedly, throwing bread at him was probably not the best way to win his trust, but I was afraid to throw anything harder. Huge plates of glass overhead.

I looked up. He was climbing again. When he wasn't dangling his feet over the side of a beam, he was climbing one, then sliding back down it. Over and over again.

Every time he slid, however, my heart ended up in my throat. The boy couldn't have been more than two years old. He was just a baby, climbing and sliding and dangling from beams that stood twenty-four feet high in the center of our living room.

But this time I was prepared. I'd hauled a ladder up from the basement. The kind that elongates and props up against whatever structure one wishes to scale.

Having finished my first cup, which was really like an appetizer, I dragged the ladder out from the butler's pantry, where I'd stashed it. It was metal and noisy no matter how quiet I tried to be. I cringed when I knocked it against a wall, waited to make sure the man of the house wasn't going to come check on me, then pulled the two parts until it was as long as it would go. The next part was a bit trickier. I tried to balance it against one of the beams overheard, but it was still too short.

The angel, who'd been ignoring me completely, looked on with something akin to mild interest, while I did some cyphering in my head. Never a good idea. Still, the way I saw it, I could use Captain Kirk to give me those extra inches I needed to reach the beam and climb up to the boy.

I put the ladder back down, almost strained a kidney moving the captain into place, then picked up the ladder again, knocking over a lamp in the process. I cringed again, but miraculously, it didn't break. And who better to perform a miracle than a celestial stalker-like being?

I glanced back at the angel. He was the ginger in the black leather kilt. "Did you do that?"

The only indication that he even heard me was the fact that one imperious brow arched.

Of course he didn't. He was far too above saving a lamp for little old me.

I tossed a blanket over the captain to protect his silky fabric, then leveraged the ladder onto one of his cushions. Still not quite enough. By the time I got done, I'd piled on an end table, a wingback chair, and a set of encyclopedias to hold it all in place. It worked. The ladder reached one of the bottom metal beams. I could get to the kid at last.

Now, if my luck held, Reyes would sleep another half hour while I tried to get to know our new roomie. I ascended my creation with the vigilance of a mountain climber scaling a wall of ice, ignoring the creaks and tiny slip to one side when I was about halfway up. Another two inches and I'd have been sipping my meals through a straw for the next few weeks. And wearing one of those hideous neck braces. Those things were impossible to accessorize.

By the time I got to the top, my arms were shaking, my feet hurt from the thin rungs of the ladder, and I had to pee. I totally should have gone before I left.

I crested the beam and wrapped both arms around it, resting my face against its cool surface. The little boy watched me the whole time. He giggled and ran toward me. Ran. On a beam that couldn't have been more than ten inches wide.

I bolted upright to catch him should he fall, but he stopped short to take me in, to assess the intruder. His smile was the sun. His blue eyes the ocean. A tiny Viking so full of life, he glowed.

He pointed to my chest, and said, "Yite," but he was not quite within arm's reach. I wanted to grab him and take him back down with me. He'd probably just climb the walls back to his playground, but I had to try. I had to coax him closer.

I offered him my best Sunday smile. "What's your name?"

He pointed to his pajamas, blue with brightly colored fish on them. He poked a goldfish. "Ishy."

"Fishy?"

He nodded and pointed to one on his chest. Then his knee. Then his elbow.

Elated we were communicating, I laughed, peeled one hand off the beam, and pointed at another one right above his heart. "That one's pretty. Do you like fishies?"

He nodded again, then pointed back at me, all the while balancing on the beam as though he were walking in the park. As though one of us wasn't in danger of plummeting to her death or, more likely, ending up in traction.

"Yite," he repeated, and it finally hit me. *Light.* He was referring to my light.

"Yes, I've been told I'm quite bright." I leaned a little closer. "Not as bright as your smile, though."

He giggled and took another step closer, his eyes sparkling with curiosity. Just a few more inches. Not that I had a clue how I was going to get down the ladder with him. And what I was attempting could be considered child abduction if he didn't want to come with me, but I had to try.

I straddled the beam, almost toppling over more than once, breathlessly out of my comfort zone, and peeled my other hand off the metal. Then I gave him the universal sign for *hug.* I lifted my arms, palms up, and coaxed him forward, hoping beyond hope he'd come close enough for me to grab.

And he did. Boy did he. But he didn't just inch closer as I'd imagined. Nope. He graced me with a nuclear smile, then sprinted forward.

"Wait!" But he'd already run right through me. He'd already entered the other side. He'd already crossed.

8

Children see magic because they look for it.
—CHRISTOPHER MOORE

The richness of the boy's memories stole my breath. The textures and scents and emotions. He loved flowers and lollipops and, yes, fish. And his name was Curren.

Oftentimes when I'm gifted with the images and feelings and most precious memories of a life once lived, it starts at the end and goes backwards, and I have to flip it. To put everything in order and create my own timeline of events. But Curren showed me the most important things first. Beginning with his family.

He showed me how his mother would snuggle and rock him every night and sing to him as he nursed. How she would tickle him before bedtime. How she would catch him trying to hide food in a pocket in his bib while she wasn't looking so they could move on to the most important part of the meal: memm-memms. M&Ms. But she always knew. Somehow she always knew. And she smelled like the flowers he loved so much.

He showed me how his dad took him to the hardware store once, and he was so proud, he kept waving to his mom and his siblings, all the way to the truck. Waving and smiling and blowing kisses even after his dad had strapped him into his car seat.

Because he wanted her to know. His mother. He wanted her to know how much he loved her. He needed her to understand.

When it happened, he wasn't so much scared as stunned. He'd crawled out of bed early one morning and decided to climb up his dresser. When it fell on him, trapping him, suffocating him, all he thought about was her. She would be in soon. He could hear her footsteps on the stairs.

He loved walks. He loved toy cars. He loved flowers. So much so that a neighbor planted a giant sunflower garden after he'd passed.

His mother had found him. He remembered her screams. Her desperate cries for help as she struggled to get the dresser off him. Her pleas as she breathed into his mouth. But he wasn't beneath her anymore. He was beside her. Trying to calm her with his hand on her shoulder.

They took him to the hospital, and she held him for hours, unwilling to let him go. Unable to. But the warmth left him and his body started to stiffen, and she had to give him up at last. Her pain was enough to seize my lungs. I could feel it through her son, they had such a strong connection.

And I saw them through his eyes now. Curren didn't understand what his mother was doing, but I did. She was educating the public about the dangers of dressers and other furniture. About the countless children who had died so needlessly. About how to anchor furniture. To secure it.

And she took heat for it. For her outreach. Idiots chastised her for not watching him closely enough. For being a bad mother. If I'd ever seen a good mother in my life, it was this woman. My heart broke for her, but she carried on. Still carries on to this day.

I wanted her to know how exquisitely she was loved. How much her youngest son adored her. How her fight was worthy and commendable and needed.

With an older departed, I could write a letter or an e-mail to get a message to a loved one, pretending to be them. But with a two-year-old, I didn't know how to get a message to the parents without upsetting them unduly. They were struggling to move on with their lives. How could I undermine that?

I would check on them. Keep an eye on them. Somehow I would let them know how loved they were. How loved they still are. Because he'll be waiting for them in his blue *ishy* jammies.

I collapsed onto the cool beam, one cheek resting against it, legs and arms dangling over the side. It was for the best. I knew that, but I'd wanted . . . I'd wanted to hold him. To rock him and sing to him and tickle him until he giggled. All the things I couldn't do with Beep. But he was with his family now, those who'd gone on before him. They deserved him much more than I did.

But I knew one thing for certain. No parent should have to go through that. No parent should have to be ripped apart like that. I had to find Dawn Brooks. I couldn't imagine what her parents were going through, but if I knew the Fosters, and if they really took her, she was still alive. Somewhere. I had to find her.

I heard a male voice from somewhere below me. "Are you okay, pumpkin?"

Prying my eyes open, I looked down at Uncle Bob. He was dressed in a dark gray suit and had a file in his hands. I nodded, hoping he couldn't see the drool I'd left on the beam. Then I realized the wetness was not drool but tears. I wiped my eyes and slowly, ever so slowly, sat up.

"Want to tell me what you're doing?" he asked.

Glancing back at the ladder, I shook my head.

He nodded. "Okay. I have the file you wanted. It's everything we have on the Dawn Brooks case." He sat it down on our coffee table, then reached up and took hold of the ladder to steady it.

I flattened onto my stomach, swung a leg over, and began feeling for the rungs with my feet. When I found only air, I glanced back over my shoulder to guide my foot to the ladder, but it was gone. Vanished into thin air. I looked down. Uncle Bob had laid it on the ground and was messing with it.

"I think that's as tall as it goes. I tried to make it taller."

"Which would explain the homemade scaffolding."

"Yeah." I looked at Captain Kirk and the gang. Probably not my best idea.

"Well, this looks really dangerous," he said, standing. "I'll just leave it here."

He'd separated it into two pieces. Two short pieces. Now the extension ladder couldn't extend.

"Uncle Bob?" I asked, my voice as shaky as my scaffolding.

He looked up and shrugged. "Guess you'll have to stay up there until we can call in rescue. That could be a while."

"What?" I squirmed back into a sitting position. "Uncle Bob, you put that back right this minute."

"Sorry." He glanced at his watch. "I have to get to work. I'll make sure someone gets over here aysap."

"Uncle Bob!" I yelled to the back of his head.

He opened the door and walked out of it. Just like that. He left me hanging. Literally.

"Uncle Bob!"

When I got no response, I looked at the angel. I smiled. I pointed to the ladder and offered him my most pathetic expression.

He didn't budge. The only sign of life I saw was his wings ruffling together as he repositioned himself.

I closed my eyes and gritted my teeth. This was not happening.

"Is there a reason you're up here?"

The sound of Reyes's voice, as close as it was, startled me. I jumped and began to slip, my bottom half proving heavier than my top. I clamped onto the beam with both arms before sliding to my death—or at the very least a painful landing—then looked over at my husband. He was crouched on the beam, his powerful legs holding him in perfect balance. He was barefoot, too, and wore only a pair of gray pajama bottoms with one arm resting casually on a knee. Casually! This was not a casual situation.

"I need the ladder. Uncle Bob moved it."

"Ah."

He glanced down. I slipped. He looked back at me. I slipped some more, sweat breaking out over my whole body.

"Reyes, the ladder."

"I see it."

"I need it."

"I see that, too."

I rolled my eyes. "Seriously?"

"I'll get it if you'll drop the case."

I tried to gape at him, but I was too scared to move. I was literally holding on for dear life with both arms wrapped around the beam and the rest of me dangling underneath. Now was so not the time.

"Reyes," I said, hoping to be heard over the grinding of my teeth, "if you don't get that ladder . . ."

I left the threat hanging. It seemed appropriate. But he only studied me from beneath ridiculously long lashes.

I slipped some more, my sweat making the beam impossible to hang on to.

Cookie's screech was both alarming and welcome. "Charley!" she yelled as she ran into the room. "Robert told me to come check on you. What are you doing?"

"Can you get that ladder?"

She looked down as Amber walked into the room and stopped short. "Aunt Charley?"

My arms were shaking so badly, I knew I couldn't hold on much longer. I tried to fling a leg over, but the act only made me slip a little more. As Cookie tried to fit the ladder pieces back together, taking out a framed picture and a fireplace stand in the process, my hold slid another few inches until I was holding on by my fingertips. At least it felt that way.

"Take my hand," Reyes said.

I looked up at him. He was still crouched down, but if I took his hand, I knew enough about the laws of gravity to know he'd fall with me.

"No," I said, shaking my head.

"Dutch," he said, cool as a cucumber sorbet, "take my hand."

"No. You'll fall, too. Cookie?"

She stepped back to observe her handiwork. "Does that look right?"

It most definitely did not. The top part was crooked. No way would that hold.

"So, you won't take my hand because you think I'll fall?"

I strained to see over my shoulder. If I could just aim for Captain Kirk.

In the next heartbeat, my hold gave. My hands slipped, and I let out a yelp. And waited. Nothing. Then I felt a pressure on one wrist. I opened my eyes and almost cried out in relief. Reyes had caught me. He was standing and held my wrist in one hand. I clasped my other hand over his and then still had to wonder how we were going to get down.

"Well?" he said.

I nodded, panting in excitement, then wondered aloud, "Well, what?"

"Are you going to drop the case?"

Oh, no, he did not.

"It's your decision." There was something about the way he said it, something a little too nonchalant that had dread creeping up my spine. The barest hint of a smirk crept across his sensual mouth. Then he said it, and it took me precious seconds to absorb the fact that he was blackmailing me. "Drop the case or I drop you." Or was that extortion?

Anger exploded inside me. I narrowed my lids, gave him a second to think about what he'd just said to me, then dematerialized my hand. The one he was holding.

With a lightning-quick strike, he tried to catch me with his other hand, but I was already out of his reach.

I hit Captain Kirk before I even knew I was falling. And I hit hard. Also an end table was taking up half of him, so I landed on Captain Kirk, then my face landed on the edge of the end table, bounced off it, then flipped me over the back of the sofa. Who knew my face had been trained in Krav Maga?

"Charley!" Cookie rushed forward. Amber stayed where she was, her jaw hanging in shock, as her mother tried to help me up by dislocating my shoulder. "Charley, are you okay?"

"I'm good. I think." I sank back to the floor. It was moving way too fast for me to try to get on at the moment, like when I was a kid and tried to time the already-spinning merry-go-round just right. It never ended well.

I heard the lyrical chime of a phone as Reyes knelt beside me. He'd clearly had no problem getting down without a ladder.

Amber checked her phone then said, "I have to get ready for school," and hurried out.

I shook off the hand Reyes offered, then turned on him. "You could have killed me."

He made clear his lack of concern with a deadpan. "You did that all on your own."

"Yeah, but you threatened to."

"Son of Satan," he said by way of an explanation.

I scrambled to my feet, assured Cookie I was fine, then headed to our bedroom. If that doorframe hadn't jumped out of nowhere, I would have made a grand exit. As it stood, I was stumbling on the spinning merry-go-round one second, then cradled in the arms of my husband the next.

He started to carry me to our room. I decided not to argue the point since I could barely walk without getting arrested for public intoxication.

"The file," I said to Cookie, pointing over Reyes's shoulder. The broad one that fit my head just right. "Ubie brought the file on the Brooks girl."

She nodded, then asked, "Are you going to be okay?"

I gave her a thumbs-up before Reyes turned the corner into our room. He dropped my legs and let me slide down the length of him. Then he examined my eye, the one that had tried to take out our end table.

"You need ice."

"I need a shower."

I pushed off him and stumbled to our bathroom. It wasn't until I stepped into George, the shower that God built—metaphorically—that it hit me. Someone in that room was not okay. I felt the remnants of anxiety. Stress. Fear. Even despair. All the things I would have felt instantly had I not been dangling from a rafter like a tea bag.

Amber. Something was very wrong with Amber.

George felt wonderful. I stepped out feeling completely relaxed and satisfied, which was more than I could say about my husband at the moment. He was brushing his teeth. As soon as I got out, he rinsed and got in.

I hurried to get dressed, not wanting another confrontation on the Foster front. He was not going to bully me into dropping the case, so why bother arguing about it? Honestly, between him and Uncle Bob . . .

Still, Ubie was really starting to worry me. In the past, he would never do something like he'd done today. He would never leave me hanging like that. He'd trapped me on purpose. Tried to get me to take the day off. To stay home. But why? Ubie and I had always been so open. So honest. Why wouldn't he confide in me now?

I had half a mind not to unmark him for hell. If I could do that. Only one way to find out, but if he didn't straighten up his act, it was a one-way trip to hellsville for him.

I didn't bother drying my hair. I pulled it into a ponytail, threw on a sweater, a denim skirt, and a killer pair of ankle boots, grabbed my jacket, and headed out the door. Then I ran back in for my bag. Then I ran back in again for my keys. I was already settled inside Misery, ready to head out—Mr. Foster owned an insurance agency, and I was suddenly in dire need of life insurance on my husband—when I realized I'd left my phone on the charger.

Holy cow. When did I accumulate so much stuff I couldn't leave home without?

I waffled back and forth on whether to go back in and risk another confrontation—I loved waffles—when a knock sounded on my window.

After jumping three feet into the air, I glared at Reyes. Then heat blossomed over my skin, partly from alarm and partly from arousal, when I noticed his attire. Or lack thereof. He stood in the parking lot in a towel. A beige towel that hung low over his hips.

Water dripped off his hair and spiked his lashes, making his dark brown irises glitter all the more. Or that could have been the anger.

I turned the key and rolled down the window, fighting the urge to chastise him. It wasn't freezing but it was damned sure too cold to be running around wet and nigh naked. Instead, I asked, "Are you going to threaten me again?"

He had both hands braced against the door. My phone was in one of them.

"We need to talk."

"We tried that, remember? You don't seem to understand the difference between a conversation and an order. And you're rubbing off on Uncle Bob."

His brows slid together. "What do you mean?"

"I mean men. Thinking they can order me around. Thinking they have a say in anything that I do." I leaned closer. "Anything."

He paused to think about what I'd said, then leaned closer, too, his warmth wafting toward me. "Your flat-out refusal is not exactly civilized conversation, either."

"I . . . you . . ." I bit down and tried again. "I seem to remember a very recent *civilized* conversation we had in which we agreed we'd no longer keep secrets from one another." I studied his face. Watched how the water pooled in his lashes and above his mouth.

He worked his jaw and turned away. "It's not that simple."

"The hell it isn't."

He glanced down at his feet.

"Reyes, just tell me why you don't want me on this case. What are you afraid of?"

And that did it. The manly part of him—no, the Neanderthal part—became incensed. Reyes wasn't the insecure type in most every aspect of his life save one: his darkness. And I was slowly realizing that the

Fosters, one of them at the very least, had some kind of perception that pierced the veil of this plane.

But still! He was dark. No shit. It wasn't like that was a big secret. I could shift onto the celestial plane anytime I chose and see that darkness for myself.

"You think I'm afraid? Of the Fosters?"

"What? No." That was an odd thing to say. "Of course not."

"Fine," he said through gritted teeth. "Do what you want. You always do."

His frustration knew no bounds. Nor did it know his own strength. He pushed off the door, but in his anger, he literally toppled Misery onto two wheels. She came back down hard as Reyes walked away.

It was my turn to be angry. I jumped out of Misery to inspect the damage. He'd caved in the side of the door. I should have been thankful I could still open it, but I wasn't. I bent to pick up the phone he'd dropped. My phone. He'd shattered her screen, but she still came on.

By the time I turned back, he was just going inside the building. "You're buying me a new phone!"

Having had about enough of men and their appalling sense of entitlement, I decided to pay a visit to another male who was on my shit list: Mr. Abraham Foster. I found his office despite my phone's shattered screen. She'd had worse. I could barely think of the tequila incident without cringing.

A bell rang out when I walked in, and I was greeted by a receptionist who'd clearly been hoping for a few moments' respite before being bombarded with customers. I felt her pain.

She put down her coffee cup, forced a silicone smile, and said, "Hello, how can I help you?"

I walked up to the tall desk. "Hi. Yeah, I need insurance?"

She replaced her smile with one more genuine. "You don't sound very convinced."

"Right, sorry." I was still seething, so I took a deep breath and started again. "Do you offer life insurance?"

"We do. Would you like to speak to an agent?"

I needed to make sure the agent I spoke with was of medium height and build, with dark hair and a penchant for child abduction. "Well, a friend recommended I speak to Mr. Foster? Does he work here?"

She quirked a humorous brow. "He owns the agency, so, yes. But he's not in at the moment."

"Oh, darn."

"Would you care to see another agent?"

Before she'd finished, I noticed a man who fit Mr. Foster's description walking across the parking lot to a coffee shop next door.

"No, thanks. I'll just come back."

"I can have him call you." She grabbed a pen. "What's your name?"

"Um, Cordelia Chase."

I tensed the moment I said it, wondering if this receptionist was as savvy as the last one. She wrote it on a message pad while simultaneously nursing her coffee, and I tried not to drool. I'd only had the one cup that morning, and in my fury-driven haste, I hadn't thought to pick up a mocha grande with extra whipped cream on the way.

I thought about asking her for a quick sip when she asked for my number.

"You know what? I'll just come back. Thanks, though." I hurried out and wandered as nonchalantly as I could in the direction of the coffee shop, praying the receptionist didn't notice me stalking her boss.

I spotted Mr. F the moment I walked inside the retro diner and sat in a booth across from him.

A menu landed in front of me, and an older lady with hair teased just enough to hold the three pens sticking out of it asked, "Would you like some coffee, hon?"

"Would I?"

She offered me a knowing grin and, carafe already in hand, poured me a cup. I fought back the moan that threatened to erupt from the back of my throat when the rich scent hit me and graced her with my most appreciative smile. It wasn't until she winked and spun away that I realized Mr. Foster had taken note of my presence.

Keeping my gaze averted, I let him take me in a solid minute before looking back at him. When our gazes locked, he schooled his expression, shaped it into one of cordial congeniality, and nodded a greeting. Then he went back to his paper, unfolding it and refolding it at a different section. But underneath, he was more shocked to see me than Mrs. Foster had been the day before.

So, once again, he either knew who I was or he could see what I was. But his surprise went deeper. Mrs. Foster had been taken aback, but he was downright astounded. Mrs. Foster must have told him about me. The last thing he was expecting was for me to show up out of the blue.

I decided to push my luck just a little further. "I'm sorry, are you Mr. Foster?"

He looked up, a shock wave punching him in the gut. "Have we met?"

"No."

"Then how—"

I grinned and pointed to the billboard outside his office. The one with his picture on it.

He had the wherewithal to look sheepish. "Of course."

"I didn't mean to bother you. I was just at your office and your receptionist said you weren't in, so I decided to get some coffee and wait."

He was staring. He caught himself and put the paper aside. "And you are?"

"Cordelia Chase. I was going to talk to you about insurance, but I can wait."

"No, please." He gestured toward the seat across from his. "Join me."

I grabbed my bag and my cup and did just that.

"You need insurance?"

"Yes. Life insurance. For my husband. He's dying."

"Oh." He didn't believe me. Not for a hot minute. But he was playing along so I went with it. "I'm sorry."

"It's okay. He doesn't know it, yet, but I have a strong suspicion he doesn't have long to live."

Mr. Foster cleared his throat and leaned back in his seat. "Can I ask who your health insurance is with?"

"That's a good question." I crinkled my nose in thought. Cookie handled all that stuff. "I don't know what the name is, but it has a red logo? With, maybe, a triangle? Or a square? Yes, that's it. It's definitely a square. Or possibly a circle."

"It doesn't matter, Ms. Chase."

"Oh, Cordy, please."

"Cordy, if I can get some basic information from you, we can go from there. See what we can come up with and get you some quotes. How does that sound?"

I nodded. "Perfect."

Sadly, I didn't get a read off him when I said my name, so I still had no clue if he knew who I was or not.

He pulled a memo pad and pen from an inside pocket just as Angel popped into the diner.

"I quit," he said, bending down so that his face was inches from mine. I had to concentrate not to look at him. "I'm only thirteen. There are some things I just shouldn't see. *Ay, dios mio.*" He turned, his agitation evident in his sharp movements. He scrubbed his head.

I dragged out my phone and held up an index finger, faking a phone call. "I am so sorry. I have to take this."

"Not at all." He'd schooled his features again and created a steeple with his fingers, but the fact that I took a call in the middle of his break, a break I was interrupting, irked him. As it should have. Rude was a bit of an understatement, but I had to see what was up with my best—not to mention only—investigator.

"Hey, Angel. What's going on? I'm kind of in the middle of something."

He spun around to face me again. "My job. Your uncle is a detective for the freaking police department. Do you know what that means?"

"Uncle Bob? Is everything okay?"

"It means he gets called to shootings and stabbings and child abuse cases and guys beating the fuck out of their wives. It means his job is screwed up as hell. And it means I quit."

I eased out of the booth. "Angel, did something happen to Uncle Bob? Is he okay?"

He railed at me. "No, he's not okay. Have you been listening?"

Alarm cinched around my throat. "You need to calm down, hon. Tell me what happened."

After taking a few deep breaths, he finally calmed enough to explain. "He's at a shooting. Happened early this morning at one of those breakfast places on Central."

"Like an IHOP or a Denny's?"

"There was a kid," he said without answering. "Just eating eggs with his mom before he went to school. What the fuck is wrong with people?"

The moment he said *kid*, dread started its slow ascent up my spine like a funeral march. I had to see for myself what would upset Angel so much. "Sweetheart, where is Uncle Bob?"

"What?" He tried to gather himself. "No, not an IHOP. It's like a breakfast place with a yellow sign. It has a sun coming up in the corner."

"Okay, I think I know which one you mean." I slammed a quick gulp of coffee, picked up my bag, and tossed a couple dollars onto the table. "Off Tramway, right?"

He nodded and I turned to Mr. Foster. "I am so sorry, Mr. Foster, but duty calls. I can drop by later, if that's okay."

"Of course." He refolded his memo pad and stuffed it inside the pocket again. "I hope everything is okay."

"Yeah, me, too."

Unfortunately, mass shootings rarely meant everything was okay.

9

Everyone complains about the weather,
but no one wants to sacrifice a virgin to change it.
—TRUE FACT

Although my meeting with Mr. Foster didn't yield much in the way of information, I did get one tidbit for certain: Mr. Foster could definitely see, even if just barely, into the celestial plane. I caught him glancing toward Angel twice, and both times it had been when Angel had moved quickly. If what he could see was anything like my friend Pari, he may have seen Angel's essence in the form of a grayish mist. Just like in the movies. Then again, he could be like Amber's main squeeze, Quentin. Thanks to a tragic demonic possession, that kid could see the departed as clearly as I could.

I hauled butt back across town to Sunny Side Up on Central. Angel had seen a lot. He'd died over two decades ago. His reaction to this crime scene, after everything he'd witnessed, made no sense. It had to be the kid. He'd said something about a kid, proof that underneath all his bravado sat a heart of gold.

But he saw dead kids all the time. Maybe it was the shooting. Maybe it brought back memories of his own death, which was shooting related, as well, the hole in his chest surrounded by a feathering of dark crimson evidence. Evidence that he would wear every day for the rest of his existence as long as he stayed on this plane.

Was that what set him off? I'd never given much thought to how Angel handled everything he saw. He'd been with me all through high school, college, and the Peace Corps. And he'd been investigating for me since I'd opened Davidson Investigations over three years ago. He seemed to take everything in stride, but clearly there was more than met the eye. I'd have to pencil in a sit-down as soon as I could.

Until then, the crime scene was easy enough to spot. Flashing lights and yellow tape were never a good sign.

I had to park at a hotel next to the café. Then I went in search of my favorite—and only—uncle. He stood behind an ambulance, speaking to an EMT. The emergency technician nodded, shook his hand, then climbed inside the van and took off, lights blazing and sirens blaring.

Ubie turned and saw me standing with the spectators behind the tape. I was just about to wave him over when he stormed toward me.

He scanned the area, then dragged me under the tape and marched me toward the café. "What are you doing here?"

I could hardly tell him I had Angel watching his every move. Because then I would have to tell him why. I would have to tell him that the man who could be responsible for his death was still at large. I would have to tell him how we thwarted the first—and hopefully only—attempt. I would have to tell him he was slated for hell. And then I would have to tell him why. That I knew what he did for me. That I owed him. That I loved him beyond measure.

"Charley Davidson, you are under arrest."

Or not. "You can't arrest me just because you want to, Uncle Bob."

He stopped just inside the doors to the café and snapped his fingers at a nearby uniform. "Watch me." He collected the officer's handcuffs and turned me around, concern drawing his brows into a hard line. "You have the right to remain silent."

I stilled when I saw the inside of the café. Overturned chairs. Broken glass. And blood. So much blood. "What happened, Uncle Bob?"

"Anything you say—"

"The kid," I said, remembering what Angel had said. I whirled to face him but kept my hands behind my back even though he'd only cuffed one wrist. "There was a kid. Is he okay? Did he get shot?"

Ubie let out a long, exhausted sigh. "How did you know there was a kid involved?"

"Spies. Uncle Bob, what happened?"

The anger drained from his body, and a sadness crept in. He walked to a chair and lowered himself into it. "Just another day in the city."

I knelt beside him and put my cuffed hand on his knee. "Is the boy . . . is he okay?"

After a long moment, he caved. "He will be. He was shot in the head and shoulder. The head wound was just a graze, and the shoulder will heal."

"Oh, thank goodness." I scanned the area again. A couple of uniforms eyed me, clearly wondering what I was doing at a crime scene as the CSS team scoured the place.

"Mass shooting," he said, taking in the scene again. "A homeless man came in and shot up the place. Killed two people. Injured five others."

"I'm sorry." It seemed like such a lame thing to say, but I had nothing else. What did one say to such a senseless act? "Did they catch the shooter?"

He shook his head. "There's a search going on as we speak. He took off toward the interstate, but that's the last anyone has seen of him."

Before he could say anything else, his phone rang. He stood, walked a few feet away, and answered it. I stood and followed him.

"Where? Just the coat? Get a field investigator over there and check the area for cameras." He hung up, then turned, surprised at first I stood right on his heels until it sank in who I was. Who I was explained a lot of my actions to those who knew me well.

"Good news?" I asked.

"Possibly. They found a coat that may have been the shooter's three blocks over."

"That's strange."

"In what way?"

"Well, if he was just some random homeless guy, why would he ditch his coat?"

"To throw us off."

"But a homeless guy on a chilly day who probably only has the one coat to speak of?"

Uncle Bob bent his head in thought as I took a closer look at the crime scene.

"Who died?" I asked.

"What?"

"Who died?"

"A woman in her midthirties and an elderly man."

I nodded. Bit my bottom lip. Started to let the emotions of the spectators I'd felt earlier soak in. A couple felt off, but I chalked that up to reporter enthusiasm. Only a reporter would get excited at a fatal shooting. Especially if he were the first on the scene. So there was definitely one reporter present. So, then, why did I get a similar reaction from another spectator who had no press credentials or cameraman to speak of?

"Who died first?"

"We don't know that yet. What are you thinking?"

"Okay, who was shot first?"

"According to a security feed and a couple of witnesses, the woman who died was shot first."

"Was the kid hers?"

"Yes," he said, fighting the urge to care on anything more than a professional level. He was usually pretty good at that. This one bothered him, though.

"What is it, Uncle Bob?"

"The kid. He jumped in front of his mother, trying to protect her." Then he looked at me as though the puzzle pieces started falling into place in his mind. "The shooter shot the woman once. Then the boy jumped in front of her to protect her. The shooter . . ." He stalked to a hall that led to the offices in the back of the place. I followed.

"What are you thinking?"

"Nothing. Not yet. It's just, it looked like the shooter tried to move the boy out of the way, but the shooter was blocking the camera's angle, so it was hard to tell exactly what happened."

We went into an office where another detective was viewing the security recording. He nodded at Ubie, then went back to his task.

"Can you rewind it?" Uncle Bob asked him.

He did, and we watched as the horrific event unfolded. I slammed my hands over my mouth as the woman was shot. When the boy lunged to protect her, my faith in humanity was completely restored. We may be a messed-up race, but there was still more good in the world than bad.

The man struggled with the kid a few seconds, then gave up and shot, very carefully, through him. After that, the shooter opened fire randomly. Many of the employees and customers had already fled. Those who were left hid behind counters and under tables, but the shooter still managed to take down several of the more unfortunate, including an elderly man who used a cane. He couldn't have run out if he'd tried.

Then, just as the man was about to flee, he stopped over the woman. Pointed the gun at her head again. Nudged her with his foot.

Satisfied, he fled the scene out the back door.

I sank into a chair. Uncle Bob looked back at me. "What do you think, pumpkin? Her husband?"

"Yes. Or ex-husband. He didn't want to kill his son. Unless he had to. But he damned sure wanted his wife dead. Enough to kill others to get her there."

The other detective frowned at us. "You got all that from the video?"

"He's out front, watching," I told Uncle Bob. "You'll probably find a wig and fake beard in his car. And he's been practicing, so he'll appear distraught. Nothing would make him happier than the news crew capturing his anguish for all to see when you tell him his wife is dead."

Ubie nodded. "You don't happen to have his name and Social Security number, do you?"

I raised my arm. "You're going to need these."

He shook his head. "You're still under arrest."

"Okay." I wasn't going to argue with him. Something was eating at him. Gnawing at him. And it definitely involved me. He had his reasons for wanting me to stay home. To stay safe. I could respect that even if I didn't listen.

He pressed his mouth together, then summoned the officer to remove the cuffs. "You want to be a part of this?" The arrest. Did I want to be a part of the arrest.

"You know what? I think I'll let you handle this one."

"Okay."

I stood and hugged him. Hard. For a long time. At least I didn't have a family member stage a fake mass shooting to murder me. My family may have put the fun in dysfunctional, but we were rarely homicidal.

When I walked back to Misery, I passed the shooter. I stopped and took a step back. It was so obvious now. His emotions were all wrong. I wanted to look him in the eye. To let him know that we knew what he'd done. I couldn't help the sneer on my face.

He was tall and beefy with a protruding beer belly that screamed heart attack.

"What?" he asked, eyeing me curiously. Then he realized I might be somebody important. His expression changed to one of concern. Desperation. "My wife. I think—I think she was in there."

I stepped closer and stared up at him. "Ya think?"

I turned back to Uncle Bob, and gestured toward the man. "This is him."

Not that I'd needed to. He'd been standing behind me the whole time, so the suspect would have been a little hard to miss.

He nodded. "Thanks, pumpkin."

The man began his efforts anew. "Please, I just want to know about my wife. She should have been home by now."

He truly thought Uncle Bob was going to tell him his wife had been fatally shot in a random, senseless attack. And he was good. His expressions were spot-on. Worry. Doubt. Agony. I got the feeling he even had a bit of denial up his sleeve for good measure.

But when Ubie pushed him against a cruiser and ordered an officer to take him into custody until they could get a warrant for his house and car, the guy's well-rehearsed demeanor crumbled.

"What—? What's going on? I'm just here about my wife." He tried to keep up the act, but the realization that he was facing a life behind bars proved a bit unnerving. Panic had seized his lungs. When the officer went to cuff him, he started to fight.

It took three officers to restrain him and get him into the cruiser.

Unable to stand the scumbag's presence any longer, I sought out Misery. Climbed inside her. Sat for a long time.

I wanted to take over this world. To run it differently from Jehovah. He gave humans autonomy, the freedom to choose to do good or bad. But what would I do differently? Heal all disease? Quell all violence? Erase all remnants of racism?

"Jehovah has a point," I said to the angel standing outside my passenger's door, looking in. "To control the human race, even a little . . . that can't be the answer. Where would it end? When people are so healthy they're living for hundreds of years? And still procreating until the world is so overpopulated we'll have to pool our resources and find another world to live on? And then what?" I raised my brows in question. "Life is a cycle. I understand that. And I get it. He can step in when asked. When prayed to. That was part of the deal."

The angel tilted his head as he listened to me rant.

"But it's those few humans that . . . that ruin it for the rest of us, you know? I mean, holy hell, why not just get divorced? And then there's the accidents. The tragic accidents that no one saw coming. They somehow seem the most unfair of all. When they are no one's fault. They just happen for no explainable reason." I glared at the celestial being. "Well, I want an explanation. What about Curren? What did he do?"

I had no idea why I was suddenly venting to an angel. I'd seen so much. Faced so much. Maybe it was the essence of that sweet boy crossing through me, a boy who was born to such worthy parents, such a loving family, to then be faced with the reality that not all parents were created equal. Not all of them were such a high caliber. Some, instead, would shoot through their own child to rid themselves of a nuisance. And still others would rid themselves of the child altogether. Or commit unspeakable acts. Or just ignore their offspring, pretending she didn't exist.

"You know what?" I asked the angel. "I'm with Angel. I quit, too."

He continued to stare, ambivalent.

The fury that had been pooling like a bucket of gasoline in my stomach ignited. The atrocious things people did to one another sickened me. He shot through his own child to kill his wife. When I couldn't even hold mine, couldn't even see her without risking her life, he shot his.

I swiped angrily at the tears that refused to be squelched and glared at the celestial being. He was here. On this plane. And he'd done nothing. A powerful, radiant being had just stood by and let that man hurt all those people.

This was where Jehovah and I parted ways. He could have done something. He could have stopped it.

I could have stopped it.

When the world began to shake around me, I closed my eyes. Filled my lungs. Tried to tamp down the rage that churned inside me. I had to slow my heart. To soothe the raw emotion that threatened to rip me apart.

Then, despite squeezing my lids shut, my fingers, white-knuckled and gripping the steering wheel, came into focus. I blinked, confused when the world tilted and began to spin. Then realization sank in. My molecules were separating.

I bit down.

Fought for control.

Lost.

Before I knew what was happening, I plunged into the celestial realm, the sensation similar to being tossed from a sauna into a frozen lake. The sudden change in temperature, like scalding ice, like blistering freezer burn, sent shock waves rocketing through my nervous system. Winds whipped around me, and I struggled to gather the cells in my body, to bring them back to the fold, but they scattered in the tempest hidden behind the veil of our world.

I doubled over, curled my hands into fists, and said quietly, "Stop."

A shift in reality shuddered through me. Time had slipped, yes, but I'd been uprooted. The ground beneath me was wet. The interior of Misery had morphed into trees and bushes and grass, and I began to realize I wasn't in Kansas anymore, unless Kansas was a thick, emerald green with icy-crisp air and an ocean crashing against rocks nearby.

Probably not.

I stood and turned in circles, trying to get my bearings. Trees. Grass-lands. Trees. Grasslands. The terrain, stunning and fierce, was the polar opposite of New Mexico.

Last time my temper got the best of me, I ended up in upstate New York, but the crashing waves convinced me I was not in New York, either. I'd learned to dematerialize, but I still had trouble controlling—as in no control at all—where I ended up. So, God only knew. Well, God and my old friend GPS.

I patted my skirt pockets and prayed, but my phone was still in Misery with my bag. And my jacket. And my ID.

A sweaty kind of panic set in. If I died here, no one would know who I was. They'd never find my body. And if they did, they would have no way to identify it. Unless they spotted the tiny tattoo Pari had given me on my wrist that said in bold script MRS. REYES FARROW. That might give them a clue.

Still.

I had to get a handle on this shit. But first, I had to get home.

I could try to dematerialize and find my way back, but knowing my luck, I'd end up in a terrorist training camp. Or a men's prison. Or a feminine hygiene commercial.

Left with little choice, I began walking.

On the bright side, no angels stalking me.

On the dark side . . .

No, I was not going to succumb to the dark side.

I repeated that mantra and channeled my inner Luke Skywalker as I walked for what seemed like hours. The landscape was like nothing I'd ever seen. Not in real life. It was rocky and grassy and woodsy and smelled fresh, like dirt and salt and ozone. I followed the sound of the ocean and came to a stunning cliff that dropped at least a hundred feet, white waves crashing against sharp, jutting rocks below. Then I turned right. It seemed like the right thing to do.

It was all so breathtaking, but I had places to view and people to do. I didn't have time to roam about, searching for signs of life.

Wait. What if I hadn't gone anywhere? What if I'd actually gone back in time? Was that possible? I went over what I knew about dinosaurs, which was basically: Flat teeth, herbivore. Sharp teeth, run.

I made a mental note to run either way.

After another seventeen hours—or possibly thirty minutes—I spotted an isolated house tucked between two rocky hills. Like a haven. Like a sanctuary for lost travelers. Or, more likely, like the den of a serial killer. Either way, it was my only choice. I started toward it.

Two years later, breathless, frozen, and near death, I knocked on the door of the quaintest little serial killer's cottage I'd ever seen. A woman in her fifties answered, her face round and rosy cheeked from the bitter winds of the strange land.

"Oh, heavens," she said—at least I think that's what she said—as surprised to see me as I was to see her. She turned and called out. "Bernie! Got a we'an on the stoop."

"It's no a tea leaf, is it?" a male voice called out.

She eyed me up and down. "Don't look like one. Closer to a drown doo."

I hugged myself to squelch a shiver as a man around the same age as the woman walked up, his eyes bright with excitement. "Got a lassie, eh?"

The woman nodded. "What're you doing out in the cold?"

Their accents were so thick, I couldn't even decipher which language they were speaking. "Um, do you speak English?"

Bernie laughed and slapped his leg as the woman, to whom I'd yet to be introduced, said, "We are speaking English, love."

"Oh." I knew every language ever spoken on the planet, both alive and dead. But every once in a while I had a little trouble with accents. The Scottish lilt being one of them. 'Parently.

"Am I . . ." I could hardly say the words out loud. "Am I in Scotland?"

The woman cackled in delight. "You're a dear we'an, aren't ye? Come in out of the cold."

"Thank you." I stepped inside as the man hustled off.

He came back with a blanket and wrapped it around me. "That's a sin about your clothes," he said, gesturing toward my apparel.

He was probably right. As wet as my clothes were, they probably looked sinful. Showed a little too much. Maybe they were really religious.

"Aye," the woman said, glaring at her husband. "Downright awful to see a bonnie lass nigh in the skuddy."

He shrugged. "Tea?"

"Lassie's American, ye wanker."

"Oh, right. Caffee then?"

Now *that* I understood. I was still running on one cup. I wouldn't last much longer.

A smile blossomed across my face. I hoped. My face was fairly numb, so I could have just drooled. "Please."

Watching the couple as they worked making "caffee" and biscuits was like watching an American sitcom. They were hilarious, their banter both loving and demoralizing. My kind of people.

After filling my belly with biscuits that weren't biscuits at all, Bertrice and Bernie offered me the use of their phone.

"Thank you so much," I said, but I had no idea how to dial to America.

Bertrice showed me how to dial the operator, and eventually, after several attempts and failed connections, a phone rang on the other side of the world. On about the third ring, however, I'd completely lost my train of thought.

I stood in a dark hallway. The cottage was actually round, and right in the middle was a wooden, octagon-shaped closet.

I stepped closer. Examined the carvings. The way the door slid open.

The Brummels were using it as a pantry, but I'd seen a closet exactly like this one in the convent Reyes had sequestered me away in for eight months. The one that took us forever to figure out how to open. The one that, when I stepped inside, made my light disappear from the celestial realm. It just vanished.

Nothing—no room, no material, no bank vault—could block out my light. Even Earth itself didn't block it. The departed saw it from any-where in the world. It was a beacon to them. A lighthouse so they could find their way to the portal when they were ready to cross.

The only time I'd ever known it to disappear was when I'd stepped into that closet a few months ago. And this one was exactly like it. Right down to the type of wood.

"Charley?" Cookie said, fairly yelling into the phone. Thank good-ness she'd accepted the collect call. I could not imagine going through all that again.

This place was completely rural, so I'd expected the bad connection. I hadn't expected the terror in her voice.

"Hey, Cook! You'll never guess where I am."

"Where are you?" she asked, panicked.

"Right. That's what I mean. You'll never guess."

"Charley," she said in her mommy voice.

"Gosh, okay. I'm kind of in Scotland. This call is probably going to cost us a fortune."

"Charley, this is no time to joke."

"No, really, this is a landline, and since I had to call you collect, beaucoup bucks, baby."

"You know what I mean. Scotland?"

"I know, right? I just kind of ended up here."

Reality sank in. "But . . . but you remember who you are?"

"Yes, Cook. I have not lost my memories. Just my marbles. I have no money, no phone, and no passport. If the coppers get me, I'm screwed. Also, I don't know how to get back. But whatever you do, you can't tell—"

"Have you tried clicking your heels together three times and saying, 'There's no place like home'?"

"This is serious, Cook. Don't tell Reyes. I'm begging you."

When I was met with a thick, drawn-out moment of silence, I said, "He's right there, isn't he?"

"Well—"

"Oh, wait." I closed my eyes and let a wave of both embarrassment and relief wash over me. I felt his heat at my back. His power. His concern. "Never mind."

"Sorry, Charley. He's been pacing around and—"

He reached from behind me and disconnected the call. Then he stepped closer, drowning me in his warmth. Saturating every cell. Filling every dark corner.

He leaned into me. Pressed his mouth to my ear. Whispered, "Care to explain?"

I turned to him at last. He towered over me. Curious. Worried. And a little angry. I didn't know what to say. I'd exploded and ended up thousands of miles away. So I decided to change the subject. "Does that closet look familiar?"

He didn't turn around. Didn't take his eyes off me. Didn't change his expression in the least.

"It's just like the one at the convent."

"Is it?" he asked, still refusing to look. "There's an angel with a sword wound explaining to Jehovah right now how he got it."

"Reyes," I said, alarmed. "What did you do?"

"What did I do?" he asked, deathly still.

"Well, yes." I pushed against him. He didn't budge. "You got into a fight with an angel?"

"Three. I thought . . ." He bit down but didn't give up his position. "I thought they took you."

"You thought they took me?" I asked, both stunned and flattered. "Why would they take me? Wait, no, *where* would they take me?"

"It's not important. Why are you here?" He glanced around the cottage just as Bernie came up behind him, his expression grave as he said, "Grab me a chib, wifey. Shite's about to get real."

"Bernie, wait," I said, pushing past Reyes and holding up my hands. "This is my husband. He came to get me."

Bernie continued to glower as Bertrice ran up behind him with a knife. "A good nip is all this'll take, I imagine."

"It's okay, really. He's a good guy."

Bernie relaxed, but just barely. "He's no right to pin ye against your will."

I turned back to Reyes. "Bernie has a point."

Reyes glared at me, then crossed his arms over his chest. What he said to the man, in a perfect Scottish accent, floored me to no end. "I would-nae refuse a square go, but I'd best warn ye, I'm solid."

It was at that point that I melted. Only a little. Mostly in the knees.

10

Thank God I don't have to hunt for my food.
I don't even know where tacos live.
—MEME

Bernie stepped closer to my husband, his chest puffing in a display of strength and fearlessness. "Solid or no, ye pin her like that again, ye'll find yourself covered in your own blood."

He and Reyes stood nose to nose for a tense minute before Bertrice slapped her husband on the back. "Let it go, Bernie. That one'll see ye to your grave afore ye ken he even moved." She looked at me and winked. "He's a braw one, aye?"

"Yes," I said, wrapping an arm in Reyes's. Since I didn't know if she meant beautiful or brave, I just agreed. "He is definitely a braw one. This is Reyes."

Bernie took Reyes's hand. Amends were made. Biscuits were eaten because who doesn't like biscuits that taste like cookies?

We said our good-byes and promised to visit again. I couldn't get the closet out of my mind. That couldn't have been a coincidence.

We walked in the dark a ways, the chill less chilly with Reyes near. It was like having my own personal traveling heater and latte maker. The man could make a latte.

Also, he'd given me his jacket. It was like a huge, comfy blanket, and it smelled like him. I struggled to keep from molding it to my face and breathing him in.

Since I had no idea how we were going to get home—Reyes basically teleported over—I turned to him. "So," I said, my breath fogging on the air, "any idea how we're getting back?"

We'd stopped in a grove of trees, and Reyes was leaning against one, watching me. Studying.

When he spoke, it was with that same Scottish lilt. The one that melted my knees. And my panties. Mostly my panties.

"Come here, lass."

I did. How could I not? He pulled me into his arms, where it was warm and safe.

"Care to tell me what happened?" he asked in his normal accent. Oddly enough, it still worked for me.

I shrugged. If he wanted a conversation, he'd get one. "Care to tell me why you want me to drop the Foster case?"

He tensed and looked off into the distance but said nothing.

"How about the fact that you're a god. I mean, you just found out. What do you think? What do you remember?"

Silence again.

"What about the god glass? It's clearly upsetting you that I have it." Nothing.

I pushed out of his arms and walked to a brook. The moon overhead glinted on the bubbling water. "Okay, we can always talk about the promise you made to Michael. Do you remember that?"

When I turned back, he was watching me again, his dark eyes glistening as though the moon danced inside them.

"You promised him you'd get all three gods of Uzan off the plane. He tricked you, since you had no idea at the time that you were one of the three. But is there like a loophole? How are we going to get around that?" I waited, but not long. "And speaking of the god glass, there are innocent souls trapped in there. Now they are trapped with an assassin demon named Kuur and a malevolent god, Mae'eldeesahn. I have to get them out. I've been racking my brain, but I don't know how. I don't know what a hell dimension is like."

At that point, I was more or less voicing my stream of consciousness. If he didn't want to chat with me, I'd chat with me. I was excellent company.

"And, according to Kuur, the only way to get a soul out is to open the pendant and say the person's name, but only the one who put them in there in the first place can release them. If that's the case, we are seriously screwed. Not to mention the fact that we don't know any of their names."

I cursed the sadistic priest who'd condemned all those people to a hell dimension in the 1400s. What would they be like now? Would they even still be there? Would there be anything left of their sanity to salvage? I had no idea what six hundred years in a hell dimension would do to one's psyche, but it couldn't be good.

"You know, I was thinking about my in-laws." I strolled closer, craving his heat. And his scent. And the power that continuously hummed through him like an infinite source of energy. "You know, from your supernatural side? By being married to you, I am Satan's daughter-in-law, Jehovah's sister-in-law, and Jesus's aunt by marriage. We're like the ultimate nuclear family. Oh, and do you know what a god eater is?

Apparently I showed something to ADA Nick Parker, something pro-phetical, and he called me a god eater."

I turned away from him, breaking the spell he was trying to cast.

"Also, hell is going to freeze over, so that's apparently a real thing."

"They didn't deserve me."

I whirled around. He'd finally dropped his gaze. "Who didn't deserve you?"

"The Loehrs."

I stepped closer, confused. The Loehrs were his birth parents. His human birth parents. He'd chosen them out of all the people in the world to be a part of. And now they were Beep's guardians, caring for her and loving her like nobody else could.

"Reyes, they're good people. They're going to take care of Beep as if she were—"

"Exactly. Good. They didn't deserve me. Bad. The Fosters did them a favor."

As his words sank in, I began to understand his misgivings about my taking the case. "So, you think that what they did was okay?"

"I think they did the right thing."

"The right thing?" I put my hand on his chest. "Is that what this is all about?"

He didn't answer yet again. His jaw flexed under the weight of his stress.

"I think they have the ability to see into the supernatural realm. Not totally, but just enough to—"

"Know evil when they see it?"

He stuffed his hands in his pocket. "No. I just think that's how they target their victims. You've talked to them, I take it? To Mr. Foster, too?"

"Yes. I went to his office this morning."

"They'll adore you," he said. "Like they do Shawn."

"Shawn? Why? What does he . . . ?"

He'd turned away from me. His profile with its perfect angles and sensual curves almost glowed in the warm light of a yellow moon. It cast shadows where his lashes fanned across his cheeks. The effect was stunning.

"What's so different about Shawn? I didn't notice anything unusual besides the pureness of his aura."

"Because you never look beyond what meets the eye. You rely too much on reading their emotions."

"It's worked pretty good for me so far. And looking beyond? You mean like when I shift onto the other plane?" I took his silence as a yes. "Okay, so if I'd looked harder, what would I have seen?"

"The opposite of me."

Fine. He was being Cryptic Man, which meant he was nowhere near comfortable talking about it. "Opposite. Like dark versus light?"

He finally met my gaze again. "He is Nephilim."

"Nephilim? You mean . . ." My jaw dropped open, and I sat there, stunned speechless, for about an hour. That a Nephilim—part human, part angel—was even possible. That it could actually happen. "They're real?"

"He is descended from the union of a Grigori and a human."

"Does he know that?"

"I doubt it."

"Holy cow." I walked back to the brook. "This is big. This is like discovering Noah's ark. Or the Holy Grail. Or a crashed UFO."

"There are more than you might think."

I spun back to him. "There are more? How do I not know these things?"

"You should come here again." A whisper of a grin played on his mouth.

"We should get back."

"In that case, you'll definitely have to come here."

I walked back to him and let him wrap me in his arms.

"Hold on tight," he said, humor in the warning.

"Wait. Would you really have dropped me this morning?"

He bent closer to whisper in my ear. "Right on your ass."

Before I could reply, the celestial world slammed into us. Whipping and howling and coursing. And then it was gone, and we were in Reyes's office.

I swayed as I got my bearings, then glared up at him.

"That's awful," I continued, picking up where we left off and wishing I had that kind of control over my destination. "You're supposed to care for me and protect me and make me tacos."

"Please." He sat behind his desk, leaned back, and watched me. Again. "The day you need anyone's protection is the day . . . well, the day hell freezes over. I don't think dear old Dad is going to take that lying down. I should probably have your back. But until then . . ."

Fine. I'd go along with it. "Any idea when I'm scheduled to transform his dimension into Ice Capades: Hell on Ice?"

"Hey, boss." Sammy poked his head in. "Fryer's on the fritz again."

I perked up. "Did you check the carburetor?" Gawd, I was so helpful.

He laughed softly and shook his head. "Davidson, did you stop taking your medication again?"

"Why? What have you heard?"

"I'll call Saul," Reyes said.

Really?

Sammy gave him a thumbs-up and me the crazy sign. I felt very judged.

I had Reyes talking. I wasn't about to give up on this conversation just because he had to call Saul.

As he picked up the phone, I continued my rant. "So, I had an idea about the god glass." I waited for his reaction. Got none. "So, there are rules, right? I don't know the names of the people the evil priest sent there, and I'm not the one who sent them, anyway. So I figure I can go to hell. I can get him back."

He shook his head, then left a message on Saul's phone.

When he hung up, he said, "You don't understand. People don't really burn for an eternity. That's a myth. He's long gone."

"But the people in this dimension are still alive. What if we just broke it?"

"The god glass, from what I can tell, is a gate. A portal to the hell dimension. What if instead of freeing the people inside, we locked it forever? Or if the entire dimension collapsed and trapped them for all eternity?"

He had some really good points. I sat across from him, defeated.

"Besides, if it really is god glass, I doubt you can just break it with a hammer."

Another good point.

"Does it bother you that I have it?"

"Should it?"

I draped my body over his desk. He could be so frustrating.

He laughed under his breath.

"I suppose you have to work."

"Nothing urgent. Do you want to tell me how you ended up stranded in Scotland?"

I shrugged, his coat heavy on my shoulders. "I just got angry."

"At me?"

"At men in general."

"Ah."

"Do you know when I was born?"

"Come again?"

"You know. Like what era? How old am I? Are we talking the Meso-zoic, or do we have to go back as far as the Paleozoic?"

"I don't know. Your dimension is much older than this one."

I bolted upright. "Older?"

"That's not how it works, anyway. Time isn't the same on every plane. This plane's chronological structure doesn't mesh with the one from your dimension. It would be impossible to tell."

"Is that a polite way of saying I'm so old, I'd have to be carbon-dated to figure it out?"

"Yes," he said, his voice dripping with sarcasm. "That's it exactly."

"Okay, what about you, then? How old are you? You and Jehovah? And how are you brothers? Like, did you have a mom and dad?"

His brows cinched together, but only for a moment. "I don't remember. I don't think it works that way."

"I'm sorry. What do you remember?"

He filled his lungs and sat back in his chair. "I remember I treated you like shit. And I know you don't remember, because if you did, you'd hate me."

"Doubt it. Why did you treat me so badly, then?"

He pulled his lower lip between his teeth in thought. "You know how in grade school a boy pulls the hair of the girl he likes?"

"You liked me? Wait. You pulled my hair?"

"You were, for lack of a better phrase, out of my league."

I snorted before I realized he was serious. "I find that really hard to believe. Have you looked in the mirror lately?"

He studied me, then asked, "If you do ever remember, will you for-give me?"

I walked around his desk. Propped my ass against it. Studied him a long moment.

He let me.

How were this perfect man and I even in the same orbit? I was out of his league? Not likely.

He reached forward, put a hand on my thighs, and slid my skirt up until it bunched above my hips. Then he looked up at me. "Say yes," he said, his voice smooth and deep.

"Yes."

Anticipation fluttered in my stomach.

He propped me against the desk again and sat back, letting his gaze travel over me, stopping at my crotch, then continuing down my legs.

The outline of his cock through his jeans quickened my pulse.

Before I could do anything about it, he lifted my booted foot and braced it on the arm of his chair. Then he did the same with the other, anchoring it before reaching up and parting my knees. He took hold of my ankles, my boots only a few inches high, and sat back to study me again.

Thankfully, Sammy had closed the door. Otherwise the patrons would be getting dinner *and* a show.

He locked his intense gaze with mine. "Wet your fingers."

I lifted a hand to my mouth.

"Not there."

Surprised, I reached between my legs and slid my fingers inside my panties, my chest rising and falling as I pushed them inside.

"Farther."

I pushed them deeper, the sensation swirling in the pit of my stomach.

His breaths grew labored as well. "Rub your clit."

I did, the hunger I saw on his face more erotic than my own touch.

He watched a long moment, shifting in his chair as though his jeans were suddenly too tight.

Then he said, his voice deep and smooth, "Come."

It was a simple command. I had never masturbated in front of anyone before. But the look on Reyes's face, the desire shimmering in his eyes, convinced me I had absolutely nothing to lose.

I rubbed my clit with two fingers, watching as his erection grew more pronounced. As his hands clenched around my ankles. As his jaw flexed. When he reached up and slid my panties aside for a better view, arousal spiked inside me. My cunt was so swollen and sensitive at that point, the softest brush of his fingers would have pushed me over the edge, but he only watched.

He turned his head and sprinkled the inside of my knee with soft, feathery kisses. My skin was so tight, the endearments were almost painful. And I wanted more. I wanted his mouth on me. His cock in me.

But he only watched as I worked. At first. I'd started slow, but as the embers sparked to life and the fire spread, my fingers moved faster.

Unable to sit idly by, he stood between my legs, opened my shirt, and slipped my bra down, giving him access to my hardened nipples. He bent and seared first one, then the other with his mouth. His tongue scorched as he covered the crest and suckled.

The sensation was like a string pulling taut nipple to clitoris. One tugged at the other, and the pressure built. His audible breaths quickened with each stroke. I grabbed the side of the desk with my other hand and held on, shaking uncontrollably, until the familiar sting exploded low in my abdomen, so sharp it seized every muscle in my body, so hot it flooded every cell.

He wrapped an arm around the curve of my back and held me as I arched against him.

I had no idea if I'd been too loud, but when Reyes unfastened his jeans, I didn't care if I'd screamed his name from the top of my lungs. He pushed between my legs, and his rock-hard erection slid easily inside me. The waves of orgasm were still pulsing in rhythm with my thundering heart, the aftermath exquisite, when his cock, so perfectly placed, coaxed a second one to rise and crest the instant he entered me, opening the floodgates again, spilling molten lava, sweet and hot and sensual, into my core, rewarding my body with the most delicious sensations on Earth.

But he didn't move inside me. He held me tight against him, clamped down on me, rendered me immobile, and let the convulsions of my climax squeeze and massage his cock, milking him until he exploded. He grabbed a handful of hair. Pulled me tighter. Rocked against me. And groaned aloud. The combination so pleasurable, so ethereal, I almost came again.

We stayed locked together, riding the last of the waves down together, enjoying each other's touch until the tremors subsided.

Reyes squeezed me to him again and whispered, "Fucking hell."

I agreed. And I was not ready to let him go. Not just yet.

Instead of getting dressed, he lifted me off the desk and sat down with me still straddling him. With him still inside me.

"Kiss me," he said, in yet another command I was willing to obey. But just this once.

I felt his smile behind the kiss as I pressed my mouth to his.

I pulled back and licked my lips. Then smacked them and licked them again. "You taste like cotton candy."

He pleasured me again with a satiated grin. "Do I?"

"You do."

He licked his own lips and put his head back in thought. "You taste like—"

"Pot roast?" I offered.

He chuckled.

"Chiles rellenos? Cinnamon rolls? Battery acid? I've got to stop eating those things."

"Salt," he said at last. "From the sea."

"From Scotland?"

He nodded, and I burrowed closer.

"I can't believe I've been to Scotland. Think about all the plane fare we're going to save. Oh, I think we should name your penis the Vampire Lestat."

"Really? I was thinking Angry Johnny."

I stifled a giggle. "Maybe we should sleep on it."

As we sat there, the door opened, just barely, and a hand slid inside and dropped a set of keys on a side table. My keys. Reyes must have had Garrett pick up Misery. That'd save me a trip.

"Thanks, Garrett!" I called out.

He gave me a thumbs-up and closed the door.

"How do you suppose he knew we were performing sexual favors on each other?" I asked, snuggling against my man again.

"Possibly because you screamed my name about seven times."

I bolted upright and gaped at him.

He'd brought out his most wicked grin. "But that's just a guess."

11

I never said I'd die without coffee.
I said other people would.
—MEME

After Cookie picked Amber up from school, she and I went over everything she'd found out so far about the Fosters before going home. She'd hit a brick wall, but apparently she had a friend on it. I didn't know she had any friends.

But she did find out about the other two adoptions that the shady adoption agency, the Divine Intervention, filed paperwork for.

"Okay," she said, handing me a sheet of paper, "they were both adopted in Albuquerque. One boy and one girl. The boy died a few years ago in a fire. The fire inspector ruled it arson, but they never found who did it." She pointed to the other name. "And this one. The girl. She's your age and still living here. Oh, and I also found whose name was on the lease for the building."

She handed me that information as well.

"Thanks, Cook."

She seemed tired, and that worried me. Cookie didn't get tired.

"How is Uncle Bob?"

She shrugged. "Not living with me."

"He moved out?" I asked, shocked.

"No, I mean emotionally. It's like he hasn't really been home in days."

I covered her hand with mine. "It's a case, Cook. Classic symptoms. I promise you."

She nodded and went home early. I went to see a girl about a building.

The woman who'd leased the building the adoption agent worked out of lived in Taylor Ranch, so I headed that way despite the hour. Nothing sucked the life out of a day like rush-hour traffic. Fortunately, it wasn't that bad. The woman, a Karen Claffey, lived off Montano in a small white stucco with faded plastic flowers lining the drive.

I knocked on the door and heard a small dog barking inside when a car pulled up. A woman in her fifties got out and went around to her trunk to grab her groceries.

I smiled and waved as she walked from her drive to the front door. "Hi. Karen Claffey?"

She nodded and shifted her bags to get the door open.

"My name is Charley Davidson. I'm a private investigator looking into the Divine Intervention Adoption Agency, and—"

"I don't know anything about that." Her brusqueness threw me, but only for a moment.

"Really?" I took out the file. "According to city records, you leased the building the agency worked out of."

"Not me. I don't know anything about it."

If she had a sign around her neck, it would be flashing LIAR, LIAR, PANTS ON FIRE.

"No problem. But I should probably warn you, I'm working with

APD on this. I have to turn in my findings, so they might show up in the next couple of days. Just routine stuff. Nothing to worry about." I started toward Misery. "Have a good day."

"I didn't have anything to do with that agency."

"Excuse me?"

Annoyance mixed with a healthy dose of fear washed out of her. "It wasn't me. They just put the lease in my name on account of I went to their church and we became friends."

"Who, Mrs. Claffey?"

"Eve and Abraham. The Fosters. They needed the building but didn't want it in their names."

I stepped back to her. "Did they say why?"

She opened her front door and stood halfway inside as though hinting she had better things to do. "Just that they were going to adopt some kids and wanted to start their own agency. As far as I could tell, no agency ever went in. The building stayed empty the whole time. I would get the mail for them and drop it off at their house. That's all. I didn't have anything to do with the rest."

"Mrs. Claffey, I have to ask: What rest?"

She bowed her head in thought. Or prayer. She was down quite a while.

After enough time passed for me to have ovulated, twice, she gestured me inside.

She had a dachshund named Marley. I only knew that because she yelled at her seventeen times to shut up. But Marley continued her reign of terror, barking at me for a good three minutes before deciding I was okay. Then it was all belly rubs and toy tubs. As in a tub of toys. She had to bring out each and every toy, and we had to fight to the death for it until she got bored and went for the next one. I wondered if Mrs. Claffey would notice her missing after I left.

Karen put the bags on her kitchen counter, then started a pot of coffee. The smell sent me skyrocketing to my happy place called Coffeeland.

"There was some hubbub a while back," she said, talking over the dog growls as we battled for a pink mouse with one ear. "An investigator came by saying he worked for a public defender and that he needed everything I had on the agency. I tried to tell him I didn't have anything. The lease was in my name, true, but that was it. I had nothing to do with the business."

After almost losing a hand, I asked, "Did he say what they were investigating?"

She busied herself putting groceries away. "A woman was arrested for the disappearance and murder of her child. But she says she didn't kill her. She said that a couple from an adoption agency approached her. Then, twenty-five years later, the remains of the baby are found not fifty yards from the house she was living in at the time."

I stood and walked to her. Or, well, hobbled. Marley took a liking to my ankle boots. Had the Fosters adopted this woman's child only to kill it? Why go to such lengths? "Do you believe the Fosters capable of such a heinous act?"

She snorted. "Of course. The woman's story is too . . . accurate."

I bowed my head in sadness and in thought. I needed to talk to that investigator. "Mrs. Claffey—"

"Just Karen."

"Karen, did the investigator leave a card or give you a contact number?"

"He did, but I threw it away. I'm sorry."

"That's okay. I can find out. Thank you so much, Karen." I took her hand and pressed a card into it. "If you think of anything else."

She took my card, and I was about 90 percent certain she'd throw it away the minute I left as well.

Right before I headed for the door, I realized I needed to warn her. To let her know she could be in danger. "Karen, I don't want to scare you or sound all dire, but please don't say anything about this to the Fosters. I don't want this coming back on you."

She bit down and I felt a mixture of outrage and animosity. "I never see them anymore. I quit going to their church a while back."

"Care to tell me what happened?"

She turned away. I'd been doing this long enough to know that I'd lost her. "No."

Fair enough. "What is their church called?"

"People of the Divine Path."

"They really like the word *divine*."

"Yeah, they think they are." She leveled a serious stare on me. "Divine. Anointed. Godly."

"Don't we all?" I asked with my best self-deprecating smile.

I gave Marley one last scrub, then left.

I had Cookie on the phone before I even got to Misery. "Cookie, I need you to find out who's on trial for murdering her baby twenty-five years ago. They just found the—"

"Veronica Isom."

I stopped. "Wow, that was fast."

"It's been all over the news."

I really needed to jump on that whole evening news movement. "Thanks, Cook. Can you find out where she's being held?"

"Sure, hon. Give me five."

"You got it."

I climbed into Misery but didn't start her up. Instead, I waited for the little beastie in the passenger seat to announce her intentions.

I knew the kid. She was a blond-haired, blue-eyed beauty who'd drowned when she was nine years old. She lived with my friend Rocket and the gang at an abandoned mental asylum, so I really didn't see her much. She had her friends and no time for boring old me.

Strawberry, a.k.a. Strawberry Shortcake based off the pajamas she wore, sat pretending to eat ice cream from a bowl. She would take a bite, then give a bite to her doll. The bald one.

Strawberry had a thing for dolls' hair. Well, hair in general. She was always wanting to brush mine or braid it or give me a quick trim. After seeing her doll collection, I decided to go to a professional.

"Do you like dolls?" she asked out of the blue.

"I like blow-up dolls. Does that count?"

"Oh, I do, too. My friend Alex had one, and we would punch it in the face, and then it would bounce back up again."

We were so not on the same page. "Hey, sweetness, what are you doing here?"

"I saw you driving and came over."

"Oh. Okay."

"Have you seen Angel?" She'd developed a bit of a crush on my thirteen-year-old investigator.

"Not for a while."

"Oh. I need you to talk to my brother."

Her brother, David Taft, was an APD officer I liked to occasionally harass. "Yeah? Dating skanks again?"

She shook her head. "He fell, and now I can't see him anymore."

I froze. "Strawberry, what do you mean, he fell?"

"I don't know. I just saw him fall, and now I can't find him. I need you to look."

Okay, if there was one thing the departed excelled at, it was the cryptic message. Strawberry was no different, but if she couldn't see him . . .

Alarm slipped up my spine. Had he really fallen? Had he died? Had he crossed?

"Okay. I'll look into it, hon."

She nodded and force-fed her doll another bite. "You've been gone forever. I was looking for you, too. I thought you left."

I reached over and smoothed her hair over her shoulder. "I'm sorry." I didn't have the heart to tell her she'd just seen me a few days prior. The departed didn't always have the best sense of time. Maybe it was the same with her brother.

She lifted a tiny shoulder. "It's okay."

"Want to ride with me a while? I'm going to visit a woman accused of murder."

After a yawn, she shrugged again. "I guess."

Kids these days. So hard to keep entertained.

I started Misery, dragged my phone out of my pocket, and called Uncle Bob.

"What are you doing?" he said in lieu of a greeting.

"I'm not driving, if that's what you mean. I was calling about Officer Taft. Is he okay?"

After a moment of silence, he asked, "David Taft?"

"That's the one. His sister can't find him."

"He has a sister?"

"Departed."

"Oh. Oh, right. I guess I didn't realize you knew him that well. David Taft is on leave."

"On leave? Since when?"

"Since about four months ago. It was really strange, though. He came in one day, talked to the captain, then cleaned out his desk and left. We haven't seen him since."

"Are you sure he didn't get transferred?"

"Not according to our records."

If Taft had just left his job, taken some time off, why couldn't Strawberry see him? Not that she was the more reliable source, but still . . .

"Okay what's your theory?" I asked.

"Theory?"

"Come on, Ubie. What are you thinking?"

"I don't know, pumpkin. He got burned out. It happens all the time."

Not to the David Taft I knew and almost respected. He loved his job and he'd only been on the force a year or two. And, last I'd checked, he was training to be a sniper. He'd had hopes. Aspirations. And probably an STD from all the skanks he'd dated, according to Strawberry.

"That just doesn't sound like something he'd do."

"I don't know, pumpkin. This life isn't for everyone."

I heard that. "Okay, thanks, Uncle Bob. Can you keep me updated on this?"

"Absolutely. Are you at home?"

I blinked. "Yes."

"Good. Stay put. I'll be home in about an hour."

"Oh-kay."

I hung up and was just about to ask Strawberry, a.k.a. Rebecca Taft, if she'd been to her brother's house lately, when she turned to me and said, "I'll be back."

Damn. Her attention span was even shorter than mine. So much for using her as an investigator. Maybe I could call—

"I'm back!"

I jumped at her unexpected appearance.

"I needed a different brush." She held up what looked like a used toothpick. She turned it over in her fingers then rolled her eyes and said, "Ugh." And she was gone again.

The David Taft sabbatical really bothered me. Why would he just leave like that? And why couldn't Strawberry find him?

Another side effect of law enforcement was the high rate of suicide. What if he really had gotten burned out? What if he'd done something or seen something he shouldn't have? What if he was gone?

I waited until I got to a red light, bowed my head. "David Taft," I said, summoning him. If he had passed and was still on this plane, he should appear beside me or in my lap or on my hood. I'd take any scenario. But he didn't appear.

Sadly, that didn't mean he hadn't passed. He could have crossed to heaven moments after he died, and I couldn't summon anyone back from heaven. Not that I knew of. Though Angel always swore I could, I'd never tried it.

Cookie called when I was only a couple of blocks away from the office.

I answered with a simple but elegant, "Hey, Cook."

"Hey, hon. So, she's been bonded out and is staying at her parents' house."

"Good for her. That seems like a good place. Help her unwind and figure things out. Who are we talking about?"

She chuckled. "Veronica Isom. The girl accused of killing her—"

"Right. Sorry." The Taft conundrum had rattled my brain.

"They live in a mobile home park called Green Valley."

"Oh, perfect. Shoot me the address, and I'll head over."

"Will do. So, why does Robert think you're at home?"

"He does? That's strange."

"Charley," she said, her voice taking on an ominous note. "I'm not going to lie to my husband for you."

"What? Why? I'd totally lie for you."

"Yes, but you like to lie. You see it as a challenge. Probably because you're so bad at it."

"Wow. And the hits just keep coming."

"Be careful," she said, her tone more amused than concerned.

"I'm not promising anything." I hung up, pulled a U-ey to hit up the closest drive-thru, then headed off to find Veronica Isom, praying she'd talk to me.

Twenty minutes and half a mocha latte later, I pulled into the Green Valley Mobile Home Park off Fourth. Her parents had a well-taken-care-of mobile. Avocado green. It made me hungry for guacamole. And in turn I realized how close the park was to El Bruno's. So close I could smell the green chile roasting, flooding my mouth with anticipation. And saliva. Mostly saliva.

My stomach growled as I journeyed up the Isoms' walk. I knocked on the metal door and waited. A TV played softly in the background, and there was a car in the drive, but I didn't get an answer at the door until I'd knocked three more times. And the greeter was not happy that I'd been so persistent.

An older gentleman jerked open the door.

"Mr. Isom?" I asked, praying he'd give me a few seconds to convince him to give me more.

He glared. He had bushy brows and a faded blue work shirt with an Auto Crafters emblem on it. He was a body man. I could totally relate to body men. And, well, pretty much any men.

"I am so sorry to bother you, but I may—and this is a big *may*—be able to help in your daughter's case."

That got his attention, but not in the way I'd suspected. "The only thing my daughter needs help with is signing the plea agreement the DA offered. Can you help her do that?"

My heart sank. He, like probably the rest of the city, believed his daughter guilty of murdering her child. Either that or he saw no way to win regardless. This could be a tough sell.

"Is she here, Mr. Isom?"

He glared again, and I felt a distinct disdain wafting off him. My gut told me he was only helping her out of loyalty. Out of a sense of fatherly duty. But his heart had been raked over the coals. I could tell.

"My name is Charley Davidson. I'm a private investigator, and I think my current case directly relates to your daughter's. Mr. Isom, I truly believe that your daughter is innocent of the charges against her."

"And what makes you so sure?" he asked. But he only did so to prove me wrong. He didn't believe for a minute she was innocent.

"Because the same people who pretended to have an adoption agency, the ones who took your granddaughter, kidnapped my husband when he was a baby, as well as at least one other boy that we know of."

He straightened but still held the screen door, barring any thought I might have of entering. "There was no agency."

"There was," I argued. "And I have proof." I didn't, not anything physical, anyway, but he didn't need to know that.

He stewed on my words a moment, then yelled, "Roni!"

A woman came to the door having just gotten out of the shower.

"This woman has bought your story hook, line, and sinker. You two should have a great time together."

Okay. Well, that'd work.

"I'm Charley Davidson," I said before he could throw any more sarcasm my way, "and I know you're telling the truth."

She went completely still. Mr. Isom walked away, the door almost closing behind him. But Veronica recovered and pushed the screen door wider.

"Come in."

Veronica had long dark hair that hung over her shoulders in wet clumps, big bourbon-colored eyes, and a curvy figure. She'd been towel-drying her hair and picked up where she'd left off, squeezing the ends with the damp towel.

I navigated the steps to a rickety porch and stepped inside. There were toys strewn about the small mobile home.

"My nephew's. He's at the store with my mother," she said, explaining the clutter. She kicked a few toys out of the way and offered me a seat. "Can I get you anything to drink?"

It was a sweet gesture. Inside, her pulse pounded like a war drum. Her hands shook as they pressed water from her hair. And there was something unnatural about her movements. They were stiff. Anxious. The strong elixir of hope and fear had rendered her partially paralyzed.

"No, thank you, I'm fine."

When she sat down, she put the towel aside and pressed her shaking hands onto her lap. Then waited. No, hoped. Prayed. Begged.

"Veronica, the couple that approached you all those years ago, do you remember what looked like?"

"How did you hear about the case?" she asked, suddenly confused. "Are you working with my public defender?"

"No. I'm sorry, I should've explained. I'm a private investigator. I'm working on another case that is peripheral to yours."

Her pretty brows cinched together. "In what way?"

"I can't tell you. Confidentiality and all. But I will say I think I know who approached you and why."

She bowed her head. "Because I was homeless with a newborn. That's why they approached me."

I wasn't about to go into the fact that her baby probably had some kind of aura that caught the Fosters' attention, so I went along with her story. "I'm sure. Why were you homeless?"

Mr. Isom stood in the kitchen, listening to every word we said.

She glanced that direction, then said, "I was a mess back then. On and off drugs. I'd stayed clean, though. Once I found out I was pregnant, I got clean and stayed that way. Then, after I had Liana, her father came back into the picture."

I felt a deep fury emanate from Mr. Isom's general direction. Clearly, his daughter's ex didn't invoke the warm and fuzzies.

"He said he wanted to help raise our daughter. Talked me into moving in with him. A month later"—she dipped her chin even farther—"I was back on the shit and we were fighting all the time. He kicked me out, but I couldn't come back home. I wasn't ready to go through that again."

"To go through—?" I stopped myself. Of course. "The withdrawals."

She bit her lip and nodded.

"He got you hooked again?"

"He didn't force me into anything." The guilt radiating out of her stole my breath.

I leaned toward her. "But he took advantage of the situation, Veronica."

"He led. Didn't mean I had to follow. And yet, here we are." Her breath hitched in her chest and I picked lint off my sweater, giving her a moment to recover.

I didn't argue with her. She was right, of course, but I'd wager he still deserved a lot of the blame.

I decided to steer the conversation back to the case. "There's a reason you're having a hard time finding evidence that the adoption agency existed. It was never licensed."

She nodded. "Yeah, that's what the investigator said, but he can't track down who actually ran the business. Or the fake business."

I pulled up the side-by-side picture I had of the Fosters that Cookie had found from around the time they'd taken Veronica's baby.

"I know this might be impossible to remember, but is this them?"

She looked at the picture. Squinted. Turned it a little to the left. "I don't think so."

My hopes plummeted. Maybe I was on the wrong track. Barking up the wrong tree. Grasping at straws. And any other cliché I could think of.

"I think . . . ," she continued, staring at the Fosters. "I think that's the couple that actually adopted her."

I straightened, hope blossoming. "You remember them?"

"No." She stood and went for her purse. "I never met them, but the agents gave me a picture of the couple who was going to adopt Liana to make me feel better about the whole thing. I was really hesitant. I dug it out when . . . when they found her."

She pulled out a picture.

I took it and almost cheered aloud. "It's them," I said, recognition rocketing through me. "So, a different couple approached you for this couple?"

"Yeah, they seemed a little too Jesus freak, but I figured anything was better than living in a drug-infested squalor."

"Except for living with us," her father said, his tone bitter.

"Dad, stop it. It wasn't you. You know that."

He turned and went back into the kitchen.

"Veronica, how old were you?"

"I was sixteen." She glanced over her shoulder. "After they took Liana, I did it. I got clean again. I decided I was going to try to get her back. I know that's a shitty thing to do, but it was so sudden. I only had a few days to think about it. I thought I was giving her a better home. All this time, I thought she was living a life I couldn't give her. A better life. And they . . . they killed her."

She covered her mouth with her hands and let a suffocating agony wash over her. Her shoulders shook and I moved beside her. Wrapped an arm around her as she tried to gather herself.

If they'd kidnapped other children, why go through the trouble of pretending to adopt Veronica's baby? Why not just take her?

"Veronica, where were you living exactly?"

"At the time, I was living in a shelter."

That could explain it. Shelters often locked their doors at a certain hour. Maybe the Fosters couldn't get in. Maybe they could only get to her when she panhandled, but there were too many people around? And it was surely during daylight hours? That had to be it.

"Okay, I'm working with a detective on this, or I will be soon. I promise you, Veronica, I'll help you in any way I can. In the meantime, send your PD to Detective Robert Davidson."

The room cooled about thirty degrees instantly, and she backed away from me.

"What?" I asked, knowing the answer before she said it.

"He's the detective that arrested me."

"Oh, sweet," I said, making a note in my phone. "Then he's already on the case." I leaned closer. "We got this. You just take care of yourself." I started for the door, then said, "And don't sign anything."

12

I talk an awful lot of shit for someone
who can't put underwear on without tipping over.
—T-SHIRT

By the time I got home with dinner from El Bruno's, Ubie had gone out again, Cookie was fretting about it, and Amber was hiding in her room. I tried calling my curmudgeonly uncle, but he had yet to return the favor. He was probably mad that I'd lied to him about being home. The weirdo.

Reyes and I went over the case, and I shared everything we'd found on the Fosters and Veronica Isom. He listened but didn't really join in the conversation. He wasn't really a joiner. Still, he wasn't ordering me about like usual.

I could find the positive in any situation. It was a gift.

But I could still feel his resistance to the whole idea. His reservations.

We'd just cleaned up after dinner when a knock sounded at the door.

I pretended to be surprised. "Who'd be knocking at this hour?"

Reyes narrowed his gaze in suspicion.

I hurried to the door and opened it. Shawn Foster stood on the other side, looking a tad sheepish and very uncomfortable with his hands stuffed in his pockets.

"Shawn, come in." I'd invited him over, thinking that if Reyes met him, if he understood the whole situation, he wouldn't be so upset that I'd taken the case.

Shawn stepped inside, took a quick awestruck sweep of the room, and then nodded his head toward Reyes in a silent acknowledgment. I hadn't realized until that moment that he'd wanted to meet Reyes. His heart-beats stumbled into one another. A mixture of anticipation and excitement radiated out of him in warm waves.

"It's so good to see you," I said. "Is everything okay?"

His brows slid together. "Yeah, you told me to—"

"Reyes!" I said, gesturing toward him. "This is my husband, Reyes. Reyes, this is Shawn Foster. You know, the Fosters' son?"

For a brief moment, Reyes looked like he was going to bolt. He glanced toward our bedroom as though calculating how many steps it would take him to stalk out.

I held my breath, hoping he wouldn't be so rude. Hoping he wouldn't dash Shawn's hopes. The same hopes he could detect as easily as I.

But Shawn had already felt it. Reyes's irritation. He started to turn toward the door when Reyes walked forward and took his hand. A wave of relief washed over me.

"Would you like some coffee?" I asked them both.

The flash of annoyance in Reyes's eyes didn't deter me.

"Coffee it is. You guys sit down. Get to know each other."

I went to the kitchen and started a pot as they sat at the dining room table. Because we wouldn't want to sit in the comfortable seats by the fire in the living room so that our guest actually felt welcome.

"Sorry to just show up like this," Shawn said.

Reyes shook his head, seeming a bit sheepish himself. "No, it's fine. I've been meaning . . ."

"Yeah, I've been meaning, too."

Reyes nodded and then noticed the ink Shawn had on his forearm. "Nice."

"Oh, thanks." He held out his arm to display a gorgeous, full-color sleeve. "Got this a few years ago. My mom—Eve—almost had a heart attack."

Reyes laughed under his breath. "So, do you know who your real parents are?"

I stilled, wondering how Shawn would take Reyes's bluntness.

"No. That's why I hired your wife."

"Then you hired the best."

Once the ice had been broken, the conversation flowed like a smooth whiskey. They talked about everything, including the fact that they were almost but not really kind of sort of brothers.

"I heard about you my whole life growing up."

Reyes cringed. "That couldn't have been good."

"Nope, which made me want to meet you even more."

Reyes ducked his head, suddenly bashful.

"How long have you known about me?" Shawn asked him.

"Few years now."

"Did you know I wasn't their biological son?"

"I suspected. But they kept you. They must've really loved you."

The look of surprise on Shawn's face was priceless. "Wow, you really don't know them at all, do you?"

Reyes grinned and shook his head. "Can't really say that I want to, either."

"I hear that," Shawn said, laughing.

They were getting along famously. After I served them coffee, I was suddenly so exhausted I could barely keep my eyes open and there was a pillow somewhere with my name on it. I went to bed early to give them time to get to know each other, then I lay awake, listening to them talk and laugh and commiserate.

Three hours later, Reyes joined me. Or he tried to. Artemis was taking up most of his side.

He slid in, scooting her over in the process, and lay in silence for a long time while I lay in agony, waiting with baited breath. But after a while, I really did get sleepy. We both rubbed Artemis's ears and I took his hand into mine. His long fingers laced into mine; then, just before his breathing evened out and he drifted into oblivion, he said, "Drop the case."

A wave of disappointment washed over me until I realized I'd learned something. His reservations had nothing to do with Shawn. He liked the guy. I could tell. So there was something else eating at him. Interesting.

Later that night, I felt an elbow at my ribs, and it wasn't my own. It was nudging me out of an incredible dream. I was on the verge of nudging it back when a hand slid around my mouth.

My eyes flew open, but Reyes held me against him, tight, and whispered, "Shhh," into my ear. Then he pointed.

Startled, I followed his line of sight and jumped again. He tightened his hold and waited for the image to come into focus. It did, and I slowly realized Amber was standing beside our bed.

I tried to rise, but he continued to keep a tight grip on both my body and my mouth, so I couldn't ask him, "What the fuck?"

Then I realized why. Amber, tall and slender with long dark hair and a graceful bearing, stood in her gown. Her hair had fallen forward, but I could see her eyes. Barely. She gazed at us from behind the curtain of locks. No expression. No emotion.

A glint lower down drew my gaze to her hands. Her right hand, to be exact, in which she held a chef's knife. Our chef's knife. The one Reyes used to chop vegetables. The one that was so sharp, I'd once accidently brushed my fingers against it, soft as a feather, and come away bloody. And Amber was slicing her leg with it.

Blood soaked her gown, creating a large, dark circle as she slid the knife across her thigh again.

I lunged forward, but Reyes pulled me back. I fought him. His hold tightened, and he whispered into my ear, "I'll go around the bed and grab the knife. Stay put."

But before I could acknowledge with a nod, Amber spoke, her voice low. Monotone. "The oceans will boil. All the sand will die, and it's your fault."

"Stay put," he said again. He eased backwards, his weight pressing into the mattress.

"The skin will slide off your bones if you don't eat him."

He inched off the bed. Then, before I could blink, he stood behind her.

"The beaches are covered in broken glass."

With the care of a snake handler capturing a cobra, he took her wrist into his hand. She'd already made another incision. Blood streaked down the front of her gown. I pressed my hands to my mouth.

"The fish are very angry."

He gently took the knife out of her hand, and I rushed forward. Kneeling on the bed before her, I took her face into my hands.

"Amber?"

Reyes tossed the knife away and held her shoulders should she fall.

"Amber, sweetheart, can you hear me?"

She'd curled her hands into fists and glared at me. "The blood is evaporating too fast, and the birds can't breathe."

I pushed her hair back. She was covered in sweat and tears. "Amber, it's Aunt Charley."

Her gaze finally locked onto mine. She stared a long moment, then said, "*Unofanira kudya iye.*"

It took me a few seconds to pinpoint the language. She spoke chiShona, a language that belonged to the Shona people of Zimbabwe. "You must eat him," she said. In chiShona. Since when did Amber speak chiShona?

Before I could say anything else, she collapsed. I yelped, but Reyes caught her.

"Take her," I said, scrambling off the bed and running for my robe.

Reyes already had on pajama bottoms. He scooped her up and headed for the door. I grabbed the first aid kit out of the bathroom and followed him.

He put her on our dining room table, then turned on the lights. I lifted her gown to assess the damage. The blood drained from my brain, and the world tilted. Just a little. She'd done some damage. Miraculously, none of the cuts looked deep enough to require stitches. There were just so many of them.

"Go," he said, taking over. He ripped open the kit and found the peroxide.

I backed away but couldn't seem to stop staring at her leg.

"Dutch," Reyes said, his voice hard. "Go get her."

I shook myself and nodded. "I'll be right back."

Both our front door and Cookie's stood wide open. I flew through them, then remembered that her husband was a detective. With a gun. I could only hope he wouldn't shoot me, because I had no intention of waking them softly.

I barged into their bedroom, turned on the light, and ran to Cookie's side.

Uncle Bob woke up instantly, his hand going for the gun locked in a holster safe on the side of his nightstand. He would have to unlock it before he could shoot me. That gave me just enough time to let him know who I was.

"Uncle Bob, it's me," I said, shaking Cookie awake.

"Charley? What the hell?"

"It's Amber." I nudged my BFF again. "Cook, sweetheart, wake up."

Cookie bolted upright, her eyes almost as wild as her hair.

"Cook, it's okay."

Uncle Bob was already out of bed. He was used to being roused at all hours. Cookie, sadly, was not.

"What?" she asked, her gaze darting wildly about the room. "What happened?"

"Cookie." I coaxed her to me. "She's okay, but you need to come to my apartment."

She finally focused on me. "What? Who's . . ." Then it sank in. "Amber!"

She scrambled out of bed, slipped on a sock, only one, then found her robe. Uncle Bob had already thrown on a pair of sweats and a T-shirt.

We hurried back, and Amber was sitting in a dining room chair as Reyes administered first aid.

"Amber!" Cookie ran to her and kneeled beside the chair. "Oh, my God. What happened?"

Uncle Bob stood back and took in the picture while I kneeled beside them.

"We woke up," I said, "and she was in our room, sleepwalking."

"What?" Cookie questioned Amber with a look of astonishment. "Amber?"

Amber shrugged. "I don't even remem—" She hissed in a breath as

Reyes poured another round of peroxide on her shaking leg. In fact, she was shaking all over.

"But what happened?" Cookie asked, taking in the bloody scene.

"Do we need to get her to a hospital?" I asked Reyes.

"No!" Amber said. Then softer, "No, really, the cuts aren't even deep."

I leaned forward. Put one hand on her face and one on her arm. Turning her arm over, I asked, "Like these?"

She pressed her mouth together. Bowed her head.

She had over a dozen cuts on her arm, all at different angles and different depths.

Cookie gasped aloud. Then threw a hand over her mouth.

"It's not what you think," Amber said.

"You're . . . are you mutilating yourself?"

"No." Amber shook her head. "No, Mom. Never."

"Then . . . then I don't understand."

Amber chewed on her bottom lip.

"They aren't deep," Reyes said. "She doesn't need stitches, but this will have to be cleaned a couple of times a day and the bandage changed for a few days. Just to be safe."

Amber put an arm around Reyes as though for strength.

He looked up at her and winked. "You'll be okay, princess."

She nodded. She melted a little first, but nodded valiantly in the face of lethal charm.

Cookie stepped closer. "Amber, what is going on?" she asked, growing frustrated.

"I'm not cutting myself, Mom. I swear."

Reyes began wrapping her leg.

I took her foot and straightened out her knee to make it easier. "You've been upset," I said. "I've felt it, especially this morning."

"Oh, that?" She shook her head as though dismissing the notion. "That was nothing. I just . . . I just got bad news."

"What kind of bad news?" Uncle Bob asked.

Amber's eyes rounded, and I felt a distinct jolt of fear. I couldn't help the anger that shot through me. Was this because of him? Because of his behavior of late? Was he somehow stressing her out?

I shot him a warning glare over my shoulder.

He mouthed, "What?"

"Amber Olivia Kowalski," Cookie said. "Explain."

Amber chewed her bottom lip a bit longer, then said, "I just woke up and I had cuts on me. I don't know why. I didn't do it on purpose."

What the hell? "Amber, do you remember speaking to us?"

My question surprised her. "What did I say?"

"Something about the oceans boiling and broken glass and then"— I looked at Cookie and Uncle Bob—"she spoke in chiShona."

Cookie flashed me a puzzled expression.

"It's a language native to a people in Zimbabwe."

"Come again?" Uncle Bob said.

"She spoke a Shona language. She said I must eat him."

"Eat who?" Amber asked, her expression a little grossed out.

I stifled a laugh. "I was hoping you could tell me."

Amber shrugged, helpless. "I'm sorry, Aunt Charley. I don't re-member."

Reyes finished taping the bandage. I scooted a chair over so he could stay close to her, then I scooted one over for Cookie and myself. Uncle Bob could just stand there and stew. The bully.

"I didn't figure you would, actually," I told her. "You've done this before."

"Done what?"

"Prophesied."

Cookie shook her head. "Charley, you don't mean that time at the school carnival."

Amber was pretending to be a fortune-teller at a school carnival, only when I went in, she didn't have to pretend. She slipped into a trance and prophesied about the Twelve, a dozen hellhounds that, we didn't know at the time, had been sent to protect Beep. And she prophesied about Beep's war with Satan. She'd nailed it, too. Every word.

"She's very powerful," I said to Cookie. "I tried to tell you."

Cookie hadn't wanted to listen when we spoke about Amber and her sensitive nature. Her gift. Cookie's cousin was also touched with a gift, but she'd gone a little insane. The thought of Amber having the same abilities terrified her.

"Surely . . . no, you can't be serious."

"I am serious. And don't call me Shirley."

Cookie deadpanned me. Maybe she hadn't seen the movie. After taking a moment to absorb what I was saying, she shook her head. "Okay, so maybe she does have . . . abilities. What does that have to do with her cutting herself in her sleep?"

I sat back in the chair. "I wish I knew. Do you remember anything, hon?"

Amber shook her head again. "I just remember waking up on your dining room table and Uncle Reyes pouring peroxide on me."

"Sweetheart, why have you been so stressed?" I asked her. "I felt it, so don't even try to wiggle out of this one."

Uncle Bob took a chair a few feet away.

She folded her arms. Pursed her lips. Lifted a shoulder to her chin.

"Stress can bring on bouts of sleepwalking and apparently self-mutilation and prophesying." Leaning forward, I tucked a strand of hair behind an ear. "You can tell us anything. No matter who is in this room. You know that, right?"

She nodded.

I let her relax a little, then hit her with, "Are you afraid of your step-dad?"

I knew if she were afraid of him, she probably wouldn't answer with him sitting right there. But her emotional reaction would give me all the proof I needed, at which point I would promptly order him to leave the room and we would get to the bottom of this. Instead, she jumped to his defense.

"What?" She straightened in her chair. "No. Not at all."

Relief washed over me like a welcome tidal wave. I was really worried. I gave him my best "You're lucky, punk" look.

He gaped at me.

I turned back to her. "Okay, sweet pea. Spill."

"It's nothing. Really."

"Amber," Cookie said, her mommy voice in top working order.

"I've just . . . I think someone is stalking me."

Uncle Bob bolted out of his chair.

I took Amber's hand. "What do you mean?"

"I've been, kind of, getting texts."

"What kind of texts?" Cookie asked.

Uncle Bob stormed out of the apartment and came back thirty seconds later with Amber's phone. He thrust it into Cookie's hands, whose face, as she read the texts, went from shock to disbelief to absolute horror.

She pressed a hand over her mouth.

"May I?" I asked Cookie.

She handed me the phone. I didn't want to embarrass Amber, but stalking should never be taken lightly.

I read three texts and sat in such shock, Uncle Bob took the phone to see for himself.

"It started when I was at the mall with Brandy." She dipped her head, ashamed. "We were taking selfies, and we stuck out our tongues. Five seconds later, I got a text that said, *Stick out that tongue again, and I'll show you what to do with it*." Amber looked at me as though pleading. "We were so scared, we called Brandy's mom to come pick us up. We went to her house and were watching a movie."

"This happened when you stayed the night with her?" Cookie asked.

"Yeah. Dad let me. About three weeks ago."

Amber had been staying with her dad because Cookie was in New York babysitting little old me. I'd gone crazy and forgotten my name. Along with everything else. She was gone when Amber needed her because of me.

"You were watching a movie?" I asked her.

"Yeah. Brandy fell asleep, and I was watching the end. We were in our pajamas, and I had my feet on the coffee table, and I get a text that says, *Let your knees fall apart so I can get a better view*."

Cookie began shaking.

"Mom, we were in her basement. There was only one tiny window in the basement. He had to be in Brandy's backyard."

"Oh, honey," Cookie said, pulling Amber to her.

Amber still had Reyes's hand in hers as she clung to her mother with the other. Reyes sat patiently, rubbing his thumb along the back of her knuckles. Warmth radiated through my chest as I watched him. He was going to be such a great dad when we got Beep back.

"I turned off the TV and didn't sleep that whole night. I was so scared, I just watched the window."

"I'm sorry, hon," I said to her.

"Everywhere I go, he's there. If I go to the movie, he's there asking me if I'm sleepy yet because he drugged my soda. If Quentin and I go to the park, he's there, saying, *If you don't stop bending over, I'm going to beat that ass*."

Cookie closed her eyes, frustration and worry coursing through her. "Then they got even worse."

I agreed. Even the few I read could have made a porn star blush. To say that to anyone, especially a thirteen-year-old.

"He started threatening to hurt me. Like, one time at school, we were eating lunch and he knew I was wearing a dress. He threatened . . ." She swallowed hard. "He threatened to cut off my legs if I spread them any farther. He called me a slut and said he could see my wet panties."

I stilled. I hadn't gotten that far. I turned to Ubie. "How did he get her number?"

"He even watches her at school," Cookie said to him.

He was still scrolling through texts. "It could be anyone," he said a microsecond before he stormed out again.

He came back in with his own phone and began making calls.

"Amber, why didn't you tell us?" I asked her.

She leaned back into her chair. "I couldn't. That's all."

The look on Cookie's face was one part astonishment, two parts determination. "That's not good enough, missy. I want an explanation."

I put a hand on her arm. I'd never heard her call Amber missy before. It was out of character.

"You were in New York, anyway," Amber continued, growing defensive. "I didn't want you to worry."

"Worry me? Amber, I can't believe you didn't tell me."

"I'm sorry, Mom."

Uncle Bob raised his voice. "Now. I need it now."

"I would block the number," Amber added, "but then he would text me from a different number. Like every day he had a new number."

"Why don't we just change Amber's number?" Cookie asked.

"And worry for the next year, if not longer, if he will come after her? Cook, these texts are brutal and violent. They may very well be from your everyday neighborhood stalker. The kind who never comes face-to-face with his victim. Completely harmless." I was lying through my teeth. No stalker was ever completely harmless. There were always ramifications. "But we need to be sure." I looked at Amber. "Did Quentin know?"

She shook her head. "No. I was afraid he would tell"—she shot a glance at Uncle Bob from under her glasses—"Mom."

Uncle Bob had stilled. He'd continued scrolling through texts while he was on the phone. He stopped and stared at one, then whirled around to Amber.

She looked down. Pulled the knee of her good leg to her chest. Squeezed Reyes's hand.

"Is this why you didn't say anything?" Ubie asked, furious. When Amber didn't say anything, he yelled, "Amber!"

I stood. "Uncle Bob, that is enough." I took the phone from him.

"Not at first," Amber said. "I was being stupid, worried you'd take my phone away if I told you, but then—"

She had texted the stalker back after a particularly nasty message, writing, *My stepdad is a detective. He will find you if you don't stop.*

The stalker's next text was possibly the most chilling: *Don't you ever threaten me, you bitch. The day that pig finds out is the day his throat is cut.* The next seven texts were pictures of Uncle Bob, either at work, at Calamity's, or in front of the apartment building, getting out of his SUV. The guy had clearly done his homework.

Uncle Bob went back to his phone. "I don't need a warrant. This man is threatening my daughter. *My. Daughter.* Do it. Now."

He hung up and curled his fingers around his phone in anger. "I have tech getting every text to and from this number and running traces. If he's been texting you from different numbers, chances are he's using burners, but even then there's a chance we can trace them to the store where they were—"

He stopped talking when Amber jumped up and tackle-hugged him. He stood stunned for a minute, then wrapped her in his arms, stroking her hair and kissing the top of her head. "You are the bravest girl I've ever met," he said to her.

She shook her head. "I wasn't brave. I was so scared. He said he'd kill you."

"I'm not going anywhere, smidgeon."

Reyes and I exchanged secretive glances, then he stood and started cleaning the urgent care center.

"I was so worried about Robert," Cookie said softly, the inevitable guilt setting in. "I completely missed this."

I patted her hand. "Yes, yes. You're the worst parent since Joan Crawford. Thank God you have me, because I have a plan."

Ubie looked over at me. "Your plans rarely end well."

"What?" I scoffed, waved him off, then turned to my homey. "What say you? Do we go after this guy?"

Cookie drew in a deep, shaky breath. "I say yes, absolutely, but I think it's ultimately up to Amber."

"Since she'll be the bait?"

Her eyes rounded in horror. "Bait?"

"Didn't I mention that?"

13

*Some days I just stay inside
because it feels too peopley out there.*
—TRUE FACT

Amber fell asleep on the couch at about two in the morning, while the rest of us hammered out the details of my plan. Uncle Bob would need some time to get a team together for the big showdown, so we couldn't implement it for another day, at least.

Cookie wanted to keep Amber home from school, but I convinced her we needed everything to look completely normal if we were going to lure this guy into a trap. That was when my IQ level, based on the elements of my plan, went from everyday smarty-pants to stone genius.

Of course, convincing a slave demon to go to a human high school, even for one day, could be difficult, but we only had six hours to find someone who could pass as a high school student and have the ability to protect Amber from pretty much any kind of attack. Too much red tape in getting an actual undercover cop, so a former slave demon it was.

And, after a careful examination of all the texts, the stalker didn't seem to have any inherent celestial abilities, so he wouldn't be able to detect that Amber's new BFF was a supernatural entity.

Now to convince said supernatural entity.

After Uncle Bob scooped Amber into his arms and carried her back to their apartment as though she were as fragile as butterfly wings, Reyes and I threw on some clothes and headed over to Osh's. Together. Like in the same vehicle.

I was a little surprised he was joining me. I should have been less surprised and more suspicious, however. He was a little too enthusiastic. A little too eager.

Thankfully, Osh was home. Always hoping for another meal, his front door wasn't locked. Reyes didn't knock. He walked in and went straight back to what I assumed was Osh's bedroom.

I hurried after him.

Reyes opened the door to Osh's room and turned on the light.

"Damn," Osh said, covering his sleep-swollen eyes from the overhead light. "Could you take the brightness down a notch, love? You'll wake the dead."

"It doesn't have a dimmer," I said, looking for one on the light switch.

"I meant yours."

"Oh." I pulled my jacket tighter. "Sorry. I can't really control that."

I could tell Osh was on the defensive the minute we walked in. Could he sense Reyes's mood, too?

Wearing only a pair of plaid pajama bottoms to bed, much like another supernatural being I knew, he kicked off a dark blue comforter and scooted up until he was using the headboard as a backrest.

Reyes was busy snooping. Like literally. Opening drawers and peeking inside. Lifting items off a dresser and examining them. Checking the closet and filtering through Osh's clothes. It was all terribly rude.

"Mind telling me what Sherlock is up to?" Osh asked.

"Oh." I waved the spousal unit off. "He's just snooping. We're here because we need you to go to high school tomorrow. As a student. To watch Amber."

"No."

"Please?"

"No. And really? High school? I'd have no idea how to act."

"Please. You know more about humans than they know about themselves. But no snacking on any souls. They're just kids."

Osh let out a long sigh and scrubbed his face with his hands.

Reyes lifted a pair of pants that were crumpled on the floor, took out a wallet, and started going through it.

I pinched the bridge of my nose, mortified.

"Are you kidding me?" he said, looking at Reyes, who continued going through the contents of Osh's wallet.

"Uncle Bob is getting it cleared with his captain as we speak, so it will kind of be an official APD operation. Just without the warrants and stuff. Hopefully, the school won't make a fuss."

"What do I have to do?"

"Go to her classes with her. Watch her back. Keep her safe. She's being stalked."

His gaze snapped from Reyes back to me. "Stalked? By whom?"

"That's what we're going to find out. But tomorrow's Friday, and we need one more day to get a team prepped. Which means one more day everything has to appear normal. If she misses school, the stalker may know something is up."

"Fine. I'll do it, but I'm not doing homework."

I laughed until Reyes opened up Osh's nightstand and brought out a *Playboy*.

"The articles," Osh said.

I rolled my eyes, then grew serious. "Did you see her again?"

He didn't have to ask whom I meant. "I was on duty all day yesterday."

I nodded, ignoring the cavernous ache in my heart.

"She's amazing," he added. "She's smiling now. It's lopsided, just like yours."

I beamed at him.

Reyes did not.

"So, you're better now?" Reyes asked.

Osh eyed him. "Right as rain."

Reyes nodded and walked over to stare down at him. They'd been getting along so famously, until I told Reyes that Osh was destined to be in Beep's life. That she would love him. That he would love her.

"Just remember," Reyes said, "anything you do to my daughter, I do to you."

"What?" Osh stared, aghast. "What the fuck are you talking about? I'm out there risking my life for her, and you—"

Reyes leaned closer, shutting Osh up, and whispered, "Anything."

The two of them nose to nose, both being temperamental demons, was all kinds of bad. And, strangely enough, disturbingly sexy.

But they couldn't get into a fight. I needed Osh to be healthy and bruise-free. Not to show up at Amber's high school looking like a scrapper-slash-troublemaker. We needed the school on our side.

"Reyes, can we discuss your opinion of Osh later?" He started to argue, but I held up a finger and said, "Amber."

He bit down, tossed Osh his wallet, and backed off.

"No," Osh said. "I want to know what the fuck that was about. If you think I can't protect her, just say so."

"That's not it at all," I said. "You're one of the few who can. Reyes just had a long day. We went to Scotland. He doesn't travel well."

Osh's expression would suggest he didn't believe me for a hot minute. I wouldn't have, either, but we didn't have time to go into it.

"Okay," I said, heading for the closet I'd just glared at Reyes for snooping in. "You need to look young."

"I do look young, considering how old I am."

"No, like, really young. You look nineteen. Amber's thirteen, but she's a freshman in high school, so we could pull this off if you—"

Osh scrambled off the bed and blocked my advance with an arm across the door to his closet. "I've been around awhile now. I know how to look young."

I eyed him doubtfully. "Are you sure?"

"Seriously?"

"Okay." I handed Osh the address and ushered Reyes out. "Be there at 7:30. We have to get it all set up in the office before classes start."

"Got it."

"And no flirting."

"What?" he asked, pretending to be offended. "I would never."

Maybe this was a bad idea after all.

Three hours later, we were in the principal's office, never a place I liked to be. Uncle Bob was giving her the details of our operation and asked her to keep it all confidential. He showed his badge and said it had all been approved by the captain, and that seemed good enough for her. Thank goodness. She could have insisted on a warrant of some kind.

Ubie and I didn't come with Amber. We wanted everything to appear as normal as possible, so Cookie dropped her off at the same spot she did every morning. Amber had walked by us, backpack in place, but pretended not to notice us. Good girl. She'd pull this off beautifully.

But the first bell was minutes away and still no sign of Osh. I poked my head into the hallway again. Nothing.

"What can I do for you?" the admin assistant asked.

I turned to see a skater kid with spiky dark hair under a grungy hoodie, baggy pants, and high-tops—untied high-tops—sitting in a corner of the main office. Although sitting would be an overstatement. He was making it his personal mission to elevate the slouch to an art form.

He shrugged as I took another peek into the hall. "I'm just waiting on my uncle to finish with the principal. He's getting me checked in."

I whirled around and gaped. "Osh?" I said, surprise shooting through me.

He lifted his chin in greeting and gave me a lopsided grin.

I hurried over and sat beside him. "Holy cow, Osh. You look . . . this is amazing."

"Yeah?" he asked. "So, you approve?"

"Osh, um, yes." I could hardly speak, then I realized the lengths he had gone to. "You cut your hair."

His gaze studied my face a moment. "Only a little. It grows fast."

"I'm . . . I don't know what to say."

"It's Amber, right? And you care for her a lot."

"Yes, I do."

"Then so do I."

It was like talking to a kid. Like a genuine fifteen-year-old kid. One that would definitely pass as a freshman, albeit a tall one.

I squeezed his hand, then led him into the principal's office. When Uncle Bob got a load of him, he was as impressed as I was. We rushed through the introductions, and the principal gave her spiel about what Osh was and was not allowed to do. Sadly, sucking the souls out of her students did not make an appearance.

"Have you ever thought about a career in law enforcement?" Ubie asked Osh. "We could use some good UCs in high schools."

He grinned. "I've seen *21 Jump Street*. I'm not sure I fit the mold."

Uncle Bob shook his head. "That's too bad."

"Okay, remember," I said, handing him Amber's schedule, "you're Amber's cousin from Denver. Your family just moved here. Your dad's—"

"Sugar," he said, his sudden Southern drawl and sensual grin stopping me. "I got this."

"Okay. Right. Sorry."

He saluted, mocking our authority over him exactly like a freshman in high school might, and headed toward Amber's first class.

Because we didn't know if the stalker had access to Amber's text messages—he could easily have cloned her phone—we instructed her to text her mom and friends as she normally would. Even her boyfriend, Quentin, who had an out-of-town basketball tournament that weekend.

Some of the texts from the stalker gave me a sneaking suspicion he did indeed have access to her text messages. He simply knew too much about her family and friends.

Something good had already come out of this whole operation. Since telling us the truth, Amber's mental state had taken a dramatic turn for the better. I could feel her relief while we were explaining the plan that morning. Knowing we were on the case. Knowing she would be kept safe.

The entire situation broke my heart. And made my skin crawl. Stalkers were a different sort and terribly unpredictable. At least the male ones were. Female stalkers rarely resorted to violence, but one just never knew about the male ones.

I watched as all eyes turned toward Osh when he passed. The new kid. The mysterious new kid who . . . crap. Every girl in school was going to be swooning over him. I hadn't thought of that. And Osh, the most irredeemable flirt I'd ever met.

Oh, well. We'd programmed a new number in Amber's phone from a burner I would carry. I would be Jess and would invite her to the mall the next day. Considering the circumstances, Amber would argue back and forth, saying she couldn't go, that she had a lot of stuff going on, but I would eventually convince her to go. And then we would be ready for the sting Saturday morning.

We'd also set up some codes, so I could secretly make sure everything was okay without tipping off Joe Stalker. I'd have to ask her about her *cousin* Osh. See how his first day of school was going. Make sure he wasn't setting up any dates for later. From what I'd seen, many of the seniors at Roadrunner High could moonlight as supermodels. Maybe there was something in the water. I didn't remember the girls at my high school looking like pop artists and movie stars.

"Okay, we're all set," Uncle Bob said, walking out of the principal's office. Underneath his very Uncle Bob exterior beat the heart of a pissed-off Uncle Bob interior. Whoever this stalker was, his life was about to take a turn for the worse.

I knew what happened to people who messed with those Ubie loved.

We were headed to his SUV. I slowed my pace in thought. I really did know what happened to such people. Damn. Now I was going to have to make it my mission to get to Joe Stalker before Ubie did. Getting away with murder was not something that happened often. For him to pull that rabbit out of his hat twice would be nigh impossible.

I watched him walk out the front doors, apprehension working a hole into my stomach.

When we emerged from the halls of medium-to-higher education, I noticed a thrill rush through the crowd like an electrical current. A telltale sign that somewhere nearby stood a very hot person of the male variety. Girls twittered as they talked quietly. They giggled and gasped. Either Osh had already made an impact, or my husband was checking out the younger crowd.

Yep. We'd turned the corner of the building, heading toward the parking lot, when I spotted Mr. Reyes Farrow standing next to his stunning '70 Plymouth 'Cuda. Classic. Dark. And all muscle. The car was hot, too.

He raised his chin in greeting to Ubie and waited for me. And he was going to cause about twenty girls to be late for class. They stood around, whispering and gazing starry-eyed. The guy took *chick magnet* to a whole new level of attraction. He was less like a refrigerator magnet and more like one of those cranes that picked up junk cars to be crushed. Substitute girls' hearts for the cars, and that was Reyes in a nutshell.

"Okay," Ubie said, "I'm getting the details worked out with the op team. You'll keep in contact with Amber all day, yeah?"

"Of course, Uncle Bob. We are going to get this guy."

He nodded, unconvinced. At least he'd stopped harassing me to take a few days off.

"Okay. Get your ass home."

"Uncle Bob, what's going on? Why the sudden need for me to take a few days off?"

He shook his head. "I just think you need a break," he said, lying through his slightly crooked teeth.

"Well, I just got back from a vigorous trip to Scotland. No more taking off for a while."

"I mean it, Charley."

"I can see that."

Not really sure if I'd agreed or not, he walked to his SUV.

What would have Ubie so upset that he couldn't tell me? He would hide it from me? Maybe he knew we were stalking him, for his own good, of course.

I looked across the street and spotted Garrett's black truck, still on Ubie duty. We had yet to catch Guerin, and I couldn't take the chance that, even though we thwarted the initial design that the man was destined to kill Uncle Bob, it would happen anyway. Fate was a fickle thing. Who knew what changing one miniscule part of it would do to the rest? I was a firm believer in the Butterfly Effect.

"Hey, handsome," I said, strolling up to Mr. Farrow.

He eyed me, a dimple appearing at one corner of his mouth, but he was mostly looking at my T-shirt, which read, *IN MY DEFENSE, I WAS LEFT UNSUPERVISED.*

"What brings you to this neck of the woods?" I asked, pulling on a sweater over my shirt.

"I thought we'd take the morning off."

"Did you?" I rose onto my toes for a kiss. He obliged, his essence warming my lips. "Are you cahooting with my uncle?"

"Cahooting?" he asked, quirking a brow. "Not that I know of."

"Okay, then this wouldn't have anything to do with a certain case I'm working on?"

"Not at all. Cookie's in full research mode, so—"

"Cookie's daughter is in danger. I'm not sure how much research she'll get done today."

"True, but one morning away from the grind isn't going to hurt your chances of nailing the Fosters."

"I guess." I waved at Uncle Bob as he drove away, and I went around to the other side of the sexy beast Reyes drove. "Any change in Ubie's status?" I asked, wondering if the guy Reyes saw in prison was still slated to murder him even though we'd stopped it. I didn't know that much about destiny. If we thwarted one attempt, was another one sure to follow?

He got in, disappointing his fans, and started the powerful engine, like a lion's purr. "It's not your uncle I need to see where that's concerned. All I see is what got *him* slated for hell. I would need to see Grant Guerin again to know if your uncle is still in danger."

"So, we're still at DEFCON 1."

"For the time being, but we've stirred up his world enough that the chances of your uncle randomly stumbling across him again are pretty slim."

"Wait. Does that mean if Grant Guerin doesn't do the deed he was slated for, if he doesn't kill Uncle Bob, he won't go to hell?"

"He's making some bad decisions, so he's on a pretty direct path to cause someone harm. I only see the initial offense. There's no telling how many other crimes he was destined to commit afterwards. The chances are still pretty good that he will end up on fire eventually."

"I wish I could see that."

"You can. You just choose not to see the evils that men do."

"I don't think choice has anything to do with it."

"Of course, it does. You're the reaper. You can see all things like that. You can even send them there yourself should you choose. You've done it before."

"Yeah, but when I marked those men, I was in a state of heightened arousal."

"Were you?"

"Well, not like in an aroused way. It's just, adrenaline was dropping by the bucketsful into my nervous system. I didn't think about it. I just marked them."

"Ah."

"Osh said I can unmark Uncle Bob."

"You can."

"That's great. As long as he stays alive long enough for me to figure out how, we'll be good. And what are our plans for today?"

The wicked grin that slid across his mouth made me rethink any protests I might have for missing half a day of work. Had I known what he really had in store, I would have begged off, anyway.

"You want me to put what where?"

Reyes didn't take me to bed as I'd thought-slash-hoped. But he did take me to the next best thing: a coffee shop. Nothing screamed "I love you" like taking your blushing bride to a coffee shop. Or an ice cream parlor. Or a tractor pull, but only on special occasions.

He leaned closer, the tiny table we'd taken in a darkish corner suddenly way too big. His deep brown irises shimmered, his five-o'clock shadow, the one making an early appearance, framed his sculpted mouth to bittersweet perfection.

Then he repeated what he'd said, and the spell was broken. "I want you to put your hand through my heart."

Oh, yeah. He'd left the station, headed for Crazyville. "Your heart. Okay, I know you're a god and all, but won't that kill you?"

"Most likely. It's a lesson in control. Here, I'll show you."

I jumped back when he reached over the table. I trusted him with my life and my heart, but when both were in jeopardy at the same time?

Then again, he'd been doing the whole dematerialization thing much longer than I had.

"So, you're giving me a lesson?"

"If you hold still, I will."

I glanced around. "Should you stick your hand into my chest in a public place? Blatant murder seems more of a dark-alley kind of activity."

"I'm willing to chance it."

"Fine." I took in a deep breath and clenched my hands on the table. "I'm ready. Rip out my heart."

He laughed and took one hand. Capturing my gaze with his, he turned my hand over and leaned closer, brushing his full lips across my palm.

I felt the soft prickle of his stubble. The smoothness of his lips. The hotness of his tongue.

He had me so focused on what he was doing to my hand, it took me a moment to realize he'd put his other hand on my chest. Let it melt. Let it sink into me.

I gasped. He didn't just pass through me like a departed would when crossing. He let his molecules separate inside me. Let his heat spill into me like warm honey. First causing a rush in my chest. Then lower. And higher. Everywhere at once.

It moved to the back of my neck, behind my ears, over my lips. At the same time, it dipped into my stomach and then my abdomen and then to the flesh between my legs.

His molecules pooled and swirled until I wrenched my hands free and gripped the table. Dug my fingernails into it. Begged for the storm to come closer. That whirlwind of pleasure. That burst of ecstasy.

I felt his arm wrap around my neck. His mouth claim mine. His tongue brush against my teeth before plunging inside. Hungry. Possessive.

But the pièce de résistance was the energy building inside my core. Like lava bubbling and boiling and ready to explode. I tried not to moan. To cry out as the energy amassed, the pressure nuclear. I failed. Which would explain the hand suddenly clamped over my mouth. The gentle shushing at my ear.

But Reyes took his time. While I almost screamed for release, he kept his strokes, his radiating heat, slow and feather light. Teasing and taunting. Coaxing me closer. Daring me to come.

Unable to sit still, I parted my legs and squirmed against the infusion of energy. I whimpered as he stimulated me from the inside out. As my center contracted and convulsed. As the friction he injected directly into my core caused tiny delightful spasms to quake through me. Until the white-hot orgasm that had started so far away rushed forward at light speed. Slammed into me. Burst inside me, dumping waves of heavenly pleasure until the wetness in my panties grew to urgent levels.

He'd clamped onto me, and when I was finally able to think straight, I realized he was beside me, holding me tight as I seized underneath his expert touch.

But then he removed his hand and grabbed the padded seat at my back. I wrapped my arms around him, partly to steady him and partly to anchor me to Earth as an orgasm rocketed through him as well. It shuddered out of him in splendid, sparkling waves that almost had me coming a second time.

When his climax receded, we sat panting for a long while.

Then I remembered where we were. My eyes flew open, but I soon realized we looked simply like a couple making out in public, which I always thought was a little brash, but holy fuck. I was more than willing to put aside the *Charley Davidson Book of Etiquette and Mud Wrestling* if it resulted in earth-shattering orgasms.

"Fuck," Reyes said, laying his head against my shoulder. "That wasn't supposed to happen."

"Which part?" I would've been heartily disappointed if he hadn't wanted me to come. Not with the fact that I came, because hell, yes. But with the part where he didn't want me to reach my maximum potential in any situation.

Still, the boy was talented. I was pretty sure he did that on purpose.

"I didn't mean to . . . that was supposed to be just for you."

"While I do appreciate the thought, I'm glad you joined me. Sex is always better with friends."

He flashed a set of dimples and leaned up.

When I focused on him, his face inches from mine, his mouth curved most sensually, I said, "That was the best lesson ever. You should teach professionally."

"I think that's illegal."

"True."

He cleared his throat and returned to his own seat.

I sat up. Took a sip of coffee. Fought to regain my bearings.

He took a gulp of his, finishing it off, then said, "I would say it was your turn, but I'm going to have to change before we go any further."

"Made a mess?" I asked.

He nodded.

I reached across and caressed his crotch. Felt the warmth. Moistened my panties even more.

"Yeah, I should probably change, too."

14

Bat-shit crazy really brings out the color in my eyes.
—T-SHIRT

An hour later, we were sitting at our kitchen table, the small one that was actually in the kitchen. Not the ginormous one that seated more friends than I had.

I'd texted Amber and got the A-okay on the current sitch, except that all her friends were falling in love with her "cousin." She didn't know exactly what Osh was, but she did know he was a supernatural being. And that it was getting annoying. Girls who had never spoken to her were suddenly her best friends.

I looked at Reyes. Amazing how that worked.

I'd also checked on Cookie, but she did not want to be disturbed. Apparently she was onto something insane on the Fosters. Any time Cookie got that excited, I got that excited. And curious.

"Okay," Reyes said, pulling me out of my musings and sidling up to me. "Hand through heart."

"Um, no?"

"Dutch," he said, trying not to grin. "How better to learn to control this than to give you dire consequences if you fail?"

Male logic at its finest, ladies and gentlemen.

"Just try it."

"Reyes, no. I'm not risking your life so that I can control where I end up in the universe when I accidently dematerialize in a fit of rage."

"Exactly. In the universe. What if you dematerialize on the dark side of the moon?"

"The album?"

"The round rock in the sky."

"Oh, yeah. That glowy thing. Still not doing it."

"Dutch, you won't kill me. We're gods, remember?"

"That's something else I want to talk to you about. How does that work exactly? I mean, what if I'm thrown into a wood chipper?"

"Later. Hand through heart."

I let out an annoyed breath and turned toward him. "This is so weird."

"Just concentrate."

"What if I materialize while I'm still in your chest?"

"You won't. That would actually take more concentration than what you'll be doing."

I put my hand on his chest. "In what way?"

"That would be purposely taking someone's life."

"I thought you said—"

"Not my life. Just in general. You can only do that if that is your strongest desire. If you really and truly want to kill someone. Otherwise, you can't materialize inside me. It's like a built-in safety switch."

"How do you know all this?"

"It took me a while to figure it out."

I drew back my hand and straightened again. "You figured out how to kill someone using this ability?"

He lowered his head. "I did."

I blinked. "And have you . . . I mean, did you ever . . . ?"

After a long moment of silence, he said, "I have. Once. I was in a maximum-security prison, Dutch." He let that sentiment hang in the air and faced me again. "Hand. Heart."

I lowered my head. Forced myself to concentrate, then let the molecules in my hand drift apart. It was like sand on the wind, and slowly, I pushed them through his chest.

I expected to feel . . . something. His muscle. His rib cage. His left ventricle. But I didn't feel anything.

"It's because you are no longer on the plane where my body is," he said, reading my mind.

Not literally. God, I hoped not literally.

"And, no, I can't read your mind."

Holy crab apples.

"You—or, more accurately—your hand is on the celestial plane while the rest of you and all of me are on the mortal one. It's all about shifting from one plane of existence to another."

"Then how did you . . . ? Why did I come earlier?"

"Ah, that's the next class. Advanced Cellular Manipulation for Fun and Profit."

I laughed, and suddenly my hand was physical, lying against his chest again. Over his heart.

I jerked it back. "I didn't do that."

"Told you." His grin was infectious. "You can't just materialize inside someone without a lot of practice."

"And a lot of anger, I suspect."

"Yeah, that, too. Try it again."

We did the hand-through-the-heart thing a few more times, then advanced to him standing still while I walked through him. Through his body. Literally. He stood in front of me, hands in his pockets, while I dematerialized my whole everything and just passed right through him.

I laughed the first time I did it and clapped my hands like a kid on a waterslide. Then I cleared my throat and returned to my normal state of absolute coolness.

Just kidding. I have never been to the state of Coolness, though Ubie told me he drove through it once.

"Meet me over there," Reyes said. He dematerialized and rematerialized on the other side of the room. It was a large room. "Your turn."

I drew in a lungful of air, then shifted onto the celestial plane. Wind whipped around me. Thunder crashed. Lightning hit. The colors were so bright I lost sight of Reyes and rematerialized where I stood.

"Again," Reyes-Wan said.

"I can't see you."

"Then you aren't looking."

That was helpful. I shifted again and tried walking to where I knew Reyes stood.

"Don't walk over here. Be over here."

I gave up. "You know, I can't tell if you're channeling Obi-Wan or Yoda more."

"Dutch, don't make me come get you."

That sounded menacing. Shifting for the seven millionth time, I tried to block out the storms raging around me. The scalding wind threatening to peel the skin from my bones. The thunderous roar. The clouds opened nearby, and a beam of light shot down to take a newly departed home.

Okay, don't walk. Be.

I could be.

Reyes appeared in the distance. Much farther than he should have been. I fought the urge to put one foot in front of the other. I was incorporeal. Utter mist. Could I float?

I tried to lift off the ground. Nope.

If I couldn't float—an activity I'd seen Reyes do countless times—how was I to get from here to there?

"Dutch, be here."

I glared at him, clenched my fists, and . . . ordered space out of my way. One second later, I appeared. Right in front of him.

"Good. Now here." He disappeared again. A second later, he was another few hundred feet away.

Ordering space to move aside, I did it again. I beamed up at him.

"Good. Now materialize."

I ordered my molecules to realign. He did the same. Sunlight burst around us, and he nodded, gesturing for me to look over my shoulder. I did. Right as a semitruck plowed into us.

Its horn blared. I screamed and jumped into Reyes's arm. Then I watched as it passed through us. Gears and rods and other mechanical stuff rushed through our incorporeal bodies. Two seconds later, a Nissan Maxima did the same. Then a Buick Enclave. Then a little white thing I couldn't identify. A Dodge Ram. A Mercedes GLE. On and on until I realized we were on the interstate. I-25, to be exact.

I turned to Reyes and hit him on the shoulder. He grinned and disappeared again. After rolling my eyes, I followed. We were at Calamity's. In the kitchen. There were two prep cooks prepping away, but they had yet to realize we were there. Which was a whole new can of worms.

When we materialized again, I threw my arms over Reyes to anchor him to the spot. He laughed, his voice soft and husky and deep.

"Okay, that was cool, but what if I want to go somewhere you are not?"

At the sound of my voice, the two cooks looked over at us, exchanged confused glances, then went back to work.

Reyes slid his arms around my waist. "You slow down. Think about where you are going. Get a mental picture of your target. It can be a person or a place. And you just go there."

"I just go there. Okay." I was actually a little thrilled that I was finally learning this stuff. Stuff Reyes had been able to do since he was little, though the dematerialization of his human body didn't come about until more recently. "What if someone sees us materialize out of thin air? Won't that be a little upsetting?"

"The human mind fills in the gaps. It is certain it saw us walk up or just come out of a closet. Whatever it needs to do to explain, it does. You only really need to be careful with children. It takes them a while to develop that skill."

"What skill? Denial?"

"Pretty much."

"I can't believe we didn't get squashed."

"You can't." He lifted me up and sat me on the counter, then took down two cups and went for the coffeemaker. I had him trained so well.

"I'm pretty sure I can be squashed. Just like a bug. Only bigger and with more entrails. Then what, Know-It-All Man? If I'm a god and can't die, then what? I'm still human, Reyes."

He walked back with two cups of coffee. I took both. He raised a single, arrogant brow.

"Oh, I'm sorry. Did you want one?"

Without answering, he leaned in, nipped at the tender skin below my jaw, then turned and started making us lunch.

I put one of the cups down. Mostly because I started feeling silly when Sammy, Reyes's head cook, walked in, took one look at me, and walked back out again, shaking his head.

In his own defense, he prolly had to pee or something.

"If I can't die, then what happens if I really am hit by a semi? Or thrown into a huge meat grinder? Or locked in a car destined for a car crusher? I'm going to die."

Reyes handed me a sandwich.

I took a bite. "Peanut butter and jelly?"

"We have places to be."

"Another lesson?"

"More or less."

He was really pushing the lesson thing today. He took a bite of his own sandwich as I continued.

"So, yeah, car crusher. You don't live through that. No amount of stitches will put me back together."

Reyes-Wan listened as he ate but didn't offer an explanation.

I took another bite and decided to talk with my mouth full. "I get that the supernatural side won't die. Everyone has a soul."

That got his attention. He shot me a quick glance, then went back to his sandwich and checking the most recent delivery invoices.

"Or not. Either way, my body will not survive." I swallowed and thought about the alternative. "At least, it had better not." When he didn't say anything again, panic rose in my chest. "Right? I would die. I do not, in any way, shape, or form, want to be a living pile of hamburger. And I don't want to be a zombie. Have you seen their skin? Not even sunscreen would help with that."

Silence. I hopped down off the counter and walked over to him. "Roda?" I asked, combining his name with Yoda's. He didn't find my sense of humor amusing. It happened.

He spoke at last. "It doesn't work that way. Not for us."

He turned to talk to Sammy as he walked into the kitchen again. Sammy had learned long ago not to put much stock in our conversations. He either thought we were bat shit or he didn't give a rat's ass one way or another.

And who came up with the animals for these euphemisms, anyway? Why bat shit? Why not cow shit or grasshopper shit? And why don't we give a rat's ass as opposed to a hamster's ass?

My point being, I could pretty much say anything in front of Sammy. He took it all in stride. The angel standing beside the walk-in freezer, however, would just have to deal.

"But I'm still human, yes? I was born a human."

"Yeah," he said to him, completely ignoring me. "Just keep an eye on the driver."

"You got it," Sammy said, noting my indignation with a barely suppressed grin "What are you going to do?"

Reyes looked down at me at last. "We're going to the beach."

Suh-weet.

As Reyes took my hand and led me out, Sammy shook his head again. Probably because we didn't have any beaches in Albuquerque. Not real ones, anyway.

The lunch crowd was vast as usual, but with Dr. Feel Good being gone so much lately, the demographics had shifted from a large percentage of women to some actual men. Or so I'd thought.

We stepped out, and the noise level dropped. A couple of women got on their phones, saying stuff like, "He's here today," and, "Get over here, stat." Still more women either texted or took his picture with their phones. He was somewhat of an Internet sensation, and he was either oblivious or just didn't care. It was fun to watch, all the while knowing he'd be going to bed with me at night.

Delight shuddered through me. Not a gloating delight. More of a delight of disbelief. If someone would have told me two years ago I'd be spending my nights with this man . . . well, I might have believed them, but only because one look at him and I would have offered my services. But to be spending those nights with him in a marital capacity? Priceless.

He walked to the men's restroom and dragged me inside.

"Hey, mister," I said, playing coy. I batted my lashes and gave him my most innocent look. "I'm not supposed to talk to strangers. Or follow grown men into restrooms. What would my daddy say?"

He pulled me against his chest, shoved a hand into my hair, and devoured my mouth with a kiss that should have been X-rated.

As soon as Donnie, our bartender, finished making pee-pee, he left without washing his hands. I could only hope the alcohol would sterilize them. In his defense, the kiss was rather sexual. With sexual undertones and a sexy, noir slant to it.

Reyes broke off the kiss and stared down at me. "You keep talking like that, and I'll have to take you into a stall."

"You romantic, you." In truth, he left me completely breathless, and the stall sounded pretty freaking good.

"Ready?"

"For stall sex? Hell, yes."

The grin that slipped across his face bore a strong resemblance to the one he'd worn the night he'd performed a vaginal exam with kitchen utensils. I melted. Or I started to until he took hold of me and said, "This time, I'll steer for both of us."

Celestial storms slammed into me and around me and through me, and then a sun brighter than I'd ever seen—and I was from New Mexico, thank you very much—blinded me. All I could see was a single shade of blue and a single shade of tan.

I cupped a hand over my eyes and kept the fingers of the other one curled in Reyes's shirt. The image around me slowly came into focus. Actually, it was already in focus, I was just now figuring it out.

"We're in a desert."

Reyes nodded. He had yet to actually look at our surroundings. Instead, he chose to look at me, and I could not fathom why.

"Oh, my God, Reyes." I turned and surveyed the area. "This is stunning."

We were surrounded by exactly two things: a sky so blue it glowed and a desert such a rich golden red it took my breath away. My feet sank into the sand. It formed little hills around them. I reached down and sifted it through my fingers, then fell onto my knees. They sank into the warmth beneath them, too.

"Are we where I think we are?"

He kneeled beside me. "If you think we're in the Sahara, then yes."

I gasped. I was standing—kneeling—in the Sahara. "Reyes, I don't know what to say. I've never seen anything so . . . so perfect in my life."

"I brought you here for a reason."

"Yeah?" I sat down and played in the biggest sandbox in the world.

He watched me, and I wondered what he must think of me. I must seem like the craziest kind of loser, fumbling around in his world, trying to navigate it like a child in a walker, running into walls and cabinets and knees.

I shook off the sudden feeling of insecurity, chalked it up to the freaking Sahara. If there were any one thing that could make a person feel insignificant, it would be this vast terrain. Beautiful and deadly at the same time.

I tossed sand, as blisteringly hot as it was, onto his jeans. "You could have warned me. Sunglasses would have been nice."

He flashed his perfect teeth and picked up a handful of sand. Let it slide through his long, strong fingers. Then he began the lesson of the day. "Pick up one grain of sand."

I picked up a handful and showed him proudly.

He grinned patiently, so I sifted it down, trying to get down to one grain. I had to wipe my hands together and start over. Finally, after much effort, I had one grain of sand in my palm. I named him Digby.

He took Digby, much to my dismay. I'd worked hard for the little guy.

After placing Digby in his palm, he held him out to me. "This is how much of you is human."

"Okay."

"Look around you."

I did and then looked back at the man I'd always believed sane.

"In comparison to this desert, this is how much of you is human."

"I don't get it. That's impossible. I'm human. I've always been human."

"So, in your mind, you believe that you are, what? Half-human and half-god?"

"Well, up until a few months ago, I believed I was 99 percent human and 1 percent reaper. Then I was told that 1 percent had been split in two: half-reaper and half-god."

"You can't be half-reaper. That's like saying a postman is half-human and half-postman."

"Or a lawyer is half-demon and half-human?" I heard that a lot.

One corner of his mouth tugged. "Something like that. Reaping is your job, not your heritage, for lack of a better phrase. But you can't be half-god and half-human. The human side of you is one grain of sand among the 3.6 million square miles that make up this desert. The god part is too powerful. You need to get past that, because it doesn't work that way."

I studied Digby. "That doesn't make sense."

"You keep talking as though your human body can die. And, yes, it can, but it would take something very powerful to achieve it."

I stood and abandoned Digby by walking a few feet away. "So, if I'm cut up and thrown into a wood chipper—"

"Did the truck kill you?"

"Well, no, but we went incorporeal. On purpose. If I were unconscious or bound—"

"Dutch, this one grain of sand doesn't control the shape of the desert. It doesn't control the drifts. The hills and the valleys. It is infinitesimal in comparison to the desert as a whole."

"Okay."

"The part of you that is a god, the whole that is you. A sentient being with immense power."

"The wind shapes it," I argued. "An outside force."

"Just like on the mortal plane, outside forces influence, but the body is still one. The more you understand that, the less your human part"—he held out Digby—"this miniscule aspect of your makeup, can control you."

"And this is important, I take it."

"There is another god loose on this plane."

Ah. Figured we'd come back around to that eventually.

"Right now he is more powerful than you are because he knows one thing to be true above all others."

"And that is . . . ?"

"He cannot die. Not at the hands of anything less than a god." He stepped closer. "And neither can you."

I nodded, trying to let it sink in, to force it to, but there was still a part of me that just couldn't believe it. "I could trap him like I did Mae'eldeesahn."

He bit down, the subject clearly raw. "You got lucky."

No way on heaven or earth could I argue that. "I agree, but—"

"We may have to fight him. But we have an advantage."

"Yeah?"

"He is one god, just like I am one god. You, Elle-Ryn-Ahleethia, are thirteen. As far as I know, you are the most powerful god to ever exist."

I nodded again, feeling about as powerful as Digby at that moment.

"You don't believe me."

"No, I do. I get it. Sort of. It's just kind of hard to comprehend the vastness of it. It's like when you take a native out of the rain forest he grew up in to the open plains and he sees cows in the distance, he thinks they're flies. His mind can't comprehend such vastness. Such distance."

He reached out, ran the back of his hand along my cheek, his touch as light as air, but it was enough. The celestial realm hit me like a tidal wave, tossing me about again, tumbling me through space. Just for a second. Then we were on pavement.

I swayed and looked down. Not pavement. After a quick scan of the area, I realized we were on top of a building. A very tall building.

I wasn't exactly afraid of heights, but they weren't my favorite of the three dimensions. I much preferred depth. Deep buildings. But Reyes had placed us on top of the Albuquerque Plaza, the highest building in the city.

Still feeling like a light breeze could send me hurtling to my death, I took hold of Reyes's T-shirt again. Curled my fingers into it as though that one article of clothing could keep me from falling off, because Reyes hadn't placed us on the center of the building top. Oh, hell, no. We were smack-dab on a nifty edge looking over a 350-foot drop.

In his defense, the very top wasn't flat. If he'd placed us there, we would have slid off. So there was that. But we were on the highest edge, and while the world looked super cool from that viewpoint, it was not a place I wanted to be.

"Reyes, this isn't funny."

"I didn't mean for it to be."

"Why are we here?"

He wrapped his arms around me. "I wanted you to see. You are the desert. You are the whole. Until you believe that, you're in danger." He looked out over the city. "You don't know what Eidolon is capable of. Everyone in this city, in this world, is in danger." Then he returned to me with a hard gaze. "Our daughter is in danger."

He was right. If I could do something, anything, to stop Eidolon, I had to try.

He set me at arm's length but held me tight. Still, for my own peace of mind, I kept my fingers curled in his shirt.

"You can save everyone here. You are the most powerful god in all the dimensions combined." He shook me. "You just have to believe it to the very depths of your soul."

I nodded. "I'll try."

He relaxed. Pulled me to him. Kissed the top of my head. "That's just not quite good enough."

And then I was airborne.

15

If at first you don't succeed,
it's only "attempted" murder.
—MEME

Few things in life are as surprising as having your husband, the man you gave your heart and soul to, throw you off a 350-foot building. I should know.

The second my feet left the building top, the moment I felt that thrust, I slowed time. And hung, quite literally, in midair. Stunned. Breathless. Slightly irked.

"Reyes Alexander Farrow!" I screamed, because it seemed like the right thing to do.

He stood on the top of the Albuquerque Plaza. Arms crossed. Smirk in place. "You stopped time quickly. That's a good start."

He had a plan. Surely he had a plan. "Okay, I get it! I'm a god. I have to know this to the marrow of my bones. But it won't do me any good if my bones are in a big squishy pile at the bottom of this building."

"You're doing great," he said, completely unmoved.

"Reyes, this isn't funny anymore. Time is going to bounce back any second—"

"You're a god. Time doesn't bounce back unless you allow it to."

"—and when it does, I will hit that pavement so hard, you will wish you could die before I'm finished with you."

His white teeth flashed against his dark skin. "Then don't hit the pavement. Become it."

"What the fuck does that mean?" I screeched.

He laughed. Laughed! "Absorb it," he said. "Stop being so human. Just be a part of all that is around you. A part of everything. Like a proper god."

"You. Are. So. Dea—"

Before I finished my threat, time did indeed bounce back, and I fell faster than I ever imagined possible.

I turned in midair. Not on purpose, because who the hell wants to see that? But I did. I barely had time to focus on the instrument of my death when I was there. Slamming into it. The excruciating pain riveted through my . . .

Wait. Where was the pain?

Then I felt it, but not my own. I felt it in others around me. Along with joy, annoyance, love . . . pretty much every emotion imaginable coursed through me like heroin.

And I saw. Everyone. Everything. I saw every blade of grass. I saw every ray of sunshine. I saw every strand of hair on every person who walked through the plaza. That worked in the surrounding buildings.

I saw good as though it were a physical thing. Bad as well, only there was less of it, thankfully. Love overshadowed hate. Altruism overshadowed greed. Confidence overshadowed jealousy. Though in each case, the margins were narrower than I would have liked.

I saw a lizard scurry along a wall two blocks away. A child trip over her ball in her living room on the other side of the mountains. An elderly man offer a homeless kid who'd been making fun of him five dollars to get something to eat in Seattle. A doctor wash the feet of his ailing mother in India.

I absorbed it all. I basked in it all. Like bathing in light.

"Well?" Reyes asked, pressing against my backside, his mouth at my ear.

I leaned in to him as though I'd been standing on the sidewalk the whole time. Astonishment, and a fair amount of shock, had taken hold.

Gazing up at him, I asked, "Have you felt that? Is this what Jehovah feels all the time? No wonder He likes us so much. We are amazing, complex beings."

"You even more so."

I shook my head. "That's where you're wrong." Stepping out of his hold, I leveled my best serious stare on him. "If this has taught me anything, Reyes, it's that humans are incredible. They are each worthy of life. Well, most of them. And each and every one deserves the right to be equal. To be safe. To be fed and sheltered. Part of me understands why He doesn't step in. Why He doesn't just make it all right. Their free will is an astonishing gift."

"One that most squander."

"No. Not most. There is more good in the world than bad. They are still learning."

"They?"

I questioned him with a tilt of my head.

"You said *they*."

"Well, yeah, but I meant—"

He grinned and turned to walk away. "Mission accomplished."

"No, I meant us. We. I'm still human. And hey!" I caught up to him and tugged on his shirt. "You pushed me off a building."

"What about it?"

"Well, that was rude."

———

Nothing made a girl hungrier than being thrown off a building. Reyes and I sat at Rustic on the Green, eating an incredible green chile burger, when Cookie called.

"Hey, Cook. How was Amber's day at school?"

"Oh, great. Thank you so much for having Osh stay with her. It really set my mind at ease."

"I'm glad. So, what's up?"

"First, how did your day with Mr. Farrow go?"

"Wonderful. We went to the Sahara. And he threw me off a building. Other than the building thing, it was fab."

"Well, that's what matters most. So, I just wanted you to know that I found something on the Fosters. Something . . . well, pretty hard to believe."

"Really?" I dipped my head as though it would help us be more secretive. "Hit me."

"As you know, I ran into a brick wall once I found out the Fosters are not who they say they are."

"Yes."

"So I asked Pari for her help."

"Oh, that's awesome. Bring her into the fold. What did she find out?"

"Right? Well, she used some kind of facial recognition software and found them. Maybe. About forty years ago, there were two teens suspected of killing a family."

"Okay. Awful."

"The kids were arrested and taken to the county jail. Where they escaped. Somehow, a deputy left their cells unlocked. I don't know. It was all very suspicious. And they were never heard from again."

"Cook, are you telling me that the Fosters killed a family when they were kids?"

"I'm saying that according to facial recognition software, they were arrested for the crime. But there's more. These kids were part of some super-religious cult. The members of this cult believed that the children were touched by God to ferret out the unholy and destroy them."

"Okay, this is all sounding eerily similar to what I'm finding out."

"So, this cult, if a bunch of nuts living together and marrying children is a good interpretation of the word—"

"I think it is."

"—believed these kids were the second coming. As soon as they escaped, the sheriff went to the compound to find them. It had disappeared. Overnight. The entire group of thirty-something members vanished. And none of them have been found again, either. Not one single member."

"Wow. So, you think the whole cult was behind the murders?"

"Either that or they condoned anything these kids did. Charley, they did everything but worship them outright."

"Stranger things have happened."

"But there's more."

"This is like a soap opera and a gossip show all rolled into one."

"The children arrested for the crime?"

"Yes."

"Charley, they were brother and sister."

Okay, that one surprised me. It surprised Reyes as well. He sat completely motionless, deep in thought.

I glanced over at a nearby table. They were eavesdropping. I could hardly blame them. Shit didn't get more bat than religious cults. And/or brother-and-sister couples. Because ew.

"Wait. You got this from Pari? Our Pari?"

"The one and only."

"And how does our Pari have access to a secure FBI database?"

Silence.

"Is she hacking again?"

"She didn't sound phlegmy."

"Websites. Databases. She's gotten into some serious trouble in the past, and she's on some kind of probation. She's not even supposed to go onto the Internet. Ever. For any reason."

"Wow, Charley. I knew she was good with computers. I had no idea she'd gotten into trouble."

"That's not on you. I'll have a talk with her. In the meantime, this is crazy stuff."

"Should we talk to Robert?"

"Yeah. I'll call him."

"Great. Talk soon."

I hung up the phone and scanned Reyes's expression. "Are you okay?"

He nodded. "Makes sense."

"It does. Well, all except the brother-sister thing. I'm hoping that one was a mistake." I picked up the phone and found Ubie in my contacts.

"Hey, pumpkin. Cookie told me you took the day off." He was so happy, I couldn't tell him he had nothing to do with it.

"I did. So, has she told you anything about the case we're working on?"

"No. She's been . . . well, I've been a little distracted lately."

"Care to tell me why?"

"No."

" 'Kay. So . . ." I filled Ubie in on the usual. It was enough to grab his interest with razor-sharp claws.

"I'll keep you updated on what I find out, but if you can check out this cold case—"

"I can do that," he said.

Reyes and I left the restaurant. It was one thing to allow eavesdropping of some random bits of research that can be found online. It's another altogether to allow information about my client to leak. I had yet to confront Shawn about his providing an alibi for the Fosters when Dawn Brooks was abducted. I would definitely need an explanation, but now was not the time.

I explained the entire case to Ubie, leaving out the details about who my client was. I focused on the Fosters and what Cookie found.

"Charley, if that is true, I'm going to need more. I don't think I can get a warrant on information obtained . . . creatively."

"Okay, so, like what? How about a confession?"

"If they are who you say they are, they've been on the run and in hiding a very long time. They aren't just going to recite you a tell-all."

"I have a plan."

"When don't you have a plan?"

"True." I looked over at Reyes as he drove home. "But it's a pretty good plan, providing I have a little help."

"Okay, well, keep me in the loop. On the stalker front—"

"Joe?"

"Joe?" he repeated.

"Joe Stalker."

"Right. On the Joe front," he said, finding it easier to go along with me than point out the many flaws of my mental process, "we are all set on this end if you're sure you still want to go through with it."

"Of course I want to go through with it. Why wouldn't I?"

"I figured you would. Just checking."

"Have you heard from Amber?"

"I've been texting Osh all day. She's fine, and he's decided he wants to go back to school."

"Oh, hell, no."

He chuckled. "I don't know what I would do without you, pumpkin."

That sounded ominous. "Are you going somewhere?"

"I don't think so. Just wanted you to know how much you mean to me. Oh, and if I'm late for any reason tomorrow, Officer Tang will be in charge."

"Late? Why would you be late?"

"I have about a hundred cases at any given moment, pumpkin. There's been movement on an old one that I need to look into. It could take me a while. But don't worry. Just go on with the plan."

"Okay. Be careful."

"Always. Be good. And stay home."

Actually, that wasn't a bad idea. I hadn't had an evening home alone with the ball and chain in a few days.

Reyes and I raided the coffeepot at Calamity's, then I hoofed it to the second floor to fill Cookie in with everything as Reyes talked to his manager, Valerie. I mistook her for a coat rack once and tried to hang my jacket on her head. I thought it was funny. She did not. But there were only so many hateful glances a girl could take. The fact that I was married to her boss, a boss with whom she was hopelessly in love, was hardly my fault. I got him first. You snooze, you lose when it comes to love. Or was that war? Either way.

By the time I got up to the office, Cook had gone home for the day. I decided to get some paperwork done. Realized that was crazy talk. And went about trying to figure out how to get revenge on Mr. Reyes Farrow. Payback was such a bitch.

I came up with a hundred ideas thanks to a website called Tortures-R-Us. Oh yeah. They had some fabulous ideas. But first, now that I could do the whole dematerialize thing, I wondered if I could spy on him. Would serve him right.

I closed my eyes and let the celestial realm wash over me. It really was stunning. Then I concentrated. Went in search of my prey. Ended up on a corner on Central, in the nonprofessional sense, and watched as the two realms collided.

I was a part of everything around me. I could always feel emotions, but this went way beyond that. I knew them. Everyone who walked through me. I knew what they were going through on a much deeper level. Not that I could read their minds or anything. More like I could feel their emotions suss out their deepest desires. Their greatest worries.

It was like a high. It was like—

I stopped and thought about what I was doing. Was I pulling an Osh? Was I feeding off them somehow? Siphoning their energy to get high?

I backed off immediately and watched from afar. Actually, from up high. Reyes used to do this all the time. He would literally float around me to keep watch. But he was always covered in a massive, black, undulating robe. I'd have to ask him how he did that.

After a few minutes of people watching and taking a couple of notes—one girl was in serious trouble and on the verge of committing suicide—Reyes stole back into my mind as he was wont to do. Probably because he was walking down the street, going in the opposite direction of me.

Reyes could be visible to me or invisible, and that part I thought I'd figured out. The more I shifted onto the celestial plane, the less visible the sentient beings of this world became. I could still see them, still see their auras, but their human forms became vaguer until they disappeared completely. Perhaps it worked the other way around. Perhaps if a human could see beyond the veil between the two worlds and I shifted more and more onto the celestial plane, maybe I became invisible no matter what they could see.

I decided to test it out.

Reyes's aura was spectacularly easy to pick out of a crowd. He was darkness and flames. I swept in behind him and watched, marveling at how his ass looked in those jeans.

Without missing a beat, he lowered his head and asked, "Are you having fun?"

I was, in fact. I brushed against him, allowing my molecules to collide with his. I wanted to feel him as I felt others. I wanted to know everything about him. All the secrets he'd tucked into the furthest corners of his mind. But it didn't quite work that way. His emotions were still so deeply packed, so thickly entwined, that making out any one was nearly impossible.

Regaining my footing on solid ground, I followed him until he stopped, turned around, and caught me to him. Plunging his fingers into my hair, he pushed me against a storefront.

"You shouldn't tempt me," he said, his voice like warm bourbon.

"I beg to differ. You are the only one I should tempt."

He'd shifted onto the celestial plane. Here his kisses were even hotter. His energy rawer. More abrasive.

He pulled at my jeans with one hand, and part of me was surprised I still wore jeans. He opened the button, ripped the zipper down, and pushed a hand inside. I bucked and grabbed his wrist. Everything was more sensitive here. Every touch more important. His fingers massaging my clit, dipping inside, had me shaking with need.

I pressed a palm to his crotch. Found the length of his erection. Molded my fingers around the outline until he sucked in a sharp breath.

"Dutch," he said against my neck. "What are you doing to me?"

I couldn't even begin to answer him, because whatever I was doing to him, he did to me first.

Without the slightest thought of there being a witness to our adventure, I pried the buttons of his jeans apart and wrapped my fingers around his cock.

"Motherfucker," he said, bracing a hand on the wall behind me. And he was right. How was it all so heightened here? So extra sensitive?

The slightest bit of friction was almost orgasmic. So much so that I could hardly control my actions. My clothes were suddenly gone, as were Reyes's, and I couldn't remember which one of us took them off. But he pressed into me, incorporeal energy against incorporeal energy. Molecules colliding. Tendrils of heat lacing around me like ribbons.

Our bodies didn't slide as they would during a regular round of aggressive cuddling, but our energy did. Hot. Fast. Frantic.

Then he shifted, just barely, onto the mortal plane, bringing me with him. And the solidness of his cock inside me rocketed through to my core. The pressure building in my abdomen with every thrust, the sheer weight of it, clawed at the delicate balance between the sweet pleasure of a slow, sensual fuck and the wild, passionate greed of a come-induced seizure.

And then the scales tipped and I seized, throwing back my head and bucking against him. Something deep inside me, something unnamable, exploded. I gritted my teeth as spasm after violent spasm slammed into me. Crashed against my bones. Trembled over my nerve endings, spilling the darkest pleasure known to man throughout my consciousness.

An orgasm in this state was a thousand times brighter and hotter and more intense. I'd never felt my atoms splitting. I'd never felt them collide and create a reaction as hot as the center of the sun.

As Reyes strained against me, his own orgasm shuddering through him, I wondered if this was how two gods merged to make one. And why did they do that, anyway? Why did all the gods from my dimension come together to make one god? What was in it for them?

Reyes collapsed against me as I floated in the aftermath of mind-blowing sex. And then I realized something pivotal. Cores. Centers. We had centers even in our most dematerialized state. Whether we had shape or not, we had centers.

And they fit together really well. Like pieces of a puzzle. Or a lock and key. Or a penis and vagina. Mostly a penis and vagina.

When Reyes stepped to the side, leaned against a storefront, and continued to stare, I realized I was humming. Like my body was literally humming, its current state utter perfection.

"Sorry," I said to him, worried he could hear it, too.

At first, he continued to gaze at me, but not just at me. All around me. Then he whispered, "Magnificent."

"What?" I floated back to the ground to join him and turned around to see what was behind me. "What do you see?"

Reyes shifted and stepped to me. "You, Dutch. I see you."

"Really? I'm trying to be invisible. How can you see me?"

"I don't know that you can be. Not to a supernatural being, anyway. Remember, you're still the light the departed are drawn to. It's just, it's different now. When you're like this."

"What's so different about it? Is it even more annoying? Pari can hardly look at me without wearing sunglasses."

"It's a shimmering white all around you. You literally glow."

"Like a glowworm?"

He grinned. "Why not?"

"You look different when I shift, too."

He lowered his head.

"Reyes," I said, readying to tease him, "give it up already. I know all about the darkness. Being created in hell—"

"You don't remember, do you?"

I ran my fingers over his sensual mouth even as he spoke. "Remember?"

"Before you convinced Jehovah to send me to your hell dimension instead of locking me up in the one He created, you knew me."

We turned and walked down the street hand in hand. Only we were both incorporeal, so people kept walking through us. Mostly college students cramming for finals. Poor kids. That, I remembered.

"I was dark even then. I was dark before Satan got ahold of me."

I stopped and faced him. "I don't remember that."

"I think my Brother, for some reason, has altered your memories. Taken some away."

"Do you know why?"

"No, I don't. I'm sorry." He reached down and slid his fingers along my abdomen.

"Oh, just so you know," I said, my muscles tensing with his touch, "I'm paying you back for that little stunt you pulled today."

His expression softened. "Are you?"

"Yes. I've been doing research. You are so screwed."

"I can hardly wait."

I snorted. "I suggest you adopt a more concerned attitude than that, Mister Man. Payback is a bitch, and her name is Charley Davidson."

He pressed his mouth together in an attempt to hide his reaction. Apparently I was funny.

"Good to know I can bring humor to any situation. I'm not even going to feel sorry for you while I torture you."

He raised a brow. "Torture? You sure you got it in you?"

"Oh, I got it and then some."

He turned his most sensual gaze toward me. "Be still my beating heart."

Part of me believed he wanted me to torture him.

16

I dreamed of starless nights and planets colliding. Of nebulae drifting too close to black holes and galaxies spinning out of control. And I dreamed of angel wings. Of their feathers brushing against my skin, sending shivers down my spine.

Then I awoke to the hushed sound of Angel. He'd shaken me gently, but there had been an urgency in his whispered voice. Either that or . . .

My eyes flew open. Reyes had Angel pinned to the floor, choking him out. If a departed could be choked out. I had no idea.

I scrambled out of bed and tapped Reyes on the shoulder. "Hon, what are you doing?"

He looked up at me, his face the picture of joy. "Wrestling."

Angel made strange gagging sounds and shook his head.

"Sweetheart, I don't think Angel wants to wrestle."

"His problem. He was standing over our bed, staring down at you. Figured he needed a lesson."

"Wait. What?" I ripped Reyes's arm from around Angel's throat. Or, well, Reyes let me rip his arm away. "Angel, what's going on?"

Now free, Angel doubled over, coughing and choking and being generally pissed off.

I knelt beside him. Patted his back. That'd help. "Rey'aziel, he probably had something to tell me. Now we'll never know. I think you crushed his larynx."

"Sorry." Reyes stood and headed for the bathroom. He wasn't sorry. Poor Angel.

Angel tried to make it to a chair in the corner. I half helped and half dragged him toward it. He tried to push me away. I slapped at his hands and helped, anyway.

"What's wrong?" I asked when he could breathe again. No idea why he'd need to. I figured it was out of habit.

He sat holding his throat and glaring toward the bathroom.

"Angel, what? Is it Beep?"

Reyes was at the door in an instant, suddenly as curious as I was.

When Angel didn't answer as quickly as he'd have liked, he stalked toward him.

I held up a hand and cast him a warning glare. "I think you've done enough, Mr. Farrow."

He stood back, every muscle in his body coiled, ready to spring into action should anything have happened.

"It's your uncle," he said, his voice hoarse.

Alarm rocketed through me. "What about him? Did he find Guerin?" Grant Guerin. The lowlife slated to kill Ubie. The whole reason we had eyes on the curmudgeonly man.

Angel shook his head. Coughed again. "No, he's at a hotel room. Some dive a few blocks from here. He's been watching one particular room all evening. Some guys just pulled up in a rental, and now your uncle is gearing up like he's preparing for World War III."

"What? Show me."

I rushed to throw on some clothes. Reyes did the same.

"You'd better hurry. When I left, he was headed for the door. If Captain America hadn't tried to kill me."

"If I'd have wanted you dead—"

"Seriously, guys?" Then I glared at Reyes again for good measure.

He lifted a shoulder. "He should learn to knock."

Before they could start arguing again, I took Angel's hand. "Show me." I dematerialized beside him. Reyes followed suit. Angel wanted to ask me about this spiffy new ability, but he remembered why he'd come, and he disappeared.

Following Angel was a little more difficult than I'd expected. Reyes took my hand and led me, and we were there in a split second, standing in front of one of the sleazier hotels Albuquerque had to offer.

"There." Angel pointed. "Room 212."

"Thanks, hon." Uncle Bob was already inside. The door was closed, so I did what any self-respecting PI would do. I dematerialized again and eavesdropped.

"He doesn't speak English," a man said.

I slipped into a tiny hotel room. Reyes appeared beside me. Angel on the other side of the room.

Uncle Bob seemed to be holding the entire place hostage. A total of nine men. Nine. And they'd been in the middle of a meeting, by the looks of it.

"Yes," Uncle Bob said. "He does." Then he aimed one of the two guns he had drawn at a man in his early fifties. Bad haircut. Hideous mustache. Like something out of a seventies discothèque. "And I know why you're here."

"Dutch," Reyes said, drawing my attention to a table.

I stepped over and took a peek. There was a briefcase open with a stack of papers inside. And on top was a surveillance photo of yours truly.

Oh, no. This couldn't be the same people. I looked at Reyes. "This can't be the same people."

"Robert killed them, but they could be from the same crew."

"He doesn't know what you are talking about," the speaker of the house said.

"Sure he does." Uncle Bob put his best grin forward. "Charlotte Davidson."

The man Ubie was most interested in let a smile slither across his face. "Is that her name?"

"Doesn't matter. You aren't leaving here alive."

"I think we might, my friend." The man started to stand.

Ubie tightened his hold on his gun.

The man raised his hands in surrender and sat back down. "I think you came here not expecting so much"—he spread his hands, indicating his cohorts—"company, no?"

"I knew exactly what I was getting into, Valencia."

"I think maybe you are lying."

"I think maybe you are nervous."

I had never seen Uncle Bob so determined. So . . . furious. It radiated out of him. Hot waves of anger.

"See, I'm the one who killed your little crew two years ago."

The man stilled, clearly not expecting that.

"They knew about her. They were going to get her for you. I found out, and, well, this is my town. I don't like it when Colombian drug barons try to steal women and eat them."

"My men knew about the witch?"

Witch?

"They did."

Witch?

"Certain people in certain crowds know about how she has some kind of extrasensory perception." Uncle Bob chuckled. "But trust me, they don't know the half of it."

"How did you find out we were here?"

"The State Department keeps tabs on people like you, El Tiburón. Of course we'd find out you came into the country."

"I did not come through the normal routes."

"You were smuggled in. I know. I have contacts."

"But maybe I am not here for this Charlotte."

Ubie didn't even acknowledge that with a comment.

The tension in the room ratcheted higher with each passing second. One man would ease toward a gun on a dresser, and Uncle Bob would shoot him a warning glare. Then another would lower one hand toward a gun in his holster. Same story. Different caliber.

But they would get the best of him and soon. He couldn't keep up the standoff for long. What the hell had he been thinking?

"I'd like you to know, I'm actually doing you a favor," he said. "Charley's husband is the son of Satan. He would've done much worse."

The man remained impassive, but I felt his pulse skyrocket. In hunger. He wanted to eat Reyes, too. Fucker.

I turned toward my husband and startled at the look of rage on his face. Pure, unadulterated rage. "Reyes, they couldn't have killed you, anyway, right? It's okay."

He all but gaped at me. "You think I'm worried about me?"

No. Of course he wasn't. "But they couldn't have killed me, either."

"There are worse things than death."

Oh. Crap. That didn't sound promising.

In a sequence of events that was so fast it took me by surprise, guns from every corner of the room were drawn.

I could barely get out the words *Be still* before several fired.

Bullets slid through the air, two from the guns Ubie held, slowing to a complete stop. He was fast. I'd give him that.

He stood frozen to the spot. Not because I'd stopped time, but because he was shocked and confused. I'd stopped time but kept him in the loop. Then Reyes and I materialized so he could see us.

He noticed me out of the corner of his eye, dropped to his knees, and swung his gun around way faster than I'd thought him capable. A defensive maneuver that left me completely impressed. But he paused, his gaze fixating on me. His brows slid together in disbelief.

I rushed forward. "Uncle Bob," I said, patting him to make sure a bullet hadn't hit its mark. "What the hell were you thinking?"

"Charley?" He glanced from me to Reyes and back. Then he scanned the truly frozen occupants of the room. "What are you . . . ? I don't understand."

I knelt beside him. "What were you thinking, coming here?"

"I . . . what are you doing here?"

"I had Angel watching you."

"Why? You knew Valencia was in town?"

Shaking my head, I said, "No. But we've had surveillance on you for a while for a completely different reason. You were supposed to be killed by a kid named Grant Guerin. We were tailing you. Trying to make sure he didn't succeed."

"I don't even know a Grant Gue—" He looked around at the statuesque figures, the blood draining from his face even more. "How did you . . . ? What happened?"

"I just slowed time. These men were going to kill you." I flung my arms around his neck. He patted my head absently, the shock settling in and growing roots.

Reyes went around collecting guns and tossing them into the brief-case.

"You can . . . you can stop time." It wasn't a question. It was said more as a matter-of-fact statement that he was trying to wrap his head around. I got that.

"Not for very long. Uncle Bob, why did you come here alone like this?"

"What?"

I thought about slapping him like they did in the movies, and I might have if he weren't holding not one but two guns. "Why did you come here alone?"

"I got word. I . . . Valencia was smuggled into the country." He nodded. "He saw that video Amber showed you."

"The puppies yawning?"

"No."

"The puppies wrestling?"

"No, the—"

"Did it have kittens?" I watched a lot of kitten videos. "Or Ellen?" And Ellen clips. She rocked so hard.

"The possessed one. The girl and the man with the machete and—"

That didn't really narrow it down much. Then it hit me. "Oh, right, the one of me exorcising a demon out of that little girl in Africa." I cringed. "Bad lighting. And when my face bounced off the floor, the sound was all wrong. It was much more of a dull thud. I swear someone overdubbed it."

He blinked at me, the lights on but nobody home. "He wanted to—"

"Eat me? Yeah, Reyes told me. He also told me what you did two years ago to those men who were going to abduct me and take me to El Jefe over there."

"El Tiburón," he corrected.

"The Shark? I like it." I hugged him again, taking complete advantage of his mental state. "Uncle Bob, you are amazing, but you were slated for hell because of what you did for me."

He finally tore his gaze off the statuesque—and not in a Michelangelo sort of way—men and focused on me. He let go of one gun and put his hand on my face as though it were a precious jewel. "Pumpkin." Or an autumn fruit. "I knew the consequences before I had walked through that door."

I gasped softly. "Uncle Bob. I don't . . . I don't know what to say." And I didn't, so I just hugged him. Again.

"What do you think?" Reyes asked, still seething. "A tragic succession of broken necks? They're all going to hell, anyway. I say we move up their arrival date."

I finally saw it. What he saw. The mark. I'd seen them before, but it was rather hit or miss. If I looked closely enough, I could see what they did, that one act that earned each of them such a fiery destiny. These were not nice boys.

I shut my eyes to turn it off, for lack of a better phrase. They'd killed entire families just to set an example for others. They'd hung them from bridges. Decapitated them. Tortured wives while husbands and children watched. I stopped there, unable to see any more. The darker side of humanity. Like toxic waste.

I focused on my husband and said, "Kill them all."

And I'd meant it. For a split second, I was ready to kill. To take human life. Like I had the right. Like I was one of them.

Just as Reyes was about to break his first neck of the evening, I yelled, "Wait!"

But it was too late. An angel appeared. An archangel, to be more precise. Michael. He materialized not three feet from me, his massive wings taking up half the already-crowded room.

I jumped to my feet. Reyes stepped away from the goon and lowered his head, his muscles poised and ready as his billowing black robe materialized. It undulated in giant waves. Made him look even more menacing, not that he needed any help. I could just make out the glint of steel underneath it—the boy really wanted a fight—then it settled around him.

And Uncle Bob, who I was surprised could see the archangel, scrambled to his feet, not sure what to do next. He couldn't decide if he was more taken aback by the angel or by Reyes.

Personally, I would have placed my bet on the prickly son of Satan, but I did marry the man. I was probably biased.

"What?" I asked Michael in my rudest tone. We hadn't always gotten along. Mostly because he tried to kill me. Or, well, hold me until Jehovah arrived to do the deed Himself.

He'd warned me. Michael. He'd warned me not to stop what was already set in motion. "I suppose He's coming for me now that I've changed human history. Now that I've saved my uncle's life."

"Not at all," he said, keeping his gaze trained on the biggest threat in the room which, sadly, was not me. "You arrived before he died. No laws have been broken."

"What?" I stepped forward, incensed and ready to throttle him. But I stopped short and took him in.

Angels had the most incredible inhuman eyes. They shimmered with the lights of the universe. Their eyes were proof that Reyes was part angelic being. The way they glistened even in the lowest of light. The way they saw straight into one's soul. The way they knew way more than they let on.

Reyes had been created from the energy of a god and the fires of hell, but part of him was angel. True, that part was fallen angel, but angel nonetheless.

And just like Reyes, they could be the most frustrating things this side of eternity.

"I thought I couldn't heal at all. Isn't that what you said?"

"You may heal on occasion. Many of the gifted in this world do."

I folded my arms, annoyed. "Yeah, I hear doctors do it all the time."

"There are laws, reaper. However, you did not break any this night."

"What laws? Remember, this whole gig came with a serious lack of instruction manuals."

He finally spared me a glance. "You are a conundrum. We've had only one reaper live as long as you have. And she was a hermit with no other abilities than what your reaper status entails. You, on the other hand, require special . . . mandates."

"So, I can heal people? Because I thought if I healed anyone or stopped Ubie's untimely demise, I'd send heaven into an uproar."

He let his gaze wander over me as though trying to place my species.

"Not that it would be the first time. Heaven seems insanely easy to uproar these days."

"You can heal," he said at last, "only very occasionally and only— and mark these words, reaper—only if the soul has not already been freed. Only if it has not left the vessel and entered our Father's kingdom. That is the most sacred law."

"So, that's the biggie?"

"Yes."

"And if I break it?"

"You will be cast from this dimension for all eternity."

"Oh. Well, that doesn't seem too difficult to follow. I can't heal dead people, which, why would I? They're dead."

He tilted his head to the side, but his attention snapped back to Reyes when the devil's spawn—in the literal sense—took a miniscule step forward. He'd been itching to get to Michael for a while now. I could feel the desire tug at him. Urge him forward.

I glared and shook my head. He ignored me.

"And no curing cancer," Michael continued.

"I didn't."

He tore his gaze off Reyes again and gave me a knowing grin. "You thought about it."

"Yeah? Well, I've thought about breaking your neck, too. Does that count?"

"No," he said, one corner of his mouth tilting heavenward.

"Wait a minute. Is that why your henchmen have been tailing me?"

His gaze grew curious. "Henchmen?"

"Are they following me because I threatened to cure cancer?" Then something else hit me. I sat in a chair when I realized what Michael had said. What he'd really said. "You were going to cast me from this plane if I healed my uncle, but you didn't. Because . . . because he wasn't dead yet? Because we'd stopped them from killing him?"

He nodded.

"So, then, he was really going to die here. We stopped Grant Guerin from killing him, so this was . . . and I was going to—"

"—find him too late," he finished for me.

I looked at Uncle Bob, my heart breaking at the mere thought of losing him, but he didn't seem upset in the least. Then again, he was still in a state of awe. Angels did that.

"You knew," I said to him. "You knew you wouldn't make it out of here alive."

He finally focused on the conversation. Bit down. Lifted one shoulder in a helpless shrug. "I had a strong suspicion."

"Uncle Bob. How can you just . . . ?" At a loss for words again, I took him in.

He bore the mark. It was unfair, especially given the circumstances. His cause had been noble. The sentence unjust. I raised my hand and then raised my brows in question to Michael.

He nodded and waited, so I waved my hand and unmarked my favorite uncle.

Then I turned to Michael. "Why can I mark and unmark?"

"You are reaper. It is your domain."

"So, I ask you again, why are your henchmen following me?"

"They are not."

"Dude, they're everywhere. Don't even try to tell me they're not following me, because . . . oh," I said when I realized how amazingly arrogant I sounded. "They aren't following me, are they?"

"They are following the god Rey'azikeen."

Right. That actually made a lot of sense.

Reyes stayed deathly still, but he let slip the barest hint of surprise on his perfect face, a reaction so minute that if I'd blinked I would have missed it.

"Now that Reyes knows he's a god," I said, "he's more of a threat? Is that it?"

"Probably no more than you, but yes."

"Me?" I asked, appalled. "What did I do?"

He deadpanned me. I didn't even know angels could do that. "Did you or did you not threaten to unseat the Father?"

Wow, did my fingernails need a good filing. I turned them this way and that when I answered. "Pfft, dude, I make threats all the time. Like I'd know how to unseat . . . wait." I stood, astonished, and stepped closer. "Are you telling me that's possible?"

He didn't answer. I couldn't blame him. Who would want something like that getting out?

"So," I said, changing the subject lickety-split, "we've been holding back time for quite a while now."

"Time is of no consequence."

"Tell that to someone in a car accident, bleeding to death."

Michael started to touch me, but Reyes was there in a heartbeat, sword drawn, the tip piercing the angel's throat.

Uncle Bob stumbled back, still freaking a bit.

Michael held up his hands. "I was just going to show her." With the sword still at his throat, he turned a hand over and offered it to me.

I reached out and brushed my fingertips along his upturned palm, and the images that flooded my cerebral cortex defied logic. The creation of Earth. The depth of the ever-expanding universe. Living creatures in the farthest reaches of space. And the gods. So many more than I ever imagined possible. Almost every dimension, and there were thousands, had at least one. Some more. A few none.

When he'd finished, I stepped back and lowered my head. Absorbed what he'd shown me. And why. It wasn't a documentary on the mysteries of our amazing universe. It was to let me know just that: thousands of dimensions. Thousands of options. And I could be cast into any one of them.

I glanced at him and nodded my acknowledgment. My understanding. We came to an accord of a sort.

Almost.

I leveled a hard stare on him and said, "These men are mine."

"Those slated for Lucifer's domain are not my concern." He offered a congenial nod and vanished.

Time slammed back into place, the sound deafening for a split second, then the men glanced around, looking for their guns.

"You know," I said to Reyes over my shoulder, "we should let Osh in on this."

He scowled but shrugged, leaving it up to me.

"Uncle Bob, you are about to see something that might be a little disorienting."

Ubie's expression went from stunned to comical in under six. He was really good at the deadpan thing, too.

"Osh," I said, summoning the slave demon to us.

He stepped from a shadowy corner as though he'd been there the whole time.

"Take your pick."

A grin far too wicked for the grim situation flashed across his handsome face. By that point, El Jefe had figured out he'd made a grave mistake.

I didn't understand men like him. So loyal and loving with his own family and yet a monster, an absolute monster to others.

Valencia gave Osh a once-over and smirked. I wanted to tell him Osh only *looked* like a kid, but he'd find that out soon enough. Osh was on him so fast, he was impossible to see. He pinned him against a wall, then lowered his mouth onto the older man's and breathed in his essence. Absorbed his soul. Fed on his aura.

It was like watching gay porn without the nudity, the whole exchange one of the sexiest things I'd ever seen.

Valencia's men scrambled to help their boss, but Reyes had been chomping at the bit long enough. He let loose. Got into a couple of fistfights for the fun of it before snapping necks one by one. They didn't know what hit them. Then again, their deaths were merciful compared to what they did to their victims. Their eternal damnations following death, however, would be another story.

I escorted Uncle Bob out under the guise of plausible deniability.

Also, he didn't need to see it all. Reyes and Osh were demons. Sometimes they enjoyed the kill a little too much.

"We have to go to hell in less than three hours," Uncle Bob said to me, as though we were walking out of a meeting or had just come from dinner.

"What? Oh, right, the mall." I suppressed a giggle. "You know, I've been. They really are very similar."

"Why am I not surprised?"

"Uncle Bob, I still can't believe what you were about to do for me. You could have died."

"Charley, I know how special you are. Or, well, I thought I knew." He raked a hand through his hair. "I guess I had no clue. Not really."

I wrapped an arm in his. "That's okay. I don't always get it, either."

"Was that . . . was that an angel?"

"Oh, him? Yeah, that was Michael the Churlish Cherub." I bent at the waist, giggling.

Uncle Bob just stared all aghastlike. Not everyone got my humor.

"Does . . . how much does Cookie know?"

"Not as much as you. Not anymore."

He nodded as Reyes stepped out.

"Feel better?" I asked him.

"You know, I think I do."

I studied the run-down hotel. "I essentially killed those men. Am I slated for hell?"

He stepped to me. Put his fingers underneath my chin. Raised it until our gazes locked. "You're a god, Dutch. And the reaper. You don't get slated. You are the slate."

"Yeah, well, I'm not sure Michael the Churlish Cherub would agree." I snorted again at my own joke. "I'm so calling him that next time I see him."

"I want to be there."

"I'll get you a ringside seat."

"No, I want to be there the next time you try to start World War III."

His statement wasn't actually the light suggestion he'd made it out to be. It was a warning. He'd paired his warning with a gentle glare. It would have been even better had he paired it with a nice chianti and a cheese ball.

I stepped into his arms and offered my own warning glare. "Push me off a building again, and you'll see Michael sooner than you'd hoped."

He pulled a lock of my hair, then tucked it behind my ear. "Unless he's visiting Lucifer, I doubt that would happen."

I eased back, surprised. "Do you really think you'd go to hell?"

"No. As a god, I'd go to a prison dimension, I suppose."

"I think you've seen the inside of enough prisons to last you a few million years. And besides, why would you go there? You've done nothing wrong, Reyes."

He offered me a sad smile and looked away.

17

My entire life can be summed up in one sentence:
"Well, that didn't go as planned."
—T-SHIRT

The next morning, I waited on the sidelines in Amber's room while Uncle Bob and a tech guy named Jimmy equipped Amber with a wire. We'd be able to hear everything. Reyes stood in the doorway with a cup of coffee. Sadly, it was not mine.

"Thanks for being here, Swopes," I said to Garrett Swopes, one of my best friends on planet earth. Or he could have been if he'd drop the macho guy routine and offer to make me tacos. He'd been explaining to Amber how the wire would work when he stood and walked over.

"Not at all." He gestured toward Amber. "How's the smidgen holding up?"

"She's nervous. I want her to be able to see either you, me, or Reyes at all times."

Garrett was the only person in our circle who I could be fairly confident Joe Stalker didn't know about. He could be there without worry that Joe would have seen them together. And while Amber and I hadn't been seen together in public for months, I had a workaround, just in case. A reason for my being at the mall. It was ingenious. I'd pretend to be a shopper. Gawd, my plans rocked.

I walked over to Amber just as the tech guy was finishing up. "Are you sure you want to do this?"

She nodded, but I could feel the elevated pulse. The tightening of her throat. The nausea churning in her stomach. Poor kid. Stress did so much more damage than people realized.

I sat beside her and took her hand.

We'd sent texts throughout the day before, so if Joe Stalker did clone her phone, he would know exactly where she'd be. I had a hard time believing he just followed her around. The texts were the only thing that made sense. Either that or he was following her on GPS. Both acts relied on her phone.

"Brandy will be there, too, right?" Amber had texted her friend Brandy as well after Uncle Bob discussed the whole thing with Brandy's parents. They'd agreed, albeit very reluctantly, to let their daughter go. I could hardly blame their hesitation. Who would purposely set up their daughter in a sting trying to catch a stalker? Yeah, I bet that wasn't an easy sell for Ubie. But he got the job done.

"According to her parents, yes. She'll show."

She nodded, relieved.

"I heard he didn't text you yesterday."

Ubie said everything went well with Osh being there, but I was worried it may have scared Joe off. Now was not the time to go into hiding, but if it happened, it happened. We would simply try again until we caught him.

She shook her head. "He'll do that, though. Go for a few days without texting me, then I get like ten in one day from a totally new number."

"Okay." I could only hope he wasn't someone who traveled for work and was out of town. This whole thing could be for naught.

Cookie's hands shook as she handed Amber a hairband. "I don't see why I can't go in. I'm her mom. I would be at the mall with her, anyway."

"We can't risk it, Cook. We don't want to do anything that will scare him off."

She agreed with a soft nod, but she wasn't happy about any of it.

"You'll be able to hear the whole thing from the van."

We'd set up a special surveillance van and, as per regulation, had an ambulance waiting in the wings.

Ubie knelt in front of her. "How does that feel?" he asked, gesturing toward the wire. Jimmy had had to reach inside her camisole to clip it to her bra. Humiliation had surged through her, poor kid. But I got the feeling that had been the worst of it.

"Fine."

He cupped her chin and waited for her gaze to meet his. "We will be right there, smidgeon. I would never let anything happen to you."

She nodded, dipped her head, then lunged forward and wrapped her arms around him. Cookie pressed a hand to her chest. Now that she knew what had been eating at Ubie—namely, a drug baron wanting to make a creole sauce with my brains and enjoy it over a nice frittata—she felt a small amount of relief. I only prayed that after today this whole ordeal would be done and over with. For Cookie's sake.

Amber sat back down, her hands still shaking so badly she had to clasp them together.

I looked at the crew, letting my gaze linger for a moment longer than necessary on the ball and chain as he leaned against the doorjamb and sipped from a black mug. Then I focused on Cookie. "Do you mind if I talk to her alone?"

"Oh," she said, a little surprised. "Not at all."

She stood and shooed everyone out, including Tall, Dark, and Sensual. He had to tease her, of course. He stood his ground until she started to step across the threshold, then he blocked her path, an evil grin widening his mouth.

She stopped and questioned him with her gaze; then, realizing he was teasing her, she physically turned him and pushed him from the room. He raised his arms in surrender.

God bless him. He was trying to help Cookie deal and it was working.

Amber relaxed, just barely, after they left. It was a lot to put on a thirteen-year-old's shoulders. This entire sting was not only for her benefit, but hinged on how well she could pull it off.

I sat on the bed opposite the desk where Amber sat. She stared at her shoes for a solid minute before glancing up at me.

"I will be right there, Amber. I'll hear everything you say. If you feel like something is wrong or you get scared, you just give the signal."

The signal was a phrase: *Don't tell your mom about the jelly.* Of course, running and screaming worked, too.

She let out a nervous laugh, the sound soft and shaky. "I don't know why I'm so scared."

I lifted a brow. "Want me to tell you?" After she nodded, I said, "Because this guy knows a lot about you. He stalked you for a while before initiating contact. He threatened your stepdad. You wish Quentin were here. And this is a big operation with a lot of people and a lot at stake, and you don't think you're worth it."

She glanced up, surprised.

"You don't think we should have gone to all this trouble, and I'm going to tell you right now, you are wrong, Amber." I took her hands into mine. "You couldn't be more wrong. Odds are this guy is just some nut who would eventually leave you alone, but we cannot take that chance, hon."

She withdrew inside herself, her shoulders going concave. "It's just a lot of fuss for what might turn out to be nothing."

"Amber, you are the most confident thirteen-year-old I've ever met."

I rethought that. "Okay, the second-most confident." Angel exuded confidence by the bucketsful. "Don't let this guy knock you off your game. That makes him the winner. Even if he never touches a hair on your head, he's still won, and that is not okay in my book. Because there is nothing on earth more important than you."

She nodded, completely unconvinced.

"Can I tell you a secret?"

A spark of interest lit her blue eyes.

"You are on her team."

Intrigue straightened her shoulders. "Whose?"

I smiled and thought about everything this amazing kid had left to do. And she'd need all of the tenacity she could get. I'd be damned before I'd stand idly by and let this asswipe drain even an ounce of that spunk and spitfire from her lovely, graceful bones.

I squeezed her hands and said, "Beep's."

Her lids rounded in awe.

"I've seen it. You're a prophet." Warmth filled me just thinking about it. "You're *the* prophet."

The look of amazement and wonder that overtook her face was my reward for confiding in her. "I'm . . . me? I'm the prophet? The one who sees into the future?"

"You already see into it better than I'll ever be able to. I think we should talk to your mom about honing those skills. You're going to need them to help Beep in the coming years, don't you think?"

She nodded, excitement and enthusiasm overpowering her fear. Her uncertainty. "I would like that."

"And I shouldn't be telling you this, because nothing is ever set in stone—things could change—but Quentin is on her team, too."

Her expression went from ecstatic to dreamy. The girl had it bad. "That would be the coolest thing ever."

"I agree." The fact that Quentin was about to turn seventeen and Amber didn't turn fourteen for a couple of months had me a little on edge. It was one thing when the kid was sixteen. There was just something about his inevitable seventeen-dom that brought out the mother bear in me.

Then again, Beep was barely two months old and I'd already peddled her off to a four-hundred-year-old demon.

Maybe seventeen wasn't so bad. And I'd had nothing to do with their inevitable hookup. That little nugget came to me the same day Amber's destiny did. The day they'd taken Beep away. The day I'd forgotten how to breathe.

"I miss him," Amber said.

"Osh?"

She giggled. "No. Quentin."

I pulled her onto the bed beside me and leaned in to her secretively. "Okay, for reals. How did Osh handle high school?"

She snorted then doubled over in a fit of the giggles. It was fun to watch.

After laughing so hard her face turned red, she told me all the gory details. Girls fell over backwards, literally, to get a look at him. And one glance was not enough for most. Since Osh hung with her all day under the guise of being her cousin, every girl in school wanted to get to know her better.

"He *is* cute," she said.

"What?" I shook my head. "No, he's not. He's . . . he's . . ."

"It's okay, Aunt Charley. I don't think of him in that way."

"Right," I said, relief washing over me. "You only have eyes for a tall blond boy who eats his spaghetti with a straw."

She burst out laughing again. "We only did that once. As an experiment. It doesn't work as well as you might think."

"Yeah, I'll take your word for it."

By the time we emerged from Amber's room, her entire demeanor had changed. She was still nervous, but the situation didn't bother her as much. Her future looked far too bright to let it.

As Uncle Bob went over some last-minute instructions with her, Cookie wrapped an arm in mine and took me aside. "How do you do it?"

"What?"

"I'm her mom and—"

"Cook, that's it. You're her mom. I'm the cool aunt." I breathed on my fingernails and polished them on my shirt.

"I suppose you're right. I'm just glad that cool aunt vibrator thing works."

"You know about Han Solo?" When she questioned me with her usual comic obliviousness, I said, "I think you mean *vibe*. And it does work. Clearly. Also, I have superpowers."

She gaped at me. "I have superpowers, too."

"Hon, blinding people with your fashion sense doesn't count."

"Oh, okay. Never mind, then." She hugged me to her, thanking me for the thousandth time since the whole thing began.

I had Swopes text Amber to make sure we'd get it, too. Something totally nonsensical. Because we would also get all of Amber's texts, we would know the minute Joe made contact.

When a text came through that read, *Do you think Justin is cute?* Amber giggled.

I punched Garrett on the arm.

"What?" he said, rubbing his biceps as though he actually felt my paltry effort. "I have nieces. I know how they think. And every school on the planet has at least one Justin. It's a statistical fact."

He had me there.

As per the instructions, Cookie dropped Amber off at Coronado Center, a.k.a. the mall, then drove to the back entrance of a convenience store three blocks away and got in the waiting surveillance van. We couldn't risk Joe seeing her slip into the van and grow suspicious.

Once Cookie was inside, an officer drove the van over and parked behind the mall.

The team consisted of me, Reyes, three officers posing as shoppers, Uncle Bob, who was stationed in the mall security booth, Garrett, who was hanging back, and Osh, who was meeting us on-site.

Reyes had been a little moody after finding out the angels who'd been stalking me were actually stalking him, so I stationed him at a kiosk that sold cologne. The salesman there was about to have his best day ever. Women flocked around the kiosk as Reyes pretended to try this cologne and that. They would spray perfume on their wrists, wave it in front of him, and ask his opinion. Subtly was none of their strong suits.

I went about my business window-shopping. Not that I needed new windows.

Amber met her friend Brandy at the entrance. We would hear every word they said over the mic. If Joe texted, she was to go to the food court, where we had the rest of the team waiting.

Two hours later, the girls were still walking around looking at clothes rather unenthusiastically. The officers were getting antsy. Osh, dressed in his high school getup, was flirting with a saleslady.

I navigated my shattered screen and called Ubie, wishing I could run over and get the screen switched out. We were so close, the store barely a hundred feet away. But conducting personal business during a stakeout was often frowned upon.

"What do you think?" Ubie asked me.

"I've noticed a pattern. I need to talk to the girls."

"Now? Charley, you could blow the whole op. If he sees you with her—"

"Which is exactly why I'm going to make it look like a total coincidence. This is a mall, after all. It's not unheard of to run into people you know."

He let out a loud sigh as he thought about it. "I guess it won't hurt."

"Okay, I'm heading in."

I bought a scarf off another kiosk just so I'd have a bag to carry around, then headed toward Amber and her friend.

"Amber!" I said, rushing to her for a hug. "What are you doing here?"

Amber's expression quickly changed from shock to elation. Girl was good. "We're just shopping. Looking at cute boys. You know, the usual stuff."

"Indeed I do. I'll let you girls get back to it. I have a couple of more things to pick up. Tell your mom hi for me."

"Okay." We hugged again, and I whispered in her ear, "Have fun. Try on silly hats. Dance to the Muzak. Stick out your tongue. If I'm right and he's here, he won't be able to resist commenting on it."

"You're right," she said as realization dawned. He seemed to only text when she was behaving in a certain way or dressed a certain way.

When I let her go, she nodded that she understood.

I gave Brandy a quick hug, too, and hurried off.

The girls started picking up the pace. They tried on sunglasses and hats and sprayed cologne on one another while Reyes and I scanned the crowd, but still nothing. Not until Amber raised her shirt like she was going to flash a cute boy walking by did she get a text. And it was not a nice one.

Joe didn't seem to appreciate Amber's sense of humor when he said, *Raise that shirt again, and I'll rip it off you and wrap it around your neck.*

I resisted the urge to pump my fist. But I did do a mental *Woohoo!*

Now the real challenge began. And Amber did beautifully. She looked at the text and burst out laughing, just like we'd instructed. Then she showed it to Brandy, and they both laughed.

I was so proud of her. Pretending to laugh when you were filled with terror was not easy. I'd had to do it before.

After they sobered, they headed toward the food court. But in their haste, and as afraid as they were, Amber forgot to put down a perfume bottle she'd picked up. An alarm rang out, and her eyes rounded.

No.

A saleswoman hurried forward. Amber didn't know what to do. She glanced around, the terror she was trying to suppress evident on every plane of her face.

My heart broke for her. We would, of course, explain, but the sting would be a bust.

Seconds before the saleswoman reached them, Osh raced by on a skateboard, snatched the perfume out of Amber's hand, and sped off. When the woman got there, she seemed confused.

Amber improvised beautifully when she pointed to Osh. "I think that boy stole something."

The woman hurried to call security. And I almost collapsed in relief. Osh didn't know it yet, but that boy was getting a big fat kiss.

The girls, after almost fainting from relief, continued to the food court, sat at an outside table, and began talking about the text again, pointing at the phone and laughing.

"Come on, Joe," I said, whispering under my breath.

A second later, another text came though.

You won't be laughing when I spread those skinny legs, bitch.

Oh, yeah, he was angry.

Two of the cops stuck to the girls like glue while I surfed the crowd. If he was in it, I'd feel the anger. A strong emotion like that would be hard to miss.

Ubie's voice came through. "Anything, Charley?"

I could only shake my head. I did a complete circle and got nothing. What the hell? He had to be here.

I glanced up toward the second floor but saw no one really watching, besides Reyes. He'd taken up position overhead to get a bird's eye.

Growing frustrated, I started to circle again. The girls kept up the game. I gave Amber the signal to amp it up, at which point they showed a total stranger the text and burst out laughing again. I needed this guy to go ballistic.

I felt anger here and there, but nothing anywhere near what he would be projecting. And then it hit me. Anger, yes. But it was more than that. I felt hatred and jealously and hostility.

Whirling toward the emotions that had now filtered through the masses and were bombarding me, I saw no one.

"What is it?" Ubie asked into the mic. I held up an index finger and walked forward through the crowd. Men of every shape and size sat around eating a variety of mall food, but when I finally spotted the source of the rage, I stopped short, unable to believe my eyes.

I shuffled closer, pretending to look at my phone, but Joe Stalker was so busy watching the girls, she paid me no mind at all when I stopped right beside her table.

It was a kid. A young girl probably no older than Amber. Chubby with short dark hair, curly and unkempt, and ghostly white skin, she looked more like a book nerd than a girl capable of such hatred.

What the hell? Maybe I was wrong. Maybe she was just pissed off at her parents for not buying her the latest copy of *Seventeen*.

She bent to type out a text, then looked up, waiting.

The whole team got it at the same time. *I'm going to stab you in the face, cunt.*

Oh, no, she didn't. She did not just use my beloved CU Next Tuesday in a negative, nonempowering way. We girls needed to stick together, not reinforce a derogatory stereotype. I bit down, vowed to have a little talk with Little Miss Miffed about her contradictory use of one of my favorite words and tried to lace this new information together with what we already knew.

First, she was a kid. For a kid, her grammar was flawless. Even though she didn't text like a typical teen, we still should have picked up on that fact. It never even occurred to me. Then again, maybe that was part of her game. To make the stalker seem older. Smarter. More cunning. To scare Amber even more.

Amber looked at the latest text and laughed again, doubling over, mirth shaking her shoulders.

The girl exploded. Her temper skyrocketed out of control. I saw the glint of metal a mere second before she stood and headed toward the girls. This was going down.

My pulse accelerated like it had rocket boosters. Without another moment's hesitation, I gave the signal. Which was basically jumping up and down and waving my arms.

The team rushed in, knocking people out of the way to get there. They'd pulled their badges out of their shirts to let people know who they were. I followed the girl, pointed at her, and yelled, "Knife!" just as she turned on her heels and plunged it into my stomach.

The sensation of cold, hard steel slicing through skin and ripping into muscle wasn't the first thing that registered. What registered first was the fact that the girl embraced me with her free arm, and whispered, "Eidolon says hi."

I stood stunned for several long moments, wondering if I'd inadvertently stopped time.

But when she slid the blade out of my stomach, reality sank in. Along with a sharp burning sensation that had my knees buckling.

People were screaming around us when Reyes appeared behind the girl. He reached up, took hold of her head, and was a microsecond away from snapping her neck when I cried out to him.

"Reyes, no!"

It was the look on her face. Pure, unadulterated horror as she looked down as her hands. Her blood-soaked hands.

He bit down and pushed the girl aside hard enough to send her sprawling across the floor. Then he rushed to me. Braced me against him. Closed my jacket, and ordered, "Shift."

I blinked up at him. Felt another set of hands at my shoulder and waist. Began to crumple again.

Engulfed in flames of rage, he jerked me back up, pulled me roughly against him, and put a hand behind my head, cupping it. Holding it steady. We stood like that for a long moment, our faces centimeters apart as someone called my name. Garrett maybe.

Then Reyes spoke, his voice deep and soft and unhurried. "Shift, Dutch. Now."

And I did. But just barely. I let my molecules drift apart. Scatter. Then realign. Knitting the cells of my body back together.

When I solidified completely, the pain had vanished.

He eased his hold and waited to make sure I could stand. I nodded and he back away while I zipped up my jacket. It was one thing to heal my flesh. Healing my clothes was another thing altogether.

Amber ran up to me then, distraught and confused. "Aunt Charley, are you okay?"

I nodded and took her into my arms, only then noticing the blood on Reyes's shirt. I'd tell the cops the girl cut me, but not bad.

Amber looked back at the girl the cops had pinned to the ground.

"Her?" she asked, surprised.

The officers had the girl facedown, one of them securing the knife and phone. The girl didn't struggle. Probably in shock. And pain. It couldn't have felt good to have a two-hundred-pound male officer on your back. The female officer bagged the evidence and cuffed her, then they hauled her to her feet. They were not gentle with her. The girl's pale face showed the horror she felt inside.

When the girl gained her footing, her gaze locked onto Amber's.

Amber shook her head and took a step back. "That's . . . no, that's . . . it can't be her."

I took her arm. "Amber, do you know her?"

"No way," Brandy said, as astonished as Amber.

"That's Thea Wold," Amber said. "Why would she send me texts? We see her every day at school. I say hi to her every day."

Brandy nodded. "Amber's nice to her. She's, like, the only one in school who's nice to her."

"You aren't?" I asked her.

Caught, she dipped her head. "No. I mean, I'm not mean or anything. I just don't go out of my way, you know?"

"But I do," Amber said. "Is this what I get for being nice?"

The girl had started shaking, and tears were now streaming down her face.

Amber put her head down, unable to watch, and I knew right then and there why she was on Beep's team. She had an incredible heart.

"Amber, I don't think this is what it looks like."

"What do you mean?"

"I think—" I stopped, trying to choose my words carefully as Reyes and Garrett moved in to create a huddle.

Uncle Bob ran up, then. He took one look at the girl then hurried toward us to complete the huddle.

"I think she was being controlled."

"Are you okay?" Uncle Bob asked first Amber and then me.

We both nodded and he wrapped an arm around Amber. Then he spotted the blood that had soaked down and into my jeans. His gaze darted back to mine, but I shook my head.

"She said something to me. She said, 'Eidolon says hi.' "

"Okay," Ubie said, "who's Eidolon and why is he sending messages through a stalker?"

"I think he was somehow controlling her."

The cops started to take Thea away. I yelled at them to stop and ran over. The gang followed, everyone except Brandy. I got the feeling she'd had enough for one day. She sank into a chair and watched from afar.

"Thea," I said, trying to get her attention.

Her shock and horror were so plain on her face, she stared absently.

"Thea, what did Eidolon say? Did he tell you to do this?"

"I was so mad," she said.

"At Amber?"

"At me?" she asked, appalled.

Her knees started to give, so we ushered her to a chair. Her hands had been cuffed behind her back. A fall face-first would not end well.

"Yes. No." She shook her head, confused. "I thought . . . someone spray-painted the number fifty all over my mom's Encore. And he said it was you."

"The number fifty?" I asked.

Amber lowered her head. "They were calling her a moron. You know, like an IQ of fifty?" She looked at Thea, her expression full of empathy. "Thea, some people are jerks. Why would you think that I had anything to do with that?"

"Because . . . I don't know." She blinked and looked up at me. "I stabbed you."

Amber gasped and Uncle Bob tightened his hold.

"I'm okay, hon." I knelt in front of her. "Thea, what do you know about Eidolon?"

I felt the heat at my back. Reyes was fuming, but his anger had finally shifted off of Thea and onto the root of our problem.

As though really seeing me for the first time, she refocused and drew in a sharp breath of air. "Oh, my God, he's keeping you busy while he searches for your daughter."

I stumbled like she'd punched me. Reyes caught me, jerked me up, and spun me around.

He was going to explain. I could see it on his face. But the situation hardly needed an explanation.

"Go," I said, the word a mere hiss under my breath.

Unable to dematerialize in front of everyone, he took off, so fast people barely saw him as he sprinted across the mall, darting in and out of the curious onlookers.

He was going to check on our daughter. I couldn't go, because that was precisely what Eidolon was hoping for. He wanted me to freak out. He wanted me, the one lugging around the bright-assed light, to lead him to Beep.

I prayed he couldn't follow Reyes in the same way. Surely, he couldn't.

I put my hand on Thea's knee to draw her back to me. "Thea, what else do you know? Is there anything—?"

"He was mad. When you got upset and"—she cinched her brows together, trying to understand her own memories—"when you dematerialized? You can do that?"

I offered a weak smile, but Amber was all over that, her lids a perfect circle.

"He was angry," Thea continued. "He wanted you to rematerialize near her. Near your daughter. He was tracking you. But he said you were too smart. You went somewhere—anywhere—else."

I had no control over my destination when I went to Scotland. Or did I? Was I truly trying to avoid materializing near Beep? And if I'd had absolutely no control, how did I end up at a house on the other side of the world that had a mystical closet exactly like the one in the abandoned convent here?

"But I just kept getting angrier and angrier. He told me the most horrible things. I texted . . ." She looked up at Amber. "I'm so sorry, Amber. I never—"

"I know." Amber dropped to her knees, too. "I know, Thea. It's okay."

She shook her head. "No, I stabbed her. I felt it go in."

"I'm not hurt, see?" I unzipped my jacket and lifted my sweater. My blood-soaked sweater, but underneath the skin was, well, also covered in blood but unmarred nevertheless. "Just a scrape," I said to explain the blood.

"But, how? I felt it go in."

I leaned toward her, bringing Amber with me. "Okay, hon, I'm trying to help you out here. You didn't stab me." I winked, the gesture about a subtle as an elephant in a pink tutu. "You with me?" I looked at Amber. "Both of you?"

Amber nodded and beamed at Thea. "It's okay, Thea. My aunt Charley will make sure you get out of this."

Ubie cleared his throat from behind us. "Oh, and my dad. Mostly my dad."

A shy sense of pride widened his mouth as he helped us to our feet while the cops took Thea away.

I was still confused. Eidolon couldn't possibly have possessed Thea. As a god, he was too powerful. She would only have lived a few hours. A couple of days at the most. Then how did he get to her?

"I didn't spray-paint her mom's car," Amber said to Ubie.

"Smidgeon, you think I don't know that?"

Just then, Cookie ran up out of breath and took Amber into her arms.

"Where you been?" I asked, already knowing the answer.

"I got lost," she said between pants. "I hate malls."

I coughed to camouflage an inappropriate laugh. Uncle Bob did the same. Then he wrapped his arms around both his girls. Cookie leaned into him and Amber buried her face in his lapel.

"Are you sure you're okay, smidgeon?" he asked her, smoothing her hair back.

Amber nodded. "I can't believe that happened to my friend."

"Can I put a picture on my InstaBlog?" Brandy asked, finally braving the crowd. When she raised her phone to snap a shot of the cops escorting Thea away, I gently coaxed her arm down.

"What?" she asked, suddenly self-conscious. "Everyone does it."

"I don't," Amber said, clearly upset.

Brandy had the decency to look embarrassed. "I'm sorry, Am. This is beyond serious, and I'm just . . . I'm being stupid."

"Brandy," I said, getting her attention. "Just out of curiosity, do you know who spray-painted her mom's car?"

Brandy suddenly became fascinated with her shoes. "No."

"Brandy, I'm sensing a lot of guilt."

"It's just, I saw a can of paint in Josie's car. I'm sorry I didn't say anything."

Amber put a hand on Brandy's arm. "If it really was Josie, I don't blame you."

"And who's Josie?" Cookie and I asked at the same time.

"Only the toughest girl in school."

Interesting.

"She has, like, this whole gang," Amber added.

"Who are these girls?" Cookie asked. "I want full names and contact information."

"They're just girls, Mom. The local bullies, but they usually leave us alone."

Brandy nodded. "Because we don't give them a reason not to."

"Well, maybe someone needs to talk to the—"

"I'm going to stop you right there," I said, holding up a hand. "This has to be handled with care. If those girls think Amber and Brandy went to the principal about them, things could get bad. They could retaliate."

Uncle Bob's temper flared. He squeezed his girls tighter. Helplessness sucked, but there wasn't a whole lot he could do in this situation without potentially making things a lot worse for Amber. For his daughter.

Brandy's mom rushed up then. "Is it over?"

I nodded.

"Did you catch him?" she asked, but before I could answer, she went on a rant. "See where this gets you?" she asked Amber. "You girls flirt with boys and wear spaghetti straps and short skirts and think there won't be any consequences. You only have yourself to blame." She pretended to be talking to both girls, but her remarks were aimed directly at Amber.

"I beg your pardon," Cookie said.

"Mom," Brandy said, "it wasn't even a boy."

"You're gay?" she asked Amber, appalled.

That was it. I turned on her with a growl a microsecond before Osh saved me from a moment that would forever live in infamy. It could've gotten ugly fast. Instead, Osh plowed into the woman with his skateboard.

The woman whirled around and glared at him.

"Sorry," he said, having way too much fun. He stepped on his skateboard and caught it in one hand. It was kind of magical.

"This is a sting, Osh. You aren't supposed to enjoy it."

He laughed and lifted his chin toward Cookie and Uncle Bob.

"This . . . boy is with you?" she asked.

"Mom, let's just go," Brandy said, now humiliated if the shade of her face were any indication. She clearly liked "this . . . boy."

Osh sidled closer to Amber. Dipped his head to look her in the eyes. "You okay, kid?"

She nodded, her smile shy when he tweaked her chin playfully. Then she waved good-bye to Brandy as her mother dragged her off.

"Finally," Osh said, easing closer to me. "I thought we'd never be alone."

"Oh, my God, what is it with teenaged supernatural beings?"

He flashed me a wicked grin, then leaned in. "She's okay."

Beep. Beep was okay. When I almost collapsed in relief, he winked and rolled off. Mostly because security had spotted him.

I tapped Uncle Bob's shoulder as I watched Osh glide in and out of the throngs of shoppers. "Did you clear up that whole shoplifting thing yet?"

Ubie chuckled. "I'll get right on that."

I stepped to Amber. Put an arm around her waist since Ubie had claimed her shoulders. "I'm so sorry, hon."

"People suck."

"Yes, they do," Osh said as he raced past us again. Kid was so going to get arrested.

But it did the trick. Amber laughed. There were tears in her eyes when she did it, but she laughed nonetheless.

I'd take it.

"No idea. It looked good."

"Hmm." He took a bite, then got to his point. "How are you doing?"

"Truth?" I asked, adding a hard edge to my voice.

He dropped his gaze. "Of course."

"I'm in awe, Uncle Bob."

His gaze drifted back up. "Awe?"

"Of you. What you did for me . . . I can't ever repay you."

"What I did for you?" The astonishment in his voice bordered on comical. "Charley, you're special. I mean, I already knew that, and I know that you know that I already knew that, but . . . you are really special."

"So are you."

"No. Not like you. Not like . . . where did you come from?"

"Well, one night, my mommy and daddy decided to play doctor—"

"That's not what I mean." He only pretended to be gruff with me. "How did we end up with you? Of all the people on the planet."

"Just lucky, I guess."

"I'll second that." He took another bite, then glanced down at my stomach and asked, "But you're good?"

I leaned forward and, just to make him as uncomfortable as humanly possible, kissed his cheek. "I'm better than good." Not that I wasn't worried about Eidolon, but Beep was safe, Amber's stalker had been ferreted out, and I no longer had a knife in my stomach. That hurt so much worse than I thought it would.

"I'm glad," he said. "Are you going to finish that?"

I pulled it back. "Yes. Go get your own." I pointed out where I got the mystery meal just as my phone rang.

"Be right back," he said, excited.

Shattered screen or not, I didn't recognize the number, so I refrained from answering with, "Charley's House of Hot Pickles," and just said hello. It was so boring, I almost fell asleep.

18

Life isn't a fairy tale.
If you lose a shoe at midnight, you're drunk.
—MEME

We were still at the mall well past two when hunger hit. According to Osh, Reyes was going to keep an eye on Beep for a while. He wouldn't get too close. Those were the rules. Our visits were very much like today: an orchestrated sting operation. We had to get in and out before anything—any supernatural being not working for us—noticed our presence.

By the time Uncle Bob took Amber and Cookie home, I had almost starved to death. I glanced around at the offerings. Mall food. I'd eaten worse.

After scoping out something that sounded only slightly less nutritious than a marshmallow cream puff, I sat down to eat. Uncle Bob sat down with me.

"I thought you were taking them home."

"I was. Then I remembered we came in separate cars."

"Want some?" I asked, scooting my delicacy closer to him.

"What is it?"

"Charley Davidson?"

Damn. What bill did I forget to pay? I was so bad at the whole bill-paying thing.

"You are going to drive to the Giant on Fourth and Vineyard."

"I am?" This person must've had ESP, because I didn't even know I was going to drive to the Giant on Fourth and Vineyard. It was uncanny. And, frankly, a little out of my way.

"You are if you want to see your client Shawn Foster alive again. Come alone. Call the cops and he dies."

The caller hung up, and I stared at my phone for a solid thirty seconds before dialing Shawn's number. It rang a few times before voicemail picked it up.

"Shawn, if you get this, please call me."

Just because they said they had Shawn didn't mean they actually did. Granted, most people wouldn't say something like that if it weren't true, but how did I know it wasn't Eidolon saying "Hi" again?

I wasn't about to call Reyes back from his mission. Beep was our number one priority, and Shawn was my client, my responsibility, not his.

I put the phone away and schooled my features, contemplating the irony of someone calling and threatening me should I call the cops when I was in the process of having lunch with one. What were the odds?

Uncle Bob sat down with his own mystery meal.

"Who was that?"

I didn't want to completely throw off my oblivious uncle. I might need him should things go south. Which, sadly, was often the case.

So, I'd give him a clue. If I ended up dead—a possibility Reyes swore impossible, but I remained far from convinced—Uncle Bob would know where to look for my body before it decayed too much.

"That was my hairdresser, Mrs. Foster." I put my phone away. "Cookie knows her."

He crinkled his brows as he chewed. "You call your hairdresser Mrs. Foster?"

" 'Parently. I gotta head that way. I forgot I had an appointment."

He nodded and took another bite. Poor guy.

"I wanted to thank you, Uncle Bob."

He swallowed and leveled a curious stare on me. He was such a great guy. Even with the seventies style 'stache.

"You know, just for being you." I leaned over and hugged him then left my trash on the table and hurried toward the exit, praying I'd see him—and his 'stache—again.

I hopped in Misery and drove to the spot Shawn's abductors had instructed, knowing that this could be my fault. I'd turned over the wrong rock when looking into the Foster case. I'd struck a nerve. The only thing I didn't know was whose nerve I'd struck.

Well, that and how the hell they knew I was working with Shawn Foster on this. I had to think. Whose milk did I spill?

The Fosters. That was it. They were the ones with the most to lose. But he was their son. So, who else? Maybe it was someone else involved in Veronica Isom's case. Or with the fake adoption agency. Or even with the missing girl we were looking for, Dawn Brooks.

While they all pointed back to the Fosters, I no longer believed they'd worked alone on any of it. They had followers. Believers who would likely do anything for them. Even abduct their son?

I thought about calling the Fosters, but what would I say? I still couldn't tip them off to the fact that Shawn had come to me.

I'd taken the fastest route. I pulled up to the Giant and put Misery in park. First, I would meet with the person on the phone, then I'd have Ubie run a trace on Shawn's.

I hadn't been sitting there thirty seconds before my phone rang again.

"Leave your phone and walk to the abandoned car wash on the other side of Dion's."

"First, let me—"

They hung up before I could insist on hearing Shawn's voice.

I clenched my jaw and contemplated if I should stuff my phone into my boot. Deciding against it, I left it on the floorboard with my bag, locked up Misery, and headed that way.

After crossing the street, I rounded Dion's and, as sure as death and taxes, an abandoned car wash sat on the other side. It looked unassuming enough. Had probably been a family-run business. How bad could it be? Then again, the Mansons had been a family.

Stepping inside one of the tall bays with weeds growing out of the cracks in the cement, I looked around and saw no one.

Then I heard a male voice. "Back here."

I whirled around and followed it to the back of the building. A mixture of weeds and ivy had grown along the chain link fence so that no one could see the back of the car wash from the restaurant next door. This just didn't bode well.

A man, clean and dressed in khakis and a baby-blue button-down, coaxed me over with a nod. He looked about as much like a kidnapper as my accountant did.

And then it hit me. Of course. I was so stupid.

He stood by a dark blue sedan, the trunk open. After motioning me over, he patted me down and told me to take off my boots. When he was satisfied, he said, "Get in."

"Look, you haven't done anything yet." He was so young. For a kidnapper, anyway. He looked in his early thirties. Clean cut. Well groomed.

It was all a ruse to get me to come along quietly. No one had Shawn. The Fosters were behind this. They'd used him to get to me.

"What do the Fosters want with me?"

So far, the guy had done two stupid things. He'd joined a cult of crazy people. And he'd worn a rope belt with khakis. Unless he was a sailor in his spare time, that was just tacky. But I was willing to forgive him his trespasses until he knocked the ever-lovin' craptastic out of me.

He backhanded me. My head whipped to the side and hit the edge of the trunk lid, sending a sharp jolt of pain rushing through me.

"Get in."

I glared at him to make my point, but he only stared, unmoved. Lifting one leg over the rim of the trunk, I crawled inside, still hoping for the best. After all, these were the God-fearing kind of abductors. How bad could this be?

I'd scared them. The Fosters. And somehow they had put two and two together. They were smarter than I'd given them credit for. My bad. Though I should have known. They'd gotten away with child abductions and murder for over thirty years. They had to be at least semi-intelligent.

After climbing in, I expected the trunk to close down on me. What I hadn't expected was the shot of electricity he'd hit me with. He'd Tasered me! Jolts of electrical currents rushed through my muscles and crashed against my bones. My body stiffened, my head jerked back, and I lost all motor control.

When he turned the gun off, I shouted a few expletives like I had Tourette's then went completely limp. I couldn't even lift my head, so when I felt a needle pierce the skin on the inside of my elbow, I could do nothing about it. Except seethe.

This guy had serious issues. I saw a promising career as a serial killer if he lived that long, because I was suddenly in a killing mood.

Still reeling from electroshock therapy, I realized I may have bitten off more than I could chew. Uncle Bob was never going to let me live this down. Reyes was going to kill me. And Cookie . . . well, at least Cookie would mourn me.

The kidnapper slammed the trunk lid closed, and I lay in total darkness as we drove. The drug didn't knock me out entirely. I remembered hitting pothole after pothole and thinking he was aiming for the things.

I thought about summoning Angel. About three seconds before I lost consciousness.

We hit another pothole. That had to be what roused me from my sleep. I blinked and tried to gain my bearings with little success. Mostly because I couldn't see shit.

My shoulder and hip ached from the hard surface I'd been riding on. And the bumps in the road didn't help. We took a sharp turn. A few seconds later, we slowed. I heard voices outside, then the trunk lid popped open, and two sets of arms reached in to drag me out.

At first, I thought we were in an underground garage. It was dark and cold. Then I realized night had fallen.

I shook my head. How long had I been in that trunk? The dried drool on my cheek would suggest quite a while. And I had to pee like nobody's business.

They dragged me into an outbuilding of some kind. Perhaps a storage building or a barn. It was lit with lanterns strewn across a dirt floor. I knew the floor was dirt because I tried to walk but couldn't quite manage it, so my feet dragged along the ground, stirring up clouds of dust.

Then they dropped me, and I fell forward, landing on my knees and palms and face. I pushed up and took in my surroundings. Mostly I just saw legs. Several sets of them. Then I saw someone very tall. I raised my head, tried to look up, but it took every ounce of strength I had not to fall face-first again.

I finally sat back on my heels and my gaze traveled the length of the really tall guy. But he wasn't so much tall as . . . hanging. Shawn Foster was hanging by his wrists, his arms over his head, his mouth gagged, his face and body bloody and bruised. They really did have him. It wasn't the Fosters after all. Then who?

A woman stepped into my line of sight. She wore Sketchers, jeans, and a button-down. But the higher my gaze traveled, the more my head spun. I couldn't seem to keep the room steady. Whatever they'd given me was powerful.

"Aren't you something," the woman said, squatting down in front of me, her smile genuine.

Mrs. Foster. It was Mrs. Foster, looking as happy as a python at a bunny farm.

"I've never seen anything like her," a man said. Probably Mr. Foster.

Around us stood a group of about fifteen people, if my leg count was correct. Mostly adult males, but a couple of women and even a teen or two. Were they watching their parents torture the Fosters' son? Because that could not be healthy.

Mrs. Foster leaned closer. She cupped my chin in her hand and asked, "What are you?"

"Wasted. What did you give me?"

She displayed a smile that was so smug, my palm itched to slap it off her. Still, violence was never the answer.

I smiled back. I'd had just about enough of the Fosters and their personal brand of crazy. "You're going to die soon."

A loud slap sounded, and I lost sight of her as my head swung way too far to the side. Apparently, she didn't get the violence-is-never-the-answer memo. The world tilted and I struggled to stay upright.

"You think we don't know how to handle your kind? We've been doing it for years, sweetheart. Decades. It's why we were put on Earth. To smite the work of the devil. To erase the abominations to God. To cleanse the Earth of your kind."

"That shouldn't take long. There's only one of me."

"Is that right?" Mr. Foster asked. I could see him more clearly now. His short brown hair wasn't as groomed as it had been at the diner and he had a layer of scruff on his jaw. But he was still an incestuous wiener. "Well, then, this should be easy."

"Why did you . . . why are you hurting your own son?"

Mr. Foster knelt before me. "You know perfectly well he's not our son. It was only a matter of time."

"We tried to do a good deed," Mrs. Foster said.

As she spoke, the Diviners clapped and shouted an occasional "Hallelujah!" or "Praise be!"

"We took him in," she continued. "Raised him. Nurtured and cared for him. He was so full of light when he was a baby, but even light can be corrupted. As you are well aware." She tsked and walked back to Shawn. "Even the brightest of lights can be swayed. He went to you. He turned to you, a corrupted soul, to investigate us, the Divine. He knew the consequences."

Somehow I doubted that. "He had nothing to do with my investigation."

She whirled around and glared. "He turned to you and your evil husband."

They knew about Reyes? "Dude, you are so much eviler than the man who's going to snap your necks like kindling." That came out wrong.

A surge of whispers erupted but then quieted just as quickly. "Please, Mrs. Farrow," Mr. Foster said. "Or do you still go by Davidson like so many of the unclean in this world?"

I didn't see the connection.

"Practically planning ahead for adultery and divorce."

"When you put it that way." Freaking psychos. "In my own defense, Mrs. Foster kept her maiden name as well." I snorted until the inevitable slap put a stop to that nonsense. "Fine. Oh, my God. What?"

"Shawn's fate was sealed the moment he sought your counsel," he said.

Mrs. Foster walked back to us as I tried to get a better look at Shawn. Was he still alive? I couldn't tell. I closed my eyes again and tried to summon Reyes. Angel. Osh. Anyone. The drugs were blocking me. It had happened before.

"He must be returned to the earth," she said. "He must learn from his mistakes and be allowed to grow again."

"You're going to replant him?"

"And you as well."

"Can I come back as an azalea?"

"But out of the darkness, brothers and sisters," Mr. Foster said, his voice booming now, "comes the light."

They shouted and clapped. A couple even fell to their knees with hands raised.

Don't get me wrong. I was all for religion. Whatever helped you get up in the morning. And a higher power, like the one Christians referred to as the God Jehovah, was definitely real. It was religion being turned into an excuse to torture and maim and kill that I had a problem with.

Mrs. Foster raised her hands as well. "And the answer we've prayed for night and day has finally arrived." She smiled down at me. "When Shawn went to you, a weak, corrupted slut—"

"Slut?"

"—we knew what we had to do."

"I think slut is a tad strong."

"See, you aren't just any corrupted. You are his corrupted. His concubine. The Dark One's. The demon from hell."

"Promiscuous, maybe."

She kneeled again. "We were never after you."

"Wanton."

"We were after the abomination," Mr. Foster said, quite proud of himself. "We've been tracking him since he got out of prison. We just had no way of getting to him until now."

When their meaning finally sank in, I focused on the crazy kids in front of me. If they thought to lure Reyes here the same way they lured me, they'd have another thing coming. Oh, they'd get him here, but he would not be in such a cooperative mood.

Whereas, I was all about cooperation. I also shared well in school.

"It's true," Mrs. Foster said. "If you hadn't come to our offices, we probably never would have known about the connection between you and The Dark One."

I fell forward in my attempt to see Shawn again. The ground kept toppling over. Thank God my hands weren't tied. I'd be eating dirt about now.

"We figured you were onto us," Mr. Foster continued. "That was why you showed up. But apparently we were wrong. Shawn, in his weakened state, sought you out."

"That's not why I went to your offices."

"Oh?"

"Not at all. I was thinking about becoming the leader of a fanatical cult and wanted some pointers."

Another crack echoed off the walls and, as my head whipped around, I noted the expressions of excitement on all those present. If anyone were there against his or her will, as was known to happen in cultish situations, I certainly wasn't picking up on it.

Mrs. Foster grabbed a handful of hair. Unfortunately, it was mine. "How do we send him back?"

"Maybe you should have thought of that before you abducted Reyes when he was a baby and gave him to a monster." People never think ahead.

Mrs. Foster bent so we'd be face-to-face, her smile so congenial, it creeped me out. "Of course we gave him to a monster. He's evil. He deserved to be raised by a man just as evil."

It was at that moment precisely that I knew I was staring into the cold eyes of true evil. Evil hiding under the guise of righteousness. It wasn't the first time and certainly wouldn't be the last, but it still astonished me. How someone could do that to an infant.

Then I thought about the baby girl they murdered and pinned on the mother, albeit twenty-five years later, and could hardly believe what I was about to say. But my curiosity got the better of me. "But why give him to Earl Walker? Why didn't you just do what you did to Baby Liana? Why didn't you just kill him?"

Mrs. Foster was surprised I'd pieced it together. No idea why. Veronica Isom, Baby Liana's mother, was telling anyone who would listen about the adoption agency, about what they did, but as a former prostitute and drug addict, her credibility was shot. No one believed her. Clearly, the Fosters knew that.

The smile she placed on me that time was full of sadness, as though she felt sorry for me. For my ignorance. "Oh, sweetheart, we did try to kill him. Several times. He just wouldn't die."

Her words hit harder than any slap could have. The air fled my lungs, and a roaring silence stretched out as the truth sank in. She said something else, but nothing could get past the shock wave pummeling my system.

They'd tried to kill him. When he was a baby, they'd tried. And I thought what he went through with Earl Walker was unfathomable. What had he gone through with the Fosters? What had they done to him? How had they tried to kill him? And what was it like for him when they failed?

I doubled over in astonishment. True evil. I was in the midst of true evil, and Reyes thought he was dark. He had nothing on the Fosters.

"The scales have been knocked off balance," Mr. Foster said, but not to me. He was back in full preach mode. Waving his Bible. "It's all over the news. The end of the world is nearing, so we have to kill. To rid the lands of evil so it can heal. So it can become strong again. So it can nourish us and support us. It is our sacred duty."

He got a whole lot of amens for his effort.

Mrs. Foster let go of my hair but stayed close. She spoke to me as her nutcase brother-slash-husband spewed his sanctimonious bullshit. "We were quite surprised he survived that horrible man," she said. "We figured he'd have killed The Dark One while he was still young."

I was certain he'd tried.

The Diviners were praying and praising God, raising their hands in celebration, asking for His blessing on the blood sacrifice to cleanse the lands. Apparently they hadn't moved on to the New Testament. Sacrifices were kind of old-school, but whatever floated your boat.

Still, how Jehovah could stand by and let others be killed in His name . . .

I tried to stop time so I could walk—or probably stumble—to Shawn and check on him. Nothing. I tried again to summon Angel. Osh. Artemis. Nothing again. What the hell had they given me?

Reyes would figure out something was wrong. I just had to stall. To buy us some time. Then again, I'd sent him to Beep. He was watching over her. And that information caused a peaceful sensation to spread through me. At least she was safe from the likes of people like this.

But I'd given Ubie a clue. Maybe he would figure it out and storm the gates. Still, deciphering my whereabouts would be next to impossible if he didn't get some supernatural help.

"Okay," I said, swaying upright, "I'll tell you how to kill him."

The crowd hushed.

"First, everyone here has to sacrifice themselves at the altar."

Mr. Foster grabbed my hair that time and dragged me closer to Shawn. At last. "Do you think because you are a woman we won't do this to you?"

"Shawn," I said to him, "the cops know everything I do. They won't get away with this."

That caught Mr. Foster's attention. He shook his Bible at me. That'd teach me. Then he said, "You know nothing about us, whore."

They really had a problem with promiscuity. The most promiscuous often did.

I snorted. "You're right. I know nothing about what it's like to have sex with my sibling."

When absolute, unadulterated surprise flashed across their faces, I knew what it must've felt like to win a gold medal at the Olympics. Or at a hot dog–eating contest. Either way. And I had more where that came from.

"How did you—"

"Find out about your incestuous relationship with your sister?" I could only hope he understood me. My words were blurrier than my vision.

"God has ordained our union," Mrs. Foster said.

"Whatever helps you sleep at night."

Shawn groaned before I could say anything else. I tried to stand, to get to him, but the blunt object slamming into the back of my skull convinced me to chillax.

So I did. I lay there for a while. Gathered my thoughts. Weighed vacation spots in my mind, arranging them according to where I'd most rather be at that moment in time.

"How do we kill The Dark One?"

"You don't."

Fury arced out of Mrs. Foster, then her expression changed. Morphed into one of absolute cruelty. "Bring him out."

Him? Who him?

I lay there, begging to get off the merry-go-round, when two men dragged out a third man who was tied and gagged. They dropped him a few feet away from me, and my vision darkened around the edges. The image before me had my head spinning even more. This was not real. This was not happening.

It was Reyes. Unconscious. Beaten and bloody and bruised.

Tears sprang to my eyes. It was the picture. The one I'd gotten ahold of a year ago. The one taken by the monster that had raised him.

He was a kid again. Bound with ropes. His hair mussed. His mouth gagged. His face swollen and discolored and bloody. And I lay in stunned silence.

We were gods. Reyes and I. How could this happen to us? To him? There was no way they could get him. Not Reyes. Not unless . . . unless they Tasered and drugged him. It had worked on me. I bit back the rage swelling inside me.

Reyes groaned, coming to, and I heard the pressure from the ropes as they strained and stretched. Was he fighting against them? I tried to look up at him, but we were suddenly in an industrial-sized dryer, tossing and tumbling. That last hit must've knocked something loose. I begged for the timer to go off, because this sucked.

"Shut him up," Mr. Foster said.

I lost sight of Reyes through the shuffling of feet. Then I heard a struggle and another loud crack, but I felt no pain that time. They'd hit Reyes. I cried out to him and, naturally, received another blunt object to the cranium for my efforts, but this time I managed to focus on him.

I saw him through the throngs of legs. He fought the restraints when they hit me. And because of that, they'd hit him again, too.

"Reyes, stop," I said.

"Shhhift," he said. Or tried to say.

"Cut out the abomination's tongue," Mrs. Foster ordered.

Two men grabbed hold of Reyes's face and tried to force open his mouth as I shot forward. I didn't get far. Reyes clamped his teeth shut so a beefy man—it was always the beefy ones—started hitting him, his fist landing punch after violent punch.

Until my stomach lurched.

Until my heart cracked.

Until my head exploded with the pain I felt drowning every cell in my body.

The man stopped at last when Mr. Foster raised a hand.

Then I heard Reyes's voice. Soft. Barely audible. And yet as clear as if he were whispering it in my ear. "You have to know."

I looked over at him. He'd passed out again. When one man forced his jaw apart and another walked forward with a knife, Mr. Foster said, "No! I want him lucid when it happens." He turned back to me, blocking my view of my husband. "How do we kill it? Answer or he will only suffer longer."

I heard it again. "You have to know."

I tried to see past the evil evangelists to get to Reyes, but the harder I tried, the thicker the air became. Time slipped. People around me sped up and then bounced back to normal speed. Then they slowed down. It had to be Reyes. "Go," I said to him. "Get out of here."

He stopped time and looked across at me, a mischievous sparkle in his eyes. "Well, I would, but the police are on the way, and it always looks better when the hostages are tied up and beaten bloody."

Relief washed over me. So much so I almost hurled. Which I felt was a strange reaction to elation. But a part of me, like nine-tenths, was horrified.

"Reyes, you're just letting them beat on you?"

"I'm sorry, Dutch. I didn't know they were going to get you, too."

"It's okay. Wait. How did they get you?"

"Taser. Then drugs."

"Me, too." I still couldn't balance and kept falling on my face. "That Taser crap hurts."

"Not as much as it hurt watching them hit you." His shirt was almost torn completely off him and hung in shreds.

"Wait a minute," I said, not buying what my husband, a.k.a. the son of Satan, a.k.a. the best liar on this plane, was selling. "They Tasered you? Just out of the blue, they walked up and got the jump on you."

"I may have let them, but it still hurt."

"Reyes, seriously, they want you dead."

"Why didn't you try to summon me the moment they came for you? I would have felt it."

"And taken you away from guard duty? You know she comes first. Speaking of which—"

"Osh is with her, now."

I let out a sigh of relief then gestured toward Shawn. "Is he okay?"

He turned to him then back to me. "He'll live."

"Thank God. But, Reyes, why? Why did you let them hurt you?"

He looked away. "You were right. They need to be behind bars. I didn't realize the extent of their crimes, Dutch. I would never have let them live this long." When he looked back at me, his expression was somewhere between admiration and guilt. "I'm sorry I'm so hardheaded."

"That's okay. I can be a little stubborn at times, too. Wait. Have you seen a little girl about three years old?"

He gestured with a nod. I followed his gaze to a beautiful little girl being held by an elderly woman. Dawn Brooks. Dawn and the woman were the only people whose expressions weren't pure delight. The woman looked scared, actually. Nervous. For us. And I was oddly grateful.

"Reyes, she's beautiful."

"I agree."

"Hey, you need to summon Angel."

"Been here the whole time, boss."

I rose onto my elbows when I tried to turn toward Angel's voice. "Okay, first I want to know why I wasn't invited to this party earlier, and second, why didn't you come get me the minute they took Reyes?"

"Ask the hell-god. He threatened to punch me in the throat."

"Reyes, that's mean."

The grin that spread across Reyes's bloody face was pure wickedness. "Your uncle is coming, but these things never end well. They'll barricade themselves in, and there'll be a days-long standoff."

"I don't want to be used as a punching bag for days," I said.

"Yeah, me neither."

"We need to get Dawn out of here, along with any other children. I'd bet my last nickel some of them are abductees as well."

"I'll see your last nickel and raise you a silver dollar that some of the adults were abductees, too. Raised here since they were kids."

"I bet you're right. We need to figure out how to get out of here."

"You don't think I could've gotten out hours ago?"

I was finally able to sit up without toppling over. Angel kneeled beside me for support. "Then why, Reyes? Why let them . . ." My voice cracked so I stopped talking.

But he didn't need me to finish. "Because these people need to go to jail, and the best way to ensure that—"

"—is to be found all kidnapped and bloody?"

He nodded.

"Reyes, they . . ." The image of him as a baby as the Fosters tried to kill him ravaged my mind again. It would be something I would never forget. I fought the sting in my eyes, but the sting kicked my ass. Like most things today. Tears pushed past my lashes.

Angel leaned into me, and I grabbed hold of him. Wrapped both my arms around his neck. Buried my face in his cool shoulder.

"Dutch," Reyes said softly. Soothingly. "I'm fine. I don't even remember it. I'm not like you. I don't have every memory from the day I was born."

But I couldn't help it. I sobbed, anyway. Angel wasn't sure what to do, so he patted my head. It was just about the sweetest thing he'd ever done. If not for the fact that I'd been bludgeoned with a blunt object on that very head not once, but twice, I might have enjoyed it.

I tried to get to my feet, to make my way to the man I adored more than caramel apples, but my legs wouldn't work right.

"It's okay," he said, gazing at me through lids swollen almost completely shut. I had a feeling his lopsided grin could be attributed more to facial paralysis than that mischievous charm he carried around like a weapon of mass destruction. "We need to make sure there's no standoff. We have to stop them from barricading themselves inside. This whole place is one big compound."

I sniffed and wiped my nose on Angel's dirty tank. "I'm all ears. Wait!" I said as a plan formed. A good one. "Okay, I've got it."

"Does it involve either of us getting our tongues cut out?"

"How'd you know? Just follow my lead."

Angel snickered. "I've had to do that a few times. It's scary."

"Why are people always dissing my plans?"

"They're almost here," Angel said.

"Is Uncle Bob with them?"

"Boss, Uncle Bob is leading the cavalry. And he is not happy."

19

I never make the same mistake twice.
I make it like five or six times, you know, just to be sure.
—T-SHIRT

I was beginning to get the feeling back in my legs. The drugs had worked their way through my system and were starting to wear off.

With Angel's help, I navigated the Diviners and checked on Shawn. He was alive. Then I returned to my earlier position and nodded. "I'm ready."

Reyes nodded and prepared to release time. "In three . . ."

"You know they're wrong about you."

"Later," he said, letting his head fall to the ground again. "Two . . ."

"You aren't evil."

"Dutch. Do you want to get hit again?"

"Are you threatening to spank me?" I teased.

He glared. "Them. If you talk . . . one . . ."

I whispered to Angel as fast as I could, "Tell me when the cops are close." Then I looked at Reyes again. At my beautiful, heartbreaking, breathtaking husband. "And they're wrong."

"No, Dutch," he said sadly. "They're not."

Time slingshot back into place just as, yep, a hand whipped across my face. At least they were back to hitting me with an open hand.

They picked up exactly where they left off. I waited for Angel to let me know when to move. If Reyes could walk, he could get to the gates and open them while I led them in the opposite direction, not that I had any idea where the gates were. But the car had left tracks in the dirt. That was enough to figure out which way not to go.

One of the men holding Reyes spoke up. "Did you hear that?"

They stopped. Everyone stood still and listened.

"What?" Mr. Foster said.

The man shrugged. "I thought I heard . . ."

"They're about two miles away," Angel said.

While their attention was elsewhere, I shot to my feet and ran. Or, well, stumbled to my feet and did an interpretive dance of autumn leaves dying and falling off a tree.

I'd expected to let them chase me. To lead them away from the front gates so the local law enforcement could get in. What I hadn't expected was the loud crack that split the air and echoed against the walls. A searing pain that burst in my back. What seemed like a hundred white-hot pokers stabbed me from behind, and I tripped, skidded onto my knees, and pitched forward, ending up barely twenty feet from where I'd started.

Reyes jerked in his constraints, but I shook my head. He had to see this through. To finish it.

But I hadn't expected them to finish it first. I lay on the ground, bleeding out, and watched as they put the shotgun to Reyes's chest.

I cried out in horror. Had he been wrong after all? Could he die? It was simply not worth the risk.

Fear consumed me to the marrow of my bones.

Blood pumped into my stomach and lungs and throat.

A pain like an inferno spread through me, but all I could think about was Reyes.

A microsecond before they pulled the trigger, Mr. Foster shushed them again. Sirens could be heard in the distance, prompting the Diviners into action.

"Close the gate!" he yelled.

Reyes and Angel had been right. My plan had sucked. The Diviners scrambled to get to the gate before Reyes could get there.

Mr. Foster turned and nodded toward his man. The shotgun exploded. Buckshot plowed into Reyes's chest at point-blank range. He shuddered and coughed before going still.

I covered my mouth with both hands. This was not happening. Blood pumped out of him in a slow and steady stream.

"You have to know," he said. Just like he had before. "Dematerialize."

"I . . . I can't." My chest ached, but not from the buckshot. "I have holes."

The grin that slid across his face was a most wicked thing. "I know. I like your holes." He really was evil. The Fosters were right! "Do it, Dutch."

"But the holes. The ones in my back."

"Dutch . . ."

"All right. Holy crackerjacks."

But before I could act, his lids drifted shut. And for a split second, I studied his face. Beaten and bloody but serene. No, accepting. Just like in that picture. He'd resigned himself to his fate as though . . . as though he deserved it. The Fosters did that to him. Earl Walker did that to him. Made him feel less than he was.

The anger that truth evoked was the catalyst I needed. I dove inside myself, struggled past the drugs, dug my heels in and forced my molecules apart.

The world exploded. Storms raged around me in both the celestial realm and the tangible. I made the Earth quake and tremble, as though trying to shake some sense into it. I bent the winds to my will, forcing them to twist and curve and spiral. Forcing them to do my bidding.

Then I saw everything. I saw the Diviners arming themselves and running for the gate, trying to close it before the cavalry arrived. I saw others barricading themselves inside the main building. I saw people running and stumbling, trying to get away from the tornado. From my tornado.

I ripped the gate from its hinges. Tore the doors off the main building. Threw men into trees and onto roofs.

Then I turned back to the barn. I lay Shawn gently on the ground and knelt beside my husband. His eyes were open and he seemed to be looking at me with something akin to admiration.

I knelt beside him and punched him as hard as I could. Not really. But Hard.

"You didn't die."

"God," he said by way of an explanation. When I rolled my eyes, he added. "You're so gullible."

I did a full-body scan. My sweater was a goner, but I was still alive and kicking. "I'm alive!" I said, raising my arms in victory. Then I looked back at Reyes. "Your turn."

"Not just yet. Remember, this has to look good."

I gave him a once-over. "It looks good. A little too good. As in, they may wonder why you're still breathing. Please, Reyes."

"Dutch, I'm fine. Promise."

Finally able to touch him, I put my hands on his face. "Why did you let them do this to you?"

"I told you—"

"I don't believe you." I set my chin and glared, but only a little. "I think you wanted to be punished. For some idiotic reason, I think you wanted them to do this. And worse."

His smile held more sadness than humor. "So, was the plan to run and stumble and get shot in the back or to call out your inner tornado? Either way, I'm impressed."

"Do you remember what they did to you?" I asked, ignoring him. "As a baby?" The very thought broke my heart. "Please tell me you're not lying."

"Have I ever lied to you?"

I closed my eyes in a pathetic attempt to block out the truth. He did remember. At some point over the last few weeks, probably when he learned his godly name, he became like me. He remembered everything.

He raised up until his mouth was at my ear and whispered, "Don't." Then he moved his mouth to my other ear. "Don't you dare."

I filled my lungs and helped him to a sitting position. "So, yeah, the tornado thing was kind of plan B. If the cops know there has been a crime committed, they don't have to wait for paperwork and the likes, right? They can just come in? Because the gate is kind of nonexistent at this point, so nothing but Johnny Law stopping them."

"Far as I know."

Angel popped back in. "There're here."

I nodded and brushed my mouth across Reyes's.

Then I stood and ran to the opening of the barn.

People were running from one building to another, carrying weapons and supplies. One guy fell out of a tree with a loud thud. My bad. And in the distance, lights flashed as cars sped toward us.

The Diviners scattered like cockroaches as official vehicles stormed in one after another. And someone invited the National Guard. Those guys were always trouble.

Most of the parishioners ran for the main building, which would lead to a similar situation. Despite the fact that I'd ripped off the doors, crazy people were still barricading themselves inside. Those things never ended well.

Cruisers and official SUVs skidded to a halt inside the compound, stirring up enough dust to give all the members time to run and hide. The officers opened their vehicle doors and took cover behind them, aiming their guns.

An ambulance waited in the wings.

"Well, crap," I said to Angel. "I'm all better. I don't have a scratch on me."

"But your clothes look messed up. Bad." Angel gave me a thumbs-up, then disappeared into the melee.

I ran back to my husband. "Reyes—"

"Behind you," he said softly.

Only this time, instead of getting bludgeoned, I shifted as the butt of a rifle slammed toward me. The man, the beefy one, almost fell forward when it passed clean through.

I stood and faced him, ignoring the confused expression on his face. "That is enough."

When he went to hit me again, Reyes was there. He hadn't dematerialized. He'd broken the ropes, as he could have done hours ago, walked behind the man, grabbed his jaw and the back of his head, and twisted.

A crack proved that he'd broken the man's neck. I'd tried to warn them. He crumpled to the floor. Then another crack, only from gunfire, echoed around us, and another, but not from any of the guns outside. These were coming from inside the main building. But they weren't firing at the cops outside. They were firing inside.

"Oh, my God, Reyes. They're killing them!"

I ran forward before Reyes could stop me and sprinted across the compound, yelling to Uncle Bob. "They're killing them! Uncle Bob, hurry!"

To the surprise of the other officers, Uncle Bob scrambled from behind a cruiser and followed me, as did Garrett, who'd apparently tagged along. I slammed against a bookcase blocking the entrance, but Reyes was right behind me. He pushed me back into Uncle Bob's arms and said, "Hold her."

With one solid thrust, he broke down the barricade and dove into the darkness inside. Two more shots sounded as I struggled against Ubie. Then nothing.

I pushed out of Uncle Bob's arms and rushed inside, but Garrett hurried past me to lead the way, flashlight on, pistol at the ready.

People were huddled in corners and underneath tables, while a woman, a teenaged boy, and two men lay dead. Rifles lay beside the two men. The woman and teen had been shot in what could have become one of the worst mass shootings on American soil. I could only assume they didn't have time to mix the Kool-Aid, so they were taking out the members with bullets one by one.

The men had clearly had their necks snapped, compliments of my husband.

I ran to the woman and boy and knelt beside them. Feeling for any sign of life. There was none.

Reyes came back through a doorway and did some kind of military gang signs to Garrett, sending him into the room he'd just come from.

"Reyes." I rushed to him but took great care when I walked into his arms, trying not to cling. Failing as my arms locked around him. As my fingers curled into his shirt.

He seemed completely unfazed by his injuries as he stared down at me. "The Fosters?" I asked.

He shook his head. "They're here somewhere. They have to be."

Damn it. I'd lost track of them when I went all tornado. Which, who knew that was possible? Show of hands.

Uncle Bob raced in then with several uniforms. They checked the bodies and began assessing the other Diviners.

Ubie took Reyes's hand in a firm shake. "You've looked better."

"So have you," he teased.

"Hey," I said, interrupting, "where the hell are we?"

They both grinned. "We're near a town called Datil," Ubie said, "just west of Socorro."

Socorro was south of Albuquerque. That part I knew. Had been to the pretty town many times. But Datil? "There's a Datil, New Mexico?"

"There is. Your dad never told you about it? The area is gorgeous. Your dad wanted to put in a ski resort and call it Ski Datil. Get it?"

I laughed into Reyes's shirt, and he pulled me closer, wrapping a large hand around my head and kissing the top of it.

Uncle Bob cleared his throat and placed an uncomfortable gaze on my husband. "I hate to be a downer, Farrow, but did you get shot?"

He shrugged and pulled me tighter. "I wasn't the only one." When I signaled him with a look of panic, he gestured toward the back room, and said, "There are three more victims in there."

"Damn," I said. "How many did they kill before you got to them?"

"Five."

"Any . . . ?" I lowered my head. "Any children?"

He gestured toward the teen. "Besides that kid, no. It looks like some of the adults were protecting them."

My heart broke. Odds were most of those people just wanted a home. A safe place to live and raise their children. They probably showed up with only the clothes on their backs, and the Fosters took advantage of that.

Medical swarmed in, and we were officially on active duty as Uncle Bob supervised the rescue efforts. We began ushering people out. I leaned down and helped an elderly woman to her feet, then I recognized her as the one who'd been holding Dawn Brooks.

"Where is Dawn?" I asked her.

Shaking a fragile finger, she pointed to a cabinet. "I stashed her in there when the shooting started."

"Bless you."

Reyes took hold of her arm as I dove for the cabinet.

"I didn't even know they had guns here," she added.

I opened the cabinet door and peeked inside. Huddled in the farthest corner was a tiny ball of curls. "Dawn?" I said gently. She shook and was crying into her dress. "Dawn Brooks? I'm here to take you home."

She dared a peek at me, her face hopeful. She wanted to trust me, but she'd been through a lot. I didn't rush anything. I sat beside the open cabinet and gave her time to adjust to my presence. After a few moments, I held out my hand. She eyed it, then slowly reached out to me. I pulled her out of the cabinet and lifted her into my arms.

"Are you uh angel?"

I laughed softly. She did have a gift. The Fosters were right. "I get that a lot. But, no, I'm not. I'm just a girl like you."

She shook her head. "I don't fink so."

Oh yeah. She rocked.

She wrapped her arms around my neck and refused to let go the rest of the night, even as I saw after Shawn, made sure he was the first one taken to the hospital. Even as I asked Diviner after Diviner where the Fosters were. None of them knew. Well, almost none. A couple of the higher-ups knew more than they were letting on, but short of torturing them with a three-year-old in my arms, I saw no way to get the information out of them.

They were devout. Not to their faith or their religion. To the Fosters. Getting information out of them would take some time.

I called Cookie, who was frantic. Worried sick. At her wit's end. And I'd better not forget it. I'd taken ten years off her life. Ten good years she could have used to explore Europe. But all that was null and void because I'd shaved those years right off.

I loved that woman so.

By 2:00 A.M., things were not calming down at all. It seemed like every emergency services vehicle in a five-hundred-mile radius was on scene as well as reporters and the average lookie-loo. A small hotel-slash-restaurant from Datil, the Eagle Guest Ranch, provided coffee and water and sandwiches to the emergency crew, and a church group from Socorro provided blankets to the Diviners since they couldn't go back inside to get their things.

Ubie walked up to me. "Pumpkin, you've had a long day. Maybe you should go home."

I was still holding Dawn. We'd wrapped her in a blanket, and she'd fallen asleep, her head on my shoulder, her warm breath on my neck. I doubted I'd ever get the feeling back in my arm again, but it was so worth it.

"I will," I said, rubbing the doll's back, "but first, how were you able to just come in? I thought you'd need a warrant or something."

"Not when you have the permission of the owner," he said, pulling a piece of paper out of his pocket. "This guy's apparently a client of yours?"

I looked over to see Shawn Foster walking forward. After a stunned moment, I rushed toward him. His face was swollen and his lip split open, but he looked good considering what he'd just been through.

"Shawn, how are you here? I thought an ambulance took you to the hospital?"

"I came back. I'm so sorry, Charley." He glanced around in shock. "If I'd had any idea they would do this . . ."

"Shawn, this is not your fault."

"No, I should have warned you. I'm no longer involved in my parents' delusions, but I have people inside who keep me informed. I knew they were stockpiling guns. I just had no idea."

"I'm the one who's sorry. I can't believe the Fosters, the people who raised you, would do such a horrible thing to you."

"Yeah, that's why they're called fanatics."

"But how are you up and walking and talking and—"

"Well," he said, suddenly uncomfortable, "I heal pretty fast."

"Of course. You're Nephilim."

"How did you—"

"Actually, it was Reyes."

The two of them shook hands. Shawn seemed a little star struck. I could hardly blame him.

"You gave permission for the authorities to come in?" I asked him.

"I did. Weeks ago. The FBI has been investigating the Diviners for years and, technically, it's all mine. The land. The buildings. Everything." He turned bitter. "Dear old Dad didn't want anything in his name, so he put it all in mine years ago."

Sounded like him.

"Do you have access to the paperwork?" I asked, praying there'd be something about the fake adoption agency the Fosters had set up.

"Every forged document."

With that paperwork, we had a chance of getting the charges against Veronica Isom dropped.

"What about your par . . . the Fosters. Any idea where they went?"

He shook his head. "I do know they were building something in the main barn."

"Building something?"

"I don't know what. My contacts weren't in the inner circle, but they did say the guys were spending a lot of time in there."

"Thanks. I'll check it out."

I strolled that way, trying to steer clear of the emergency crew as Uncle Bob spoke with Shawn. I hadn't noticed any new construction in the barn, but I'd been pretty out of it.

"Want me to take her?" Reyes asked, scanning the yard for any sign of danger.

"I'm good." I hugged her to me, seemingly unable to put her down. I buried my face in her curls and breathed in her scent before asking, "Do you feel them?"

"The Fosters? No. But there's a lot of emotion here to sort through."

"True."

However, the moment we walked into the barn, we felt them. They were hiding like little rats, and I realized the bales of hay in the corner were covering something up. The Diviners had built a hidden room.

We eased closer. Reyes, who still didn't want to shift, to heal himself instantaneously, put a finger over his mouth, motioned me to stay back, and stepped toward the wall of hay. He went around what we could see but found no door.

I gestured to him that I would go around back. He lowered his head and gave me a warning scowl.

"What?" I mouthed. Fine. I stayed put for Dawn's sake.

She stirred, and I bounced her as Reyes pushed, testing the hay in this place or that. When nothing worked, I checked the dirt floor. Maybe there was an underground access point. But before I got too far, we heard a click.

Reyes had pushed on the side and found a panel of some kind. I stepped over to him as he pulled. A door gave way to total darkness, but they were inside. I could feel them. I patted my jeans for the flashlight Garrett had given me, found it, then jumped when a gunshot splintered the air.

Without thought, I shifted and slowed time at once. The gun had not been aimed at me. Nor at Reyes. The bullet traveling at what seemed like light speed headed straight toward the back of Dawn's head.

I clutched her to me and closed my eyes, only I'd shifted so I could still see. Could still watch as the bullet entered her skull, traveled through it, continued through my neck, and stopped only when Reyes closed his hand around it.

Anger ignited inside me like the splitting of an atom that set off a nuclear bomb. I turned on them. The evil beings who hurt. Who took advantage of and destroyed. Who murdered in His name. If that wasn't taking God's name in vain, I didn't know what was.

I had no control over the rage that boiled inside me, the power that burst out of me in one blinding flash. So hot it scorched my skin and singed my hair. So cold it froze the air around us.

Reyes stepped between me and the Fosters. Wrapped his arms around both Dawn and me. Soothed my soul with his warm breath fanning across my ear. He cupped my chin and his fingers brushed my cheek.

Then I realized it wasn't his fingers, but the feathers of his massive, black wings. He was blocking the scene before me. The scene I'd caused. But I was too busy being fascinated with the musical sound I heard when his wings brushed me. A tinkling melody, like ice defrosting under the heat of the sun. And I realized it was ice. His wings were brushing across the ice on my arm. On my face. And then, just as quickly as it had appeared, it evaporated. His heat had melted it.

Uncle Bob ran in, followed closely by Garrett and Shawn. I knew Ubie and Garrett couldn't see Reyes's wings, but I wondered if Shawn could.

"Take her," Reyes said, and I realized he'd dematerialized when the gun went off. He'd ruined his injured look, not that we needed it. We had enough on the Fosters to put them away for a very long time.

It was Garrett's horrified expression that finally dragged me out of my thoughts. Shawn looked inside and paled. I leaned to see past Reyes, but he wouldn't let me. He kept himself between me and the room behind him.

I glared. Then I tensed. Then I worried. What had I done? A spike of anxiety rushed through me, causing an electrical surge to shoot over my skin.

"Reyes," I whispered as Garrett wrapped his hands over my shoulders, "what did I do?"

Garrett urged me back, gently leading me away. But I had to know. I pulled out of his grip and rushed past my husband. Mr. and Mrs. Foster lay in a pile of twisted and mangled limbs, as though every bone in their bodies had been shattered from the inside out. Their heads lay at unnatural angles and it was almost impossible to tell where one Foster sibling ended and the other began.

I threw a hand over my mouth and turned to Reyes. "I didn't do that. Did I do that? How could I do that?" Then to Shawn. "I'm so sorry."

Reyes bit down and gestured for Garrett to get me away. Several other officers were filing in, wondering where the gunshot had come from, as Garrett led me outside.

Shawn came out first. A resolved sadness had overcome him. I wanted to talk to him, but say what? Sorry for horridly mangling the people who raised you?

Reyes came out a while later, but everyone else was taking turns getting a glimpse of the Fosters, as though they were a sideshow attraction.

He walked up and covered me with a blanket.

"Dawn should have woken when the gun went off," I said to him.

"You shifted her," Reyes said as though proud of me.

"That's why she didn't wake up?"

"That would be my guess."

I had the feeling her comalike state had something to do with our shift onto a celestial plane as well. If she wasn't different before, she danged sure would be now.

"I killed them."

"If you hadn't, I would have. You also saved that little girl's life. Along with who knows how many others."

"But I didn't just kill them. I . . . mutilated them."

"Dutch—"

"I really am a monster."

He took my shoulders and turned me toward him. "You, Dutch, are by no means a monster. If anything, they got off easy."

I didn't buy it for a minute, but another conundrum popped into my addled mind. "How can I explain this to Uncle Bob?"

"You don't have to. The official report will say the Fosters were hiding in a secret room when a wall of cinderblocks they'd stored there fell on them. There was a whole pile out back. It's taken care of."

I didn't know what to say. I lowered my head and rocked Dawn. An ambulance was waiting to transport her to a hospital in Albuquerque, but I couldn't put her down just yet. Reyes sat with me, wrapped his arms around both of us, and took some of Dawn's weight off my back.

The sun crested the horizon when I noticed a couple, frantic and searching, standing behind the crime-scene tape. They were talking to a young deputy, trying to convince her that they'd been called to the scene by APD.

I stood, shaking Reyes out of a light slumber, and walked closer.

"Please, they said they were going to transport our daughter to a hospital, but we couldn't wait. She's still out here."

"Sir, I can't let you through either way."

But the deputy's words weren't getting through. As the man argued with her, the woman spotted me walking forward with my bundle. I recognized them from news articles, so I pulled the blanket off Dawn's hair. Mrs. Brooks cried out, ducked under the tape, and ran for dear life, dodging one officer after another like a professional running back.

Dawn must've heard her mother's cries. She blinked awake and rubbed her eyes.

"Is that funny woman your mommy?" I asked her.

She finally looked over. After a moment, recognition set in. She took the thumb out of her mouth and bucked her legs in the international signal for *put me the hell down*. Then she ran as fast as her twelve-inch legs would carry her, meeting her mother at the thirty-yard line.

Her father wasn't far behind. They scooped Dawn up and formed a huddle. Only they cried a lot more in theirs than most huddlers do.

Mrs. Brooks looked over at me just as I started to walk away. "Charley?" she asked.

Good guess. I nodded and walked back to them.

"I spoke with your uncle on the phone. He said you helped solve this case."

"Only a little."

This was definitely a convergence of anomalies. Shawn hiring me. Dr. Schwab's receptionist, Tiana, opening up to me. Reyes getting abducted. Again.

"We can't thank you enough." Her voice cracked, and her shoulders began to shake.

I shook my head. "You know who you should really thank?" I stepped closer and told her all about Tiana from Dr. Schwab's office, where Mrs. Foster had worked. "If not for her, I would never have known about Dawn. Tiana suspected the Fosters had something to do with her disappearance and had even reported them to the police. They just couldn't find anything on them."

"Until now," Mr. Brooks said. He exuded gratitude, but this was a bizarre case of blind luck and coincidence.

Then again. I looked toward the heavens. I was beginning to believe less and less in coincidence.

20

Two days later, I sat outside Calamity's, having lunch with Shawn, who was still a little beaten up, and possibly a little sad, but no worse for the wear. Cookie had found his parents, and I wanted to give him the information in person. And to thank him.

"I can't believe it," he said, staring down at the paper. "They really did die in a fire."

"I'm sorry. It was most likely set by the Fosters. They didn't want to risk the authorities coming after them again."

"But they did, anyway, right? The authorities?"

"Yes. When it was discovered that you didn't die in the fire, they suspected it had been set to cover up your abduction. They just had so little to go on, and the Fosters were clearly good at what they did."

He stared at the pictures Cookie had found of them. Ran his fingers over his mother's face.

"But you have family. You have an aunt and two uncles and several cousins. I'm sure they'd love to meet you."

He nodded, not quite ready to take that step. "Their information is in the file?"

"It is. And if you need me to make the initial contact, should you decide to meet them, I'd be happy to."

"Thanks. I'll think about it."

Uncle Bob had found enough evidence to exonerate Veronica Isom. The Fosters may have been psychotic, but they'd kept meticulous records. We were still working on the other children they'd abducted. One was living in Albuquerque. Two more were found at the compound. And countless others were still unaccounted for.

The press had dubbed them the Divine Siblings. Even above the atrocities they'd committed, the fact that they were married siblings was what caught national headlines.

Shawn filled his lungs, closed the file, and took a sip of his iced tea. "This is a nice place."

"It is. It belonged to my dad before Reyes bought it."

"So, Reyes."

I thought he might broach that subject eventually.

"He's kind of like a brother in a weird, demented kind of way."

"I agree."

He wanted a brother. I could sense it. He wanted someone he could talk to. Someone he could confide in like he had the other night. They'd gotten along so well, I felt Reyes would benefit from such a relationship as well.

"Shawn, I have to ask. Why did you give the Fosters an alibi the night Dawn Brooks was taken? You told the police they had been home that night."

"Because they really were home. But as you can tell, they had a lot of followers who would do anything they told them to." He dipped his chin and bit down. "Anything."

I could only wonder what he meant by that. "Why not tell me about the compound?"

He lifted a shoulder. "I grew up out there. Spent my summers there. Those people were like family. They were just . . . lost."

"And murderous."

He nodded. "I didn't know. Mom—" He cleared his throat. "Eve kept that part private. All I knew was that I loved going out there even though the adults were crazy. That's what we thought growing up."

"We?"

"Us kids who were raised at the compound. We always knew something wasn't quite right there."

"Did you know the Fosters were brother and sister?"

He froze. Pressed his mouth together. Grew even paler.

Crap. "You know what? Let's just save that for later."

He shook his head. "Please tell me you're kidding."

Apparently he hadn't seen the paper. I looked down and gave him a moment to deal. But I eventually let my gaze wander up and went back to staring.

Knowing what Shawn was, the product of a union thousands of years ago between an angel and a human, had kept my gaze locked onto him through most of lunch. Like, I couldn't stop staring. He was a blond version of Reyes. Absolutely beautiful, though not as compelling. Not as . . . what was the word? Sexy? Exotic? Dripping with sin? But still. The coolness factor sitting across from me rated right up there with pumpkin spiced lattes and Chuck Norris.

Shawn chuckled, probably trying to cover up for the awkward silence of my thousand-yard stare.

"What?" I snapped out of it. "Wow, I'm so sorry, Shawn. It's just, I didn't know your kind existed. It's so cool."

"Well, in all fairness, I didn't know your kind existed, either. I mean, have you looked in the mirror?"

"Do I have something in my teeth?" I turned to look at my reflection in the window behind us.

"No, I mean, your light. It's crazy bright."

"Yeah, I can't really see it, though I did force it into a former slave demon from hell so that I could sneak up on a god incognito, and I saw it then. Really bright."

"Is that how you did it?"

I turned to an elderly man standing beside us, stunned that he'd gotten that close without my feeling his presence. His essence.

Then again, he emanated zero emotion. That wasn't what I did feel. I felt the staggering power radiating out of him. The waves of energy.

Shawn knew something about the man was different. I felt interest from him. And confusion.

"How I did what?" I arched a brow as arrogantly as I could. "How I snuck up on your bestie and took him out in a matter of minutes?"

Shawn grew alarmed. He glanced over his shoulder, wondering if he should go inside and get Reyes.

The man shuffled toward us, barely able to walk, but we both knew that was not the case. When he came around, a little girl stepped out from behind him. He held her hand, the smile on her face forced there, plastic like a Barbie's.

"Eidolon, I presume?"

He was corporeal. He'd taken a human body. He had blood that could be used to trap him. I slid a hand inside my pocket and wrapped my fingers around the god glass.

He held up a palm to stop me. "Please. I am not half as stupid as my . . . bestie? If you even think of taking the glass out of your pocket, I'll snap the girl's neck." He sat down and hugged the girl to him, his hand tight around her jaw. But her smile stayed in place. Her eyes remained unblinking. "And if you summon him, she won't live long enough to see him materialize."

I could only assume he meant Reyes.

"You've already lost one of your precious humans. Although all I see is old leather and a bag of bones."

The poor man whose body Eidolon had confiscated had died the moment he took it over. The power was too much for the human system. And it would start to decay immediately. Eidolon didn't have much time.

"I only took him because he was close by and he could hold me long enough to have this chat." He pointed an aged finger at me. "I know how much you humans like to chat." He smiled wide and indicated the girl. "Plus, this body came with a ready-made bargaining chip. She is his granddaughter. Two for the price of one."

The walls of my chest tightened. As did his grip on her jaw. Tears slipped past her lashes and slid like silver ribbons down her face.

"Please let her go. Take me instead."

"Posh." He waved off the notion. "You think I don't know what you are?"

"You're one, too. You could kill me. Just let her go."

"Don't patronize me," he ordered from between gritted teeth. "I told you. I know what you are, Elle-Ryn."

I blinked in confusion. A god could kill another god. What did he mean?

"You are thirteen strong. You have gifts passed down from the original seven, made stronger every time you"—he leaned in and chuckled—"conquered another of your brethren. I'll wait for the right moment, if that's okay with you."

"Conquered? I don't understand. The seven original gods from my plane melded together."

He burst out laughing. Because of the host he'd chosen, it came out more as a cackle. Did he choose an elderly man to set our minds at ease? To make himself appear harmless? 'Cause it wasn't working.

"They melded? Who told you that, little god?"

"I'm not little. If what you say is true, I'm stronger than you."

"That you are. I meant no offense. I only meant that, of all the gods to exist, you are the youngest. Have you not heard what you are called?"

I knew it before he said it.

"You are the god eater. The one to survive a war that raged for eons. The lone survivor, for you eventually ate them all. You are the victor, and to the victor goes the spoils." He gestured toward Reyes, who was inside working the bar. "And what lovely spoils they are."

When Shawn inched closer, Eidolon tightened his hold on the girl's throat. He held her in some kind of a trance. On the outside, she looked perfectly calm. But on the inside, terror ripped her mind to shreds. He was torturing her. Terrorizing her.

Shawn backed down but didn't relax.

"You're lying," I said, racking my brain for some kind of plan. No way could I get to the girl. He'd snap her neck before I got two inches. "My dimension is peaceful. I've seen it."

He roared at that, his false teeth almost flying out. He stuffed them back in. "Jehovah really did a number on you, did He not? A number. Where do they come up with such witty phrases, do you suppose?"

"I wouldn't know."

"You are the most violent of all the war gods from your dimension. And the most cunning. Which would explain why you are here instead of Al-Deesh or Ran-Eeth or Ayn-Eethial or . . . I could go on. Or perhaps you don't remember the gods you ate?"

I ate gods? I really was a god eater? In the literal sense? Was I any different than the Colombian who wanted to eat my flesh to absorb my power?

No. He was wrong. Ran-Eeth and Ayn-Eethial merged to form me. That much I did remember. He was lying.

"Why do you think you're here?" he continued. "Jehovah is baby-sitting you. Nothing more. Do you think He needed to outsource for the reaper position? He had His choice among billions."

"You know, every time I talk to one of you gods or an angel or a departed who might know a little more than most, I get a different take on what I am. I'm Charley Davidson. That's what I am. I don't go to war. I don't eat gods. I'm the least violent person you'll ever meet."

"Oh yes. I could sense your peaceful nature when you had the Razer kill all those men the other night."

I startled, surprised he knew about the Colombians.

"It is in every fiber of your being. You devour your enemy without remorse. You make war look like child's play. The generals of this world would do well to recruit you."

I wasn't going to argue with him.

"Then why are you here?" I asked as if I didn't know. But I had to stall. To come up with a plan. I couldn't just stop time to try to get to her. It wouldn't work on him. He'd be right there with me. I didn't dare try to get Reyes's attention, although he'd probably figure it out sooner rather than later.

"Ah. Well, as you know, we are gods. We can go anywhere and become anything we desire on any plane as long as we have a way to get there. A portal? And therein lies my problem. Lucifer got us into this dimension. He used Rey'azikeen to do it. But the Razer only works between this dimension and Lucifer's. Doesn't do me much good. Therefore, I need a portal that can get me anywhere."

"I'm a portal."

"Yes, well, your Jehovah and I are not on speaking terms at the moment. He owes me a few thousand soldiers. Never paid up on a contract." He leaned closer. "Just between us, don't trust the Guy. No, I need your daughter."

Every muscle in my body tensed in a knee-jerk reaction.

"I am not here to kill her, Elle-Ryn," he said, rushing to appease me. "I would not be so base."

"I thought you were helping Lucifer for that very reason."

"Not at all. I just need her to get back to my home dimension. True, I'm going to kill every living being there when I get back, but you don't know how they treated me."

"What makes you think my daughter is a portal to your dimension?"

"Please, Elle-Ryn. Isn't deceit beneath us?"

How the hell did he know? I just barely found out myself. I braced myself. Forced myself to calm. To think of something to say to stall him longer. "Then . . . then why are you helping Lucifer if you just want to leave?"

"Public relations. I scratch his back sort of thing. Her death is inevitable, either way."

"You just said—"

"I don't want to kill her. I did say that. And I don't. But an everyday traveler using a portal is one thing. A god, however . . . we tend to destroy them. Portals. They're usually only good for one trip, us being so vast and powerful.

"So, yes, I will end up killing your daughter, thus fulfilling Lucifer's greatest desire. But I won't kill her out of spite or malice. I mean her no harm. Harm is just an inevitable part of who she is. It's in her genetic makeup."

I eyed him curiously, trying to keep the anger from my expression. "Perhaps I'll use your heart as a candy dish."

"Perhaps I'll split your skull while Rey'azikeen watches."

We could do this all day. Hurl threats and insults at each other. I crossed my arms. "So, again, why are you here? Did you expect me to hand my daughter over to you?"

He cackled again, thoroughly enjoying himself. "Oh, no. We'll find her eventually. We are hundreds. Thousands. If she is still on this plane, we'll find her. I just need you out of my way first."

"Do you?"

"You are proving more cumbersome than we'd imagined. Though I must say, Lucifer did warn us."

"Who is *us*?"

"Lucifer's army, of course. You didn't think he'd forgotten about you? Or your daughter? He's a little obsessed with all those prophecies that swear she is going to bring him down."

"He's just a fallen angel. I could bring him down with my little finger."

"Yes. And you should have when you had the chance. He's in his home dimension now. Safe from you."

I let the barest hint of a smile slip across my face. "Never."

He cackled again and clapped his free hand on the table.

People began to notice the hold he had on the girl. They whispered to one another. Weighed their options. Tried to decide if they should intervene.

"I'm sorry," Eidolon said. "It's just been so long since I've been around a power like yours. I'm getting—what do they call it?—a rush just being near you."

"You mean a hard-on?" I asked, trying to insult him.

"In the worst way." Before I could comment, before my next heartbeat, before the next ray of sunshine found its way into my hair, he moved. Fast, like Reyes. And just as deadly.

I threw both hands over my mouth when the girl's head whipped around. Her neck cracked, and she crumpled to the ground, her tiny body like a doll's.

I sat there, stunned, my vision blurring instantly.

Shawn moved first. He lunged for the thing that only looked like an elderly man. I barely got out the word *No!* before I heard another sharp crack. Shawn fell onto the sidewalk. His head on backwards.

People started screaming and running in the opposite direction.

Even more so when Eidolon brought out a revolver. "I have to make an impression."

He raised the gun to his head and pulled the trigger. The body he'd inhabited fell, bringing the total count up to three.

I slid to my knees beside them and stared, aghast. Why? The man was already dead.

Then it hit me. While I sat confused and focused on the bodies, Eidolon burst into a cloud of smoke—shattering the windows nearby—and enveloped me. Forced himself inside.

A blinding pain, beginning in my chest and spreading through my whole body, clawed its way into every cell. Shredded my tendons and cracked my bones. I couldn't breathe. I couldn't see. He was trying to rip me apart from the inside out. He concentrated his efforts on my heart, digging as though searching for something.

I clutched at my chest. Fought to take in air, but my lungs were cement. Just as I started to lose consciousness, I felt Reyes close by. Furious. Powerful.

I blinked, tried to focus past the pain, then wondered if I were seeing things, because he had transformed. In my blurred vision, he looked angelic. But there was nothing angelic about Rey'aziel. Colossal black wings. Solid body. Muscles cording with each movement.

He raised his sword and bought it down in one defining stroke.

Eidolon shattered. Swirled. Tried to regroup.

I gulped at the air around me and held my arms to my chest before realization dawned. Everything I felt, every ounce of pain, every spike of fear, was only the human part of me. The miniscule part. The grain of sand.

He had yet to see the rest of me. So I showed him.

The essence that was Eidolon turned to face Reyes. That seemed to make my husband happy. Reyes lowered his head. Watched him for that split second from beneath hooded lids before Eidolon launched forward.

The instant Eidolon reached him, prepared to overpower him with his energy, the malevolent god jerked back as though a dog reaching the end of a chain.

Surprised, Eidolon took an almost human shape. He gazed back at me. And if mist could look surprised, I imagined that's what it would look like.

I plunged a hand into his center. That part of him that had more mass than the rest. It was what he'd tried to get from me. My heart. The core of my being. The very center of it.

In one quick movement, I ripped it out of him, this beast who was after my daughter. I devoured it. Swallowed it whole. Then I absorbed what was left of him, the feeling one of euphoria as his molecules melted into mine.

Reyes looked on, not surprised in the least. When I turned to jelly, he was there. His arm wrapped around me. His face inches above mine.

I reached up and brushed my fingers against his wings. Astonished.

Then I remembered the girl and her grandfather and . . . and Shawn. Not to mention the pedestrians around us. Were they caught in the cross fire?

Reyes and I emerged onto the mortal plane, and I scrambled to my feet.

People were injured all up and down the street. One woman was hemorrhaging blood by the bucketsful. A piece of glass had pierced her jugular. Others were screaming and running away, their faces bloodied but otherwise okay.

I knelt beside Shawn. He was draped over the girl as though trying to protect her, but his eyes faced heavenward.

I reached down to touch him. I'd heal him first. Then the girl. Then the woman and anyone else. I didn't think I could bring the elderly man back. Once a god took up residence, there wasn't much left to bring back.

"You are forbidden," came a familiar voice.

I didn't bother looking back. Michael's energy, along with that of his spies and a few reinforcements, undulated around me. Pressed into me. Suffocated.

"They died because of a supernatural fuckup. They deserve their lives back."

"You may restore only if the soul has not already been freed. Only if it has not left the vessel and entered our Father's kingdom."

I stood and turned to him. "Their deaths were not natural. The blame lies at the feet of a god. This is on us."

He drew his sword.

And Reyes drew his as his wings slowly unfolded.

"Rey'azikeen, we have no quarrel with you."

Reyes's mouth formed a ravenous smile. "Sure you do."

Michael refocused on me. "You forget your place here. You are reaper. Nothing more. You have no right to use godly powers in a dimension that already has a God. It's"—he looked up in thought—"cheating."

"Somehow I can't seem to care."

"But it is what you agreed to when you became the portal of this world."

"I didn't agree to Jehovah stealing my memories," I said, pulling arguments out of my ass. Searching for a loophole.

"You did, actually. You made a deal. Jehovah sends the rebel to your prison instead of the hell He created for him, and you serve as reaper in this world until your term is complete."

"Yes, Mae'eldeesahn told me that much. But why take my memories?"

"Prior knowledge of where you came from would influence your duties here."

"In what way?"

"Father considers this a probationary period. If you cannot obey His laws, you will be banished. And what better way to make you follow the rules than to take your memories, the memories of what you are and what you've done? You were at war for hundreds of thousands of years in your dimension. You came out the victor even though you profess to crave peace. Still, you won. That knowledge could influence your decisions here, as they are now." I shook with anger until he added, "It was your idea, after all."

My brows slid together in disbelief. "Why would I do such a thing?"

"Do you know what war does to a being, even one as powerful as yourself? The memories are excruciating. Perhaps you are who you are now because of their absence. Perhaps you wanted to forget what you did to win."

"Why? What did I do?"

Reyes had stepped beside me. He wrapped a hand around my arm.

"That is not my concern. What you do in this world is—as is restoring a soul that has already been freed. One that has already left the vessel. It is forbidden."

"These people would not have died if Eidolon had not killed them. It is not just."

"That is not for you to decide."

"So"—I kneeled down, threateningly close to the girl—"if I restore these people, I will be banished?"

"Cast from this world forever."

Anger shook me so hard, my teeth chattered.

"Dutch," Reyes said, trying to bring me back.

I felt the anger in him as well. Felt it tighten his skin and crave release, but I also felt concern. For me. For Beep.

Michael tilted his head, waiting for my answer.

But the rage that had been bubbling suddenly sprang forth. A sword manifested in my hand and in one blinding movement, I sliced into Michael.

A thin red line spread across his chest, and one corner of my mouth tugged heavenward. "There you are," I said, mesmerized.

Despite the depth of the cut, he didn't flinch. His men, however, drew their swords and readied for battle. Reyes did the same.

I was seconds away from summoning my own army when I realized what I was doing. Risking other beings, righteous beings, because . . . why? I was angry? I was spoiled? Was I throwing a tantrum because I didn't get my way?

Maybe they were right. Maybe I was a god of war. Maybe I craved it. Lived for it. How incredibly irresponsible.

I shook out of my musings and focused on Michael. "Did you give Jehovah my message?" I asked him, referring to our earlier conversation where I'd promised to take over the world.

"I did."

"And?"

"He will meet you on the battlefield at your leisure should you name the place and time."

I stood taken aback. The battlefield? Fight? Jehovah? God? The same

God I grew up worshiping and talking to when no one else would listen? I'd always known He was there, watching over me.

Still, I was angry. To wield such power only to have it suppressed. To have it caged when it could do so much good. I wanted to spout something super sassy, but nothing came out.

Michael seemed to sense my sudden inability to form a complete sentence. He stepped closer despite his angels tensing.

Reyes stepped closer, too.

"Elle-Ryn-Ahleethia, perhaps you'd like some time to think about it."

"Yes," I said, nodding. I glanced down at the sword in my hand. It was ancient, and I got the feeling it had already seen many battles. Too many. I was here for a reason, and that reason was probably not to take over this world.

The sword disappeared, and I shouldered past Michael to do what I could, what I was allowed to do. I knelt beside the woman with the plate of glass in her neck. Since we were still incorporeal, she couldn't see me. She held on to the glass, knowing that removing it meant certain death. Blood bubbled out of her nose and mouth, and the fear in her eyes, the sheer terror, wrapped its tendrils around my heart and squeezed.

Before she knew what was happening, I melted the glass, put my hand on her throat, and healed her. If that was all I could do, that was all I could do.

Michael stood over me. Reyes at his side, making sure he didn't get too close.

"It will be harder for you now," Michael said, "knowing what you know. What you are capable of. You are like an addict who has gotten a taste of heroin after years of sobriety. Only if you fall back into old habits, you will lose your family forever."

21

"What did he mean by *old habits*? If I am this god of war and I crave the blood of my enemies like others crave, say, coffee—just thinking off the top of my head—why would righting a wrongful death be forbidden? Wouldn't that be a step in the right direction? I can see war being forbidden, or starting a revolution, or . . . whatever else war gods do, but righting a wrong?"

Dr. Mayfield sat on Spock, a logical armchair that cattycornered Captain Kirk, taking notes. I hadn't seen her since I'd left her with Logan, the mischievous Native American vampire. She'd checked on her sister, traveled the world a bit, and now worked as a psychiatrist for the departed. And, apparently, for me.

"It makes no sense," I continued. "But this bottle of tequila sure does."

I turned it upside down and let the liquid scorch my throat. I'd never really understood why people drank when they were miserable. It only made matters worse in the long run. But for some reason, tequila seemed like the answer.

Surely, I was meant for more. And why would I agree to have my data banks deleted?

"Are you going to be okay?" she asked me. She had a blunt force trauma who needed her to analyze his recurring nightmare tugging on her shirtsleeve. My time had been up half an hour ago, anyway.

I nodded. "I'm glad you're still working."

She closed her notebook. "Me, too. I'll check in on you tomorrow."

I saluted her with the near-empty bottle as she vanished. Then I took out the pendant, the god glass, and held it in my hand. Rubbed the glass cover. Studied the intricate design.

If I couldn't save people in this world, how could I save any in the next? The next being a hell dimension created by Jehovah for His rebellious brother, Rey'azikeen. My husband.

Two questions arose immediately when I'd first come upon this information: First, what kind of god builds a hell dimension for the sole purpose of imprisoning His brother? Second, what the hell did Reyes do that was so bad his own Brother built a hell dimension just for him? It was kind of like his very own Holiday Inn, only without the pool or room service.

Then again, what did I know? It could have been created with all kinds of luxuries. All kinds of amenities to make the long, lonely hours of an eternity in solitary confinement more bearable.

But my gut reaction to the words *hell* and *dimension* would suggest otherwise.

I ran my fingers along the warm surface of the pendant. I used to think that it was always warm because I carried it in my pocket, against the heat of my body. I later came to realize its warmth was probably more a product of what it housed. Maybe all hell dimensions were hot. I would think there would be a need for a cold one, or perhaps a really humid one, just to add a little variety.

The image of the little girl Eidolon had killed, so utterly terrified and unable to even move, flashed in my mind again. But Jose Cuervo came to the rescue. He was such a great guy.

I realized Reyes had been watching me spill my guts to Dr. Mayfield and get wasted at the same time from the comfort of Captain Kirk. He'd been drinking, too, but his tastes were a little more uptown. He was probably drinking scotch or bourbon or some other drink that sounded sexy when it rolled off the tongue.

I was pouting. I'd refused to take the comfort any of our furniture had to offer. Instead, we sat in a corner, Jose and I, brushing up on our bladder-capacity skills. So far, so good.

I stopped studying the pendant and studied my husband instead. Studied how he always folded his shirtsleeves in the evenings, or pushed them up, depending on the shirt, to expose his forearms. He did it on purpose. He had to know what his forearms did to me. And his biceps. And his shoulders. And pretty much every other part of him.

He sat, bathed in fire. His legs outstretched. His shirt and jeans unbuttoned. Boots thrown under the coffee table.

Just when I was going to give in, to throw in the towel and seek out the porcelain pot, Reyes spoke. "Send me."

"Okay, but I don't know how that's going to help. It's my bladder that needs emptying."

He didn't look at me when he said it. He was busy studying the fire while I was busy studying him. "Send me inside. I was born and raised in a hell dimension. I can go in and bring them back."

The god glass? Was he honestly suggesting I send him into the very dimension for which the god glass had been created?

"No." I rose and stumbled to the bathroom. Not because I was drunk but because I had a cramp in my left butt cheek. I always forgot to stay hydrated when fighting evil gods and arguing with arrogant angels.

Then again, all angels were arrogant. I was 99 percent certain.

I peed, did a drive-by in the kitchen on the way back to my corner, and sank down to curl up with a fresh bottle of my new BFF.

"Is it me, or is it harder to get drunk all of a sudden?" Normally I'd be puking my guts up after even half a bottle of Jose. But I was pretty good. Aside from that whole world-tilting-to-the-left thing, I felt great.

Reyes pushed off the captain and walked up to me. No, he swaggered up to me, a severe expression on his beautiful face, his shirt open, showing the expanse of his chest. He stopped and towered over me. "Send me."

Now I was just getting annoyed. "No. Kuur is in there. You remember Kuur? The supernatural assassin who has killed beings from dozens of dimensions just because he can? Yeah, him. And let's not forget the god that killed your sister."

"You don't think I can take them?"

"I'm not willing to risk it either way."

"It was meant for me, anyway. I'd like to see what my Brother had in store for His sibling. What kind of god He is."

What kind of god indeed. I wondered that, too, but I wondered it even more so about myself. Clearly, I was not the girl I thought I was. I only pretended to want peace? I was in the Peace Corps, for heaven's sake.

He sat beside me, drink in hand. "It can be an experiment."

"Reyes, I cannot tell you how hard of a no this is. It is not going to happen, so give it up."

"Send me in, wait sixty, then call me back. I'll scope out the place."

"I may not be Miss Know-It-All when it comes to all this god stuff, but I do know that time works differently in every dimension. Sixty seconds here could be six hundred years there."

He sank down beside me, our shoulders touching. "The time slip isn't that much. If anything, it could be maybe a year. Or it could be the opposite and I'd come back so fast I didn't get to see anything. At which point we can reevaluate and decide what to do next."

"No, I think Kuur said a few seconds was years there."

"We'll never know until you send me in."

I sat Jose aside. "Reyes, why? Is this some kind of quest for revenge against Mae'eldeesahn?"

His smile held about as much humor as a pit viper's. "No."

"And what if something goes wrong and, I don't know, I can't get you back?"

"The priest did it. You told me."

"Yes, but, there are no guarantees. This information came from an evil demon assassin."

"What part of life is guaranteed? It's all a guessing game, including this glass. This dimension."

"Do you resent Jehovah for it?"

"Yes. I'd like to know what I did that was so bad He had to create an entire dimension just for me."

"I'd like to know that, too. Only I want to know why I agreed to have my memories erased. What did I do that was so bad I wanted to forget?"

He took my hand and brushed the backs of my fingers over his mouth. His eyes shimmered, and for a moment I forgot what I was going to say. I wished Shawn'd had the opportunity to get to know him better. His almost brother.

"Shawn was kind of fascinated with you. He wanted to get to know you."

He nodded and looked down in thought. "Thirty seconds."

I laughed. It was so like him to skip over the emotional parts of any

conversation. Or any part that cast him in a positive light. "We're nego-
tiating now?"

"That's all I need. Thirty seconds."

"Reyes, no." I turned to face him. "I'm not risking your life on a fool's
errand."

"Fool's? You said there were innocent people in there. That the priest
would send people of his village there whom he couldn't control or
whom he got angry with."

"Or obsessed with. Remember, he sent Joan of Arc. She was never
the same coming out as going in."

"But she was in there for how long?"

"I don't know. Kuur made it sound like weeks. Possibly months. And
she was only twelve."

He took the god glass out of my hand. Unlike every other celestial
being that gazed upon the pendant, Reyes seemed only mildly interested. Most, including yours truly, became instantly mesmerized. I'd always assumed Jehovah had done that on purpose in order to lure Reyes
closer so he could be trapped. Perhaps I was wrong. Reyes seemed the
opposite of mesmerized. Though he was curious. Who wouldn't be?

"I want to see it. The dimension."

"According to Kuur, you already have."

He straightened.

"He said they trapped you, Mae'eldeesahn and Eidolon, to transport
you to Lucifer. When you came out, you were disoriented."

Astonished, he laid his head back against the wall. "I don't remember."

"I'm sorry."

"Well, it couldn't have been that bad, right? If I've already been there
and came back normal."

Someone snorted. I was pretty sure it was Jose. "Normal? Got a pretty
high opinion of yourself, eh, Mr. Farrow?"

His grin, that wicked, sensual thing he wielded like a weapon, touched me in all the right places. "I guess you're right."

I climbed onto my knees, then climbed him. Or, well, straddled him. "I have a better idea, anyway. You send me."

All traces of humor vanished in an instant. "No."

I started to climb off him. He clasped my hips and held me to him.

"Why not send me?" I asked, sounding a bit like a petulant child. But it was my glass now. If anyone had a right to go in . . .

"It's not safe."

"Oh, but it's safe enough to send you? That's logic for you. Of the penis-wielding variety."

"We'll flip for it."

"If I had a penis . . ." I thought for a moment. "I've got it! We'll send Cookie, but only for a few seconds. Wait. What did you say?"

One corner of his mouth battled for control. Grin versus scowl. Which would come out on top?

I raised my arms in victory. "And the grin takes the gold."

He gave me a moment, the grin taking on a personality of its own.

"Okay. Sorry. Yeah, let's flip."

I shifted to the side so he could reach into his pocket. He took his time, his fingers brushing against Virginia, stirring her.

"Wait a minute." I narrowed my eyes in suspicion. "This is a trick."

"It's a coin." He held it up and showed me both sides of the quarter. "How is this a trick?"

I settled back on his lap, his crotch wedged against Virginia, my unruly vajayjay. "I don't know, but it is. I can feel it."

He tossed the coin. It flipped over and over in the air, then he slowed time, reached up and wrapped it in his hand.

"I knew you'd cheat," I said.

"I'm going. I can't risk losing you."

"But I can risk losing you?"

"You can. And so can Elwyn. She needs you."

"You're the stronger of us, Reyes. You can protect her."

"First, that's not true. Second, all the prophecies are about you. Not me. I'm going."

When I started to argue again, he lifted me off his lap and went to the kitchen for a knife. I'd expected him to come back with a paring knife. Instead, he brought a chef's. Twelve inches of glistening metal.

"We don't need that much blood," I said to him, worried.

He shrugged. "Just in case."

He ran the tip of one finger along the razor-sharp edge. Then he smeared the dark red blood on my finger.

I curled my hand into a fist to keep it safe. To keep that miniscule part of him safe. Then I lifted my chin and pretended to be brave.

"Okay, this is your basic reconnaissance mission. Go in, scope out the lay of the land, then come back no worse for the wear. It's just a trial run. A test to see if it can even be accomplished. I mean, I've seen entities go in. I've never actually seen one come back out."

"You're stalling."

"I'm—" I started to argue, but it was hard to argue with someone who was right. I soaked him in. His image. His scent. His feel.

He pulled me to him. Dipped his head. Pressed his mouth to mine in a kiss I could only hope would not be our last.

Then he stepped back, and I unfastened the catch on the glass-covered pendant. The six-hundred-year-old, glass-covered pendant. The second it sprang open, thunderstorms and lightning bolts shot out around us. Winds whipped and howled as though in mourning.

Reyes still seemed barely interested. But I stood in awe. Not of the glass. I'd seen it opened before. Of him.

The glass had devoured two preternatural beings in my presence—a demon assassin and a god—but I had yet to see the reaction Reyes was getting from the glass. Lightning crackled around us, but it did more than that to Reyes. It . . . caressed him. It explored him. Tiny spider-webbed currents of electricity pulsed over his skin, traveling over every curve, every line of his body. As though seducing him. As though luring him inside.

He sucked in a sharp breath. Threw back his head. Let the sting wash over him.

Then he leveled a hard gaze on me. "Say my name."

I wiped his blood on the surface of the glass, drew in a lungful of air, and sent my husband to hell.

Scared beyond measure, I kept my gaze riveted to the clock on the wall. The one with a second hand.

I'd said his celestial name. His godly name. His true name and the only one that would work to send him through the portal.

"Rey'azikeen."

The bolts of electricity had danced around him, had jumped as though in joy at the prospect of pulling Reyes into their domain. They'd curled and arced all the way to the metal rafters overhead in a joyous symphony. He'd offered me one last glance and winked a microsecond before he was gone.

I'd closed the pendant and my eyes, wondering what I'd just done.

I looked at the clock again. Fifteen seconds. It'd seemed like hours. I couldn't wait any longer. I opened the pendant, held the raging storm in my palms, and offered up a little prayer to the God I may or may not meet on the battlefield one day before saying his name.

"Rey'azikeen."

Then I waited. Not sure what to expect. Winds whipped around me, lightning crashed and traveled up the walls, but nothing else happened.

Alarm started a slow, agonizing ascent up my spine.

I repeated his name. "Rey'azikeen."

The storms seemed to grow stronger. More furious. I screamed it so I could be heard above the roar.

Nothing.

Fear shot through me so fast I almost passed out. Panic closed my throat. I tamped it down and tried again. With every name he'd ever gone by that I knew of. He'd been alive a long time.

"Rey'aziel." His celestial name, the one he used in hell.

Nothing.

"Reyes Alexander Farrow." His human name.

Nothing.

"Razer." His godly nickname. The one they called him in Uzan, a prison from my home dimension.

Nothing.

This was not happening. This could not be happening.

I sank to my knees. No clue what to do. Perhaps the glass had to be clean and blood-free to bring someone out. I scrambled up and ran into the kitchen. I cleaned it with soap and water. The lightning bolts punishing me. Water and electricity didn't mix.

I dried it and tried again.

I said his name.

I screamed it.

I whispered it.

I held the god glass so close to my face the electricity scorched my eyes and said it again. "Rey'azikeen."

Nothing. Nothing. Nothing.

Bombarded with idea after idea, I tried everything I could think of. I tried versions of Razer in every language that came to mind. I tried chanting it. I tried opening and closing the pendant, in a sense, rebooting it.

Nothing.

An hour later, I lay on the living room floor, clutching the god glass to me, the storm as strong as ever. I could hear nothing else but the howling winds. Could see nothing else but white hot flashes of lightning behind my closed lids.

I could break it. I could break the god glass, but what would that accomplish? It would either set everything inside free—including a malevolent god and a demon assassin—or lock the only gate to the hell dimension in existence.

Kuur had told me. One way in. One way out. Of course, the fact that he was an evil demon and an assassin kind of transferred anything he said into a folder called Reasonable Doubt, but . . .

Then it hit me. I sat up. The perfect plan. I would go in after him. I would have Cookie say my name and send me inside.

Sadly, I would have to trick her. She'd never do it if she knew the truth. But I could leave her a note explaining how to get me back out. In theory. Obviously the whole process was a little flawed.

I hurried to the bedroom for my robe. She would be asleep. Actually, I was a little surprised my screaming didn't wake anyone. Or the tempest currently residing in my apartment.

Just as I was about to head out the door, the storms changed. They became darker. Thicker. Angrier. Heat welled up around me. Energy. Power. It rushed over my skin like an electrical shock wave. Fierce and raw and furious.

The pendant became too hot for me to hold. I dropped it and stepped back in anticipation. Something was happening. It was just hard to say exactly what after the earsplitting explosion.

It threw me against a wall, almost knocking me unconscious. I lifted my lids but didn't dare move. Thick black smoke pooled around me. I looked up just in time to see a dozen souls rush into me, wanting only to escape. Wanting to be free.

I gasped as life after life flashed before my eyes.

A widow with two children. She'd spurned the priest's advances.

A man who refused to sign over part of his land to the church.

A young boy who saw the priest in a compromising situation.

On and on. Life after life destroyed by one man.

I knew the priest had been locked inside as well by a group of monks who took him to task for his evil deeds. But I didn't feel him. Of course, he would never have gone to heaven. Perhaps he was already in hell.

After more than a dozen souls crossed through me, all from the same time period, the 1400s, I waited. Three more beings were inside the dimension. The demon assassin. The god Mae'eldeesahn. And my husband.

The smoke filled the room, lit occasionally by quick flashes of lightning. The entire apartment spun slowly, churning like a supercell.

And then Reyes walked out of it, the billowing smoke falling from his wide shoulders and settling at his feet.

I jumped up, elated, and started toward him. But I skidded to a halt just as quickly, stopped short when I recognized something amiss.

Smoke and lightning curled around him as though it were alive. Like an animal. Like a lover. If he shifted, it shifted. It flowed and ebbed at his will, the lightning crackling over his skin.

He wasn't in the storm. He was the storm. The tempest. The squall. He was his own element.

I stood astounded as he walked toward me, eating the ground in three determined steps.

I stumbled back, caught myself, then whispered, "Reyes?"

He narrowed his eyes on me. As though curious. As though he had no idea who I was.

I reached up to touch his face and got a whole lot of wall for my effort.

He shoved me against it so hard I bounced back a little. Then he ran his gaze down the length of my body, his hand at my throat. Then my jaw. Wrapping his fingers around it, he talked to me, his voice low and husky. "Elle-Ryn-Ahleethia."

Why would he use my celestial name?

He seemed . . . surprised. Astonished to find me there. Then he gave me another once-over. His gaze filled with both lust and contempt.

And then I remembered. Kuur had told me Rey'Azikeen had only contempt for the humans his Brother loved so much. And I was human. At least a grain-sized portion of me.

I studied him as he studied me. Something came out of that dimension. It looked like my husband. Smelled like him. Felt like him. But the being standing in a pool of billowing black smoke was not the man I married. He was a feral version of him. A beast.

This truly was Rey'azikeen. I was meeting him at last.

And then I realized the truth. I may have just made the biggest mistake of my entire existence. I may have unleashed hell on earth.